I0632337

Richard Cecil Stone

Genealogy of the Stone Family

originating in Rhode Island

Richard Cecil Stone

Genealogy of the Stone Family
originating in Rhode Island

ISBN/EAN: 9783337378349

Printed in Europe, USA, Canada, Australia, Japan

Cover: Foto ©Andreas Hilbeck / pixelio.de

More available books at **www.hansebooks.com**

GENEALOGY

OF THE

STONE FAMILY

ORIGINATING IN

RHODE ISLAND.

By RICHARD C. STONE.

———

PROVIDENCE:
KNOWLES, ANTHONY AND COMPANY, PRINTERS.
1866.

PREFACE.

No one can estimate the labor and difficulty and perplexity of collecting and arranging the genealogical statistics of a large family, of a growth of more than two hundred years, until they have tried it. Few individuals are interested in their ancestry; its knowledge will give them neither bread, butter nor tobacco, and hence, unless "something is coming," they care not

"To whom related, or by whom begot."

Many keep no records at all, and those which are kept are often so imperfect that little can be gathered of value. Some, not intending to mislead, profess a knowledge they do not possess, and hence dates and names are given which prove, in the end, partially incorrect. The "Stone Family," in this work, not including the posterity of daughters beyond those whose mothers were named Stone, numbers nearly three thousand, including those with whom they intermarried. There are, undoubtedly, some mistakes in a work so extensive, and yet the author is gratified that he has collected so much that is reliable. No pains have been spared to make it what it professes to be, a genealogy of the "Stone Family" of Rhode Island,—though now widely scattered in Connecticut, Pennsylvania, and more or less throughout the Union. The author would do injustice to the "family" should he omit to state, that of all his widely extended correspondents but one only has failed to respond; every writer has manifested an interest, and given him some valuable facts, and regretted only, as also did the author, an inability to do more. To some, the author and the "Stone family" are deeply indebted for much elaborate information. Their assistance is especially called to mind in the Biographical Notes, in which their names are mentioned.

In the Biographical Notes, the author has aimed to give something more than isolated facts and dry annals; and although he has not, in conse-

quence of the narrow limits assigned him, been able to set the reader down to the family fireside, or to introduce much of personal anecdote and private adventure, or to fling any very enticing charm over the annals and statistics of our family records, yet, he feels that he has the satisfaction of introducing you to our fathers and mothers and to one another, and thus binding together the ties of family and kindred. The biography of any good man is always elevating and purifying in its influence on the reader; it must be still more so when strengthened by the ties of brotherhood. It is thus the author feels, if he gains no money, he has collected, somewhat, the relics of individual and family life, and shaped the scattered remains of our ancestors into memorials, not only improving to ourselves but to our children.

INTRODUCTION.

THE STONE FAMILIES IN AMERICA, which emigrated from the Fatherland to this, cannot be traced to "THREE BROTHERS WHO CAME OVER," but are distinctly traced to ten or more importations, ranging from the years 1635 to 1840.

Samuel Stone came to Boston in 1633. He was educated at Cambridge, England, and probably originated in Hertford, about twenty miles from London. He remained a short time in the vicinity of Boston, but accompanied Hooker and the first settlers on the Connecticut River. They called their settlement Hartford, from Hertford, the name of the town from which Samuel Stone emigrated. He was associate Pastor with Hooker until his death, when he became sole minister of the Hartford Church, which he sustained many years, and was then gathered to his fathers in a good old age. Samuel Stone left four children,—one son and three daughters. His son, Samuel, was educated for the ministry; but, becoming intemperate, fell, before middle life, from the high river bank upon the rocks below, was killed, and the family became extinct.

John Stone, aged forty, came to Salem in April, 1635, from Hawkhurst, Kent county, England, in the ship Elizabeth. He remained, some years, in and around Salem; but finally settled in Guilford, Conn., where he probably died. His son Timothy was educated and settled in the ministry, in Goshen, Conn., where we believe he spent his whole life. A son of his, Timothy, junior, was educated and settled in Cornwall, Conn., —a man of piety and literary talent. A grandson of his, probably, is the William Stone who had commenced a literary course, and, at the opening of the Revolution, though quite young, enlisted. He was in many severe engagements; was always foremost in any hazardous enterprise; was present at the execution of Andre, and continued his services up to the establishment of peace. He then resumed his studies and entered the ministry. He was a useful man, and his labors confined to the border settlements. He was fond of adventure; several times left his field of labor and moved up to the border line. His son, William Leet Stone, commonly called Col. Stone, was a man of education and literary taste; was editor of the New York Commercial Advertiser, and published the History of Wyoming and some other works. He has a son, William L. Stone, connected with the Journal of Commerce. The family of John Stone, or Stou as spelled in the early records, is not extensive, though a few may be found scattered in the different States.

Richard Stone left England, in the ship Alexander, for Barbadoes, in May, 1635, but left when the ship touched at Boston. He was but thirteen years old when he came to New England, where he resided until he was killed in a skirmish with the Indians, at Hatfield, Mass., 1670, when forty-eight years old. He has left no descendants.

Symon Stone, aged fifty, his wife and five children, came to Boston, in

the ship "Increase," and settled in Watertown, Mass., in 1635, whither he was soon followed by his younger brother, Gregory. The descendants of this family are very numerous in Massachusetts, Maine and many other States. Generally among the most virtuous and respected, not a few hold high positions in the gifts of their fellow citizens. The Speakers of the Houses of Representatives, in both Maine and Massachusetts, were from this family, and both elected on the same day, January 1st, 1866.

Hugh Stone, whose genealogical record may be herein found, came to this country, from England, about 1657. See Note 1.

Rev. A. L. Stone, the talented minister of Park Street, Boston, now removed to California, we understand, traces his pedigree to Sweden.

Hon. William Stone came to this country about 1635; was Governor of Maryland, appointed by Oliver Cromwell. He died in that State; has left some descendants, among whom was John Haskins Stone, late Governor of Maryland, Thomas Stone, one of the signers of the Declaration of Independence, and probably, David Stone, late Governor of North Carolina.

James Stone, an artizan in one of the manufactories in Rhode Island, came to this country about 1850.

Nesson Stone, a Hebrew dry goods merchant of St. Louis, Mo., came to this country from the south of Russia—or Polish Russia—a few years since. He informed the writer that his Russian name was long, crooked and difficult to pronounce, and he assumed the name of Stone, to use his own words, "because it was easy, and meant the same thing."

Richard Stone, of New Boston, Conn., came to this country a few years since. The following are extracts from a letter received from him by the author: "My father lived in Luton, Bedfordshire, England, where I came from to America. I have a brother Charles somewhere in Ohio, but have not seen him in six years. My father had a clothes-chest, very nicely carved all over, which he said was his father's great-great-grandfather's, and that his name was Richard Stone." Thus, the two Richard Stones mentioned here—the one who wrote me and the one who owned the chest—were seven generations apart.

The name of Stone appears in the Royal Navy of England. Lieut. James Stone, Commandant, was one of the twelve children of Isaac and Mary Stone, of Devonshire, England, and was born 1775. He was a man of courage, distinguished in the wars with the French, and commanded a sloop-of-war on the Irish coast during the time of the expected landing of Napoleon at Bantry Bay.

Lieut. John Stone, of Kent county, England, is now an efficient officer in the British Navy, and married Miss Anna Watson Johnson, in 1836.

William Stone was master shipwright of the Royal Navy Yard, Chatham, England. His son, William, is Captain in the naval service, and was Lieutenant in the war of 1812. He was one of the officers of the Peacock, when she was taken by the United States sloop-of-war Hornet, and was wounded in the engagement.

Nicholas Stone was statuary and architect to James I. He left two sons, Henry and John, who were both artists. Henry was a very skillful

painter, especially a copyist, and has left several admirable copies of Vandyke and the old Italian masters, which are still preserved among the English works of art in the royal household. His younger brother, John, was a man of less ability as an artist, and mainly followed the profession of his father,—a statuary, carver and sculptor. He died in the early part of the Restoration.

Frank Stone, an eminent painter of England, was born in the year 1800. In 1827, he became a contributor to the Royal Academy, in natural history and the subjects of sentiment and imagination. He was very successful, and some of his pieces became, deservedly, very popular. His "First Appeal" and "Last Appeal" are among the most highly prized engravings in England. In 1851, he was elected "Associate of the Royal Academy," an honor conferred only on artists of high rank. He died in 1859.

It might be interesting to know more of our connexion and ancestry here and in the fatherland. Tradition has connected some of the different families together. Hugh has been said to have been a younger brother to John, and born of the same parents after John came to America; that they accidentally met, and found out their relationship; but the author finds for the story no foundation but tradition. It may be inquired, is there any family device or coat of arms pertaining to the name? There is. The family claim a "coat of arms" bearing "four stars," a "lion rampant," two "argents." Crest, a "spread eagle." Something like this is the device, so far as the author is able to explain the ensigns and armorial bearings. To this, however, he attaches but little consequence, as in Republican America, every man is the artificer of his own escutcheon, and far distant be the day, in our beloved land, when this grand feature of American life shall be removed or obliterated. I am by no means, however, insensible to the value of a worthy, a talented or even a distinguished ancestry; I regard it, however, as an incentive, a call, a demand even upon their posterity, to stand up and live to the high elevation upon which they were born. Shame to the man that has descended! Shame to the bird, hatched from an eagle's egg, that quacks and swims! As you read this introduction, trace this genealogy and cast your eye over the names and characters and facts therein noted, it may not detract from your interest in our widely extended race (more than seven thousand) to know that not one of the name, up to the war of the Rebellion, ever suffered for crime by imprisonment or death.

R. C. S.

WORKS AND RECORDS CONSULTED IN COMPILING THE FOLLOWING.

Records of Providence, Warwick, Cranston, Foster and Coventry, Rhode Island.
American Encyclopedia.
Drake's Early Passengers, a copy of English Records.
Calender's History, a Sermon.

Updike's History of Narragansett Church.
Biography of English Artists.
Biography of English Naval Officers.
Stiles's History of Rhode Island.
Staples's History of Rhode Island.

For facilities of access to the above works, the author is indebted to the town and probate clerks; to Hon. J. R. Bartlett, Secretary of State, Rhode Island; to Dr. E. M. Snow; to the Librarian of Brown University, and to the gentlemen in charge of the City Library of Boston and the Library of the Massachusetts Historical Society, at Boston, Mass.

EXPLANATION.

The husband and wife always stand on the same line. The age of the first person named stands at the right of the name. Every person named Stone, or the descendant of one named Stone, is numbered, beginning at 1 and ending at 1814. These numbers stand at the left of the name to which they belong, when the number and name first appear. The same name and same number always appear together through the book, but the number in a parenthesis, thus: John Stone (4); Samuel Stone (19). You will find Samuel Stone (19), page 17, and in Biographical Note, 57. So, wherever *this* Samuel is mentioned, he will always be Samuel Stone (19). So of every numbered name. Wherever a name appears as a parent, it is in *Italics*. See the four parents, Hugh (1), Hugh (2), Peter (3) and Peter (12), on page first. The numbers occasionally found near the right margin, are the pages where the same person appears as a parent. See page 17, and you will find Samuel Stone (19) there, a parent. Wherever a child appears on the *same* page with the father, no page is given,—it is directly before you. See page first. The numbers at the left help trace any descent, thus, top of page 63: Harrie Stone (1300) is child of Stephen Dexter Stone (1292). Who is he? Find his number,—he is child of Daniel J. Stone (1276). Who is he? Find his number,—he is child of Daniel Stone (1246). Who is he? Find his number,—he is child of Jabez Stone (1050). Who is he? Find his number,—he is child of William Stone (658). Who is he? Find his number,—he is child of John Stone (4). Who is he? Find his number,—he is the child of Hugh Stone (1). To find the generation, count these names. There are eight; hence the boy Harrie Stone (1300) is the eighth generation from Hugh (1), our first ancestor. The number of the cousin is always two less than the generation, e. g.: trace back Pamelia S. Stone (1146), found at the head of page 56. She also is the eighth generation from Hugh (1), and consequently Harrie Stone (1300) and Pamelia S. Stone (1146) are sixth cousins.

GENEALOGY.

1   HUGH STONE, 1638. Abigail Busecot. (Common ancestors.)

Children of Hugh Stone (1) *and Abigail Busecot.*
2a Abigail Stone, 1667.
2   Hugh Stone, 1669. Mary Potter.
3   Peter Stone, Jan. 20, 1671. Elizabeth Shaw.
4   John Stone, 1674. —— Barnes; 2d, Abigail Foster. p. 35
5   Anne Stone, 1679. William Potter, mar. 1705.   80
6   George Stone, 1681.

Children of Hugh Stone (2) *and Mary Potter.*
8   Hugh Stone, 1692. Died in early life.
9   Thomas Stone, 1695. Wife unknown. No descendants of the name.
10 Oliver Stone, 1701. Wife unknown. Name extinct in third generation.

Children of Peter Stone (3) *and Elizabeth Shaw.*
11 Elizabeth Stone, 1697
12 Peter Stone, 1698. Patience Printing, mar. 1725.
13 Sarah Stone, 1699.
14 Abigail Stone, 1700.
15 Pressilah Stone, 1702.
16 John Stone, 1704.

Children of Peter Stone (12) *and Patience Printing.*
17 Betsey Stone, 1727. Jeremiah Angell. No children.
18 Peter Stone, 1727. Mary Hammond.
                   2d, Patience Hudson.   2
19 Samuel Stone, 1733. Mary Blanchard.   17
20 Patience Stone, 1735. Thomas Hammond.   16

NOTE.—To determine the degree of relationship of any two, trace back each one, setting each name and their number in a line till you find the common ancestor, or the one in whom both meet, e. g.: How is Emma E. Hawkins (1036) related to Henry Gay (945)? Trace by the numbers back, thus:

Emma E. (1036)	Sarah E. Stone (912)	John (814)	John (820)	Ezra.
Henry (945)	Almira Stone (1019)	Asahel (997)	George (828)	Ezra.
Third cousins.	Second cousins.	First cousins.	Brothers.	Com. an.

See another line traced, Note 121, page 131.

Sub-Branch of Peter Stone (18) descended from Peter Stone (12).

Children of Peter Stone (18) and Mary Hammond.

22 Mary Stone, 1754. Samuel Roberts. No children?
23 Patience Stone, 1756. James Westcott.
24 Phebe Stone, 1757. Elisha Westcott.
25 Peter Stone, 1759. Patience Westcott.
26 Andrew Stone, 1762. Mary Westcott.
        2d, Mary Battey—Bowdich. p. 3
27 Amos Stone, 1764. Diedama Burlingame.
        2d, Mercy King.   9
28 Mehitable Stone, 1766. Joshua Strait.
29 Deliverance Stone, 1768. Reuben Horton.
30 Freelove Stone, 1770. Charles Thornton.
31 John Stone, 1772. Mary Joy.   9
32 Whipple Stone, 1773. Henrietta Collins.
        2d, Catharine Carder. 13
33 Lydia Stone, 1774. Died in infancy.

By Second Wife, Patience Hudson.

34 Hopkins Stone, 1776. Amy Salisbury; 2d, Mary Corey. 15
35 Welcome Stone, 1778. Lydia Corey.   16
36 Mary Stone, 1780. Not married.
36a Rebecca Stone, 1782. David Patt.   84 A.
37 Eseck Stone, 1782. Died, about 1802, at sea.

Children of Patience Stone (23) and James Westcott.
38 James Westcott.
 Others, if any, unknown.

Children of Phebe Stone (24) and Elisha Westcott.
39 Elisha Westcott, 1784. Wife unknown.
40 Josiah Westcott, 1786. Mary Hayward.
41 Reuben Westcott, 1789. Not married?
41a Charles Westcott, 1791.

Children of Peter Stone (25) and Patience Westcott.

42 Peter Stone, 1784? Died when about 25.
43 Sophia Stone, 1787. James Strait. No children.
44 Sylvester Stone, 1790. Not married; went West.

Children of Andrew Stone (26) and Mary Westcott.

45a Peter Stone, 1785. Died aged about 17 years.
45   Henry Stone, 1787. Anne Battey.
45b Polly Stone, 1789. Died aged 14 years.
46   William Stone, 1793. Phebe Stone (676).   p. 39
46b Andrew Stone, 1795. Died in childhood.

By Second Wife, Mary Battey.

46c Alice Stone, 1802. Died in childhood.
46d Patience Stone, 1807. Elisha Keach.
46e Phila Stone, 1812. Died in childhood.

Children of Henry Stone (45) and Anne Battey.

47 Alice B. Stone, 1817. Nathan Eddy.
48 Peter Stone, 1819. Roxana Bryant.
49 Josiah Stone, 1821. Died in early life.
50 Laura Stone, 1823. W. Harrison; 2d, J. Bryant.

Children of Peter Stone (48) and Roxana Bryant.

50a Sarah Ann Stone.
50b John H. Stone. Died in the War, 1862.

Children of Amos Stone (27) and Diedama Burlingame.

51 Dutee Stone, 1787. Barbara Collins.
52 Nancy Stone, 1789. John Pratt; 2d, Job. Waterman.   4
53 Freelove Stone, 1791. Sheldon Colvin.
54 William Stone, 1796. Susan Pratt.   4
55 Sarah Stone, 1797. Sylvester Claflin; 2d, Paris Parker. 6
56 Waterman Stone, 1799. Abby Thornton.   6
57 Charles Stone, 1804. Caroline Remington.   7

By Second Wife, Mercy King.

58 Henry A. Stone, 1808. Mary Ann Rounds.   8

Continued on next page.

Children of Amos Stone (27) *and Mercy King.* (*Continued.*)

59   John Stone, 1812.   D. Fenner; 2d, D. Goudy;
                     3d, Bridget ——.   p. 8

60   Amos Stone, 1813.   Hannah Pierce.

61   Sylvester C. Stone, 1815.   Eliza King.   9

62   Joseph Stone, 1817.   Susan King.   8

Children of Dutee Stone (51) *and Barbara Collins.*

63.   Horace Stone, 1810.   Died, 1824.

Children of Nancy Stone (52) *and John Pratt.*

64   Freelove Pratt, 1809.   Died young.

65   Joseph Pratt, 1812.   Died young.

66   Serene Pratt, 1816.   Amasa Waterman.

        By second marriage, Job Waterman.

67   Albert Waterman, 1824.   Adelia Luther.

68   Mary S. Waterman, 1827.   Calvin Luther.

Children of William Stone (54) *and Susan Pratt.*

69   Mary Stone, 1818.   Thomas Nutting.   5

70   Nehemiah Stone, 1820.   Elizabeth Tanner.   5

71   Alfred Stone, 1822.   Ann M. Budlong.
                    2d, Lydia Budlong.   5

72   Louisa Stone, 1822.   Emerson Whipple.   No children.

73   Maria Stone, 1824.   Not married; died, 1848.   ·

74   Philip Stone, 1827.   Juliana Jenks.   5

75   Calvin Stone, 1829.   Harriet Blake; 2d, Helen V. Blake. 6

76   Isaac Stone, 1831.   Amey W. Randall.   6

77   William Stone, 1833.   Anna Darling.   6

78   Lyman Stone, 1836.   Amanda Morse.   6

Children of Mary Stone (69) *and Dr. Thomas Nutting.*

79 Julia Ann Nutting.
80 Minerva M. Nutting.

Children of Nehemiah Stone (70) *and Elizabeth Tanner.*

81 Susan P. Stone. 1841. George Pitts.
82 Harriet N. Stone, 1842. Frederick Phillips.
83 Louisa Stone, 1844. Died young.
84 Ann Maria Stone, 1846. William R. Spink.
85 George Albert Stone, 1847. Not married.
86 Eliza T. Stone, 1848. Jesse Webster.
87 Julana J. Stone, 1850.
88 Jesse Stone, 1853.
89 Edgar Stone, 1854.
90 Ida Stone, 1855.

Children of Susan P. Stone (81) *and George Pitts.*

91 Frank Pitts, 1858.
92 George Pitts, 1861.

Children of Harriet N. Stone (82) *and Frederick Phillips.*

93 Lyman Phillips, 1863?

Children of Alfred Stone (71) *and Anna M. Budlong.*

94 Emma Stone, 1849. Died same year.
95 Ellen Stone, 1855.
96 Clara Stone, 1862. By 2d marriage, Lydia Budlong.

Children of Philip Stone (74) *and Julana Jencks.*

97 Anne Stone, 1851.
98 Nellie Stone, 1855.

Children of Calvin Stone (75) and Harriet Blake.

99   Edgar Stone, 1852.   Died when infant.

100 Arthur C. Stone, 1853.

101 Helen Stone, 1857.

Children of Isaac Stone (76) and Amey W. Randall.

102 Carrie I. Stone, 1856.   July.

103 James R. Stone, 1859.   November.

Children of William Stone (77) and Anna F. Darling.

104 Ella J. Stone, 1855.

Children of Lyman Stone (78) and Amanda Morse.

105 Louisa Stone, 1864.

Here closes the present descendants of William Stone. (54)

Children of Sarah Stone (55) and Sylvester Claflin.

106 Charles Claflin, 1817.

By Second Marriage, Paris Parker.

107 William Parker, 1814.   Betsey Pierce.

108 Rosanna Parker, 1811.   Mowry Barnes.

109 Russell Parker, 1818.   Caroline Taylor.

110 Hannah Parker, 1823.   Died 1831.

111 Susan Parker, 1825.   Libbeus Bennett.

112 Avery Parker, 1829.   Not married.

Children of Waterman Stone (56) and Abby Thornton.

113 Mary Stone, 1817.   Stephen B. Esten.

114 Stephen Stone, 1818.   Waitstill Greene Arnold.   p. 7

115 Sophronia Stone. 1820.   Died 1821.

Children of Stephen Stone (114) *and Waitstill G. Arnold.*

115 Hannah A. Stone, 1841. Died at two years.

116 Elisha A. Stone, 1842. Died at 19 years.

117 Mary A. Stone, 1844. Died at 9 years,

118 Nathan T. Stone, 1845.

119 Abbie G. Stone, 1847.

120 George H. Stone, 1848.

121 Charles E Stone, 1849.

Children of Charles Stone (57) *and Caroline Remington.*

122 Sylvester C. Stone, 1825. Sarah J Carpenter.

123 Lucy Stone, 1827, Died 1846.

124 Phebe Lavina Stone, 1831. Wm. R. Cranston.

125 Harriet Stone, 1833. Joseph G. Brown.

Children of Sylvester C. Stone (122) *and Sarah J. Carpenter*

126 Iabel Stone, 1850.

127 Lucy Jane Stone, 1852. Died 1853.

128 Charles Stone, 1855. Died 1862.

129 Lucy Ann Stone, 1857.

130 Charles Stone, 1861.

Children of Phebe Lavina Stone (124) *and William R. Cranston.*

131 Luey Ann Cranston, 1849. Died in infancy.

132 Frank L. Cranston, 1851.

133 William A. Cranston, 1855.

134 John I. Cranston, 1864.

Children of Harriet Stone (125) *Joseph G. Brown.*

135 William H. Brown. 1851.

136 Charles H. Brown, 1857.

137 Julia M. Brown, 1863.

Children of Henry A. Stone (58) and Mary Ann Rounds.

138 Henry Stone 1823.
139 Maria Stone, 1825. David Patt.
140 Amos Stone, 1830. Not married.
141 Charles Stone, 1841.

Children of Maria Stone (139) and David Patt.

142 William Patt, 1855.

Children of John Stone and Diana Fenner.

143 George Stone, 1829. Phebe Salisbury.
144 John Stone, 1832. Died 1863.

By 2d wife, Deborah Goudy.

145 William Stone, 1840. Not married.
146 Joseph Stone, 1842. Died 1865.

By 3d wife, Bridget ——

147 Sylvester Stone, 1851.
148 Eliza Stone, 1853. Died in infancy.

Children of Amos Stone (60) and Hannah Pierce.

149 Almanzo Stone, 1845.
150 Henry Stone, 1849.

Children of Joseph Stone (62) and Susan King.

151 Almy Stone, 1840. Samuel Burlingame.   p. 9
152 Ellen Stone, 1846. Moses Cheney.   9
153 Susan Stone, 1850. Cornelius Miller.
154 Albert Stone, 1852. Died in infancy.
155 Charles Stone, 1855.

Children of Almy Stone (151) *and Samuel Burlingame.*

156 Anna Burlingame, 1859.
157 William Burlingame, 1861.
158 Frank Burlingame, 1863.

Children of Ellen Stone (152) *and Moses Cheney.*

159 Byron Cheney.

Children of Sylvester C. Stone (61) *and Eliza King.*

160 Melissa A. F. Stone, 1838. Pardon Williams.
162 Thomas H. B. Stone, 1839.
163 George W. Stone, 1841. Charlotte Dugan.
164 Benjamin F. Stone, 1843.
165 Henry J. M. Stone, 1845. Died in infancy.
166 Mercy M. Stone, 1847. Died in infancy.

Children of Melissa A. F. Stone (160) *and Pardon Williams.*

167 Eliza Frances Williams, 1858.
168 Herbert A. Williams, 1860.
169 Seca Estelle Williams, 1862.
     Here closes the present descendants of Amos Stone, (27.)

Children of John Stone (31) *and Mary Joy.*

170 Seneca Stone, 1792. Martha Congdon. 2d, Amy Stone. p. 10
171 Sally Ann Stone, 1795. Died in infancy.
172 Mary Ann Stone, 1797. S. Harris. 2d, Jer'h Fenner. 12
173 Daniel C. Stone, 1800. Mary A. Cole.   12
174 William Joy Stone, 1803. Abbie Albro. No children.
175 Catherine Stone, 1806. Not married.
176 Phebe Stone, 1808. S. D. Cole.   13
177 John Stone, 1811. Died 1835.

3

Children of Seneca Stone (170) *and Martha Congdon.*

178 Raymond Stone, 1812. Anne Gorton.
179 Thomas C. Stone, 1813. Died.
180 Albert Stone, 1815. Josephine Smith.

By Second Wife, Amy Stone.

181 Amy Stone, 1818. Died in infancy.
182 Edwin Stone, 1819. Maria Bussey. 2d, Mary Draper. p. 11
183 Jeremiah Stone, 1821. Sarah Burdick.   11
184 Otis Stone, 1823. Huldah Whitaker.   11
185 Adaline Stone, 1824. Died 1833.
186 Clark Stone, 1826. Rhoda Graves.   11
187 Cyrus Stone, 1828. S. M. Jencks. 2d, M. Phillips.   11
188 Lorenzo Stone, 1830. Maria Jennison.   12
189 Infant, 1833.
190 Esther Stone, 1834. Thomas H. Jennison.   12
191 Mary Stone, 1836. G. W. Andrews.   12
192 Jerome Stone, 1838. Fanny Crandall. No children.
193 Abbie S. Stone, 1840. T. J. Bates.   12
194 William Henry Stone, 1845. Julia Orman.

Children of Raymond Stone (178) *and Anne Gorton.*

195 Gilbert W. Stone, 1838. Ellen S. Hobson.
196 Richmond J. Stone, 1840. Ellen M. Ronian.
197 Thomas L. Stone, 1847. In Navy.

Children of Albert Stone (180) *and Josephine Smith.*

198 Virginia A. Stone, 1854.
199 Josephine Stone, 1856.
200 Emma Stone, 1858.
201 Fanny E. Stone, 1863.

Children of Edwin Stone (182) *and Maria Bussey.*

202 Albert Stone, 1845.
203 Charles Stone, 1847.
204 Adaline Stone, 1849.
205 Lucy Frances Stone, 1851.
206 George Stone, 1854.
207 Esther Stone, 1854.

Children of Jeremiah Stone (183) *and Sarah Burdick.*

208 Laura M. Stone, 1854.
209 Charles H. Stone, 1863.

Children of Otis Stone (184) *and Huldah Whitaker.*

210 Amanda M. Stone, 1844.   Smith Greene.   p. 12.
211 Clark Stone, 1846.
212 Maria Stone, 1848.
213 Leander Stone, 1851.
214 Mary Stone, 1853.
215 Joseph Stone, 1854.   Died 1858.
216 William Stone, 1860.
217 Otis Stone, 1862.   Died 1864.

Children of Clark Stone (186) *and Rhoda Graves.*

218 Amy Ann Stone, 1849.   Died in infancy.
219 Frank Pierce Stone, 1854.
220 Chauncey Wesley Stone, 1857.
220a Lawton Belmont Stone, 1862.

Children of Cyrus Stone (187) *and S. M. Jencks.*

221 Walter Stone, 1851.
222 Almoran Stone, 1855.
223 Americus Stone, 1855.
224 Seneca Stone, 1857.   Died 1859.
225 Henrietta Stone, 1859.   Died 1865.
      By Second Wife, Mary Philips.
226 Susan M. Stone, 1862

Children of Lorenzo Stone (188) *and Maria Jennison.*
227 Byron Stone, 1853.
228 Ada Maria Stone, 1856.

Children of Esther Stone (190) *and Thos. H. Jennison.*
229 Frank M. Stone, 1856.
230 Amy M. Stone, 1859.
231 Everett B. Stone, 1862.

Children of Mary Stone (191) *and G. W. Andrews.*
232 Willard Irving Stone, 1856.

Children of Abbie S. Stone (193) *and T. J. Bates.*
233 Thos. J. Bates, 1857.
234 Amy A. Bates, 1862.

Children of Amanda M. Stone (210) *and Smith Greene.*
235 Byron Greene.
Here end the present descendants of Seneca Stone, (170.)

Children of Mary Ann Stone (172) *and Stephen Harris.*
236 Almorn Harris, 1815. Emily Kellar.
By Second Marriage, Jeremiah Fenner.
237 Sullivan Fenner, 1826. S. Saunders. 2d, M. King.
238 Priscilla Fenner, 1829. S. A. Pierce.

Children of Daniel C. Stone (173) *and Mary Ann Cole.*
239 Lucy C. Stone, 1829. E. C. Grant. 2d, J. Baldwin. p. 13
240 Catherine R. Stone, 1831. Caleb W. Hopkins. 13
241 Abel T. Stone, 1833. Sarah E. Peckham.
241a Daniel C. Stone, 1836. Died in infancy.
242 Esther A. Stone, 1839. Died 1854.
243 Abbie E. Stone, 1839. Not married.

Children of Daniel C. Stone (173) *and Mary Ann Cole, continued.*

244   Mary H. Stone, 1842.   Not married.
245   Daniel C. Stone, 1851.   Not married.

Children of Lucy C. Stone (239) *and Erastus C. Grant.*

246   Emily J. Grant, 1850.
247   Erastus C. Grant, 1856.

Children of Catherine R. Stone (240) *and Caleb W. Hopkins.*

248   Anna Hopkins, 1852.
249   Esther A. Hopkins, 1854.
250   Mary E. Hopkins, 1860.
251   Charles L. Hopkins, 1865.

Children of Abel T. Stone (241) *and Sarah E. Peckham.*

252   William Clarke Stone, 1855.
253   Mary E. Stone, 1858.

Children of Phebe Stone (176) *and S. D. Cole.*

254   Desire D. Cole, 1830.
255   Mary Joy Cole. 1835.
256   Lucy Virtue Cole, 1840.
Here end the present descendants of John Stone. (31)

Children of Whipple Stone (32) *and Henrietta Collins.*

257   Phebe Stone, 1795.   Zara Pratt.   p. 14
258   Temperance Stone, 1797.   Samuel R. Potter.   14
259   John W. Stone, 1799.   Clarissa Holcom.   14
260   Roby Stone, 1804.   Elijah Taylor.   14
261   Orin Stone, 1806.   Maria Holden.   No children.
      By Second Marriage, with Catherine Carder.
262   Ann Stone, 1809.   William Haven.
263   Whipple Stone, 1811.   Cynthia Weaver.   14 & 15

Children of Phebe Stone (257) and Zara Pratt.

264 Henrietta Pratt, 1820. William Snow.
265 William W. Pratt, 1822. Unknown.
266 Orin S. Pratt, 1825. Unknown. No children?

Children of Temperance Stone (258) and Samuel A. Potter.

267 Freelove A. Potter, 1825. E. B. Strange.
268 Phebe S. Potter. 1827. David Hill.
269 Lyman R. Potter. 1829. Died in childhood.
270 Caroline M. Potter, 1731. Charles Phillips.
271 Henrietta C. Potter, 1833. Olney W. Arnold.
272 Adaline E. Potter, 1837. Thomas Bassett.
273 Ann Frances Potter, 1839. Walter H. Johnson.

Children of John Stone (259) and Clarissa Holcom.

274 Warren Stone, 1823.

Children of Roby Stone (260) and Elijah Taylor.

275 Maritta Taylor, 1821?
276 Orin S. Taylor, 1823?
277 Mary Taylor, 1825?
278 Roby Taylor, 1827?
279 Abijah Taylor, 1829?
280 Sullivan Taylor, 1831?
281 Daniel Taylor, 1833?
Another child but name unknown?

Children of Whipple Stone (263) and Cynthia Weaver.

282 Whipple Stone, 1834. Died in infancy.
283 Whipple Stone. 1835. Died in infancy.
284 Rilla Stone, 1838. William Brown. p. 15
285 Ann E. Stone, 1841. Amos Briggs. 15
286 Emeline J. Stone, 1844. Not married.

Children of Whipple Stone (263) *and Cynthia Weaver, continued.*

287 Alice Stone, 1847. Not married.
288 Fannie H. Stone, 1849, Not married.
289 Horace Whipple Stone, 1854. Not married.

———

Children of Rilla Stone (284) *and William Brown.*

290 Emma F. Brown, 1856.
291 Clara E. Brown, 1859.
292 Ida M. Brown, 1861. Died in infancy.
293 William S. Brown, 1862.

———

Children of Ann Eliza Stone and Amos Briggs.

294 Nettie Briggs, 1856.
295 Anna Briggs, 1862.
      An infant, name not known.
Here end the descendants of Whipple Stone. (32)

———

Children of Hopkins Stone (34) *and Amy Salisbury.*

296 Sarah Stone, 1801.
297 Infant, 1803.

By Second Marriage, Mary Corey.

298 William A. Stone, 1812. Eunice Burlingame.
299 Rebecca Stone, 1814. Died in childhood.
300 Infant, 1816.

———

Children of Sarah Stone (285) *and Lyman Aldrich.*

301 Amy S. Aldrich, 1820. John D. Cranston.
302 Thankful W. Aldrich, 1822. T. W. Hill.
303 Tamar Aldrich, 1824. J. H. Cranston.
304 William L. Aldrich, 1827. S. E. Farnsworth.
305 Sarah E. Aldrich, 1830. Ray Greene. p. 16
306 Robert H. Aldrich, 1833. Unknown.

Children of Sarah E. Aldrich (305) and Ray Greene.

307 Waller Hoppin Greene, 1861.

———

Children of Welcome Stone (35) and Lydia Corey.

308 Adaline Stone, 1807. Died in infancy.
309 Esek Stone, 1809. Phebe Ann Brownell.

———

Children of Esek Stone (309) and Phebe Ann Brownell.

310 Lydia Ann Stone, 1830. Died in childhood.
311 William H. Stone, 1833. Died in infancy.
312 Mary E. Stone, 1835. Died in infancy.
313 Esek A. Stone, 1837. Died in infancy.
314 Daniel F. Stone, 1838. Died 1856.
315 Lucy B. Stone, 1840. Truman Sisson.
316 Martha B. Stone, 1843. Daniel Young.
317 Ann E. A. Stone, 1845. Died in infancy.
318 Violetta M. Stone, 1846. Not married.
319 Evelyn A. Stone, 1849. Not married.

———

Children of Lucy B. Stone (315) and Truman Sisson.

320 Adaline Louisa Sisson, 1862.

———

Children of Martha B. Stone (316) and Daniel Young.

321 Daniel Fenner Young, 1862.

Here ends the sub-branch of Peter Stone. (18.)

———

Children of Patience Stone (20) and Thomas Hammond.

322 John Hammond, 1758.
323 Amey Hammond, 1763. Nathan Wood.

Sub-Branch of Samuel Stone, (19) descended from Peter Stone (12) and Patience Printing.

Children of Samuel Stone (19) *and Mary Blanchard.*

324	Almy Stone, 1756.	Peter Potter.	
325	Nathaniel Stone, 1759.	Mercy Gorton.	
326	Rufus Stone, 1760.	Sarah Lewis.	p. 22
327	James Stone, 1762.	Mary Webb.	25
328	Samuel Stone, 1766.	Hannah Sweet.	28
329	Mary Stone, 1767.	William Hill.	30
330	Edmands Stone, 1770.	Amy Ralph.	31
331	Betsey Stone, 1773.	Thomas Hill.	30

———

Children of Almy Stone (324) *and Peter Potter.*

332	Mary Potter, 1785?	James Salisbury.
333	Nathan Potter, 1787?	Elizabeth Albro.
334	Rufus Potter, 1791.	Mary Albro.
335	Almy Potter, 1794.	Olney King.
336	Betsey Potter, 1796.	David Stone.
337	Kezia Potter, 1800.	George Vickery.

———

Children of Nathaniel Stone (325) *and Mercy Gorton.*

338	Mercy Stone, 1783.	George Phillips.	18
338a	William G. Stone. 1785.	Died in infancy.	
339	Samuel Stone, 1787.	Lydia Angell.	18
340	Nathaniel Stone, 1789.	Lucy Round. 2d, Zilpha Round.	19
341	Sally Stone, 1791.	Nathaniel Phillips	20
342	William G. Stone, 1793.	Eley Hopkins	20
343	Lydia Stone, 1795.	Samuel H. Hopkins.	21
344	Charles Stone, 1797.	Died in infancy.	
345	Polly Stone, 1799.	Alpheus Bowen.	21
346	Charles Stone, 1800.	Jerusha Hill.	21

Continued on next page.

4

18

Children of Nathaniel Stone (325) and Mercy Gorton—continued.

347 Daniel Stone, 1803. Eleanor Eddy.   p. 22
348 Eliza Stone, 1808. Barton Randall.   22

Children of Mercy Stone (338) and George Phillips.

349 Hannah A. Phillips, 1808. George Round.
350 George W. Phillips, 1822. Mary A. Sweet.
351a Salvana Phillips. 1825. Abijah B. Sweet.

Children of Samuel Stone (339) and Lydia Angell.

351 Lucinda A. Stone. 1810. Miles Brown.
352 Mercy G. Stone, 1812.
353 Peleg A. Stone, 1814. Hannah M. ——
354 Samuel E. Stone, 1816. Rebecca Anthony, 1863.   19
355 Lydia A. Stone, 1818. Lorenzo Hinkley   19
356 Zilpha P. Stone, 1821. —— Cobb.   19
357 Jared C. Stone, 1826.
358 William N. Stone, 1835. Not married.

Children of Lucinda A. Stone (351) and Miles Brown.

359 Leander Brown.
360 Lovisa Brown.
361 Mary Brown.
362 Isaac Brown.

Children of Peleg A. Stone (353) and Hannah M. ——

363 Ella Stone, 1860.
364 Frederick Harvey Stone, 1865.

Children of Samuel E. Stone (354) and Rebecca Anthony.

365 Julia A. Stone, 1850.
366 Ella A. Stone, 1851.
367 Albert A. Stone, 1853.
368 Edwin A. Stone, 1855.
369 Samuel E. Stone, 1857.
370 Allen Stone, 1860.

———

Children of Lydia A. Stone (355) and Lorenzo Hinkley.

371 Maria Hinkley, 1847.
372 Addie Hinkley, 1849.
373 Delos Hinkley, 1852.
374 Ella Hinkley, 1859.

———

Children of Zilpha P. Stone (356) and —— Cobb.

375 Lydia Cobb, 1847.
376 Eliza Cobb, 1853.
377 Henry C. Cobb.

———

Children of Nathaniel Stone (340) and Lucy Round.

378 Maria Stone, 1810. Died in early life.
379 Clarissa Stone, 1813. Not married.
380 Lucy Stone, 1814. Died in early life.
381 Roxana Stone, 1817. Henry Anthony.   . p. 20

Children by Second Marriage—Zilpha Round.

382 Charlotte Stone, 1827. Died, 1860.
383 Hiram Stone, 1830. Susan S. Simmons.   20

Children of Roxana Stone (381) *and Henry Anthony.*

384 Lucy J. Anthony, 1843.

385 George II. Anthony, 1856.

Children of Hiram Stone (383) *and Susan S. Simmons,*

385 Sidney S. Stone, 1856.

387 Minnie M. Stone, 1863.

Children of Sally Stone (341) *and Nathaniel Phillips.*

388 George A. Phillips, 1815. Died in early life.

389 William N. Phillips, 1817. Died in early life.

390 Almira N. Phillips, 1818. Thomas O. H. Carpenter.

391 Roby Phillips, 1819. James Bennett.

392 Sally M. Phillips, 1821. Almoran Salisbury.

393 Horace Phillips, 1822. Orra Eddy, 1862.

394 Warren Phillips, 1824. Died in early life.

395 Elizabeth Phillips, 1828, George Franklin.

396 Hannah P. Phillips, 1829. John Howard.

Children of William G Stone (342) *and Elcy Hopkins.*

397 Amy H. Stone, 1859. Died in 1836.

398 Lyman B. Stone, 1824. Died in 1829.

399 William G. Stone, 1841. Emily M. Stone, (738)

Children of William G. Stone (399) *Emily M. Stone.* (738)

400 Elmer Franklin Stone, 1861.

In this son of William G. Stone (399) and Emily M. Stone, the branches of Peter Stone (3) and John Stone (4) meet in the eighth generation.

Children of Lydia Stone (343) and Samuel H. Hopkins.

401 Miranda Hopkins, 1818. George V. Bennett.
402 Milite Hopkins, 1819. Edmund Wight.
403 Henry S. Hopkins, 1822. Phebe Cahoone.
404 Harley H. Hopkins, 1824. Eliza Randall.
405 Catherine Hopkins, 1826. Stephen Simmons.
406 Albert H. Hopkins, 1827. Susan Wood.

Children of Polly Stone (345) and Alpheus Bowen.

407 Horace Bowen, 1820. Died in childhood.
408 Henry Bowen, 1821. Elsie Ann Cole.
409 Lucinda Bowen, 1823. Earl D. Barden.
410 Cyrus Bowen, 1824. Rhoda D. Cole.
411 William Bowen, 1826. Eliza Ann Shippee.
412 Almira Bowen, 1828. Olney C. Cole.
413 Mary Bowen, 1833. Died in childhood.
414 Alpheus Bowen, 1834. Died in childhood.
415 Vincent Bowen, 1837. Julia E. Greene.
416 Leonard Bowen, 1840. Sarah J. Randall.
417 Maritta Bowen, 1843. Not married.
418 Horace Bowen, 1845.

Children of Charles Stone (346) and Jerusha Hill.

419 Randall H. Stone, 1822. Lydia M. Cole.
420 Edmund Stone, 1824. Julia Round. p. 22.
421 Sophia Stone, 1826. Died in 1839.
422 Eliza A. Stone, 1828. A. J. Sweet. 22

Children of Randall H Stone (419) and Lydia M. Cole.

423 Alonzo B. Stone, 1851.

Children of Edmund Stone (420) and Julia Round.
423   Charles A. Stone, 1849.
424   Walter I. Stone, 1859.

Children of Eliza A. Stone (422) and A. J. Sweet
425   Rowena Z. Sweet, 1850.
426   Emogen E. Sweet, 1852.
427   Medora J. Sweet, 1856.

Children of Daniel Stone (347) and Eleanor Eddy.
428   Henry W. Stone, 1833.

Children of Eliza Stone (348) and Burton Randall.
429   Charles S. Randall, 1835.
430   Roxana M. Randall, 1840.   Died in childhood.
431   Lester B. Randall, 1845.
432   Stedman. A. Randall, 1848.
Here end the present descendants of Nathaniel Stone. (325)

Children of Rufus Stone (326) and Sarah Lewis.
433   Mercy Stone, 1782.   Died in infancy.
434   Richard Stone, 1784.   Died in childhood.
435   Martha Stone, 1786.   George Hawkins.   p. 23
436   Richard Cecil Stone, 1798.   Alma Stone.   23

The marriage of Richard Cecil Stone (436) and Alma Stone, united the branches springing from Peter Stone (3) and John Stone. (4) Their children found on page 23, are the seventh generation from Hugh Stone and Abigail Bussecot, common ancestors, running back through both branches.

Children of Martha Stone (435) and George Hawkins.

436a Philip P. Hawkins, 1807.   Sarah Weaver.
437 Benoni Hawkins, 1809.   Abbie Grinnell.
438 Sarah Hawkins, 1812.   Benoni Lewis.
439 Sabin L. Hawkins, 1815.   Maria Scott.
440 Elisha Hawkins, 1816.   Rhoda Comstock.

Children of Richard C. Stone (436) and Alma Stone.

441 James L. Stone, 1818.   Elmira Lothrop.
442 S. Hollis Stone, 1821.   Betsey Copeland.
443 George B. Stone, 1823.   Lucy Edson.   p. 24
444 Sarah Stone, 1826.   Stephen C. Arnold.   24
445 Alma Stone, 1828.   Thomas Metcalf.   24
446 Richard.B. Stone, 1829.   Ellen Russell.   24
447 Martha Stone, 1829.   Robert C. Metcalf.   25
448 Mary Stone, 1836.   Thomas Slade.
449 Charles H. Stone, 1840.   Maggie M. Barber.   25

Children of James L. Stone (441) and Elmira Lothrop.

450 Eudora Stone, 1848.

Children of S. Hollis Stone (442) and Betsey Copeland.

451 Aben L. Stone, 1847.
452 Winslow Cecil Stone, 1849.   Died in childhood.
453 Warren Stone, 1852.   Died in childhood.
454 Waldo Hodges Stone, 1855.
455 George Lewis Stone, 1860.   Died in childhood.
456 Mabel Stone, 1863.

Children of George B. Stone (443) and Lucy Edson.

457   Frank Charlton Stone, 1848.

458   Charles Morville Stone, 1855. Died at Minneapolis, 1858.

459   Two infants, not named. Died in early infancy.

460   Harry Winthrop Stone, 1860. Died at St. Louis, 1862.

———

Children of Sarah Stone (444) and Stephen C. Arnold.

461   Alma Stone Arnold, 1847. Died 1857, aged nearly 10.

462   William Edmonds Arnold, 1850.

463   Frederic Richard Arnold, 1858.

464   Ernest Warner Arnold, 1861.

———

Children of Alma Stone (445) and Thomas Metcalf.

465   Florence Metcalf, 1852. Died 1857, aged 5.

466   Walter Boyden Metcalf, 1855. Died 1857.

467   Herbert Cushman Metcalf, 1857.

468   Merton Pennell Metcalf, 1861.

469   Alice Metcalf, 1864.

———

Children of Richard B. Stone (446) and Ellen Russell.

470   Inez Alma Stone, 1854.

471   William Loring Stone, 1856. Died in infancy.

472   Ella Elizabeth Stone, 1857.

473   Frank Burrill Stone, 1860.

464   Mary Stone, 1863.

Children of Martha Stone (447) *and Robert C. Metcalf.*

475 Jennie Elizabeth Metcalf, 1857.
476 Mariella Metcalf, 1859.
477 Gertrude Metcalf, 1864.

Children of Charles Henry Stone (449) *and Maggie M. Barber.*

478 Cola Ephraim Stone, 1863,
479 Lillian Lincoln Stone, 1865.
Here end the present descendants of Rufus Stone. (326)

Children of James Stone (327) *and Mary Webb.*

480	Eliza Stone, 1788. Died in childhood.		
481	Nancy Stone, 1790. Miles Hill.		
482	George Stone, 1792. Naomi Bennett.	p. 26.
483	Betsey Stone, 1794. Thomas Hill.	26
484	John R. Stone, 1796. Sarah Harness.	26
485	William Stone, 1798. Died in 1812.	
486	James Stone, 1800. Phebe Greene—2d, Mary Whitford.	27
487	Asahel Stone, 1802. B. Harrington—2d, Dolly Burnham.	27
488	Israel Stone, 1804. Eliza Burlingame.	28
489	Jeremiah Stone, 1806. Ellen Barber.	28
490	Mary Stone, 1808. Aldis Borden.	28

Children of Nancy Stone (481) *and Miles Hill.*

491 Eliza Hill, 1810. Died in childhood.
492 Richard Hill, 1812. Mary Glass.
493 Anna Hill, 1814. George Smith.
494 Samuel Hill, 1815. Died aged 19.
495 William Hill, 1819.

Children of George Stone (482) and Naomi Bennett.

496　Joshua Stone, 1815.
497　George Stone, 1817.
498　Jonathan Stone, 1819.
499　Zebulon Stone, 1819.

George Stone (482) lives in the State of New York, in or near New Berlin, where he has married a second wife, by whom he has one or more children.

———

Children of Betsey Stone (483) and Thomas Hill.

500　Laurania Hill, 1812.　Horace Phillips.
501　William Hill, 1814.　Cynthia King.
502　Jonathan Hill, 1816.　Phebe Smith.
503　Priscilla Hill, 1818.　Thomas Nutting.
504　James Hill, 1820.　Died 1838.
505　Roby Hill, 1822.　Obadiah King.
506　Thomas Hill, 1825?
507　George Hill, 1830?

It is believed there were two other children, but their names are not known to the writer.

———

Children of John Rice Stone (484) and Sarah Harness.

508　George Stone, 1823?
509　Sarah Stone, 1826?
510　Betsey Stone, 1826?
511　James Stone.

This family lived in Lower Sandusky, Ohio. Of the branches and connection but little has been learned.

Children of James Stone (486) and Phebe Greene.
512 Phebe Stone. 1827. Married, but died 1845.
513 Louisa Stone, 1830. —— Howard.
Several children of this family died in infancy. Names not known.

———

Children of Asahel Stone (487) and Betsey Harrington.
514 Mary Stone, 1824. Died in childhood.
       By Second Marriage, Dolly Burnham.
515 Lyman B. Stone, 1828. Emily Trowbridge.
516 Almira G. Stone, 1830. Edmund Potter.
517 Betsey M. Stone, 1833. Thomas Burgess.
518 Charles A. Stone. 1837. Celinda Howard.   p. 28
519 Sarah A. F. Stone, 1841. Died 1855.
520 George A. Stone, 1846. Not married.

———

Children of Lyman B. Stone (515) and Emily Trowbridge.
521 Andrew Lyman Stone, 1856.
522 Mary Frances Stone, 1861.

———

Children of Almira G. Stone (516) and Edmund Potter.
523 Charles W. Potter, 1854.
524 Linden T. Potter, 1856.
525 Sarah M. Potter, 1858.
526 Hattie Jane Potter, 1862.

———

Children of Betsey M. Stone (517) and Thomas Burgess.
527 Mira F. Burgess, 1849. Died in childhood.
528 Everett Burgess, 1862. Died in infancy.

Children of Charles A. Stone (518) *and Celinda Howard.*
529   Sarah Stone, 1861.
530   Lucy M. Stone, 1863.

———

Children of Israel Stone (488) *and Eliza Burlingame.*
531   Mary Ann Waterman Stone, 1830.   Died in 1846.

———

Children of Jeremiah Stone (489) *and Ellen Barber.*
532   Anna Stone, 1830.   Died in childhood.
533   George Stone. 1831.   Died in infancy.
534   Caroline Stone, 1833.   Leander Burlingame.
535   James Stone, 1835.
536   Frank Pierce Stone, 1853.

———

Children of Mary Stone (490) *and Aldis Borden.*
537   Henry Borden, 1840.
538   George Borden, 1842.
539   James Borden, 1844.
540   Ann Maria Borden, 1847.
541   Aldis Borden, 1849.
542   Mary Emily Borden, 1851.
543   Luther Borden, 1853.
544   Nancy Miranda Borden, 1855.
        Here end the descendants of James Stone. (327)

———

Children of Samuel Stone (328) *and Hannah Sweet.*
545   Cyrus Stone, 1792.   Eleanor Smith.   p. 29
546   George K. Stone, 1794.   Susan Child.   29
547   Amasa Stone, 1796.   Sarah T. Dana.   30
548   William Stone. 1798.   30
549   Almira Stone, 1803.   Daniel Greene.   30

Children of Cyrus Stone (545) *and Eleanor Smith.*

550　Henry Stone, 1822.　Elizabeth Hodson.
551　Charles Edward Stone, 1824.　Caroline Sweet.
552　Cyrus Stone, 1827.　Died in California, aged 32.
553　William G. Stone, 1831.　Sophia Ann Fiske.
554　John H. Stone, 1833.　Died aged 18 years.
555　Benjamin B. Stone, 1836.
556　Caroline Stone, 1838.　W. Lapham. 2d, E. P. Littlefield.
557　Charlotte A. Stone, 1843.　Died aged 16 years.
558　Eugene Smith Stone, 1845.　Died aged 19 years.

———

Children of Charles Edward Stone (551) *and Caroline Sweet.*

559　Walter A. Stone, 1848.　Died in infancy.
560　Edgar N. Stone, 1852.　Died in 1865.
561　Eleanor S. Stone, 1856.　Died in infancy.
562　Frank G. Stone, 1858.
563　Charles Frederick Stone, 1860.
564　Orville E. Stone, 1863.

———

Children of William G. Stone (553) *and Sophia Ann Fiske.*

565　John Emery Stone, 1854.
570　William Eugene Stone, 1860.
571　Eleanor Sophia Stone, 1862.

———

Children of George K. Stone (546) *and Susan Child.*

572　Albert Stone, 1819?
573　George Stone, 1822?
574　Abbie Stone, 1826?
None other of the descendants of Geo. K. Stone (546) are known.

Children of Amasa Stone (517) *and Sarah T. Dana.*
575 Walter W. Stone, 1847.

———

Children of William Stone (548) *and Wife unknown.*
576 William Stone.

———

Children of Almira Stone (549) *and Daniel Greene.*
577 Abbie Ann Greene, 1823. Albert Earl.
578 Charles Henry Greene, 1825. Marion Buck.
579 Phebe Greene, 1827. Stephen P. Henry.
580 Andrew Jackson Greene, 1829. Emma M. Chapman.
581 Ray Greene, 1831. Sarah E. Aldrich.

———

Children of Abby Ann Greene (577) *and Albert Earl.*
582 Emma Greene Earl, 1859. Died in childhood,

———

Children of Phebe Greene (579) *and Stephen P. Henry.*
583 Dutee Greene Henry, 1860.

———

Children of Ray Greene (581) *and Sarah E. Aldrich.*
584 Walter Hoppin Greene, 1861.

———

Children of Andrew J. Greene (580) *and Emma M. Chapman.*
xx   Frank Truman Greene, 1852.
xix Frederick William Greene, 1855.
     Here end the present descendants of Samuel Stone. (328)

———

Children of Mary Stone (329) *and William Hill.*
585 Alice Hill, 1780? —— Bennett.
586 Mary Hill, 1794? Husband not known.

———

Children of Betsey Stone (331) *and Thomas Hill.*
587 Jonathan Hill, 1794? Wife unknown.

Children of Edmands Stone (330) and Amy Ralph.
388 Betsey Stone, 1788. Henry King.
589 Sarah Stone, 1791. Isaac Leach. p. 32
590 David Stone, 1793. Betsey Potter. 32
591 Mary Stone, 1795. Jeremiah Matteson. 32
592 Richard Stone, 1797. Roby Fiske. 32
Second Wife, Lucy Abbott.—Third Wife, Eliza Rogers.
593 Amey Stone, 1799. Seneca Stone. 33
594 Edmands Stone, 1801. Julina Congdon. 33
595 Joseph R. Stone, 1803. Catherine Congdon. 33
596 Robert Stone, 1805. Sarah Taylor. 33
597 Samuel Stone, 1807. Abbie Bennett. 33

Children of Betsey Stone (588) and Henry King.
598 Alma King, 1814. Andrew Moffatt.
599 Eliza King, 1816. Sylvester C. Stone.
600 William H. King, 1818. Celia Taylor.
601 Joseph W. King, 1820.
602 Susan H. King, 1822. Joseph Stone.
603 Jonathan King, 1824. —— Baker.
604 Sarah G. King, 1826.
605 John E. King, 1828. Not married.
606 A. J. King, 1830. Died in infancy.
607 Freelove King, 1831.
608 A. J. King, 1832.

Children of Sarah Stone (589) and Isaac Leach.
609 Amy Leach, 1816. Ezra Barnes.
610 John Leach, 1817.
611 Edmands Leach, 1818.
Continued on next page.

Children of Sarah Stone (589) *and Isaac Leach—continued.*
612 Roby Leach, 1819 ?
613 Mary Leach, 1820 ?
614 Sarah Leach, 1821 ?
615 Lydia Leach, 1823.
616 Samuel Leach, 1826.
There were two more children names unknown.

———

Children of David Stone (590) *and Betsey Potter.*
617 Jason Stone, 1814.
618 Nathan Stone, 1816.
619 Edward Stone, 1818.   Died in early life.
620 Laura Stone, 1829.
For the posterity of the above family, see Appendix.

———

Children of Mary Stone (591) *and Jeremiah Matteson.*
621 Eliza Matteson, 1818.   Not married.
622 Amey Matteson, 1816.   Died 1850.
623 Maria Matteson, 1821.
624 Asa Matteson, 1823.   Out West.
625 Frances Matteson, 1826. —— Walker.

———

Children of Richard Stone (592) *and Roby Fiske.*
626 James Stone, 1819.   Died in infancy.
627 Sarah Stone, 1820.   Died in 1837.
628 William' Stone, 1822.   Died in 1834.
629 Albert Stone, 1824.   Died in early life.
By Second Marriage, Lucy Abbott.
630 Lydia Stone, 1826.   Josiah Lawton.   p. 33
631 Edmands Stone, 1829.   Not married. Killed at Antietam.
632 Olissa Stone, 1832.   Died in childhood.
633 Amey Stone, 1834.   Died in infancy.

Children of Lydia Stone (630) *and Josiah Lawton.*
634   Richard Edmands Lawton.
        By Second Husband, —— *Sherman.*
635x James Sherman.
        Four other children died in infancy.

Children of Amey Stone (593) *and Seneca Stone* (170).
See page 10.

Children of Edmands Stone (594) *and Julina Congdon.*
635   Louisa Stone, 1827. S. Johnson. No children,
636   Harriet B. Stone, 1832. Roswell Baker.   p. 34
637   Emma M. Stone, 1843. Matthew Harigan.   34

Children of Joseph R. Stone (595) *and Catharine Congdon.*
638   Ritner W. Stone, 1836. Died in infancy.
639   Christopher C. Stone, 1839. Died when aged 19 years.

Children of Robert Stone (596) *and Sarah Taylor.*
640   Robert Taylor Stone, 1832. In war; enlisted in Illinois.

Children of Samuel Stone (597) *and Abbie Bennett.*
641   Samuel Stone, 1836. Roxana Shippee; 2d, H. Fiske. 34
642   Albert Stone. Died in the war—at Portsmouth Grove.
643   Abbie E. Stone. John Blanchard.   34
644   Amy Stone. Not married.
645   William Stone, 1853.
646   Amasa Stone, 1855.
               See Appendix.

6

Children of Samuel Stone (641) *and Roxana Shippee.*

647 Maria Stone, 1857.
648 Emma Stone, 1859.

By Second Marriage, Harriet Fiske.

649 Albert Stone, 1863.
650 An infant daughter, born 1865.

———

Children of Abbie E. Stone (643) *and John Blanchard.*

651 An infant son, born 1865.

———

Children of Harriet B. Stone (636) *and Roswell Baker.*

652 Inez Baker, 1857. Died in childhood.
653 Dwight Baker, 1860. Died in infancy.
654 Ezra Baker, 1862.

———

Children of Emma M. Stone (637) *and Matthew Harigan.*

655 Julietta Harigan, 1861.

———

Here ends the sub-branch of Samuel Stone (19) and Mary Blanchard. Samuel (19) was the fourth generation from Hugh Stone (1), the common ancestor. Here ends, also, the branch of Peter Stone (3) and Elizabeth Shaw, to whom is traced (with a small exception) all the persons named in the first thirty-four pages.

Branch of John Stone (4), third son of Hugh Stone (1).

Children of Hugh Stone (1) *and Abigail Bussecot.*

2 Hugh Stone, 1668. Mary Potter.
3 Peter Stone, January 20, 1671. Elizabeth Shaw.
4 John Stone, 1674. —— Barnes; 2d, Abigail Foster.
5 Abigail Stone, 1677. Husband unknown.
6 Anne Stone, 1679. William Potter; married 1705.
7 George Stone, 1681. Wife unknown.

————

Children of John Stone (4) *and* —— *Barnes.*

656 John Stone, 1705. —— Olney. Was shot—see note.
657 George Stone, 1709. Rest Clarke. p. 42
658 William Stone, 1711. Eleanor Westcott. 52

By Second Wife, Abigail Foster.

659 Anne Stone, 1716. William Colgrove.
660 Abigail Stone, 1718. Amos Hammond.
661 Jonathan Stone, 1720. Elizabeth Westcott. 80
662 Alice Stone, 1723. Daniel Fiske.
663 Benjamin Stone, 1725. Mary Strait.
664 Joseph Stone, 1727. Anne Kent. 80
665 Lydia Stone, 1730. Wilson Spencer.
666 Prudence Stone, 1732. Robert Vaughan.

————

Children of John Stone (656) *and* —— *Olney.*

667 Oliver Stone, 1738. Phebe Brown. 36
667a Caleb Stone, 1739. Drowned in early life.
668 John Stone, 1741. Phebe Greene. 40
668a Olney Stone, 1743. Went west, to parts unknown.
668b Rhoda Stone, 1744. —— Hammond.
668c Zilpha Stone, 1746. —— Goodrich.
668d Ezekiel Stone, 1746. Drowned when two years old.
668e Phebe Stone, 1748. John Gorton.
668f Anne Stone, 1749. Husband, if any, unknown.

Children of Oliver Stone (667) *and Phebe Brown.*

669 Russell Stone, 1763. Elizabeth Bullock.
670 Waity Stone, 1765. James Durfee ; no children.
671 Caleb Stone, 1767. Amy Thornton.
672 Polly Stone, 1769. J. Colburn ; 2d, John Reynolds.
673 Benoni Stone, 1770. Susan M'Intire.
674 William Stone, 1774. Elizabeth Brown.   p. 37
675 Anne Stone, 1780. Edmund Colvin. No children.
676 Phebe Stone, 1784. P. Randall ; 2d, Wm. Stone (46). 39

Children of Russell Stone (669) *and Elizabeth Bullock.*

677 Lydia Stone. ——— Crayton.
678 Phebe Stone. Gardner Horton.
679 Robert Stone. Wife unknown.

Russell Stone (669) probably had a number of children, but
nothing has been known of them for the last forty years. Russell
(669) lived in the State of New York, near the Catskill Mountains. See Appendix.

Children of Caleb Stone (671) *and Amy Thornton.*

680 Delinda Stone. Unmarried.
681 Caroline Stone. Unmarried.

Children of Polly Stone (672) *and Joseph Colburn.*

682 Waity Colburn, 1798. George Kirk.

Children of Benoni Stone (673) *and Susan M'Intire.*
683 Oliver Stone, 1800. Rachel Steere ?
684 Lewis Stone, 1804. Lydia Tinkham.
685 Maria Stone, 1805. Samuel Farris.
686 Lydia H Stone, 1809. James M'Intire.
687 Joseph Nelson Stone, 1817. Not married ; died, 1837.

Children of Charles E. Stone (712) and Eliza Darwin.

688   Henry J. Stone, 1857.
689   Ella M. Stone, 1859.   Died in childhood.
690   Lizzie Stone, 1861.   Died in childhood.
691   Ida J. Stone, 1864.   Died in childhood.
692   Lottie M. Stone, 1865.

Children of William Stone (674) and Elizabeth Brown.

695   Waity Stone, 1796.   Daniel Greene ; no children.
696   Mary Stone, 1798.   Died in 1836.
697   Simon Stone, 1800.   Sally Smith.   p. 37
698   Rhoda Stone, 1802.   Silas Smith ; no children.
699   William R. Stone, 1804.   Amy Grayson.   38
700   Abbie Ann Stone, 1806.   Silas Cole.   38
701   George N. Stone, 1808.   Died in 1830.
702   Eliza Stone, 1810.   Died in 1824.
703   Richmond Stone, 1812.   Susan Cheney; 2d, Sally Haven. 38
704   James Stone, 1815.   Sarah Grayson.   39
705   John R. Stone, 1822.   Susan Grayson.   39

Children of Simon Stone (697) and Sally Smith.

706   Lucy Stone, 1825.   Charles Biggs.   38
707   Henry Stone, 1827.   Alma M. Morse ; no children.
708   Eliza E. Stone, 1828.   John Putney.
709   Sarah Stone, 1830.   James Barlow.
710   Mary Stone, 1832.   J. Richardson ; 2d, G. L. Avery.
711   Rhoda M. Stone, 1833.   Otis Barlow.
712   Charles E. Stone, 1835.   Eliza Darwin. (See top of this p.)
713   Daniel S. Stone, 1837.   Laura Richards.
714   George N. Stone, 1839.   Lottie A. Roper.
714a   Jacob Stone, 1841.   Died in infancy.
715   William J. Stone, 1843.   Jennie Spencer ; no children.
716   Susan Stone, 1846.   Martin L. Phillips.
717   Samuel A. Stone, 1849.   Not married.
For other descendants of Simon Stone (697), see Appendix.

Children of Lucy Stone (706) and Charles Biggs.

a   Henry C. Biggs, 1846.   Died in war, 1863.
b   Elma A. Biggs, 1848.   Levi W. Richards.
c   Simon Biggs, 1850.   Died in childhood.
d   Waity Biggs, 1854.
e   Orville Biggs, 1856.
f   Lucy Biggs, 1859.
g   Luther Biggs, 1859.
h   Gilson B. Biggs, 1863.

Children of William R. Stone (699) and Amy Grayson.

718   George A. Stone, 1833.   Melissa C. Stone (930).
719   Urana Stone, 1835.   Died in childhood.
720   Samuel H. Stone, 1837.   Julia A. Stone (931).
721   William G. Stone, 1839.   Ellen M. Stone (932).
722   Henry C. Stone, 1841.
723   Albert R. Stone, 1843.   Died aged 19 years.
724   Ellen Stone, 1845.   William Marchant.
725   Julia A. Stone, 1849.

Children of George A. Stone (718) and Melissa C. Stone (930).

726   George Orlando Stone, 1856.
727   Ange Ella Stone, 1858.
728   Harriet Elizabeth Stone, 1861.
729   Elice Janet Stone, 1863.

Children of Samuel H. Stone (720) and M. E. Adams.

730   Vidella Jane Stone.
            By Second Wife, Julia Ann Stone (931).
731   Charlie Francis Stone, 1861.
732   Amos Winfield Stone, 1863.

Children of Abbie Ann Stone (700) and Silas Cole.

733   Nelson G. Cole.
For children of Richmond Stone (703), see Appendix.

Children of James Stone (704) *and Sarah Grayson.*
734 Richard G. Stone, 1844.
735 Frederick A. Stone, 1846.
736 James Allen Stone, 1851.

Children of John R. Stone (705) *and Susan Grayson.*
737 Laura E. Stone, 1845. Gilbert Hopkins.
738 Emily M. Stone, 1847. William G. Stone (399).
739 Louisa A. Stone, 1849. Thomas M. Hopkins.
740 Ella E. Stone, 1857.

For children of Emily M. Stone (738) and William G. Stone (399), see page 20.
Here end the present descendants of William Stone. (674) and Elizabeth Brown.

Children of Phebe Stone (676) *and Phineas Randall.*
741 Elizabeth Randall, 1805. Ira Blackmar.
By Second Marriage, William Stone (46).
742 Lydia A. Stone, 1810. William Joyce.
743 Andrew J. Stone, 1813. E. M. Cone.
744 George W. Stone, 1815. Lucinda M'Peake.

Children of Elizabeth Randall (741) *and Ira Blackmar.*
745 Susan M. Blackmar, 1822. W. T. Dodge.
746 Henry R. Blackmar, 1824. Died in childhood.
747 Burrill H. Blackmar, 1826. Jane Barrows.
748 Jason A. Blackmar, 1828. N. Olney ; 2d, Sarah Packard.
749 Nelson E. Blackmar, 1830. Anna Newhall.
750 Perry L. Blackmar, 1832. Died in childhood.
751 Wheaton O. Blackmar, 1835. Sarah Capwell.
752 Israel L. Blackmar, 1839. Louisa M. Dyer.
753 Mary C. Blackmar, 1842. E. D. Freeman.

Children of Andrew J. Stone (743) *and E. M. Cone.*
754 Betsey J. Stone.

Here end the present descendants of Oliver Stone (667).

Children of John Stone (668) *and Phebe Greene.*

755 William Stone, 1772. Abigail Randall; 2d, Lydia Arnold.
756 Sally Stone, 1776. Joseph Wheaton. p. 41
757 Phebe Stone, 1779. John Dixon ; no children.
758 Stephen A. Stone. 1792. Prudence Morse ; 2d, Lucy 42
Johnson; 3d, Lydia Douglass.

———

Children of William Stone (755) *and Abigail Randall.*

759 Olney R. Stone, 1797. Alpha Sheppardson.
760 John Stone, 1799. Mary Colwell.
761 Godfrey G. Stone, 1801. Polly Mowry.

By Second Wife, Lydia Arnold.

762 Maria Stone, 1806. Died aged 14 years.
763 Sally Stone, 1807. Not married.
764 William A. Stone, 1809. Charlotte Dutcher. 41
765 Elisha Stone, 1811. Olivia P. Eastman. 41
766 Abbie E. Stone, 1816. John W. Richards. 41
Ten numbers omitted.

———

Children of Olney R. Stone (759) *and Alpha Sheppardson.*

777 Francis Stone, 1821. Died young.
778 An infant, 1823. Died in infancy.

———

Children of John Stone (760) *and Mary Colwell.*

779 Julia Frances Stone, 1829. James A. Brown. 40, 41
780 William Stone, 1831. Died in childhood.
781 Maria Louisa Stone, 1833. Daniel Marvin ; no children.
782 Harriet Angeline Stone, 1836. Thomas Gardner. 41
783 John Abbott Stone, 1838.
784 Alpha Amanda Stone, 1844.

———

Children of Julia Frances Stone (779) *and James A. Brown.*

785 Charles Albert Brown, 1851. Died in 1859.
786 Mary Louisa Brown, 1856.

Continued on next page.

Children of Julia Frances Stone (779) *and James A. Brown,*
continued.
787 Emma Harriet Brown, 1858.
788 Julia Amanda Brown, 1860.
789 Sarah P. E. Brown. 1861.
790 Henry Eastman Brown, 1864.

Children of Harriet Angeline Stone (782) *and Thomas Gardner.*
791 Mary Lucy Gardner, 1858.
792 Sarah Frances Gardner, 1859.
793 George S. Gardner, 1864.

Children of Godfrey G. Stone (761) *and Polly Mowry.*
793a Maria Stone, 1823.

Children of William A. Stone (764) *and Charlotte Dutcher.*
794 Henry Arnold Stone, 1843.
795 Eliza Richmond Stone, 1845.

Children of Elisha Stone (765) *and Olivia P. Eastman.*
796 Clarence E. Stone, 1852.
797 Kate Olivia Stone, 1856.

Children of Abbie E. Stone (766) *and J. W. Richards.*
797a Adaline Frances Richards, 1835. George Leavens.
798 Mary Elizabeth Richards, 1841. Charles Haven.
799 William Stone Richards, 1843.
800 Helen Olivia Richards, 1847.
  Here end the present descendants of William Stone. (755)

Children of Sally Stone (756) *and Joseph Wheaton.*
801 George Wheaton, 1811?
802 Lucius Wheaton, 1813?
803 Joseph Wheaton.
804 Mary Wheaton.
805 Jeremiah Wheaton.

Children of Stephen A. Stone (758) *and Prudence Morse.*

806   Phebe Ann Stone, 1816. Henry Dresser.

806a Stephen Morse Stone, 1817. Died in infancy.

By Second Wife, Lucy Johnson.

807   Pardon M. Stone, 1819. Mary F. Mason.

808   Noadiah Mason Stone, 1820. Died in 1844.

809   Tyler Putnam Stone, 1823. Died in 1840.

810   Edwin Hamilton Stone, 1824. Died in childhood.

811   Maria H. Stone, 1827. William O. Darling.

Second Marriage, John Howson.

812   James Edwin Stone, 1830. Died in childhood.

———

Children of Phebe Ann Stone (806) *and Henry Dresser.*

813   Henry C. Dresser, 1837.

814   Mary Emily Dresser, 1839. Died 1864.

Here ends the sub-branch of John Stone, (656) who was the third generation from Hugh Stone (1) common ancestor. John Stone (656) was first son of John Stone. (4)

———

Children of George Stone (657) *and Rest Clarke.*

815   Ezra Stone, 1736. Freelove Howland.   p. 42 and 43

816   Rest Stone, 1738. Husband, if any, unknown.

817   John Stone, 1740. Wife, if any, unknown.

818   Jane Stone, 1743. James Field. Married 1763.

819   George Stone, 1748. Married and lived in N. Y. state.

———

Children of Ezra Stone (815) *and Freelove Howland.*

820   James Stone, 1759. Ruth Hopkins. No children.

821   John Stone, 1761. Hannah Eddy.   43

822   Freelove Stone, 1763. Arnold Mann.   47

823   Ezra Stone, 1764. Lucina White.   47—48

Continued on next page.

Children of Ezra Stone (815) *and Freelove Howland—Continued.*

824 Asahel Stone, 1766. Lois Brown.
825 Oziel Stone, 1767. Nabbie Bowen.
826 Mary Stone, 1769. Not married. Died aged 70.
827 Martha Stone, 1771. Nahum Humes.
828 George Stone, 1773. Mollie Humes.   p. 49
829 William Stone, 1786. Died aged 22 years.

Children of John Stone (821) *and Hannah Eddy.*

830 Bathsheba Stone, 1779. Daniel Chase. 2d, J. Lynch.
831 Joseph Stone, 1781. Anne Foster.
832 Betsey Stone, 1785. Caleb Brown.   44
833 Ruth Stone, 1787. Ransom Upham.   44—45
834 John Stone, 1789. Esther Curtiss.   35
835 Anne Stone, 1792. Not married.
836 Mary Stone, 1794. John Corbin. No children.
837 James Stone, 1802. Abbie Larkin.   47

Children of Bathsheba Stone (830) *and Daniel Chase.*

830 John Chase.
839 Elisha Chase.
840 Daughter, name unknown.
841 Daniel Chase.

Children of Joseph Stone (831) *and Anne Foster.*

842 Hannah Stone, 1801. Not married.
843 Polly Stone, 1803. Not married.
844 George Stone, 1806. Olive Cundall.   44
845 Enoch Stone, 1807. Diana Humes.   44
846 Isaac Stone, 1808. Died in 1835.
847 Ebenezer Stone, 1810. Died in Infancy.
848 Bathsheba Stone, 1810. Died in infancy.
849 Ann Stone, 1816. Not married.

Children of George Stone (844) and Olive Cundall.

850 Joseph W. Stone, 1830. Caroline Leach.
851 William J. Stone, 1832. Frances P. Sharpe.
852 Mary C. Stone, 1834. Nathaniel H. Lippitt.
853 Betsey A. Stone, 1836. George L. Sears.
854 Georgiana F. Stone, 1839. Died in childhood.

Children of Joseph W. Stone (850) and Caroline Leach.

855 Ella C. Stone, 1852.
856 George M. Stone, 1857.

Children of William J. Stone (851) and Frances P. Sharpe.

857 Charles I. Stone, 1861.

Children of Betsey A. Stone (853) and George L. Sears.

858 Georgiana Frances Sears, 1859.

Children of Enoch Stone (845) and Diana Humes.

859 Mary J. Stone, 1844.
860 Martha A. Stone, 1846. Died in infancy.
861 Sarah J. Stone, 1848.
862 George Stone, 1850.

Children of Betsey Stone (832) and Caleb Brown.

863 James Brown.   Sarah Shelly.
864 Ezekiel Brown.   Wife, if any, unknown.
865 Caleb Brown.   Mary Stone. (911)

Children of Ruth Stone (833) and Ransom Upham.

866 Erastus Upham, 1812. Zoa Bradford.
867 Emeline Upham, 1814. Phineas Copeland.
868 Orin Upham, 1816. Lucy Ann Wilson.
869 Hamilton B. Upham, 1819. Sally Copeland.
900 Angeline Upham, 1821. William Arnold—see next page.

Between the last two numbers 30 omitted ; from 869 to 900.

Children of Ruth Stone (833) *and Ransom Upham—Continued.*

901   Elmira M. Upham, 1824.   William Arnold.
902   Carlo C. Upham, 1827.   Eleanor Reynolds.
903   Joseph N. Upham, 1829.   Mary E. Knapp.

———

Children of John Stone (834) *and Esther Curtiss.*

904   Marvin Stone, 1808.   Zilpha Dunham.
905   Charles E. Stone, 1810.   Susannah Vinton.
906   Otis E. Stone, 1811,   Emily Child.   p. 46
907   Esther M. Stone, 1812.   Daniel F. Hubbard   46
908   Pardon F. Stone, 1814.   Chloe Taft.   46
909   Rebecca B. Stone, 1817.   Wilson Cutler.   46
910   Maria M. Stone, 1819.
911   Mary Stone, 1821.   Caleb Brown. (865)
912   Sarah E. Stone, 1823.   Horace Gay.   47
913   Hannah E. Stone, 1826.   Eddy Pray.   47

———

Children of Marvin Stone (904) *and Zilpha Dunham.*

914   Otis P. Stone, 1840 ?   Amanda Hall.

———

Children of Otis P. Stone (914) *and Amanda Hall.*

915   Eddy Stone, 1861.
916   Irving Stone, 1863.

———

Children of Charles E. Stone (905) *and Susannah Vinton.*

917   Lucy Ann Stone, 1841.   Died aged 17 years.
918   Esther Stone, 1843.   Orin Hill.
919   Sarah Stone, 1848.
920   Andrew J. Stone, 1851.
921   Susan Stone, 1854.

Children of Otis E. Stone (906) *and Emily Child.*
922   James Stone, 1837.   Lydia Greene.
923   John Stone, 1839.   Nellie Cogswell.
924   Emma Jane Stone, 1851.

Children of Esther M. Stone (907) *and Daniel F. Hubbard.*
925   Maria Hubbard. 1840.
926   Frank Hubbard, 1843.   Maria Metcalf.
927   Lewis Hubbard, 1850.
928   Ira Hubbard, 1852.
929   Marcia Hubbard, 1856.

Children of Pardon F. Stone (908) *and Chloe Tuft.*
930   Melissa C. Stone, 1837.   George A. Stone. (718)
931   Julia Ann Stone, 1840.   Samuel H. Stone. (720)
932   Ellen M. Stone, 1843.   William G. Stone. (721)
For the grandchildren of Pardon F. Stone, (908) see page 38—
being the children of Melissa C. Stone, (930) and Julia Ann Stone,
(931.)

Children of Rebecca B. Stone (909) *and Wilson Cutler*
933   Orin W. Cutler, 1842.
934   Sarah E. Cutler, 1845.   Died in infancy.
935   Otis Byron Cutler, 1847.   Died in infancy.
936   Lizzie Maria Cutler, 1849.

Children of Mary Stone (911) *and Caleb Brown.* (865)
937   Emily Brown, 1846.   Died in childhood.
938   Nelson Brown.   Was a soldier in the war.
939   Curtiss Brown.
940   Charles Brown.
941   Henry Brown.
942   Stetson Brown.
943   Alphonso Brown.
944   Frederick Brown,
The last five of this family are probably not set in the order in
which they were born.

Children of Sarah E. Stone (912) and Horace Gay.

945 Henry Gay, 1846.
946 Sarah E. Gay, 1848.
947 Anna Maria Gay, 1851.
948 Otis Byron Gay, 1854.
949 Ernest Laforest Gay, 1857.
950 Ada Estella Gay, 1859.

Children of Hannah E. Stone (913) and Eddy Pray.

951 Augusta Wilson Pray, 1857.

Children of James Stone (837) and Abbie Larkin.

952 Marcus F. Stone, 1821. Harriet Reed.
953 Dacy Stone, 1824. Smith Jones.
954 Bathsheba Stone, 1826.
955 Appleton Stone, 1827. Sarah Castle.
956 William Stone, 1829. Jennie Fox.

Here end the present descendants of John Stone (821) and Hannah Eddy.

Children of Freelove Stone (822) and Arnold Mann.

957 Arnold Mann.
958 Lucy Stone Mann.

There were other children whose names are not known.

Children of Ezra Stone (823) and Lucina White.

959 James Stone, 1791. Abigail Paine. p. 48
960 Hannah Stone, 1793. Richard Thayer. 48
961 Samuel Stone, 1795. —— Paine.
962 Lucy Stone, 1796. Arnold Mann.
963 Nathan Stone, 1798. Ada Phillips. 48
964 Olive Stone, 1799. Amasa Esten. 48
965 Roxana Stone, 1801. Hiram Wentworth.

Continued on next page.

48

Children of Ezra Stone (823) and Lucina White—Continued.

966 Lois Stone, 1803. Amasa Esten.
967 William Stone, 1807. —— White.
968 Hiram Stone, 1809. Mary Metcalf.
969 Freelove Stone, 1811. Died in early life.
970 Ezra Stone, 1812. Died in infancy.

Children of James Stone (959) and Abigail Paine.

971 Orin Stone Paine.
972 Samuel Paine.

Children of Hannah Stone (960) and Richard Thayer.

973 Sylvia Thayer, 1826 ?
974 Eliza Thayer, 1829.
975 Huldah Thayer, 1832.
976 Richard Thayer, 1836. This son is blind.

Children of Nathan Stone (963) and Ada Phillips.

977 Ezra Stone, 1818.
978 Alzada Stone, 1820.
979 Harley Stone, 1822.

Children of Olive Stone (964) and Amasa Esten.

980 Hannah Esten, 1827? Leprelate Salisbury.
981 Moses Esten, 1828.
982 Lucina Esten, 1830. Died aged 18 years.

Children of Lois Stone (966) and Amasa Esten.

983 Betsey Esten, 1832. Died 7 years of age.
984 Amasa Esten, 1834. Rhoda Young.
985 William Esten, 1837. Adaline ——
986 Elisha Esten, 1840? Hannah Wilson.
987 Elvira Esten, 1843 ?
988 Alexander Esten, 1846.
989 Adalaide Esten, 1848. Died aged 14 years.

For children of Roxana Stone, (965) and Hiram Wentworth, see Appendix.

———

Children of Hiram Stone (968) *and Mary Metcalf.*
990 Henry Stone, 1828? Wife unknown.
991 Charles Stone, 1830? Wife unknown.
992 Amanda Stone, 1832? Not married.
Here end the present descendants of Ezra Stone. (823)

———

Children of George Stone (828) *and Molly Humes.*
993 Amos Stone, 1798. Julia Angell.
994 Dacy Stone, 1800. Died aged 12 years.
995 Chloe Stone, 1801. Erastus Robinson. No children.
996 Azuba Stone, 1804. Brown Angell.   p 50
997 Asahal Stone, 1806. Sarah Battey.   50
          By Second Wife, Polly McDonald.
998 Candace Stone, 1810. Olney Fairfield. See below.
999 Alice Stone, 1812. William Clarke.   51
1000 Phebe Stone, 1815. Not married.
1001 Cynthia Stone, 1818. Stephen Emerson See below.
1002 Arnold Stone, 1821. Philinda Aldrich.   51

———

Children of Amos Stone (993) *and Julia Angell.*
1003 Nancy Stone, 1823. Hiram Ross.
1004 Mercy Stone, 1825. William Ross.
1005 Susan Stone, 1827. Marvin Wilson.

———

Children of Candace Stone (998) *and Olney Fairfield.*
1006 Eliza Fairfield, 1836. ——— Staples.
1007 George Fairfield, 1839.
1008 Emma Fairfield, 1850.

———

Children of Cynthia Stone (1001) *and Stephen Emerson.*
1009 C. H. Emerson, 1849.

Children of Azuba Stone (996) *and Brown Angell.*

1010 George Angell, 1827.   Lydia Ross.
1011 Luther Angell, 1829.   Amanda Lee.
1012 Nelson Angell, 1830.   Sarah Greene.
1013 Amey Ann Angell, 1832.   Seth Ross.
1014 Enoch Angell, 1834.   Abby Tinkham.   Died 1856.
1015 Alfred Angell, 1837.
1016 Sylvester Angell, 1839.
1017 Adaline Angell. 1841.
1018 Wilson Angell, 1847.

Children of Asahel Stone (997) *and Sarah Battey.*

1019 Almira Stone, 1829.   Henry Timothy.
1020 Emeline Stone, 1831.   Edmund W. Hawkins.   p. 51
1021 George Stone, 1833.   Mary F. Mott.   51
1022 Marcella Stone, 1835.   Died in 1856.
1023 Stephen Stone, 1837.   Carrie Carpenter.   51
1024 Fanny Stone, 1839.
1025 Emily A. Stone, 1841.
1026 Clovis Stone, 1843.
1027 Maria Stone, 1845.   Died in 1846.
1028 Albert F. Stone, 1847.
1029 Charles Stone, 1849.

Children of Almira Stone (1019) *and Henry Timothy.*

1030 Walter Scott Timothy, 1855.
1031 Gertrude Timothy, 1857.
1032 An Infant, 1858.
1033 Annie Timothy, 1860.
1034 Frederick Timothy, 1862.
1035 Henry Timothy, 1864.   Died in infancy.

Children of Emeline Stone (1020) *and E. W. Hawkins.*
1036   Emma E. Hawkins, 1854.   Died in infancy.

———

Children of George Stone (1021) *and Mary F. Mott.*
1037   Frederick Stone, 1864.   Died in infancy.

———

Children of Stephen Stone (1023) *and Carrie Carpenter.*
1038   Lizzie H. Stone, 1865.
Here end the present descendants of Asahel Stone, (997)

———

Children of Alice Stone (999) *and William Clark.*
1039   Olney Clark, 1830.
1040   Emeline Clark, 1835.
1041   Seria Clark, 1842.
1042   Jeremiah Clark, 1850.

———

Children of Arnold Stone (1002) *and Philanda Aldrich.*
1043   Marcus M. Stone, 1846.
1044   Ellen F. Stone, 1848.
1045   Jane M. Stone. 1849.
1046   Phebe E. Stone, 1853.
1047   John G. Stone, 1857.
 x 8   Emeline A. Stone, 1859.
 x 9   Adda E. Stone, 1862.
 x 10 Louis N. Stone, 1865.

Here ends the sub-branch of George Stone (657) and Rest Clarke, who was the second son of John Stone. (4)

Children of William Stone (658) and Eleanor Westcott.

1048   William Stone, 1733. Lydia Westcott.
1049   Freelove Stone, 1736. Ephraim Westcott.   p. 63
1050   Jabez Stone, 1740. Sarah Taylor, 2d, W. Greene.   60
1051   Jeremiah Stone, 1745. Dinah Knight.   64
1052   James Stone, 1753. Rebecca Sheldon.   74

Children of William Stone (1048) and Lydia Westcott.

1053   William Stone, 1758. Lucy Scott.
1054   Westcott Stone, 1761. Abbie Smith.
1055   Lydia Stone, 1764. Asa Knight.
1056   Ruth Stone, 1768. Daniel Bennett.
1057   Arthur Stone, 1772. Died 1797.
1058   Asa Stone, 1777. Phebe Greene.

Children of William Stone (1053) and Lucy Scott.

1059   Welcome Stone, 1783. Susan Hudson.
1060   Artemas Stone, 1786. Mahala Henry.   p. 53
1061   Benoni Stone, 1788. Aurilla Blanchard.   54
1062   Lucy Stone, 1793. Earl Manchester.   57
1063   Sally Stone, 1795. Died in early life.
1064   William Stone, 1797. Candace Henry.   58

Children of Welcome Stone (1059) and Susan Hudson.

1065   Nancy W. Stone, 1808. Charles Bailey.   53
1066   Eliza Stone, 1810. James Williams. See below.
1067   Ira B. Stone, 1812. Content Ryan. 2d, Olive ——   53
1068   Ethan A Stone, 1814. Lucinda ——   53

Children of Eliza Stone (1066) and James Williams.

1069   Calvin Gay Williams, 1832.
1070   Mary E. Williams, 1835. Henry L. Dean.
1071   Lucetta Williams, 1845.

Children of Nancy W. Stone (1065) *and Charles Bailey.*

1072 Susan E. Bailey, 1829. Charles A. Colvin.
1073 Lucy M. Bailey, 1831. Norman Leach.
1074 Abbie C. Bailcy, 1834. H. Coonrod.
1075 Nathan W. Bailey, 1836. Catherine Leach.
1076 Lovisa N. Bailey, 1839. F. D. Tingley.
1077 Polly O. Bailey, 1841. Died in childhood.
1078 Lydia A. Bailey, 1844. L. M. Bennett.
1079 Edwin T. Bailey. 1846.

———

Children of Ira B. Stone (1067) *and Content Ryan.*

1080 Susan A. Stone, 1837. William H. Marcy,
1081 Halina Stone, 1839. —— Angell.
1082 Laura Stone, 1841.
1083 Delia Stone, 1846.
            By Second Wife, Olive ——
1084 Charles B. Stone, 1856.

———

Children of Ethan A. Stone (1068) *and Lucinda* ——

1085 Nancy Stone, 1834. Died in childhood.
1086 Ira B. Stone, 1836.
1087 George Stone, 1838. In war.
1088 Eliza C. Stone, 1840.
       Several children, not mentioned, died in childhood.

———

Children of Artemas Stone (1060) *and Mahala Henry.*

1089 Dexter G. Stone, 1812. Elizabeth Lillibridge.   p. 54.
1090 Sheldon H. Stone, 1814. Died 1825.
1091 Leonard R. Stone, 1817. See note.
1092 Benoni Stone, 1819. Harriet Emerson.
1093 Sallie Stone, 1821. Edwin Manchester.   54
1094 Ruth Stone, 1824. Charles Hawkins.   54
1095 Susan R. Stone, 1827. Died in childhood.

Children of Dexter G. Stone (1089) *and Elizabeth Lillibridge.*
1096   Mahala Stone, 1834.   Died in infancy.
1097   Dexter S. Stone, 1836.
1098   Angenette Stone, 1839.   Edgar G. Winsor.
1099   John T. Stone, 1842.   Clara Briggs.
1100   Mary E. Stone, 1847.

Children of Angenette Stone (1098) *and Edgar G. Winsor.*
1101   Edgar Windsor, 1858.
1102   Harrie Windsor, 1864.

Children of Sallie Stone (1073) *and Edwin Manchester.* (1188)
1103   Clarence Hartwell Manchester, 1863.

Children of Ruth Stone (1094) *and Charles Hawkins.*
1104   Annie Hawkins, 1843.
1105   Mary F, Hawkins, 1845.   Died in childhood.
1106   Charles L. Hawkins, 1848.
1107   Clarence A. Hawkins, 1855.
1108   Frank S. Hawkins, 1859.

Children of Benoni Stone (1061) *and Aurilla Blanchard.*
1109   Sidney T. Stone, 1813.   Mary Decker.   No children.
1110   Pamelia B. Stone, 1814.   Stephen A. Taylor.   p. 55
1111   Welcome Stone. 1816.   Arabella Stanton.   55
1112   Rasselas Stone. 1818.   Amanda M. Cottrell.   55 & 56
1113   Almeda C. Stone, 1820.   William Franklin, 1865.   56
1114   Artemas Stone, 1821.   Sarah Tuthill.   56
1115   Solon S. Stone, 1824.   Died 1850.
1116   Hiram L. Stone, 1826.   Sarah M. Myers.   57
1117   William M. Stone. 1829.   Emily Cure.   57
1118   Lucy A. M. Stone, 1831.   Charles Taylor.   57
1119   Oscar F. Stone, 1833.   Alvira Mitchell.   56
            By Second Wife, Catharine M. Miller.
1120   Julia S. Stone, 1857.

Children of Pamelia B. Stone (1110) *and S. A. Taylor.*

1121 Leonora B. Taylor, 1837. Thomas B. Grosvenor.
1122 Victoria A. Taylor, 1840. Died 1844.
1123 Angeline V. Taylor, 1844. Stephen Miller.
1124 Helen A. Taylor, 1847. Harrison Gardiner.
1125 Abigail A. Taylor, 1850.
1126 Eunice A. Taylor, 1854. Died in infancy.
1127 Napoleon E. Taylor, 1855. Died 1858.
     Infant,   1857. Died in infancy.

Children of Welcome Stone (1111) *and Arabella Stanton.*

1128 Caroline H. Stone, 1844. Theodore Taylor.
1129 Henry C. Stone, 1845.
1130 Norman E. Stone, 1847.
1131 Catherine E. Stone, 1849.
1132 Isabella A. Stone, 1853. Died 1865.
1133 Arabella A. Stone. 1853.
1134 Helen G. Stone, 1855.
1135 Frederick L. Stone, 1857.
1136 Andrew C. Stone, 1863. Died in 1865.
    Two infants not named.

Children of Caroline H. Stone (1128) *and Theodore Taylor.*

1137 Ralph E. Taylor. Died in infancy.
1138 Carrie A. Taylor, 1866.

Children of Rasselas Stone (1112) *and Amanda M. Cottrell.*

1139 Susan C. Stone, 1841. Jessie Cobb.   p. 56
1140 Esther A. Stone, 1843.
1141 Sarah E. Stone, 1844. Elisha Lane.   56
1142 Laura M. Stone, 1846. Francis Finch.
1143 James Stone, 1848.
1144 Mary A. Stone. 1850.
1145 George W. Stone, 1852.
            Continued on next page.

Children of Rasselas Stone (1112) *and Amanda M. Cottrell,*
Continued.

1146   Pamelia S. Stone, 1854.
1147   Winfield S. Stone, 1856.
1148   Josephine Stone, 1860.
1149   Emogene Stone, 1863.

Children of Susan C. Stone (1139) *and Jesse Cobb.*

1150   Clarence Cobb, 1861.
1151   Ida Cobb, 1862.
1152   Georgiana Cobb, 1863.
1153   Susan Cobb, 1865.

Children of Sarah E. Stone (1141) *and Elisha Lane.*

1154   Francis Lane, 1865.

Children of Artemas Stone (1114) *and Sarah Tuthill.*

1155   Lucy A. Stone, 1850.
1156   Daniel A. Stone, 1853.
1157   William C. Stone, 1856.
1158   Emery A. Stone, 1860.   Died 1862.
1159   Emery D. Stone, 1864.

Children of Almeda C. Stone (1113) *and William Franklin.*

1160   Rosella A. Franklin, 1841.   Collins Wetherbee.
1161   Benjamin Franklin, 1843.
1162   Josephine Franklin, 1845.   Died 1849.
1163   Francis M. Franklin, 1849.
1164   Oscar Franklin, 1853.
1165   Sarah Franklin, 1856.   Died 1864.

Children of Oscar F. Stone (1119) *and Alvira Mitchell.*

1166   Victor B. Stone, 1856.
1167   Lucy Stone, 1860.   Died 1861.
1168   Arthur K. Stone, 1862.
1169   John M. Stone, 1864.

57

Children of Lucy A. M. Stone (1118) and Charles Taylor.

1170   Jasper C. Taylor, 1857.
1171   Florence E. Taylor, 1859.
1172   Charlotte A. Taylor, 1861.   Died 1861.
1173   Ada M. Taylor, 1862.   Died 1866.
1174   Maud, or Matilda E. Taylor, 1865.

Children of Hiram L. Stone (1116) and Sarah M. Myers.

1175   Angeline A. Stone, 1849.   Died 1852.
1176   Jacob W. Stone, 1851.
1177   Emery C. V. Stone, 1854. .
1178   Charles E. Stone, 1856.
1179   William H. Stone, 1859.
1180   Lyman H. Stone, 1862.   Died 1863.

Children of William M. Stone (1117) and Emily Cure.

1181   Julia E. Stone, 1849.
1182   Norman C. Stone, 1851.
1183   John M. Stone, 1852.   Died 1858.
1184   Mary E. Stone, 1855.

Children of Lucy Stone (1062) and Earl Manchester.

1185   Samuel G. Manchester, 1813.   F. P. Reynolds.
1186   Henry W. Manchester, 1815.   Sarah Hodges.
1187   Amy S. Manchester, 1818.   A. A. Nichols.
1188   Edwin H. Manchester, 1820.   Sarah Potter,
      -                    2d, Sallie Stone. (1073)
1189   Almira Manchester, 1825.   Myron Dean.
1190   William E. Manchester, 1827.   Mary Hazzard.

9

Children of *William Stone* (1064) *and Candace Henry.*

1191 Lucinda Stone, 1819.
1192 Harris H. Stone, 1820. Abbie Ann Parker.
1193 Celia R. Stone, 1822.
1194 Amarilla A. Stone, 1824. Edwin W. Potter.
1195 Susan R. Stone, 1828.
1196 William A. Stone, 1830. Sarah Whipple.

Children of *Amarilla A. Stone* (1194) *and E. W. Potter.*

1197 Frank Potter, 1858.
1198 Mariella Potter, 1859.

Children of *William A. Stone* (1196) *and Sarah Whipple.*

1199 Frederic William Stone, 1852. Died 1857.
1200 Frank Stone, 1855. Died in infancy.
1201 Walter Delmont Stone, 1859.
1202 Henry Harris' Stone, 1859.
1203 Clara Janette Stone, 1861. Died in childhood.
1204 Charles Thomas Stone, 1865.

Children of *Westcott Stone* (1054) *and Abbie Smith.*

1205 Achsah Stone 1805. J. Potter, 2d, H. Hubbard.
1206 Earl Stone, 1806. Rebecca Hierlehigh. p. 59

Children of *Achsah Stone* (1205) *and Joseph Potter.*

1207 Ellery Potter, 1830 ?
   By Second Husband, Henry Hubbard.
1208 Eudora D. Hubbard, 1832? Abel Squires.
w 9 George S. Hubbard, 1835 ?
w 10 Westcott S. Hubbard, 1838? Married—himself & wife dead.
w 11 Jerusha Hubbard, 1841 ? James C. Carpenter.
w 12 Demaris M. Hubbard, 1845 ?
w 13 Janette A. Hubbard, 1848.

Children of Earl Stone (1206) *and Rebecca Hierlehigh.*

1209   Westcott Stone, 1849.
1210   Winfield C. Stone, 1852.
1211   Eva L. Stone, 1855.
1212   Ella E. Stone, 1858. Died 1863.
1213   Isham G. Stone, 1861.
1214   Carrie I. Stone, 1864.

Children of Lydia Stone (1055) *and Asa Knight.*

1215   Archibald Knight, 1796. Margaret Blanchard.
1216   Benjamin Knight, 1798. Died aged 15 years.
1217   Asa Knight, 1801. Elvira Rice.
1218   Anna Knight, 1804. William Hierlehigh.
1219   Darius Knight, 1807. Roscinda Howland.
1220   Irene Knight, 1810. James Simmons.

Children of Asa Stone (1058) *and Phebe Greene.*

1221   Lydia Stone, 1805.
1222   Arthur F. Stone, 1806. Died in early manhood.
1223   John Enos Stone, 1808. Susan Potter.
1224   Lowry Stone, 1810. Mary Arnold.   p. 60
1225   Lovicie Stone, 1810. Died in childhood.
1226   Earl M. Stone, 1812. Died 1826.
1227   Asa Stone, 1816. Diantha Eames. 2d, Judith Hodges. 60
1228   Mason P. Stone, 1818. A. E. Bowen. 2d. Amy Parker. 60
              3d, Cyrene Chase.

Children of John Enos Stone (1223) *and Susan Potter.*

1229   Phebe Stone, 1836. Joseph Ledward.
1230   Amanda M. Stone. 1841. Edwin G. Fry.
1231   Susan A. Stone, 1843. D. H. Beckwith.
1232   Ellen M. Stone, 1849.

Children of Phebe Stone (1229) *and Joseph Ledward.*

1233   Charles H. Ledward, 1860.

Children of Lowry·Stone (1224) *and Mary Arnold.*

1234   Lucetta A. Stone, 1847.
1235   Robert Earl Stone, 1849.

Children of Asa Stone (1227) *and Diantha Eames.*

1236   Arthur F. Stone, 1842.
1237   Edward L. Stone, 1845.
          By Second Wife, Judith Hodges.
1238   Annie Stone, 1859.

Children of Mason P. Stone (1228) *and Amy Parker.*

1239   Ann Eliza Stone.   Died in childhood,
          By Third Wife, Cyrene Chase.
1240   Byron Stone.
   M. P. Stone (1228) married a fourth wife, and has several children. See biographical note.
   Here end the present descendants of William Stone (1048) and Lydia Westcott.

Children of Jabez Stone (1050) *and Sarah Taylor.*

1241 Eleanor Stone. 1759. Joseph White.		
1242 Joseph Stone, 1761. Mary Bowen.		
1243 Jabez Stone, 1764. Freelove Manchester.		p. 61
1244 Ambrose Stone, 1767.		
1245 Sarah Stone, 1770. Matthew Manchester.		61
1246 Daniel Stone, 1773. Polly Gorton.		61
1247 Isabella Stone, 1778. J. Hammett. 2d, D. C. Goff.		63

          By Second Wife, W. Greene.
1248   Stephen Stone, 1801.   Phebe Comstock.   63

Children of Eleanor Stone (1241) *and Joseph White.*

1249   Charles White, 1786?   Cynthia Potter.
   It is believed there were other children,—not as yet traced.

Children of Jabez Stone (1243) *and Freelove Manchester.*
1250   An infant, 1788.
1251   Wanton Stone, 1790.   Freelove Knight.
1252   Jabez T. Stone, 1806.   Died in infancy.
1253   Freelove M. Stone, 1806.   Nathan R. Colvin.

Children of Wanton Stone (1251) *and Freelove Knight.*
1254   Lorenzo D. Stone, 1815.
1255   Edwin K. Stone, 1816.
1256   Amasa A. Stone, 1816.   Died in infancy.
1257   Maria Stone, 1820.   Isaac Walling.
1258   Hannah M. Stone, 1822.   Pardon Shippee.
1259   Elizabeth W. Stone, 1825.   George Smith.
1260   Harriet K. Stone, 1830.   Henry Sheppard.
1261   Henry C. Stone, 1832.
1262   Charles D. Stone, 1836.   Almira A. Arnold.

Children of Sarah Stone (1245) *and Matthew Manchester.*
1263   Earl Manchester, 1791.   Lucy Stone. (1062)
1264   Job Manchester. 1796.   P. Fry, 2d, —— Congdon.
1265   Almira Manchester, 1799.   —— Gorton.
1266   Phebe Manchester, 1802.   Thomas R. Greene.

Children of Daniel Stone (1246) *and Polly Gorton.*
1267   Sarah Stone.   Shuman Baldwin.   p. 62
1268   Jabez Stone.   Zilpha Adams.   62
1269   Adelia Stone.   Henry Taylor.
1270   Benjamin G. Stone.   Mary Blanchard.
1271   Mary Stone.   Died in childhood.
1272   James W. Stone.   Caroline Shippee.
1273   Caroline Stone.   William Bunyer.
1274   Ambrose Stone.
1275   Thankful A. Stone.   William H. Budlong.   62
1276   Daniel J. Stone.   Harriet E. Chase.   62

Children of Sarah Stone (1267) *and Shuman Baldwin.*
1277 Lodena Baldwin. Deceased.•
1278 Mary Baldwin. Deceased.
1279 William Treat Baldwin. Deceased.

———

Children of Jabez Stone (1268) *and Zilpha Adams.*
1280 Sphina Stone, 1829. A. L. Daskam.
1281 Lucinda Stone, 1830. R. N. Holden.
1282 B. F. Stone, 1833.
1283 Emeline Stone, 1834. Died 1836.
1284 P. J. Stone, 1835. Addie Erkenbrack.
1285 Sarah J. Stone, 1840. Albanus Little.
1286 James A. Stone. 1841.
1287 Addison B. Stone, 1844. Mary Doyle.

———

Children of Sarah J. Stone (1285) *and Albinus Little.*
1288 George Lyman Little, 1860. Died in childhood.
1289 Jerome Little, 1862.

———

Children of Thankful A. Stone (1275) *and William H. Budlong.*
1290 Caroline Budlong, 1838. William Morgan.   •
1291 William H. Budlong, 1840. Ellen Kinnecom.

———

Children of Daniel J. Stone (1276) *and Harriet E. Chase.*
1292 Stephen Dexter Stone, 1840. E. H. Burgess.   p. 63
1293 Alonzo P. Stone, 1846.   •
1294 Abbie F. Stone, 1848.
1295. Solomon Stone, 1850.
1296 Nelson P. Stone, 1852.
1297 Consola Stone, 1854. Died in infancy.
1298 Flora Stone, 1855. Died in childhood.
1299 Massina Stone, 1858.

Children of Stephen Dexter Stone (1292) *and Elizabeth Burgess.*
1300 Harrie Stone, 1861.
1301. Edwin Stone, 1863.

Children of Isabella Stone (1247) *and John Hammett.*
1302 Alexander R. Hammett, 1799. Eunice Ledyard.
1303 Clorinda Hammett, 180?. William E. Rice.
By Second Husband, D. C. Goff.
1304 Alzada A. Goff, 1806.
1305 Betsey Rhodes Goff, 1808.
1306 Horatio Goff, 1811. Louisa Maxen.
1307 Amy Goff. Warren Weaver.
1308 Raymond Goff. Eleanor Whaley.
1308a Sallie Goff, Joseph Capwell.

Children of Stephen Stone (1248) *and Phebe Comstock.*
1309 Charles H. Stone, 1819. Catharine A. Brightman.
1310 An infant, 1821. Died in infancy.
1311 Almon Stone, 1823. Sarah Brown.
1312 Elias S. Stone, 1826. Susan Walden.
1313 Isaac H. Stone, 1830. Elvira Rhodes.
1314 Sarah V. Stone, 1832. William R. Northup.
1315 Julia A. Stone, 1836. Henry A. Dorrance.
For grand children of Stephen Stone, (1248) see Appendix.
Here end the present descendants of Jabez Stone. (1050)

Children of Freelove Stone (1049) *and Ephraim Westcott.*
1316 Ephraim Westcott, 1760. Freelove Stone.
1317 Silas Westcott, 1765. Wife unknown.
1318 Jeremiah Westcott, 1772. Eunice Potter.
2d. O. Burlingame.
1319 Samuel Westcott, 1776. Wife unknown.
1320 Lucy Westcott, 1781. Nichols Whitford.

Children of Jeremiah Stone (1051) and Dinah Knight.

1321 Freelove Stone, 1761.   Ephraim Westcott. (1316)
1322 Charles Stone, 1764.   Rachel Knight.
1323 Hannah Stone, 1766.   Darius Knight.   p. 67
1324 Henry Stone, 1770.   Lydia Blackmar.   67
1325 Abigail Stone, 1773.   John Whipple.   73
1326 Mercy Stone, 1775.   George Knight.   73
1327 Dinah Stone, 1778.   Silas Weaver.   73
1328 Jeremiah Stone, 1781.   Died in infancy.
1329 Knight Stone, 1784.   Died in infancy.

———

Children of Freelove Stone (1321) and Ephraim Westcott. (1316)

1330 Zilpha Westcott, 1782 ?   Nathan Bailey.
1331 Asahel Westcott, 1784 ?   Sarah Cole.
1332 Gardner Westcott, 1788 ?   Wife unknown.
1333 Zina Westcott, 1792 ?   Hannah Albro.
1334 Susan Westcott, 1794 ?   Clarke Greene.
1335 Nathaniel Westcott, 1798.   Abigail Albro.
1336 Amy Westcott, 1800.   Gorton Parker.

———

Children of Charles Stone (1322) and Rachel Knight.

1337 Nehemiah Stone, 1783.   Died in infancy.
1338 Nathan K. Stone, 1785.   Cilda Matteson.
                              2d, Rhoda Cooke.
1340 Phebe Stone, 1787.   Wanton Chase.
1341 Allerson Stone, 1787.   Sarah Burlingame.   p. 67
1342 Jason P. Stone, 1791.   Alice Hazzard.

———

Children of Nathan K. Stone (1338) and Cilda Matteson.

1343 Alban M. Stone, 1807.   Mary A. Morse.   65
1344 Cynthia P. Stone, 1808.   Horace King.   65
1345 Minerva Stone, 1811.   David H. Wightman.   65
1346 Phebe Stone, 1812.   E. B. Smith.   66

Continued on next page.

Children of Nathan K. Stone (1338) and Cilda Matteson.
Continued.

1347   Horatio A. Stone, 1814.   H. Lamphier,
      2d, E. Almy.   3d, Ann Eliza Whitman.   p. 66
1348   Jason P. Stone, 1816. Eliza Albro. 2d Sarah Weeks.   66
1349   Melissa C. Stone, 1818.   Stephen Whitman.   66
1350   Alice H. Stone, 1820.   Died 1853.
1351   Harriet P. Stone, 1822.   Stephen Whitman.
1352   James B. Stone 1826.   Died in infancy

Children of Alban M. Stone (1343) and Mary A. Morse.

1353   George Alban Stone, 1833.   Died in childhood.
1354   James Burrill Stone, 1836.   Julia A. Greene.
1355   Charles Johnson Stone, 1838.   Died in infancy.
1356   Sarah Adams Stone, 1840.   James H. Disbrow.
1357   Charles Johnson Stone, 1841.   Died in infancy.
1358   George Alban Stone, 1843.   Died in infancy.
1359   Rebecca Adams Stone, 1844.   Died in childhood.
1360   Mary Melissa Stone, 1846.   Died in childhood.

Children of James B. Stone (1354) and Julia A. Greene.

1361   Charles Greene Stone, 1860.
1362   Lillian Adams Stone, 1864.

Children of Sarah A. Stone (1356) and James H. Disbrow.

1363   Charles Stone Disbrow, 1862.
1364   Frederick Alban Disbrow, 1865.

Children of Cynthia P. Stone (1344) and Horace King.

1365   Catharine King.   Died in childhood.
1366   John King, 1833.   Maria Knight.

Children of Minerva Stone (1345) and David H. Wightman.

1367   Almy S. Wightman, 1839.
1368   Eliza M. Wightman, 1840.   William N. Allen
1369   Horatio A. Wightman, 1843.
1370   Charles S. Wightman, 1850.

10

Children of Phebe Stone (1346) *and E. B. Smith.*

1371   Emily J. Smith, 1828.   Died 1844.
1372   Susan Smith, 1832.
1373   Phebe B. Smith, 1834.
1374   Marion Smith, 1836.

Children of Horatio A. Stone (1347) *and H. Lamphier.*

1375   Infant son, 1842.   Died in infancy.
1376   Edgar A. Stone, 1846.   Died in infancy.

By Second Wife, Elizabeth Almy.

1377   Elizabeth A. Stone, 1848.

By Third Wife, Ann Eliza Whitman.

1378   Frederick W. Stone, 1852.   Died in infancy.
1879   Henry H. Stone, 1854

Children of Jason P. Stone (1348) *and Eliza Albro.*

1380   Eliza Jane Stone, 1841.   Died aged 15 years.
1381   Adelaide M. Stone, 1843.
1382   Jason P. Stone, 1846.
1383   Emily A. Stone, 1848

By Second Wife, Sarah Weeks.

1384   Herbert P. Stone, 1854.   Died in infancy.
1385   Alice E. Stone, 1856.
1386   Frederic C. Stone, 1858.
1387   Minerva Stone, 1860.

Children of Melissa C. Stone (1349) *and Stephen Whitman.*

1388   Harriet Melissa Whitman, 1842,   Peleg Kinyon.

Children of Allerson Stone (1341) *and Sarah Burlingame.*

1389   Lovice D. Stone, 1807.
1390   Charles M. Stone, 1810.   Mary E. Holden.
1391   Rachel K. Stone, 1822.

Children of Charles Morgan Stone (1390) *and Mary E. Holden.*

1392   Anna M. Stone, 1833.   Albert O. Baker.
1393   Charles M. Stone, 1837.

Children of Anna M. Stone (1392) *and Albert O. Baker.*

1394   Anna F. Baker, 1858.
1395   Emily S. Baker, 1858.
1396   Catharine M. Baker, 1860.
1397   Albert A. Baker, 1862.
1398   Pardon H. Baker, 1862.
Here end the present descendants of Charles Stone, (1322).

Children of Hannah Stone (1323) *and Darius Knight.*

1399   Jeremiah Knight, 1791.   Amy Waterman.
1400   Mary Knight, 1795.   Joseph Parker.
1401   Joseph Knight, 1798.   Olive Colvin.
1402   Abigail Knight, 1800.   Welcome Fiske.
1403   Dinah Knight, 1804.   Daniel Atwood.
1404   Elizabeth Knight, 1807.   Philip Salisbury.

Children of Henry Stone (1324) *and Lydia Blackmar.*

1405   George Stone, 1788.   M. Carpenter,
                        2d, Mahala Mason.   p. 68
1406   Waldo Stone, 1790.   Betsey Johnston.   '68
1407   Knight Stone, 1792.   Zilpha Matteson.   69
1408   Betsey Stone, 1794.   Died in infancy.
1409   Ellen Stone, 1796.   Owen Arnold.
1410   Cyrene Stone, 1798.   Joseph Burlingame.   70
1411   Alma Stone, 1800.   Richard C. Stone, (436)   71
1412   Clarissa Stone, 1803.   Died in 1821.
Continued on next page.

Children of Henry Stone (1324) *and Lydia Blackmar.* *Continued*
1413 Roby Stone, 1805. Joseph Briggs.   p. 71
1414 Melina Stone, 1808. C. J. Westcott. 2d, J. West.   72
1415 Rachel K. Stone, 1810. W. Andrews.
                            2d, G. Brownell.   71
1416 Henry B. Stone, 1812. Louisa Johnson.   71
1417 Charles G. Stone, 1815. Sophia P. Sprague.   72

Children of George Stone (1405) *and Lydia Blackmar.*
1418 Julia Stone, 1807. Charles Burlingame.
1419 Waldo Stone, 1809. Not married.
1420 Sallie Stone, 1813. Eric Walker.
          By Second Wife, Mahala Mason.
1421 Emily Stone, 1832. Joel Vaughan.

Children of Julia Stone (1418) *and Charles Burlingame.*
1422 Henry Burlingame, 1826. Mary Stone, (1493).
1423 Mary E. Burlingame, 1828. Thomas Fuller.

Children of Sallie Stone (1420) *and Erie Walker.*
1424 Arnold B. Walker, 1843. Died in early life.
1425 George A. Walker, 1847. Died in early life.
1426 Mary E. Walker, 1850.
1427 Elbridge E. Walker, 1853.

Children of Waldo Stone (1406) *and Betsey Johnson.*
1428 Orren Stone, 1813. Died 1831.
1429 Asahel Stone, 1815. Died 1834.
1430 Esther Read Stone, 1818. Died 1835.
1431 Alzada Stone, 1820. Henry B. Arnold.

Children of Alzada Stone (1431) *and Henry B. Arnold.*
1432 Orren Stone Arnold, 1837.
1433 Denham Arnold, 1839.

Children of Knight Stone (1407) *and Zilpha Matteson.*

1434   Lydia Stone, 1811.   F. C. Colvin.
1435   Job M. Stone, 1813.   Elizabeth Dicker.
1436   Orrilla Stone, 1815.   John Bailey.
1437   Knight Stone, 1817.   Fidelia P. Clarke.   p. 70.
1438   Abigail W. Stone, 1820.   Henry M'Clarrin.   70
1439   Clarissa Stone, 1824.   G. A. Carr.   70
1440   Alzada M. Stone, 1830.   Albert Whitman.

————

Children of Lydia Stone (1434) *and F. C. Colvin.*

1441   Melina Colvin.
1442   Laura J. Colvin.
1443   Joab Colvin.
1444   Horatio V. Colvin.
1445   Lydia Colvin.

————

Children of Job M. Stone (1435) *and Elizabeth Dicker.*

1446   Melissa Stone.   Philander Potter.
1447   Emily Stone.   Died in childhood.
1448   Delania Stone.   Henry Peck.
1449   Ann Stone.   Henry Taylor.

————

Children of Orrilla Stone (1436) *and John Bailey.*

1450   Margaret Bailey, 1836.   Thomas Smith.
1451   Fidelia Bailey, 1837.   Augustus Colvin,
1452   Almira Bailey, 1839.   William R. Smith.
1453   Lucinda Bailey, 1841.   Died in childhood.
1454   Levi M. Bailey, 1844.
1455   Adelaide Bailey, 1847.   Charles L. Spencer.
1456   Hollis B. Bailey, 1850.
1457   Arthur C. Bailey, 1855.

Children of Knight Stone (1437) *and Fidelia P. Clarke.*

1458   Mary E. Stone, 1846.   William Doyle.
1459   Alvira Stone, 1847.
1460   Noel Stone, 1849.
1461   Charles E. Stone, 1851.
1462   Fernando C. Stone, 1853.
1463   Albert W. Stone, 1854.
1464   Nicholas Stone, 1856.
1465   Cenora Stone, 1859.
1466   Benjamin F. Stone, 1861.   Died in infancy.
1467   Alzada M. Stone, 1864.

Children of Mary E. Stone (1458) *and William Doyle.*

1468   Emma Doyle, 1865.

Children of Abigail W. Stone (1438) *and Henry McClarrin*

1469   Agnes McClarrin, 1856.
1469a   William McClarrin. 1859.

Children of Clarissa Stone (1439) *and G. A. Carr.*

1470   John W. Carr, 1851.   Died in childhood.
1471   Isabella A. Carr, 1853.
1472   George A. Carr, 1855.
1473   John S. Carr, 1858.
1474   Lucy Carr, 1861.
1475   Nelson B. Carr, 1863.
1476   Alzada M. Carr, 1865.

Children of Cyrene Stone (1410) *and Joseph Burlingame.*

1477   Alfreda Burlingame, 1818.
1478   Betsey Burlingame, 1820.   I. H. Whitaker.
1479   Nelson A. Burlingame, 1822.   Mary Sherman.
1480   Richard S. Burlingame, 1824.   Mary Ann Cole.

Continued on next page.

Children of Cyrene Stone (1410) *& Joseph Burlingame.—Contin'd.*

1481   Cynthia G. Burlingame, 1826. E. O. Potter.
1482   Owen A. Burlingame. 1828. Mary J. Stanley.
1483   Leander S. Burlingame, 1831. Caroline Stone, (534)
1484   Albert O. Burlingame, 1834. Lydia Stanley.
1485   Charles M. Burlingame, 1836.

For the children of Alma Stone, (1411), and Richard C. Stone, (436), and the connexion of the branches of John Stone, (4). and Peter Stone, (3), in the seventh generation. See pages 22 and 23.

Children of Roby Stone (1413) *and Joseph Briggs.*

1486   Clarinda M. J. Briggs, 1831. E. P. Thurston.
1487   Angenette F. Briggs, 1835. Charles Parrott.
1488   Daniel W. Briggs. 1841. Died in childhood.
1489   Almira F. Briggs, 1844.

Children of Rachel K. Stone (1415) *and William Andrews.*

1490   Lydia Andrews, 1840. Died in infancy.
1491   Harriet N. Andrews, 1842. Edwin Baker.

Children of Henry B. Stone (1416) *and Louisa Johnson.*

1492   Jane Stone, 1833. Truman Brown. 2d. D. Carter.
1493   Mary Stone, 1835. Henry Burlingame, (1422).
1494   Alma Stone, 1837. Died in childhood.
1495   Caroline Stone, 1837. —— Martin.   p. 72

Children of Jane Stone (1492) *and Truman Brown.*

1496   George Brown, 1854.
1497   Frank Brown, 1856.

       By Second Husband, Daniel Carter.

1498   Martha Carter, 1864.

Children of Mary Stone (1493) *and Henry Burlingame,* (1422).

1499   Henry Burlingame, 1856.

Children of Caroline Stone (1495) *and ——— Martin.*

1500   Sophia Martin, 1865.

———

Children of Charles G. Stone (1417) *and Sophia P. Sprague.*

1501   Susan M. Stone, 1835.   Eugene D. Burt.
1502   Edwin D. Stone,'1836.   Died in childhood.
1503   Charles D. Stone, 1838.   Died, 1858.
1504   Martha S. Stone, 1841.   Charles Tillinghast.
1505   Lydia F. Stone, 1843.   Died in childhood.
1506   Henry B. Stone, 1846.
1507   Frank F. Stone, 1848.

———

Children of Susan M. Stone (1501) *and Eugene D. Burt.*

1508   Mary B. Burt, 1864.

———

Children of Martha Stone (1504) *and Charles Tillinghast.*

1509   Charles B. Tillinghast, 1861.   Died in childhood.

———

Children of Melina Stone (1414) *and Charles J. Westcott.*

1510   Edwin J. Westcott, 1829.   Lucy B. Barnes.
1511   Cordelia Adeliza Westcott, 1831.   Allen Chilson.
1512   Charles J. Westcott, 1833.
1513   Mary H. Westcott, 1836.   S. Round.   2d, G. E. Lyman.

By Second Husband, J. West.

1514   Lydia West, 1845.   Died in infancy.
1515   George West, 1848,
1516   James West, 1850.

———

Children of Edwin J. Westcott (1510) *and Lucy B. Barnes.*

1517   Melina Westcott.
1518   Charles Westcott.

Children of Cordelia Adeliza Westcott (1511) *and Allen Chilson.*

1519   Ellen M. Chilson, 1850.   Died in childhood.
1520   Henry A. Chilson. 1852.   Died in childhood.
1521   Charles A. Chilson, 1854.
1522   Mattie B. Chilson, 1859.
1523   Alice Chilson, 1863.   Died in infancy.
1824   Eddie Whiting Chilson, 1865.   Died in infancy.

Here end the present descendants of Henry Stone, (1324).

Children of Abigail Stone (1325) *and John Whipple.*

1525   Nehemiah K. Whipple, 1793.   Died in childhood.
1526   Polly Whipple, 1795.   Richard Howard.
1527   Alfred Whipple, 1798.   Lucy Ellis.   2d, D. Corpe.
1528   Cynthia Whipple, 1801.   Olney Williams.
1529   Selinda Whipple, 1803.   Gardner Howard.
1530   Robert Whipple, 1806.   Orilla Hill.
1531   Jason S. Whipple, 1810.   Emeline Smith.

Children of Mercy Stone (1326) *and George Knight.*

1532   William Warren Knight, 1796.   Elizabeth Colvin.
1533   Penelope Knight, 1798.   S. P. Taylor.
1534   Betsey Knight, 1802.   Welcome Matteson.
1535   Daniel Knight, 1805.   Susan Colvin.
1536   Tirza Knight, 1809.   Remington Strait.
1537   Lyman B. Knight, 1811.   L. Parker.   2d, P. Parker.

Children of Dinah Stone (1327) *and Silas Weaver.*

1538   Owen B. Weaver 1798.   Mary Arnold.
1539   James P. Weaver, 1801.   Almira Rice.
1540   Charles S. Weaver, 1803.   Diana Northup.
1541   Sallie C. Weaver, 1805.   Joseph L. Bennett.
1542   Nehemiah K. Weaver, 1807.   Freelove Peck.
1543   Celia Weaver, 1809.   Thomas D. Bentley.

Continued on next page.

11

Children of Dinah Stone (1327) *and Silas Weaver.—Continued.*

1544 Alston Weaver, 1811. Ruth Cornell. 2d, Lovisa Spalding.
1545 Silas G. Weaver, 1814. Susan Weaver.
1546 Sterry A. Weaver, 1816. Jane Clute.
1546a Harriet R. Weaver, 1819. Enoch Cox.

Here end the present descendants of Jeremiah Stone, (1051), commencing on page 64.

Children of James Stone (1052) *and Rebecca Sheldon.*

1547 Robert Stone, 1776. Sybil Dean. 2d, Almira Greene.
1548 John Stone, 1777. Rhoda Barney. p. 75
1549 Mary Stone, 1779. Stephen Parker. 75
1550 Lemuel Stone, 1781. Anna Colvin. 2d, S. Miles. 76
1551 Samuel Stone, 1784. S. Hall. 2d, P. Colvin. 78
1552 Celinda Stone, 1785. Sampson Wright 78
1553 James Stone, 1789. Polona Greene. 2d, C. Ackley. 78
1554 Rebecca Stone, 1795. Samuel Clarke.
1555 Asenath Stone, 1798. Died 1813.

Children of Robert Stone (1547) *and Sybil Dean.*

1556 Almira Stone, 1804. Horace Tripp.
1557 James Stone, 1805. Sarah Stone.
1558 Betsey Stone, 1806. Nathan Sherman.
1559 William Stone, 1808. Irene Nichols.
1560 Ezra Stone, 1809. Frances Wright. 75
1561 Lora Stone, 1811. Died in 1816.

Children of James Stone (1557) *and Sarah Stone.*

1562 Althema Stone, 1831. Joseph P. Northup. See note.
1563 Hannibal Stone, 1835. Clesia Parker. See note.
1564 Columbus Stone, 1837. Died in 1857.
1565 Foster Stone, 1840.
1566 Almond Stone, 1843.
1567 Andrew Stone, 1852.

Children of Ezra Stone (1560) *and Frances Wright.*

1568   Dewitton Stone, 1836.   Kate Shields.
1569   Robert M. Stone, 1840.
1570   Frank L. Stone, 1843.
1571   Alton Murray Stone, 1848.

Children of John Stone (1548) *and Rhoda Barney.*

1572	Riley Stone, 1802. Ruth Onsterhoudt	p. 81
1572a	Rachel Stone, 1803. Died 1819.	
1573	Rebecca Stone, 1805. Isaac Sherman	81
1574	Jeremiah Stone, 1808. Louisa Rice. 2d, Laura Rice.	81
1575	Sabra Stone, 1811. William C. Greene.	81
1576	Aurilla Stone, 1813. William C. Greene.	81
1577	John Stone, 1815. Esther L. Sisson.	
1578	Rhoda Stone, 1817. H. W. Nicholson. 2d, L. Jones.	82
1579	Rachel Stone, 1820. William Hawthorne.	82

Children of Mary Stone (1549) *and Stephen Parker.*

1580   Alvah Parker, 1800.   Polly Chambers.
1581   Delilah Parker, 1802.   Job A. Northup.
1582   Sheldon Parker, 1804.   Susan Phillips.
1583   Charles Parker, 1806.   Susan Hall.
1584   Mary Parker, 1810.   Daniel Van Fleet.
1585   Rebecca Parker, 1813.   William Hull.
1586   Asenath Parker, 1814.   Stephen Parker.
1587   Celinda Parker, 1816.   Ezra Colvin.
1588   Lucy Ann Parker, 1821.   Died in 1849.
1589   Damaris Parker, 1823.

Children of Lemuel Stone (1550) *and Anna Colvin.*

1589a Harriet Stone. 1803.   Died in childhood.
1590 Philip Stone, 1805.   Sarah Northup.
1591 Meriam Stone, 1807.   Reuben Sherman.
1592 Pardon Stone, 1810.   N. Clark.   2d, Ellen Tripp.
1593 Edwin Stone, 1812.   Louisa Smith.   p. 77
1594 Hannah Stone, 1816.   Leonard Bachelder.   77
1595 Lora W. Stone, 1818.   Delia Griffin.
              2d. Celinda C. Reynolds.   3d, Julia Gorman.   77
1596 Anson J. Stone, 1820.   Rachel Stephens.   77
1597 Lovisa L. Stone, 1823.   Joseph Chase.   77

Children of Philip Stone (1590) *and Sarah Northup.*

1598 Emanuel Stone, 1829.
1599 Ann M. Stone, 1830.

Children of Emanuel Stone (1598) *and*

1600 Clifton E. Stone, 1853.
1601 Anna J. Stone, 1855.

Children of Meriam Stone (1591) *and Reuben Sherman.*

1602 Caroline Sherman.
1603 Amy Ann Sherman.   Judson Clark.
1604 Lemuel Sherman.

Children of Pardon Stone (1592) *and Nancy Clarke.*

1605 Theodore E. Stone, 1834.   Elizabeth Sherman.
1606 George L. Stone, 1836.
1607 Watson D. Stone, 1837.
1608 Sarah Stone, 1839.   Died in childhood.
1609 Silas L. Stone, 1841.   Died 1848.

By Second Wife, Ellen Tripp.
1610 Lydia A. Stone, 1846.   John Taylor.

Children of Hannah Stone (1594) *and L. Batchelder.*

1611 Delia Batchelder, 1842.
1612 Lemuel Batchelder, 1844. Died in childhood.
1613 Joseph Batchelder, 1847. Died in childhood.
1614 Ward Batchelder, 1850.

Children of Lora W. Stone (1595) *and 2d Wife, Celinda C. Reynolds.*

1615 Charles W. Stone, 1846. Died in childhood.

By Third Wife, Julia Gorman.

1616 Delia C. Stone, 1849. Died in childhood.
1617 Ida A. Stone, 1851. Died in childhood.
1618 John L. Stone, 1852.
1619 Eddie E. Stone, 1857. Died in childhood.
1620 Hattie Stone, 1863.

Children of Anson J. Stone (1596) *and Rachel Stephens.*

1621 Charles A. Stone, 1851.
1622 Almor Stone, 1853.
1623 Sterling B. Stone, 1855.
1624 Fannie M. Stone, 1863.

Children of Lovisa L. Stone (1597) *and Joseph Chase.*

1625 Lyman Chase, 1847.

Children of Edwin Stone (1593) *and Louisa Smith.*

1626 George A. Stone, 1834. Died in childhood.
1627 Benjamin M. Stone, 1835. Olive E. Newton.
1628 Thomas W. Stone, 1838.
1629 S. Lovisa Stone, 1841. George W. Crocker.   p. 78
1630 Mary L. Stone, 1850.

Children of Benjamin M. Stone (1627) *and Olive E. Newton.*

1631 Henry L. Stone, 1861. Died in infancy.
1632 Edwin N. Stone, 1862.
1633 Burton Stone, 1865.

Children of Lovisa Stone (1629) *and George W. Crocker.*
1634   Lucius Crocker, 1861.   Died in infancy.
1635   Hattie L. Crocker, 1862.
Here end the present descendants of Lemuel Stone, (1550).

Children of Samuel Stone (1551) *and Susannah Hall.*
1635a Alice Stone, 1806.   Henry Thompson.   Died 1860.   p. 82
1636   Susannah Stone, 1807.   Alfred Fisk.   82
            By Second Wife, Prudence Colvin.
1637   Mary Stone, 1809.   Peter Cole.   82
1638   Sallie Ann Stone, 1810.   Thomas R. Purdy.   82
1639   Robert Stone, 1812.   Died young.
1640   Harrison Stone, 1815.   Esther Ackley.
                          2d, Catharine Phillips.   82
1641   Hugh Stone, 1816.   Harriet Miles.   82
1642   Gilbert A. Stone, 1816.   Orpha Shaw.   83
1642a Lavina T. Stone, 1820.   Lyman Wight.   83
1642b Mary Elizabeth Stone, 1823.   Amos B. Gorman.   83
1642c Samuel R. Stone, 1824.   Died 1836.
1642d Joseph C. Stone, 1826.   Laura Hobbs.   No children.

Children of Celinda Stone (1552) *and Samson Wright.*
1643   Lucy Wright, 1805.   Thomas Chambers.
1644   Wheaton Wright, 1807.   Aurora Clark.
1645   Stephen Wright, 1809.   —— Dean.
1646   Sophia Wright, 1813.   John Crane.
1647   Sarah Wright, 1813.   —— Phelps.
1648   Ruby Wright, 1818.   John B. Allworth.

Children of James Stone (1553) *and Polona Greene.*
1649   Merit Stone, 1813.   Sarah Franklin.   83
1650   Lemuel Stone, 1814.   Eliza West. 2d, S. C. Gaylord. 83
1651   Robert Stone, 1816.   Sarah Smith.   79
1652   Nancy Stone, 1819.   John Miller.   79
1653   Alfred Stone, 1821.   Artemesia Miller.   A 84
1654   Emory E. Stone, 1823.   Catharine S. Hudson.   79
            By Second Wife, Catharine Ackley.
1655   William H. Stone, 1826.   Sarah I. Wight.
                    Continued on next page.

1656   Benira Stone, 1828.   Died 1853.
1657   Samuel Stone, 1829.   Elinda White.   79

Children of James Stone (1553) *and Catharine Ackley.—Continued.*

1658   Byron Stone, 1832.   Angeline Miles.   p. 80
1659   Milo Stone, 1835.   —— Giles.
1660   Eleazer Stone, 1837.   Died 1858.
1661   Melissa Stone, 1842.

Children of Robert Stone (1651) *and Sarah Smith.*

1662   Delphine Stone, 1845.
1663   Celestia Stone, 1847.

Children of Nancy Stone (1652) *and John Miller.*

1664   Maralda L. Miller, 1843.   Silas C. ———.
1665   Jerusha Miller, 1845.
1666   Mary E. Miller, 1849.
1667   John I. Miller, 1852.
1668   Judson Miller, 1859.   Died in infancy.
1669   George L. Miller, 1862.

Children of Emory E. Stone (1654) *and Catharine S. Hudson.*

1670   Frank Hudson Stone, 1848.
1671   Margaret Gertrude Stone, 1850.
1672   Mary Inez Stone, 1851.
1673   Eva Augusta Stone, 1853.
1674   Arthur Jessup Stone, 1856.
1675   Charles Rice Stone, 1858.
1676   Oscar Hudson Stone, 1860.
1677   Henry Stansbury Stone, 1863.
1678   Hattie Foster Stone, 1865.

Children of Samuel Stone (1657) *and Elinda White.*

1679   Anna Stone, 1858.
1680   Milton Willis Stone, 1861.
1681   Myron H. Stone, 1865.

Children of Byron Stone (1658) *and Angeline Miles.*

1682　Allison M. Stone, 1855.
1683　Charles L. Stone, 1858.

Children of Jonathan Stone (661) *and Elizabeth Westcott?*

1684　John Stone, 1747.　Phebe Daly.
1685　Abigail Stone, 1751.　Daniel Strait.

Children of John Stone (1684) *and Phebe Daly.*

1686　Oliver Stone, 1768.　Elizabeth Bassett.
1687　Avis Stone, 1769.　Caleb Arnold.
1688　Hannah Stone, 1771.　John Vickry.

Children of Joseph Stone (664) *and Anna Kent.*

1689　Abigail Stone, 1753.　Nathan Salisbury.

Children of Abigail Stone (1689) *and Nathan Salisbury.*

1690　Wait Salisbury, 1771.
1691　Sally Salisbury, 1776.
1692　John Salisbury, 1778.
1693　Jos. Martin Salisbury, 1780.
1694　Anne Salisbury, 1782.
1695　Mary Salisbury, 1785.
1696　Ambrose Salisbury, 1789.
1697　Cynthia Salisbury, 1791.
1698　Nathan Salisbury, 1793.
1699.　Phebe Salisbury, 1796.

Children of Anne Stone (6) *and William Potter.*

1700　Sarah Potter, 1707.
1701　William Potter, 1709.
1702　Benjamin Potter, 1711.
1703　Ailis Potter, 1713.

The above Anne Stone (6), Joseph Stone (664), and Jonathan Stone (661), refer back to page 35.

Children of Riley Stone (1572) *and Ruth Ousterhoudt.*
1704 Barney Stone, 1824. Twice married. See Note.
1705 Esther E. Stone, 1826. Ira Gardner.
1706 Mary Ann Stone, 1828. George B. Nicholson.
1707 Mortimer Stone, 1831.

Children of Esther E. Stone (1705) *and Ira Gardner.*
1708 Frank Gardner, 1857.

Children of Mary Ann Stone (1706) *and G. B. Nicholson.*
1709 Emma Nicholson, 1849.
1710 Ruth Nicholson, 1852.

Children of Rebecca Stone (1573) *and Isaac Sherman.*
1711 Louisa Sherman, 1824. Died 1844.
1712 Lydia Sherman, 1826. Died 1844.
1713 Delana Sherman, 1828. Anderson Reynolds.
1714 Orlando Sherman, 1830. Died 1862.

Children of Jeremiah Stone (1574) *and Louisa Rice.*
1715 Almira L. Stone, 1834. Nicholas Northup.
1716 Emily A. Stone, 1836. George Perry.
By Second Wife, Laura Rice.
1717 Melbourne Stone, 1846.
1718 Adelia Stone, 1847.
1719 Florence Stone, 1849.
1720 Isadore Stone, 1852.

Children of Almira L. Stone (1715) *and N. Northup.*
1721 Esther L. Northup, 1855.
1722 Horace G. Northup, 1857.

Children of Aurilla Stone (1576) *and William C. Greene.*
1723 Maria L. Greene, 1837. Smith D. Dean.
1724 Benjamin M. Greene, 1839.
1725 Josephine A. Greene, 1841. Andrew J. Smith.

Children of Sabra Stone (1575) *and William C. Greene.*
1726 Hortense B. Greene, 1843. Thomas C. Kennedy.
1727 Rhoda A. Greene, 1847.

Children of Rhoda Stone (1578) *and H. W. Nicholson.*

1728   Oscar Eugene Nicholson, 1838.   Died 1861.
1729   George Stone Nicholson, 1846.   Mary Brooks.

Children of Rachel Stone (1579) *and William Hawthorne*

1730   Horatio Hawthorne, 1847.
1731   Margaret Hawthorne, 1851.
1732   Rhoda Hawthorne, 1854.

Here end the present descendants of John Stone, (1548).

Children of Alice Stone (1635a) *and Henry Thompson.*

1733   Susan C. Thompson, 1840.   Thomas Murphy.

Children of Susannah Stone (1636) *and Alfred Fisk.*

1734   Rhodes P. Fisk, 1832.   Letta Gritman.
1735   John A. Fisk, 1834.   —— Johnson.
1736   S. Oscar Fisk, 1836.
1737   Susan Fisk, 1844.

Children of Mary Stone (1637) *and Peter Cole.*

1738   Prudence Cole, 1829.   Arnon Westcott.
1739   Henry Cole, 1831.   M. Stephens.   2d, M. Hortman.
1740   Uriah Cole, 1835.   Nancy Lancaster.
1741   Samuel Cole, 1838.   Emeline Warren.
1742   Catharine Cole, 1841.   Charles Anderson.
1743   Philemon Cole, 1843.   Alice Cook.

Children of Sally Ann Stone (1638) *and T. R. Purdy.*

1744   Adelia Purdy.
1745   Latitia Purdy.
1746   Adelaide Purdy.
1747   Joseph Purdy.

Children of Harrison Stone (1640) *and Esther Ackley.*

1748   Renselaer Stone, 1835.
            By Second Wife, Catharine Phillips.
1749   Joseph Stone, 1853.

Children of Hugh Stone (1641) *and Harriet Miles.*

1750   Malvina Stone, 1837.   George L. Thompson.

Children of Gilbert A. Stone (1642) and Orpha Shaw.

1751   Orson Stone, 1838.   Died 1861.
1752   Washburne Stone, 1840.   —— Higgins.
1753   Hannah Stone, 1842.   —— Chambers.
1754   Lydia Stone, 1848.

Children of Lavina T. Stone (1642a) and Lyman Wight.

1755   William Wight, 1839.   Albina Laton.
1756   Harriet Wight, 1842.   —— Holmes.

Children of M. Elizabeth Stone (1642b) and Amos B. Gorman.

1757   Lamartha Gorman, 1843.   William Geddes.
1758   Amos Beecher Gorman, 1855.

Here end the present descendants of Samuel Stone, (1551).

Children of Merit Stone (1649) and Sarah Franklin.

1759   Polona G. Stone, 1837.
1760   Horace N. Stone, 1839.   Died 1853.
1761   Lotta Stone, 1840.   Died 1854.
1762   James A. Stone, 1843.
1763   Waldo Stone, 1845.
1764   John C. Stone, 1847.   Died 1852.
1765   Sarah D. Stone, 1850.
1766   Florilla E. Stone, 1852.
1767   Arthur Stone, 1855.
1768   Melissa R. Stone, 1858.

Children of Lemuel Stone (1650) and Eliza West.

1769   Ellen Stone, 1837.   Robert Emmett Bennett.   A. p. 84
1770   Julia Kezia Stone, 1840.
1771   Elbert B. Stone, 1844.   Lizzie A. Giddings.
1772   Mary Melissa Stone, 1852.
1773   George W. Stone, 1855.

By Second Wife, Susan C. Gaylord.

1774   Jasper N. Stone, 1861.

APPENDIX.

Children of Ellen Stone (1769) *and R. E. Bennett.*

1775 Maurice Marion Bennett, 1857.
1776 Myra Josephine Bennett, 1861.
1777 Walter Emmett Bennett, 1864.

Children of Alfred Stone (1653) *and Artimesia Miller.*

1778 Lester S. Stone, 1849.
1779 Stephen J. Stone, 1851. Died 1859.
1780 Martin M. Stone, 1862.

Here end the present descendants of James Stone, (1553).

The genealogical statistics in this Appendix, do not follow the regular course of lineal descent; they were collected since printing the first part of the work; some of them are detached and uncertain. The pages and numbers are regularly continued, and may be found in the regular index of names, and regular numbered notes.

DESCENDANTS OF PETER STONE, (18).

Children of Rebecca Stone (36a) *and David Patt.*

1781 William W. Patt, 1797. Killed in a corn mill.
1782 Barbara S. Patt, 1798.
1783 Patience P. Patt, 1799. Died in childhood.
1784 Anthony B. Patt, 1801. Cynthia Carpenter.
1785 Welcome A. Patt, 1802. Mary Angell.
1786 William N. Patt, 1808. Britania Baxter.
1787 Rebecca Ann Patt, 1811. William Carsboon.
       Two Infants.

Children of William N. Patt (1786) *and Britania Baxter.*

1788 David A. Patt, 1827. Amy Andrews.
1789 Rebecca Patt, 1831. A Clarke.
1790 William W. Patt, 1834. Phebe A. Clandler.
1791 Adaline E. Patt, 1840. George L. Place.
1792 Edward N. Patt, 1843.

DESCENDANTS OF SIMON STONE, (697).
Children of Eliza E. Stone (708) *and John Putney.*
1793   Ann E. Putney, 1860.   Died 1863.

Children of Sarah Stone (709) *and James Barlow.*
1794   George Barlow, 1857.
1795   Clara Barlow, 1859.

Children of Mary Stone (710) *and Isaac Richardson.*
1796   Allen G. Richardson, 1851.   Died in infancy.
1797   Edico F. Richardson, 1854.   Died 1856.
         By Second Husband G. L. Avery.
1798   Mary E. Avery, 1864.   Died 1865.

Children of Rhoda M. Stone (711) *and Otis Barlow.*
1799   Charles C. Barlow, 1856.

Children of Daniel S. Stone (713) *and Laura Richards.*
1800   William E. Stone, 1865.

DESCENDANTS OF STEPHEN STONE, (1248).
Children of Charles H. Stone (1309) *and Catharine A. Brightman.*
1801   Fannie Stone.
1802   William Edward Stone.

Children of Almon Stone (1311) *and Sarah Brown.*
1803   David Waldo Stone.

Children of Sarah V. Stone (1314) *and William R. Northup.*
1804   Abbic Frances Northup.
1805   William Henry Northup.
         DESCENDANTS OF DAVID STONE, (590).
Ages of his four Children incorrectly inserted.   Page 32.
617   Jason Stone, 1814.   Rhoda Fry.
618   Nathan Stone, 1819.   Elipha Mahala Potter.   p. 86
619   Edward Eddy Stone, 1822.   Died in 1840.
620   Laura Stone, 1838.

Children of Jason Stone (617) *and Rhoda Fry.*
1806   Eliza Stone, 1839.   Charles Chesboro'.   86
1807   Mary Wilbour Stone, 1842.
1808   Maria Stone, 1846.   James F. Thurston.

Children of Eliza Stone (1806) *and   Charles Chesboro'*

1809   Isabella Chesboro', 1863.

Children of Nathan Stone (618) *and E. M. Potter.*

1810   Sarah Elizabeth Stone, 1842.   Abel G. Tillinghast.

Nathan Stone (618) is found on pages 32 and 85, Appendix.

Children of Sarah E. Stone (1810) *and A. G. Tillinghast.*

1811   David Stone Tillinghast, 1861.

1812   Anna Elizabeth Tillinghast, 1864.

Family of Joseph Stone (1242) *and Mary Bowen.*

The following extract of a letter from a nephew, Jabez Stone, (1268), gives all the information the writer can collect of the above.

" My Uncle Joseph lived in Paris, Oneida County, N. Y., where a part of his family married and lived.

John Stone, with a large family.

Cyrus Stone, with a family.

Henry Stone, with a large family.

Anna Stone married Elder James Rhodes.

Betsey Stone married a Phelps.

Martha Stone married a Willard—these remained in Oneida County; my uncle removed to Weathersfield, in Gennessee County, N. Y.   Two of his sons, Charles and Joseph, are now living at Grand Rapids, Michigan."

1813   Richard Stone, 1805.   The grandson of Peter Stone (18) lives in Olneyville, and is by trade a mason.

1814   William Potter, 1782.   Died 1789, and was the son of Almy Stone (324) and Peter Potter, and was, we believe, their eldest child.   See page 17.

BIOGRAPHICAL NOTES.

Note 1.

Hugh Stone (1) whose descendants are traced in this volume, was an Englishman, and came to this country a young man (unmarried) between the years 1655 and 1665. A tradition, partially obtained among some of his descendants that he came from Wales, but the writer has, for the last thirty years, conversed upon that point with every Welchman whom he has met in his extensive travels, in twenty-five of the United States, and has *not found one* who ever knew, or heard of the name of "Stone," in Wales. Nor is that name in any Welch History, Biography, or Encyclopedia ;—moreover, in that period of English advancement, when surnames were generally adopted, the formation of Welch names then, and is now, peculiar to themselves, and almost entirely from three sources. 1st. There were a few general family names—these were retained : Lloyd, Vaughan, Llewellyn, Glendower, and a few others. 2d. Those formed by adding "*s*" to the Christian name—thus, William became Williams ; John, Johns or Jones ; David, Davids or Davis ; Richard, Richards ; Peter, Peters ; Hugh, Hughes,—and that whole class of names, very extensive, are, in their origin, Welch. Another, and a 3d class, are those which came from the Welch prefix Ap, which signifies son, as, Ap Owen means the same as the son of Owen ; Ap Richard, the son of Richard ; Ap Hugh, the son of Hugh ; Ap Allen, the son of Allen. These names, with their prefixes Ap became contracted—Ap Owen became Bowen ; Ap Richard became Prichard ; Ap Hugh became Pugh ; Ap Allen became Pallen ;—from these three sources almost every Welch name may be traced. Not so in England. Almost every word has been manufactured into a surname ; things—as Stone, Wood, Steel, Iron, Silver, Gold, Water, Glass, excepting things exceedingly repulsive, almost everything, with a slight change of spelling, has been manufactured into a surname. So of qualities—Strong, Short, Bright, Long, Loud, Broad, Little. Of color—White, Gray, Black, Brown, Red. Of offices—Sargeant, Squire, Forester, Clarke. Of trade or occupation—Weaver, Farmer, Carpenter, Smith, Mason, Baker. Of manner—How, Wild, Swift, Strange, Straight, and so on to the end. The writer has also pursued his inquiries, relative to the Scotch and Irish, with about the same results as with the Welch ; the most extended Biography of Scotland, Ireland, Wales and England, including general Biography, Biography of European Artists and English Naval Biography, afford but one name, except those found in England, and that is in Scotland,—Edmund Stone, the self-taught mathematician : and his father was probably an Englishman. While,

in all the departments of Biography, England affords many of the name of
Stone. (See Introduction to this work). Nor can any evidence be derived
from the name of Hugh. It is common to the Norman-French. Hugh Capet,
was founder of the French monarchy; Hugh De La Hays, a Norman-English
Baron, was Secretary to Edward II., and himself, or brother Gilbert, taken
prisoner by Bruce, at Bannockburn. Hugh, as a christian name, and Hughes,
as a surname, is common in the four kingdoms. The name of "Stone" is
derived from the Anglo Saxon "Stan," the "a" pronounced nearly as in
Star : that, also, is derived from the old Saxon "Sten" pronounced exactly
as the Anglo Saxon "Stan"; this name, Anglicised to "Stone," is scattered all
over England ; and, in some ot the Counties, is nearly as common as the
name of Smith. More than this, we trace seven different emigrations directly
to different counties of England, (See Introduction). Hugh Stone (1) we
find in the town of Warwick, Colony of Rhode Island, in the year 1665,
engaged in that very interesting matter which has engaged so many of his
posterity since, taking a wife ; he had probably been there several years ;
since, in 1665, he married Abigail Buscoot, the daughter of Peter Buscoot, of
Warwick. Their first child, Abigail Stone, was born early in 1667, and the
family remained there till about 1723, when he sold his farm and most of his
property, and moved to Cranston, then Providence, where three of his sons
were then living. The records show Peter Buscoot, the father-in-law of
Hugh Stone among the earlier settlers of Warwick. His name is associated
with Samuel Gorton, Randall Houlden, Ezekiel Holliman, (the man who
baptized Roger Williams), Richard Carder, and some thirty original proprietors and share-holders in the arrangements, settings off, and grants from
1643 to 1670. Peter Buscoot was by trade a blacksmith, and though possessed of a small landed estate was never affluent. He was evidently restless
in his disposition, occasionally engaged in lawsuits, frequently petitioning
the town authorities for privileges, and almost a land broker, judging by
the frequencies of his sales and purchases. The following is a sample of
some of the Deeds of that age, of the town of Warwick : "Know all men
by these presents, that I, Peter Buscoot, of the town of Warwick and Providence Plantations, have soulde unto Thomas Relph of said town, all that my
dwelling house and housen and lands that I bought of George Belden, a part
of which was given for maintaining a water power to serve Quinnimicote
and Warwick. Dated 1655." This was bought of Belden in 1654, and by
him bought of Thomas Thornicraft, to whom it was originally granted, in
1647. It will be remembered that Warwick was settled in 1642, being the
last of the four principal settlements in Rhode Island. Providence in 1636,
by Roger Williams: Porthmouth, in 1638, by John Coddington ; Wickford,
in 1640, by Richard Smith, and Warwick in 1642, by Samuel Gorton. Of
the nationality of our maternal grandfather we cannot determine with certainty, it is, however, most probably French. His name is spelt variously,
Bazacot, Buzicot, Bussecott and Buscoot, and is probably pronounced ac-

cording to the French ending of *t*, as if written Buseco, and that he emigrated to this country and State with the Tourtelots, Frys, Nichols, Tarbeaux, Tourjes, and other Huguenots, driven from their own country by the Revocation of the Edict of Nantz. Be that as it may, we find him in Warwick, in 1643. Notwithstanding the restless character of our common ancestor, we find him much beloved and respected ; every petition of his which came before the court and council of Warwick, was granted ; and when his only son, Peter, junior, was wounded in the leg by the accidental discharge of a gun, in the hands of another boy, a town meeting was called, and funds were raised, and the young man sent to Newport that he might receive the best surgical aid the country afforded,—and when, in spite of all attention and care, the young man died, the town was again convened, resolutions tendering their sympathy to the afflicted parents and sisters were passed, and the expenses of the funeral paid by the generous colonists. The death of this young man left Peter Busecot with but two surviving children, Mary, the wife of Peter Spencer, of Norwich, Conn., and Abigail, who, as we have before stated, was the wife of our ancestor.

The probability is, that Hugh Stone came to Rhode Island in the ship Deborah, which was in Narragansett bay, in the year 1657. A ship of that name sailed from London for New England, in the early part of the same year, with many emigrants ; their names and their number we are not furnished, but soon after this, Hugh Stone is mentioned among the inhabitants of Warwick, and continued, in some connexion or other, till he left for Providence, the part which is now Cranston, nearly sixty years afterwards.

In 1704, the following singular instrument passed upon the records of Warwick : " Know all men by these presents, that I, Hugh Stone, of Warwick, Colony of Rhode Island and Providence Plantations, for and in consideration of what is hereafter expressed, do grant and pass over to my son, John Stone of the same town, my mansion house, fencings, orchards, meadows, and all my whole right and title to all my lands and tenements, with the privileges and appurtenances lying in the town of Warwick aforesaid, to have and to hold forever without molestation ; in witness whereof I have hereunto set my hand and seal this twelfth day of March, in the fourth year of the Reighne of our Souvreighne Lady Anne, by the grace of God Queen of England, Anno Domin nostri 1704. For consideration, it is the condition of this deed, that if I, or my wife, or both of us, should, by the Providence of God be disabled in our, or either of our persons, or by old age or nonability to get our living and sustenance. and if our said son John shall do his utmost endeavour, to see and provide for us during the time of our natural lives sufficient maintenance, and behave himself as a dutiful son ought to do to his parents, in all respects, and pay to his brother, Hugh Stone, the sum of fifty shillings, in money or in good merchantable pay equal to money ; and also fifty shillings to his brother, our son George Stone, of like money, or pay equivalent to money, then, after our decease, the above premises to be his

13

own forever,—but if otherwise, this deed shall be utterly void and of none effect." Two years afterwards this instrument was given up,—John Stone (4) in 1712, moved to Mashantatack, then in Providence, now Cranston, near to where his brothers, Hugh and Peter, had bought and settled a few years before. At this place, and on John Stone's land, afterwards owned by his youngest son, Joseph Stone (664) commonly called Deacon Joe, was built the first church in the town of Cranston, then Providence; the worshippers were Baptist, and although the house is now, and has been for many years, away, still, there are those living who have, in their childhood, worshipped in that ancient sanctuary. The father, Hugh Stone (1), remained some twelve years longer in Warwick, when, in 1723, he deeded the same property as above to Barlo Greene, bought an improved farm of Susan Lawrence, the widow of the late William Lawrence, the same year, and when nearly ninety years old, made his last remove to the place known as the Doctor Aldrich farm, where, some two or three years afterwards, he died. On this farm is the " Old Stone burying ground." There, our common ancestor, and three of his sons, Hugh, Peter and John, all rest together,—there, too, some of every generation, as far as the sixth, lie side by side. Of the decease of his wife there is neither record nor tradition ; the probability is, she was living when he bought the Lawrence farm, in 1723. He passed through a long life beloved and respected, died at the age of 90, or over, and his posterity, a few of whom have reached the ninth generation, probably number over three thousand.

NOTE 2.

Hugh Stone, (2), though not the oldest child, was the oldest son of Hugh Stone (1), and born in Warwick, in 1669. He left the town of Warwick and purchased a farm, of some thirty acres, in Mashantatack, where he lived and closed his life,—his deed bounds him west by Pochasset river. If there is no mistake in the boundaries given in this deed, the localities of " Hugh's cellar," " Hugh's hole," and " Hugh's meadow," were not in his purchase, but it is probable that east in the boundary is the proper word, instead of west. His wife was the daughter of Abel Potter, of what is now Cranston, by whom he had three sons. One died in infancy ; the other two, Thomas and Oliver, married, but left no descendants of the name farther than grandchildren of Hugh Stone (2), consequently the name in that branch has become extinct. The following receipt of a legacy was found among the ancient records of Providence :—

march ye 10th 17$\frac{20}{21}$

Then received of my brother-in-law Abill Potter the sum of ten pounds, being in full of that part of my wife's legacy that her Honored Father Abill Potter, deceased, in his last will and testament ordered and appoynted

should be payed to her by the Ex. Abill Potter and his brother George Potter. I say we have now received the said sum in full satisfaction as witness our hands the day and year above written

Signed and delivered   HUGH STONE
in presence of us   ✦   her
THOMAS KILTON,   MARY ✗ STONE.
NATHAN WATERMAN.   mark.

NOTE 3.

Peter Stone (3), the second son and third child of Hugh Stone (1), was born in Warwick, January 20, 1671, and was married to Elizabeth Shaw, daughter of John Shaw, Esq., of Providence, now Cranston, June 16, 1696. Eight days after his marriage, he took a deed of E. Relph, of twenty-five acres of land, in what is now Cranston, then called by the Indian name of Mashantatack,—on this purchase, comprising all the "woods, swamps, meadows, waters," profits, privileges, rights, commodities, hereditaments or benefits, therein contained, he built him a house and lived quietly and respectably. On this same premises his son and grandson, Peter (12) and Peter (18) lived and died. This little farm, on the easterly slope of Sockonossett hill, is about a mile south of the recent Coal-Shaft, which has been opened in Cranston, and in full view. He died December 26, 1725, aged almost 55 years,—from him has descended a numerous posterity, arranged in the first thirty-four pages of this work. At his death, letters of Administration were granted to his son, Peter (12), an inventory of which is recorded in the Probate of Providence.

NOTE 4.

Anne Stone (5), the youngest daughter of Hugh (1), married William Potter, of Warwick, from whom was a large family, and of whom but little is known,—while of the eldest daughter, Abigail (2a), no record at all appears except the fact of her birth.

NOTE 5.

George Stone (6), the fourth and youngest son of Hugh Stone (1), was born in Warwick. He married, and the impression is he died in middle age, leaving two sons, George and Obadiah,—probably his descendants are found in Thompson, Woodstock and Putnam, Conn , though the writer has not been able to trace the connexion with absolute certainty. Among them are found the names, George, John, Reuben, Obadiah, Simeon, David, William, Mary, Anne, most of which are common names among the other branches.

NOTE 6.

Peter Stone (12) was born in what is now Cranston, and, when 27 years of age married Patience Printing, probably of Providence. With her connex-

ions and history we are entirely unacquainted. The record of the marriage is found in the City of Providence. The same year that the son was married, the father, Peter Stone (3), died, and removing into the house vacated by his father's decease, he there reared his family of four children. He survived his wife some years, and when quite aged married a widow Burlingame, of nearly his own age. They lived but two or three years after their marriage, when both died aged about 80.

Note 7.

Of Elizabeth Stone (11), and her sisters, Sarah, Abigail and Pressilah, nothing is known, except they were born in Providence, now Cranston.

Note 8.

John Stone (16) was the youngest son of Peter (3)—was a cooper by trade, and married and settled in Pawtuxet, on forty acres of land which he bought February 7th, 1731. He has left no posterity that bears the name.

Note 9.

Peter Stone (18), was born, lived and died, on twenty-five acres of Mashantatuck "woodes" and "meadowes," which his grandfather purchased a few days after his marriage, in 1696. Here he reared seventeen children, whose numerous offsprings are scattered in almost every town in Rhode Island. In him is seen, strongly marked, the leading characteristics of the race—love of home—quick nervous temperament—active industry—mechanical genius, but never aspiring—contentment with their condition—a love of domestic life—a large degree of cautiousness—the Yankee character of progress not strongly marked—rather inclined to utter the German prayer, "God grant that we may be no worse off to-morrow than to-day,"—very little disposition to travel, or see aught beyond home—immediate relatives loved—uncles and aunts fade out—cousins forgotten or not known—strong social feelings—faithfulness in friendship—very little secretiveness, and a strong religious faith. Where different character is strongly marked, it may be traced to other than the staid, contented, home marked disposition, which pervaded the early stock. His first wife was Mary Hammond, a woman of strong mind, and industrious habits; she lived about twenty-five years after their marriage, was the mother of twelve of his children, eleven of whom married and settled in life;—the last, an infant of a few brief days, slept in the same grave with its mother. He soon formed a second connexion with Patience Hudson. By this marriage were born five children, all of whom lived to maturity, and except the youngest, Esek, who died at sea, and Mary, who lived to an advanced age in single blessedness, all married. He died when about 64 years old. The family remained at the old homestead, for a time, but an arrangement was made between the widow and

heirs, the son, Hopkins Stone (34), removed the house, the estate passed into other hands, and only an aged elm now points to the spot, where three Peter Stones—father, son and grandson lived and died.

NOTE 10.

Peter Stone (25) was born in Cranston. There he married Patience Westcott, being one of four, of the brothers and sisters who intermarried with the descendants of Stukely Westcott, who came with the first settlers to Providence. He was much respected by his fellow townsmen, and was at an early age appointed a Magistrate in Providence County. He died in about 1790, and has left no descendants.

NOTE 11.

Andrew Stone (26) was born and spent his early life in Cranston ; but, when between thirty and forty moved to Scituate, near what is now called Rockland Village. At that place he married, for a second wife, Mary, the daughter of Josiah Battey, with whom he lived some twenty years, and by the first and second marriages he had eight children. His attention was early called to the subject of religion, and to the work of the ministry. He was consecrated to the ministerial work previous to 1798, as, in the June of that year he was on the Council which ordained the Rev. Charles Stone (1322), and was selected as one for the laying on of hands. When nearly 60 years of age he married a Miss Bowdich, and moved to Burrillville, where he died, leaving a character, of integrity ability, and Christian faith.

NOTE 12.

Amos Stone (27) was born and spent his whole life in the town of Cranston, where, by industry and economy he brought up a family of twelve children. A large posterity of industrious artizans, and enterprising manufacturers, trace their descent to this quiet and industrious man.

NOTE 13.

John Stone (31), son of Peter (18), was born in Cranston, and inherited the sobriety, industry and virtues of his father ; the various labors of the field became his early companions, and he had the pleasing satisfaction of knowing that his winter shoes, (his summer shoes never wore out), were faithfully earned. Like most Cranston boys, he early thought of marriage. That thought developing into action, he married Mary Joy, a woman every way worthy of him, and might have filled a higher station in life. Her education, very limited, was all brought out into practical use in her family of seven children, and each winter and autumn evening saw, for about an hour and a half, that little groupe conning their lessons in reading and spelling, under

a mother's instruction and care; more than this, the privilege granted and enjoined upon her own, was extended to the whole neighborhood, and many is the child in "Cucumber town," (the hamlet where they lived), who could trace their first knowledge of reading, and their last, even, to this good woman;—many a boy and girl not only entered, but graduated from her seminary of simple literature. Before middle life, the husband bought the lot called the "old Meeting-house Lot, the old church before alluded to in Note 1, having long since gone to ruin; with the intention of building a family dwelling—a difficulty arose about the title, and long years of controversy in the law, dissipated his hard earned dollars, and the final decision destroyed all hopes. He afterwards built a house in the same vicinity, but poverty. although it never dared to enter among that groupe of children, always kept within hailing distance through the life of this worthy couple. He died in Cranston beloved and respected.

Note 14.

Seneca Stone (170), was born, lived and died in Cranston. His parents did the best in their power for their children; this however was but little, except a good example of industry and honesty; and, although Seneca started in the race of life with but few hindrances, he had few helps. The early training, in the evening schools of his mother, gave him some taste for learning above the boys of his position, and he sought and obtained in the schools, got up from time to time in the town, an addition to his early stock of knowledge. His literary taste and capacity was appreciated, and he was employed to teach several terms of school in his native town. He devoted most of his years to agricultural pursuits with a good degree of success. His disposition was cheerful, and even in advanced life lost none of the genial warmth and sportiveness of his early days. As a public man, he had the confidence of his associates. From time to time he was elected a member of the Town Council, and several times represented his District in the General Assembly of Rhode Island. An important part of his existence was music, both vocal and instrumental;—he taught singing and music in his own town, and was leader for some time of a military band. He was twice married, first to Martha, daughter of Thomas Congdon, and subsequently to Amy Stone, daughter of Edmands Stone, and has left a numerous progeny, mostly living in Rhode Island. One son, however, is in St. Louis, Mo.

Note 15.

Rebecca Stone (36a) was married to Mr. David Patt, and reared a worthy family. Mary (36), her sister, lived unmarried, and died old and full of years, much esteemed: and, to this day,. "Aunt Mollie" is never mentioned among those who knew her without awakening a tender regard.

NOTE 16.

Whipple Stone (32), married for his first wife Henrietta Collins, by whom he had five children. His second wife was Catharine Carder, by whom he had two. He lived in Warwick, and has left a numerous and respected posterity.

NOTE 17.

Hopkins Stone (34), first son of Peter (18), by his second wife, married Amy Salisbury, a very worthy woman, by whom he had only one daughter, who lived to maturity. He afterwards married Mary Corey, by whom he had one son, who arrived at manhood. He was a carpenter by trade, and spent most of his life in Scituate, Cranston, and Warwick. His son, William A. Stone (298), now resides in Apponaug, where he keeps a large boarding-house for the accommodation of the Bleaching Company, for whom he is now engaged.

NOTE 18.

William Stone (54) was born in Cranston, but passed most of his life in Warwick. In him was happily combined the elements of the good citizen, the wise and loving parent. His opportunities for early culture, though small, were all well improved; and his strong mind, united to his love of truth and justice, rendered him the friend and wise counsellor of the young and old,—retiring in his disposition he sought no destinction, and allowed more ambitious aspirants to take what was tendered to him. In this spirit of retiracy he neither sought nor would accept office, and refused the appointment of Judge of the Court, in Kent County. When sixteen he enlisted for a year, and was in the war of 1812. When about twenty-one he married Susan Pratt, the daughter of Phineas Pratt, of Massachusetts, a gentle, yielding, loving spirit, whose uniform kindness and amiability endeared her to all who knew her. William Stone (54), though very domestic in his habits, genial and social in his temperament, was, nevertheless, of marked decision of character, and unbending in the course which he considered right,—he was one of the best of fathers, and, of his large family of ten children, all of whom reached maturity, not one would tinge the parental cheek with the blush of shame. He was never wealthy but always in comfortable circumstances, and left some $2000 at his decease, which happened in 1854. His wife died in 1852.

NOTE 19.

Nancy Stone (52) married John Pratt, and lived in Johnston. She had three children by the first marriage: Serena Pratt (66) married Amasa Waterman; they reside in Providence, where he is connected with the Post Office. The second husband of Nancy was Job Waterman, by whom she had two children.

Note 20.

Waterman Stone (56), married Abby Thornton, of Cranston. He died in middle age, leaving two children, who lived to become the heads of families;—Stephen Stone (114), who married Waitstill G. Arnold; and Mary Stone, who married Stephen B. Esten. Waterman's widow, now in green old age, lives on a portion of the land owned by John Stone (4), with her daughter, Mrs. Esten. They are in comfortable circumstances. Mr. Esten is in the employ of the Mining Company, and boards the engineer and other employees. ̄

Note 21.

Charles Stone (57) was born in Cranston, and there was married to Caroline Remington, a worthy and intelligent woman, by whom he had one son and three daughters. The son, Sylvester C. Stone (122), is married to Sarah J. Carpenter, and resides in Providence, where he is engineer of the Lumber Manufactory, near Mill Bridge; the father resides in Scituate, and is esteemed as a worthy citizen farmer.

Note 22.

Henry A. Stone (58), the first son of Amos (27), by a second marriage resides in his native town, near the well known " Fenner Ledge," where he has spent most of his life.

Note 23.

Sylvester Claflin Stone (61), like all the brothers in the large family of Amos (27), started in life with the motto before him—"work and win." That motto he has ever kept in view,—now a farmer, now a travelling trader now a dealer in paper and paper stock, now a gardener for the city market, evincing a versatility unusual to the name ;—but, like the rest of his race he goes home to sleep ; he has purchased, and now lives on a valuable estate in old Mashantatack, and in sight of the farms owned by his ancestors 170 years ago. He married Eliza King (599), whose energy and industry has truly helped her husband onward and upward in life, and now, as she is beginning to descend its down-hill, her busy hands and ornamental taste has stored, and is storing her house with quilts and counterpanes of elaborate workmanship and unusual skill and beauty. They have six children ; two passed away in infancy, four have reached maturity, one is in California, the rest around them.

Note 24.

Mary Stone (69), married Dr. Thomas Nutting, who has been in successful practice, in Clayville and Georgiaville, where he now resides. Mary died in 1844.

Note 25.

Nehemiah Stone (70) received a mercantile education, and was book-keeper several years in Providence, but remembering his early training as a farmer boy with his father, he, after marriage with Elizabeth Tanner, purchased a farm in Warwick, near the old home of his early days. He was successful; but circumstances favoring, he sold out, moved to Providence, went into a successful grocery business, and died of pneumonia at the age of 39, universally beloved and respected, leaving a widow and ten children.

Note 26.

Alfred Stone (71) has, for fourteen years, been engaged extensively in the baking business, with good success; he received a mercantile education, has a fine business talent, often striking out from the regular routine of organized trade, and entering into successful schemes and enterprizes in which his foresight and judgment usually directs him aright. He married two sisters, 1st, Miss Ann M., and 2d, Miss Lydia Budlong. He owns a valuable real estate in Providence, and a very productive cranberry meadow in Warwick.

Note 27.

Maria Stone (73) died of consumption at the age of 24 years;—she was a young lady of fine appearance, superior education, strong mind, and died a member of the Baptist communion, universally beloved and lamented.

Note 28.

Louisa Stone (72) married Emerson Whipple. She was truly her mother's child, and, like her, a gentle, clinging vine, which held and directed stronger minds by love, rather than strength. She died in 1846, and has left no children.

Note 29.

Philip Stone (74) was a carriage maker, and in successful business in Attleboro', Mass.;—receiving an internal injury, by some accidental strain, he died, aged 36, as has been remarked, without an enemy. Marriage relation on page 4.

Note 30.

Calvin Stone (75) learned the trade of a jeweller; but his native talent fitting him for the manufacturer and trader rather than the artizan, he soon became one of a firm, " Briggs, Hough & Stone," and subsequently " Briggs & Stone." After several years successful operation, this firm was dissolved, and he entered into business with his brother Isaac (76), who had also learned the same trade. They are now in successful operation as manufac-

turers, in Providence, under the firm of " Stone, Brothers," and are well adapted to each other. Isaac is every inch a mechanic, a thorough workman, a successful designer ; and Calvin, a thorough business man, in-door and out. In Calvin, more than in either son, is the father, William (54), again living and acting. The marriage connexions of these brothers are found on page 4.

NOTE 31.

William Stone (77) was born in Warwick, and being less robust than his brothers, was somewhat more favored with educational privileges. He received the advantages of the best schools of Pawtuxet, and completed his studies at Smithville academy. He too, learned the trade of a jeweller, but his mathematical and financial genius soon manifested itself in an aptness for handling gold and silver coin, rather than gold and silver ornaments ; and he soon found a situation adapted to his taste. He was appointed Receiving Clerk, to the Providence and Worcester R. R. Co., which post he retained six years, till his country called him to its defence in the battle field. He enlisted a private, in Company E, 10th Regiment R. I. Volunteers, and rose successively, in one year, through every grade of office,—Corporal, Sergeant, 2d Lieutenant, 1st Lieutenant,—until the same Company in which he enlisted, elected him, without a dissenting voice, to its Captaincy. After many war scenes, he was, at the expiration of his enlistment, honorably mustered out, and on his return to Providence he was elected Cashier of the Harnden Express Co., which position he now sustains. His marriage connexion is found on page 4.

NOTE 32.

Lyman Stone (78) married Amanda Morse, and engaged in business, as carpenter and architect, in the city of Providence. He was an active, energetic, virtuous man, and life before him, for a time, appeared a success; but the consumption, slow but sure, arrested his course, and, in 1865, carried him down to the grave.

NOTE 33.

Melissa A. F. Stone (160), eldest daughter of Sylvester C. (61), married Pardon Williams, in 1856, and lives in Cranston, almost in sight of the spot where her ancestor, Hugh (1), spent the closing years of his life. George W. Stone (163) married Charlotte Dugan, in 1860, and died in 1864, leaving no children. Thomas H. B. Stone (162) has been for some time in California. Benjamin F. Stone (164) married Lizzie Ramsden, and is building a house near his father's, in " Meshantatack," alias " Cucumber Town," alias " Stoneville."

NOTE 34.

Mary Ann Stone (172) married S. Harris, by whom she had one son, Almoran Harris (236), and subsequently Jeremiah Fenner, the owner of the well known " Fenner ledge." Her children appear in the statistics, page 12.

NOTE 35.

Daniel C. Stone (173) was trained to industry and economy, by his worthy parents, John (31), and his estimable wife, Mary (Joy). When 21 he earned his first dollar by making shoes, to which trade he had been apprenticed; this, and custom work manufacturing, he followed through life. He married Mary Ann Cole, daughter of Dea. Thomas B. Cole, of Cranston ; and in that town reared his family and spent his days. In character, he was industrious and upright, generally silent and thoughtful, and inclined to look on the dark, rather than the bright side of life ; still he was not gloomy ; his heart beat genially to every throb of suffering humanity, while clear perception, and deep thought, always made him a wise counsellor, if not a sportive, humorous companion. He was fond of music, domestic in his habits, and for many years before his death, walked hand in hand with his companion, onward and upward toward the shining shore, which, with a Divine Faith, he beheld in clearness " over the River." He died in 1860.

NOTE 36.

William Joy Stone (174) was educated in the worthy, but humble home, of his parents, and worked with his brother Daniel C., till 21 years of age ; soon after this he engaged as Clerk in a store, in Providence ; finally he went into the dry goods business, in which he continued to the close of his life. His genial spirit, his ready wit, his social turn, his sunny smile, his honest openness of heart, admirably fitted him for a salesman, in which department he was almost universally engaged. Of the large circle of his acquaintance, none knew him but to love him, and few are more extensively remembered, or with greater affection or respect. He married Miss Abbie Albro, but has left no children. He died January 20th, 1861.

NOTE 37.

Catharine Stone (175) was the daughter of John Stone (31) and Mary Joy, and born in Warwick, about five miles from Providence. Unlike the children of the present day, she had but few opportunities for gaining an education, since Public Schools, in her early days, were unknown in Rhode Island. There are some children who *will* be taught, some children who will see " sermons in stones and good in everything." Catharine cannot remember when she learned to read ; her first recollection of books, is reading them, and the evening schools of her mother only gave her an impulse for higher attainments. She succeeded in attending most of the schools of her neighborhood, and generally brought with her from the schools about all the knowledge the teacher had to dispose of, which, however, was not often a large stock in trade ;—ordinarily the rhetoric and oratory of the " American Preceptor "—the mathematics of Daboll—the writing of the teacher—and—well—that is all. To this small stock of knowledge she has been adding

600047B

through life. In her earliest maturity she taught school four or five years, when her health failed, and she was obliged to entirely abandon her favorite employment;—during these years of feebleness, however, she never gave up the strong ruling desire to instruct the young. It seems, the importance of early culture seen in her mother, Mary Joy, when she gathered her own and her neighbor's children into her humble home for instruction, was multiplied and re-multiplied in the daughter, and in that season of weakness became a consecration ; yes, a consecration to the cause of education. During two years of her feebleness she was governess in a wealthy family of the city, in which her serious and devoted labors are remembered with gratitude,—and now, in the waning years of life, brings the earnest and grateful invitation to a long yearly sojourn in the bosom of that family, and among those to whom she once imparted the germs of a virtuous education. Subsequently regaining her health, she taught in Cranston, Johnston and North Providence, with unusual success, and laid down the sceptre only a few years since, when about sixty years of age. In the Sunday School of the church of which she is a member, at Olneyville, N. P., she has been principal of the infant department for eighteen successive years. There the little ones, who first learned the name of God and Heaven from her lips, are now men and women, sustaining the burdens and honors of the day, while their venerable and venerated teacher is teaching *their* children, and herself, like pure metalic coin, growing brighter and brighter the longer it is used.

NOTE 38.

Phebe Stone (176) should be Phebe W. Stone, was genial and happy in her temperament, always diffusing the rays of peace and joy among her friends,—how could she do otherwise, her mother was "Joy" by name and joy by nature ! She married S. D. Cole, and lived for a few years, the first of their married life, in Cranston. While there, Mr. Cole was Cashier of the Cranston Bank, and a member of the Council; but he soon left for the city, where, for many years he was engaged in merchandising, and died of a paralysis, in 1863. This worthy couple have left three daughters, whose names are on page 13, virtuous and well educated, they have been, from time to time, connected with the schools of the city, and are among its most efficient instructors.

NOTE 39.

Raymond Stone (178) was born in Cranston, where he has lived to the present time. In early life, he married Anne Gorton, who is still living; their home is near that beautiful attractive village in Cranston, called Elmwood, a suburb of Providence, where is located the record office of the town, in which he is assistant, and where he is mostly employed. He has three sons, Thomas L. (197) is in the U. S. Navy; Gilbert L. (195) is conductor on a city railroad, and Richmond J. (196) is out West.

NOTE 40.

Albert Stone (180), was born in Cranston, where he lived till about 22. At that time, contrary to the course of his relatives, who seem to have the organ of locality strongly developed, he left the home of his childhood and went West. Stopping from time to time in the cities of the Rivers and Lakes, he finally made his home in the great commercial metropolis of the west, St. Louis. There he now lives, is a man of good reputation, and a pilot on the Mississippi. He married Miss Josephine Smith, a lady from Philadelphia, by whom he has four daughters.

NOTE 41.

Edwin Stone (182) is, by trade a wagon-maker, and resides in Spragueville. Otis Stone (184), resides in Buffalo, N. Y., and is, by trade, a mason. Jerome Stone (192), is engaged in the river fisheries, and lives at Pawtuxet. William Henry Stone (194) is a machinist, and lives in Roxbury, Mass.

NOTE 42.

Clark Stone (186) married Miss Rhoda Graves, of Brooklyn, Conn. He is by trade a wagon-maker, and, during the first part of his married life, resided in Danielsonville, Conn. Subsequently he removed to the city of Providence, and has been engaged in the fish trade for several years.

NOTE 43.

Cyrus Stone (187) was born in Cranston, and resided there until he engaged in business for himself, in Providence. A lingering desire for the farm-life of his boyhood, led him to purchase a farm in Foster, and remove from the city. There he lived but a few years, when we again find him back in the city engaged in his old employment, the fisheries. The reasons for this last change we know not, but rather suspect the dollars were not as plenty among the Foster rocks as among the Narragansett oysters. He has now sold his farm, and is in successful business in the city. Marriage relations found on page 10.

NOTE 44.

Lorenzo Stone (188), in early life, removed to Providence, where he engaged in business. For some years he has been extensively engaged in the fisheries, and kept an extensive fish market. He is marked for his commercial talent, thorough temperance, integrity, energy and promptness in all business matters; though a young man, he already owns valuable improved real estate in the city, and bids fair to make life, in its pecuniary relations, a success. Marriage relations found on page 10.

NOTE 45.

Amanda M. Stone (210) married Smith Greene, and resides in Cranston. Their son, Byron Greene (235), is the ninth generation from the first ancestor, Hugh Stone (1).

NOTE 46.

Sullivan Fenner (237) is the eldest son of Mary Ann Stone and J. Fenner. His integrity, and financial ability, has made him Cashier of the Northern Bank, in the city of Providence, a post which he fills with ability and fidelity. He has been twice married; to Miss Sarah Saunders, and to Miss Mary King.

NOTE 47.

Lucy C. Stone (239), the daughter of Daniel C. Stone (173), is a woman of marked intelligence and good sense; there are some that the world educate, some that the world around them is continually instructing. She is one. In 1849, she married a worthy and intelligent man, Erastus C. Grant, and moved to Nashua, N. H. Mr. Grant was the confidential clerk and book-keeper for a Mr. Baldwin. Her married life was, however, short, the consumption removed the husband to a higher sphere, for which his faith and holy life had well prepared him, leaving his widow and two children to mourn his loss. The acquaintance of the husband disclosed the character of the widow to the husband's employer, and a few years after, himself a widower, he proposed marriage, was accepted, and Lucy C. became the wife of the Hon. Josephus Baldwin, Mayor of Nashua.

NOTE 48.

Abel T. Stone (241) was married to Miss Sarah E. Peckham, and his sister, Catharine R. Stone (240), married Caleb W. Hopkins, and both families removed to Delavan, Illinois, where they now reside.

NOTE 49.

Temperance Stone (258) is now the widow of Samuel R. Potter, and resides in Pawtucket. John W. Stone (259), her brother, married Clarissa Holcom, and moved into the State of Ohio, he ceased to communicate with his friends in 1824, at that time he had one son, whose name appears on page 14; since the above date nothing is known. Phebe Stone (257) married Zara Pratt, and lives in Middleboro' Mass.

NOTE 50.

Sarah Stone (296) married Lyman Aldrich, of Scituate, where she spent most of her married life. Since the death of her husband, she has resided in Providence, and is now descending life's down hill surrounded by her children, her children's children, and a large circle of loving friends.

103

NOTE 51.

Sarah E. Aldrich (305) married Ray Greene (581), and lives in Providence. Energy, virtue, and a devotion to domestic duty marks her character, and a genial, social temperament, renders her among her friends, ever a welcome and agreeable companion. Fortune has smiled upon this household, and affluence has cast her mantle over them, to cheer their pathway amid life's duties and trials.

NOTE 52.

William L. Aldrich (304) is married, and lives in Providence,—as also is Tamar (303), and Amy S. (301),—all are successful in life, and enterprising, respected citizens.—See page 15.

NOTE 53.

Thankful W. Aldrich (302) married T. W. Hill, and lives in Iowa.

NOTE 54.

Robert H. Aldrich (306) entered the U. S. Navy, and remained in that connexion a year or more, when he was transferred to the Army, where he served with honor to the close of the war. He is unmarried, and has recently returned to New England, with the proud satisfaction of having served his country in the hour of her peril.

NOTE 55.

Esek Stone (309) married Phebe Ann Brownell, and lives at Quidnec Village, (Coventry), he is a steady, industrious man,—keeps a boarding-house, and is assistant in the Quidnec store.

NOTE 56.

John Hammond (322), in early life, made a profession of religion, and entered into the work of the ministry. He married, and removed to Foster, now "Foster Centre," and soon gathered around him a large, flourishing church. A spacious meeting-house was erected, and there this worthy man, and pious Christian, spent his life. His talents were of a superior order, and his sound sense, fluent expression and vital piety, made ample amends for any lack of education in his early life. He has left many worthy descendants in the town.

NOTE 57.

Samuel Stone (19) was born in Cranston, on the same little 25 acre farm, in "Mashantatack," "Cucumber town," or Stoneville, which his grandfather, Peter Stone (3), bought about the first days of his married life. Having learned the trade of a carpenter, he commenced work in the town of Warwick, where he soon found a mate, one who journeyed and labored with

him through a long life. He was married in 1756, and when, some ten years afterwards, he had scraped together a small pile, sufficiently large to purchase a home, with the true instincts of the family he left Warwick, and bought his first real estate in sight of his old home. Unusual energy and economy marked the course of this worthy pair, and twenty years from the time of their marriage, he was able to purchase, and pay for that valuable estate, on Sockonossett hill, now known as the " Howard Farm," lying both sides of N. L. turnpike. This location is one of the most beautiful in the State of Rhode Island. The site of the house commands a view of Providence, Bristol, Warren, Fall River, Newport, and in fact almost the whole of. Narragansett Bay for twenty miles or more, with all its villages, and its varied, meandering shore scenery on both sides, and, what is more, it overlooks every part of " Cucumber Town," and the several farms on which his ancestors and relatives had, for more than 100 years, labored and lived. In this beautiful locality, on this excellent farm, he spent most of his days, and died in 1810, much beloved and respected, a man of excellent judgment, of. high moral worth, of great industry, economy and prudence. He left an estate worth, at least twelve thousand dollars, mostly to his youngest two sons, and each one of the family inherited the industry, integrity, and moral worth of their parents. In stature, he was five feet ten inches, of robust make, and toward the close of life inclined to corpulence. His early opportunities for education were limited. At no time of life was he inclined to reading or study, and yet, through observation and conversation, he was well posted on most practical subjects. His wife outlived him but three years, and both sleep together, on " Sockonossett Hill," on the farm where they spent so large a portion of their lives. His five sons were all carpenters.

Note 58.

Almy Stone (324) married Peter Potter, in 1778, and lived in Scituate, reared a large family, and died at an advanced age. Mary Stone (329) married William Hill. Betsey Stone (331) married Thomas Hill; both lived in Foster, and both died at an early age, much esteemed, for their social worth and moral virtue.

Note 59.

Nathaniel Stone (325) was born in Warwick, but passed the time of his early manhood in Cranston. He married Mercy Gorton, a descendant in the sixth generation of " Samuel Gorton," the eccentric but liberal Christian, and founder of the Colony of Warwick, in 1642.—[See Staples' history of R. Island.] His energy and prudence enabled him, before middle life, to purchase a large and valuable farm, in Foster, R. I., about twenty miles from Providence. There he lived till the close of life. He was a man of great vigor of mind, and entered into the affairs of life, military, political, financial, with earnestness and ability. He was colonel of the R. I. Militia, and, for a

number of years, represented his town in the General Assembly of the State, he was strongly attached to the old Federal party of his day, and one of its leaders, in opposition to the French democracy, or Jeffersonian democracy, as it was then called. In his old age, he interested himself deeply in securing to the State the advantage of common schools, and gave that noble, but too long neglected measure his hearty support. He was an able financier, aided in the establishing of a bank in his own town, the Mount Vernon Bank, and was its first President, in which office he continued up to nearly the time of his death. His wife was a worthy woman, a good mother, and a faithful wife, and died when nearly 80, beloved and respected by all who knew her. To this active pair, life was a success, they lived to a good old age, made themselves felt in every department of life, while living, and left from ten to twelve thousand dollars to their posterity.

Note 60.

Rufus Stone (326), was second son of Samuel Stone (19), and, like most Rhode Island boys, began work in early life. A few weeks of winter school was all that came within his reach, nor did his natural inclinations especially incline him to more; he studied, but not books—not nature in its grandeur—not nature in its sublimity—not nature in its beauty, but nature in the practical relations of life. He, too, was a carpenter, and for some ten years closely applied himself to that business. He married Sarah Lewis, in 1781. She was the daughter of Capt. Benajah Lewis, of Providence, whose wife, dying in early life, he found homes for his children among their relatives, and sailed out of Providence master of a privateer, in the earlier years of the war of the Revolution. He never returned, and tradition, founded on what, we are not informed, says he died on the "Jersey prison ship," in the harbor of New York. Sarah was brought up with her aunt Mary, her mother's sister, the wife of Josiah King, Esq., and grandfather of Samuel W. King, late Governor of Rhode Island. In this worthy family she spent her early years, was married when 19, and soon went to reside in Providence, where her husband had purchased a lot and built a house. Here they lived some six years, when he sold his house and lot, and, gathering together his funds and "traps," moved to Chester, Vt., 140 miles from Providence,—a mighty remove this in those days;—they had then a boy of four years, and a girl of two. But a few years had been passed among the green hills of Vermont, when the boy, Richard (434), was killed with a log. The charm of the new and improving farm was then all gone,—'twas home to the father no longer; the bright sunny slopes, the beautiful and fertile vales, were all shrouded in gloom,—he sold his farm, and with sad and lonely steps returned to his native State. Here he made several removes, buying and selling, first in Cranston, then in Coventry, then in Scituate, occasionally travelling to find a home in the States of Connecticut and New York, until, in 1805, he settled down in Coventry, R. I. He entered largely into farming and stock raising,

15

was a man of great industry, of indomitable perseverance, and his judgment on all matters with which he was conversant was regarded almost as oracular. Remarkably temperate in all his habits, he enjoyed almost uninterrupted health, till his decease, in 1824. He had no love for study, rarely read book or paper, and yet he was well informed on all practical points connected with politics, theology, law, and practical life. He was a man of great observation, and, having a good memory, joined to a peculiar social tact, he made himself master of the general neighborhood information without the trouble of books. He was a steady thinker, and indefatigable worker; thinking with his head upon one subject, working with his hands upon another. He was always talking to himself. On some points his wife resembled him—in fine constitution—in industry and economy—in temperate habits. In some points they differed;—she was a great reader, had a strong memory, and would, if opportunities had favored, been a fine scholar. She lacked his sound judgment, being governed much more than he was by impulse ; their life was attended with success He died in 1824, leaving to his two surviving children at least fourteen thousand dollars, and the memory of both is cherished with increasing veneration and respect by those with whom they were best acquainted. His wife survived him twenty years, and died in Bridgewater, Mass., at the ripe age of 82. Their remains now rest, side by side, in Coventry, R. I., in a small wall-enclosed cemetery, near Potterville, on the farm where he lived and died.

Note 61.

James Stone (327), one of the five carpenters reared by Samuel Stone (19), married Mary Webb, of Warwick, and commenced his married life in Scituate. After a few years he bought a farm in Foster, where most of his children were born, and where he lived till they had all reached maturity. Like the rest of his brothers, he left house-building for farming, in which occupation he spent most of his life. He was a man of clear perceptions, somewhat opinionated, fond of controversy, but withal, a man of kind feelings, and honest and upright in all his ways. Toward the close of life, his first wife dying, he found a second connexion, moved to Coventry, and spent the remaining portion of his days on the farm now owned by his son Israel (488), near Coventry Centre.

Note 62.

Samuel Stone (328), the fourth son of Samuel (19), was born, and lived, in Cranston, until his marriage with Hannah Sweet, when he moved to Johnston, where he spent most of his days. After the death of his father, in 1810, he came into possession of the old homestead, on Sockonossett Hill, but we believe, never lived there ; subsequently he bought, of his brother Edmands, a valuable estate in Scituate, called the " Leach Farm," upon which he removed, and there died, aged 58. He was an athlethic, robust man, in

size and appearance, almost the transcript of his father. In character, he was industrious, virtuous, much esteemed by his neighbors, and died beloved and lamented. His wife survived him 24 years, and died, aged 88.

NOTE 63.

Edmands Stone (330), youngest son of Samuel (19), received his name from his maternal grandmother, " Mary Edmands," and lived with his father till 1810, the time of his decease. In the division of the real estate, left to him and his brother, by the father, Edmands quitted the beautiful homestead, on " Sockonossett hill," and removed to Scituate ;—subsequently he owned a large farm in Killingly, Conn., where he lived a short time, but finally returned to the old neighborhood, the home of his early days. His temper was genial, sportive, very social, and his conversation vivacious, and strongly spiced with wit. This trait in his character, in fact, caused his death. Passing through a way with gates and bars, his youngest son, Samuel (597), got out to open the gates; starting from one they had just passed, he called out— " Sam, I'll beat you to the next gate." Sam ran ; the horse started off at speed ; through unevenness of the ground, the seat was thrown into the bottom of the wagon,—in trying to replace this while the horse was in motion, he was thrown from the wagon, and the spine so injured that he never spoke after, and lived but 24 hours. He was a man of industry, sobriety, integrity and moral worth, though his trafficking in real estate was unsuccessful, and by these means he lost most of his property. He died aged 67 years. His remains sleep by the side of his father and brother Samuel, on the old homestead, on " Sockonossett Hill."

NOTE 64.

Mercy Stone (338), eldest daughter of Col. Nathaniel Stone (325), married Capt. George Phillips, of Foster,—a man of respectability and moral worth. She died in 1859. Their only son, George, W. Phillips, is Town Clerk of Foster, and enjoys the confidence of his fellow townsmen, having been re-elected for successive years, almost without a dissenting vote. He married Miss Mary A Sweet, a lady of fine talent and religiously cultivated mind. Their residence is Foster Centre, within two miles, and in full view of the old homestead, where he was born.

NOTE 65.

Samuel Stone (339) was born in Cranston, but removed with his father to Foster in early life. He married Miss Lydia Angell, and lived in his native State till nearly 40 years old, when he moved to Columbus, Chenango Co., N. Y., where he spent the remainder of his life. He was early engaged in military affairs, and was a Major of the R. Island Militia. He died in 1863·

Note 66.

Nathaniel Stone (340) was born in Cranston, we believe, but lived in Foster his whole life, except his infancy. Industry and integrity marked his continued course;—no man was more respected and beloved; he was appointed Justice of the Peace, chosen from time to time a member of the Town Council, elected to the State Legislature, commanded an independent company of Cadets, and was, for many years, a deacon of the Baptist Church. He was twice married,—first, to Miss Lucy Rounds,—secondly, to her sister, Zilpha. He died in 1861. Few men have performed their duties, and filled their sphere in life, better than Dea. Nathaniel Stone; few men of the same proportionate acquaintances, have left more friends and fewer enemies.

Note 67.

Sally Stone (341) was born, lived and died, in Foster. Her husband, Nathaniel Phillips, was a respectable farmer, always in comfortable circumstances, and, from the very nature of the soil on which he was reared, a portion of the bone and sinew of the little State, which, by birthright, he could call his own. Most of this family remains in Rhode Island. Horace Phillips (393) died in 1862, while on the Pacific Ocean.

Note 68.

William G. Stone (342) was born in Foster, and received, in common with the boys of that age, the educational opportunities of Rhode Island schools, we cannot say Free Schools, for in those days all were private schools throughout the State. Such schools as that age of Rhode Island afforded, he enjoyed, and improved them to the best advantage. In early life he was chosen captain of a company of Cadets, and when a young man appointed a Justice of the Peace, which office he held for more than twenty years, issuing more writs, and conducting more trials, than all the other Justices in the town ;—he was chosen, from time to time, to fill every important town office ; was three years a Representative in the State Legislature, and three years a member of the State Senate. He has carefully studied the political history of our country, and with a clear head, and loyal heart, plants himself on the topstone of American Liberty. When Rhode Island threw aside the old Charter of Charles II., under which she had lived so long, and sought an embodiment of Republican Freedom in a State Constitution, the Hon. Wm. G. Stone was chosen a member of the Convention which formed the present Constitution, that well arranged and satisfactory disposition of executive, judicial and legislative power, under which the little State has become great. He resides in North Foster, near the Baptist church, which he has done much to build up and sustain ; a church which is now, and has been for fifty years, under the care of the venerable and Rev. Daniel Williams, a descend-

ant in the sixth generation of Roger Williams. William G. Stone (342).
married Miss Elcie Hopkins, of Foster, they have but one surviving child.

NOTE 69.

Lydia Stone (343) married Major Samuel H. Hopkins. They reside in
Foster, where the husband is the owner of saw-mills and corn-mills; Major
Hopkins is much respected, is in good circumstances, and has several times
been chosen a member of the General Assembly of the State. Several of
their children are settled in Minesota.

NOTE 70.

Polly Stone (345) married Alpheus Bowen, of Foster, a wheelwright and
carpenter, a man of sound mind and elevated moral principle. They have
twelve children, nine of whom are living and in mature life; three have
passed away. Henry Bowen (408) is a mechanic, in Nashville, Tenn. Lucinda Bowen's husband, E. D. Barden, is engaged in putting up steam saw-
mills in the South. Cyrus Bowen (410) is in company with Barden in the
same business. William Bowen (411) lives in South Brookfield, Mass., is a
carpenter. Vincent Bowen (415) has been a successful teacher. Almira
Bowen (412) married Olney C. Cole, who is a blacksmith. Leonard Bowen
(416) is a carpenter, and married Sarah J. Randall, who is now, and has
been, a teacher most of her life. Maritta Bowen (417), and Horace Bowen
(418), are unmarried, and reside at home.

NOTE 71.

Charles Stone (346) married Miss Jerusha Hill, of Scituate, and was
elected, in early life, captain of a company of Cadets, as two of his brothers
had been before him. He died before he was 30, leaving a widow and four
children, three of whom are married,—Randall H. Stone (419) lives in
Providence. Edmund Stone (420) resides in Foster, and Eliza A. Stone
(422) married A. J. Sweet, and lives at Foster Centre. Charles Stone
(346) died regretted and lamented by a large circle of friends, and his children now honor his memory by a high moral and religious stand among the
most virtuous and esteemed in their own native State.

NOTE 72.

Daniel Stone (347) married Eleanor Eddy, and resides on a part of the
large farm owned by his father. He is peculiar for his domestic habits; more
than sixty summers, and as many winters, have passed over his head, but his
sleepings and wakings have all been upon the same spot;—he was never
thirty miles from home. He has one child, a son, Henry W. Stone (428),
unmarried, and resides at home with his parents.

Note 73.

Eliza Stone (348), the youngest daughter and child of Col. Nathaniel Stone (325), married Barton Randall, who has purchased and lives upon a portion of the farm where his wife was born. Mr. Randall is the grandson of the Rev. John Hammond (322) Note (56), and a man much esteemed for virtue and moral worth; his wife, Eliza, is a woman of strong mind, clear perception, active social feeling, a person to be remembered and loved by all her acquaintances.

Note 74.

Roxana Stone (381) married Henry Anthony, the son of Dr. J. Anthony, of Foster, with whom she lived some fifteen years, when he died, leaving two children; Roxana still remains a widow, and is now in feeble health. She resides at the home of her childhood, as does her sister Clarissa Stone (376), near Hopkins' Mills (so called), they are in good circumstances, inheriting the virtues of their parents, and commanding the esteem of all who know them.

Note 75.

Hiram Stone (383) resides on the estate where his father, Dea. Nathaniel Stone (340), lived and died. His opportunities for education have been above the ordinary boys around him, and he takes rank among the teachers of the present day. The Dutchman's prayer does satisfy; he is looking for improvement; hoping and expecting to be *better* off to-morrow than to-day; he is decidedly a young man of promise. He married Susan S. Simmons,— they have two children.

Note 76.

Martha Stone (435) enjoyed more than ordinary facilities for study and mental improvement; her uncle, Sabin Lewis, was Principal of an Academy; she attended several terms at that institution, and well improved her opportunities. When eighteen years of age she married the Hon. George Hawkins, a man whose strength of mind, slow but safe in all its conclusions, made up for any want of early culture which he lacked. Early in life he passed through the subordinate military ranks till he held a Major's commission, and was honorably discharged. Repeatedly he was chosen a representative in the General Assembly, and was several times elected a Senator under the Charter of Charles II., when the State Senate consisted of but *ten*. For more than forty of the last years of his life he was deacon of the Christian Baptist church, in Coventry. In many respects, Dea. Hawkins was the reverse of his wife,—she was quick in thought and expression, he slow and deliberate; she was ardent, hasty, demonstrative, unreserved; he cool, deliberate and reserved; she was a social, genial, companion, binding her friends to her by cords of love gushing out in warm expressions; he was a warm-hearted companion, binding his friends around him, not by what he did say, but by what

they saw were the out-gushings of a heart surcharged with love and truth. Dea. Hawkins was never a public speaker, either as a political or a religious man, but he always carried with him the balances to weigh what was written or spoken by others, and few that knew him, doubted the correctness of his decisions. He died in 1863, having survived his wife more than 20 years. They were both baptized into the Christian Baptist communion in 1812, exemplified their faith by a holy walk, and were pillars in that branch of the Christian church.

Note 77.

Philip P. Hawkins (436a) married Sarah Weaver, and lived in Coventry and West Greenwich. He was a man of more than ordinary education, of clear perceptions, but unsafe conclusions. He was a man of great industry, of superior argumentative powers, but lacked the judgment which marked his father's whole life-course. He died in 1866.

Note 78.

Sarah Hawkins (438) married Benoni Lewis, and now lives in Coventry. They for many years lived in Providence, where the husband built a large house, and for years followed the trade of carpenter and builder. He is an industrious and worthy man, and his wife an excellent and intelligent woman, beloved and esteemed by all who know her.

Note 79.

Elisha Hawkins (440) lives on a portion of the farm owned by his father, in Coventry. He married a very worthy girl of the same town, Rhoda Comstock, by whom he had three sons. The eldest, Richard S. Hawkins, heard the call of his country, when the Union Flag was first trampled, at Fort Sumter, beneath traitor feet; and he was among the earliest to respond to her voice. He died of consumption contracted by exposure in the army of the Potomac. He was a noble boy, and his memory is cherished with tearful esteem by all who knew him.

Note 80.

Richard Cecil Stone (436), the only surviving son of Rufus Stone (326), and Sarah Lewis, was born in Scituate, from which town his father removed to Coventry, when he was six years old. He, at an early age, gave evidence of a love of study, his earliest recollection of books is reading them; his father gratified this desire by purchasing the juvenile books, of that day, such as " Peter Pipin, king of the good boys,"— " History of George Graceful,"— " The Easter Offering,"—" Entertaining Stories," and books of a similar character, he had quite a library ; from one of these he read, before he was five years old, the story of Parnell's poem, " The Hermit," rendered into

prose, which made a deep impression upon his mind, as, portraying in clearness and beauty the movement of the Divine hand by second causes; before he was eight, he read the entire poem, and through reading and meditation upon the ideas and events, unconsciously committed the whole to memory. It had a marked influence on his life and character. He never attended school till he was seven years old, when he read in the first class in Bingham's " American Preceptor." During the next ten years he attended the schools of the neighborhood, with part of two terms at " Plainfield Academy,". less than thirty-three months; in which time, with his home study, he completed English Grammar and Composition ; Daboll's and Pike's Arithmetic; Flint's Surveying; Blunt's Practical Navigator; with a slight attention to Latin Grammar and Translation. At this time he commenced teaching winter schools, and improving a farm in summer. At the age of nineteen he married Alma Stone (1411), daughter of Dea. Henry Stone, of Scituate, and when twenty-two, with the advice and consent of his father, he moved to Worcester County, Mass., upon a valuable farm, in the town of Charlton. Two years from this time his father died, and he came into possession of some eight thousand dollars. Three things were now before him; his property was to be taken care of and improved; his family was to be cared for, and his education was to be pursued. His success in teaching gathered around him those who urged him to give up all other business, and devote himself to literary pursuits ; to this course he bent his energies, and four years after, having arranged his pecuniary matters, he built convenient rooms on " Oxford Plain," and opened a High School, for young Ladies and Gentlemen. This school he continued six years, until he was settled in the ministry, in Bridgewater, Mass. ; in fact it became a kind of Normal School, out of which from twenty to thirty, yearly, went as teachers. While in this school, and the few years previous to his entering it, while engaged in detached terms of teaching, he had read most of the Latin and Greek authors, and written out an interlineal translation (The Greek on one line, the corresponding English on the other,) of Jacob's Greek reader ; added to this, he had mastered several treatises on Algebra and the higher branches of Mathematics, and attended two courses of lectures, of thirteen each, making copious notes, on Philosophy and Chemistry. In this school he constantly employed one or more assistants, among whom was J. H. Gallup, A. M., a graduate of New Haven, and Miss Eliza Whittemore, of Leicester, whose practical mathematical knowledge, and high classical attainments materially aided in giving instruction and character to the Oxford High School. After he retired from the school, it was continued more or less successfully by Orlando Chester, A. M., a graduate of New Haven, James L. Stone (441), A. M., a graduate of Brown University, Jeremiah Moore, of Oxford, and John Burleigh, of Plainfield, Conn., son of the late Rinaldo Burleigh, A. M., the learned Preceptor of Plainfield Academy. Richard C. Stone's attention was not entirely given to literary pursuits, and the sciences demanded in the school-room. When

first a resident in Massachusetts, he was elected an officer in the Military, and rapidly rose up through the several grades until he held a Colonel's commission in the Massachusetts Militia, when he was honorably discharged. He was also Surveyor in Worcester County, and held a Magistrate's commission for fourteen years, transacting a large business as Land Surveyor, conveyancer and appraiser. In the first temperance movement, in Massachusetts, he took a decided stand. Lectured and wrote in favor of total abstinence, and through his whole life has been unsparing towards those " who give their neighbors drink, who put the bottle to them." His indomitable energy and perseverance has stopped the sale of intoxicating liquors in the town of Sherbourn and West Bridgewater, where he has lived, and to his personal efforts, many a man now owes his sobriety and respectability. His efficient course in this cause necessarily awakened a violent opposition from " vipers who creep where man disdains to climb," and brought around him a host of rum-sellers and rum-drinking persecutors, whose chief power lay in their noise. He entered into the ministry before he relinquished his school, and was ordained in 1834 pastor of the Congregational Church, in West Bridgewater, Plymouth County, Mass. He was subsequently settled in Middlesex County, the city of Boston, and Manchester, N. II. While in Manchester, his eyes, being weak, became inflamed, insomuch that he was obliged to abandon his profession. In this situation, he received and accepted an agency which enabled him to travel in the West, making his home in St. Louis, Missouri, where he has been for the last ten years. More than twenty-five years ago, impressed with the desire of learning the history of his ancestors, he visited several of the aged of the name, learned what he could of their connexion and early history, committed it to writing, and collected about four hundred names; this record, made at that time, has enabled him to collect and arrange these Genealogical Statistics now. His home is in the West, though he is, at present, the Pastor of the Christian Union Church, Washington Village, Coventry, R. I., the town where he was raised from six, till he left the State when nearly twenty-two. His wife is still living; her whole life of industry and care flashes brightly over the widespread homes of her children, from Boston to St. Louis, and lights up with radiant joy the hearts of nearly forty children, and children's children. They have pecuniarily contributed largely to the comfortable condition of their children, and are still in affluent circumstances. R. C. Stone (436) has been a voluminous contributor to various periodicals, among which are—

Discussion of the principles of the Death Penalty—written in 1825. Published in the " Worcester Spy."

Discussion of the principles of Total Abstinence, controversial—written about 1828 or 9. Published in the " Independent Inquirer."

Sermon, preached at Mansfield, Mass., at the Ordination of Rev. James L. Stone. Title; " Duties and Responsibilities of the Christian Ministry."

Address, to the Plymouth County Agricultural Society—delivered at Bridgewater, Mass.

Sermon : " The Hereditary Depravity of Man," preached at Manchester, N.H.

Discussion : "What Constitutes Christian Liberality?"—Parkerism and Transcendentalism—a controversy with Rev J. F. Clarke. Published in the " Christian World."

History of Joseph—dramatized, in twelve Acts.

Graphic description of the " Victoria Regia," or Mammoth Lilly. Published in the " Manchester American."

" Scribblings on a Journey," eighteen Letters, including a graphic description of Niagara Falls. Published in the " Manchester Mirror."

"Amoskeag, Fifty Years Ago," 31 numbers. Published in "Manchester Mirror."

" Letters from the White Mountains," eleven in number. Published in the " Manchester Mirror."

Sermon : " The Christian Citizen in the Impending Crisis." Preached at St. Louis, Mo., in 1861.

" Graphic description of Mammoth Cave, Kentucky," eight numbers. Published in the " Calhoun County Union."

Correspondence—Political and Literary. Published in the " Stars and Stripes."

NOTE 81.

James L. Stone (441) was born is Coventry, R. I., but was removed in his early childhood to Charlton, Mass., where, under the instruction of his father, he ripened into a manly boy ; and, although not large, he at fourteen taught a district school with good success; pursuing his classical studies through the summer and autumn, the winter following found him, when but fifteen years old, teaching school in the town of Rutland, twenty miles from home ; this school he taught two years. The succeeding fall found him a Freshman in Brown University. The school at Oxford, the next year becoming vacant by the removal of Mr. Chester to the State of Ohio, he left College for one year, and took it under his charge. At the close of one year he entered the Sophomore Class at the University, and, continuing his studies, graduated when he was twenty-two. Soon after, he received a call from the First Congregational Church, in Mansfield, and was ordained in 1840. He married Miss Elmira Lothrop, the daughter of Capt. Spencer Lothrop, of West Bridgewater, a lady of good education, of genial, domestic disposition and habits, and who, by her industry and economy, has contributed her share to that affluence with which they are now blessed. He was subsequently pastor of the churches in Brewster and Sharon, Mass., and when about thirty-seven, retired from the ministry. He, for a short time, had the Principalship of one of the Grammar Schools in Providence, but soon opened the English and Classical School in the beautiful town of Foxboro', where he remained for a number of years with marked success. His health becoming impaired, he

Yours very truly
Jas L. Stone,

bade adieu to the recitation-room, to the school-house, and the lecture-room, forever, and now, connected with the Connecticut Life Insurance Company, hopes, by exercise and travel in the fresh air of New England, to regain the health which he has lost.

NOTE 82.

S. Hollis Stone (442) was born in Coventry, but when an infant removed to Massachusetts; he early had a desire to engage in the labors of the field. When eight years old, he asked his father, one Monday morning, if he might work that summer on a farm. The answer was, "yes, if you can find any one to employ you;" without farther conversation he left the house and did not return, except for call or visit, for more than two years. He lived, this time, with a worthy neighbor, about a mile from home, where he learned all farm work, and acquired habits of industry and sobriety. He attended all the public schools of the town, and one or two terms in his father's school, but manifested no particular aptness for study, or interest in education, till fifteen or sixteen years old, when he seemed to catch a glimpse of educational beauty. Though mostly engaged in field labor, he improved every opportunity to add to his stock of knowledge, and although not well prepared, taught school at seventeen. His success was unusual, and strongly marked by faithfulness and personal exertion. He taught the same school a second winter, and ever after enjoyed the reputation of a superior instructor. He learned the mason trade, at which he worked for a few years, but abandoned it, on being offered the High School, in North Bridgewater. Here he taught till his health obliged him to relinquish teaching altogether. Subsequently he removed to Olean, Alleghany County, N. Y.; was agent and part owner of a sash and door manufactory, firm, "Stone, Genthner & Co." The manufactory was burned in 1859; he went West, and finally settled in Illinois, on the East bank of the Mississippi, some seventy miles above St. Louis. He owns a farm of nearly 300 acres, and is mostly engaged in stock raising, and fruit growing. He married Miss Betsey Copeland, of West Bridgewater, and they have buried one half of six children. Miss Copeland taught several terms of school before marriage.

NOTE 83.

George Burrill Stone (443) was born in Charlton, Mass., and in early childhood removed to Oxford. His education commenced at an early age; he read Virgil in Latin, and the New Testament in Greek, readily, when eight years old, and could have entered College at twelve. He entered Brown University when fourteen at as early an age as their regulations permitted, and graduated at eighteen, the year of the memorable Dorr war. Undecided in his course of life, he entered the law office of the Hon. P. C. Bacon, then of Oxford, now of Worcester, where he remained some months. No law office was better calculated to give a moral young man elevated ideas

of the legal profession, than was Lawyer Bacon's; still, he was dissatisfied, feeling that he could not practice law without lowering his standard of morals, and, the following year, with the consent of his father, he opened a private school, in Fall River, Mass. He met with good success; but a few years after, when the increase of the town warranted a gradation of schools, and the establishment of a High School, he was offered the Principalship. His labors were satisfactory, and he remained in the Fall River High School several years; at length he became impressed with the idea that he had remained long enough in Fall River. He was soon offered the superintendency of the Public Schools, and Principalship of the High School, Indianapolis, Ind. This he accepted, and went West. The decisions of the Supreme Court of Indiana, relative to public school money, materially affected the schools of Indianapolis, and rendered his situation less pleasant and less remunerative, and he accepted the same position in Minneapolis, Minesota, which he had held in Indiana. Here he remained until three years since, when he was invited by the Trustees of " Washington University," St. Louis, Mo., to his present position, Professor of Oratory and Rhetoric, and Principal of the Academic Department. While in Indianapolis, he was editor of the " Indiana State Journal," an educational periodical, published there. As a classical scholar he holds a high rank, and his capacity for governing and awakening in the youthful mind a love of literature, has rarely been equalled. He married, while in Fall River, Miss Lucy Edson, daughter of Den. Nathaniel Edson, a lady of taste, refinement, and good sense. She taught school several terms in Mansfield and Bridgewater. They have had five children, four have passed away to the "better land," one only remains, Frank Charlton Stone (117) is a member of the Junior Class, in the University of which his father is Professor.

NOTE 84.

Sarah Stone (444) was born in Charlton, and removed in infancy to Oxford, where she received the rudiments of education in the school of her father, and her education was continued subsequently, in the schools of her brother, and the Normal School, at Bridgewater. Like her brothers and sisters, she commenced teaching at an early age, in Mansfield, in Natick, and in Brighton, Mass. She taught yearly schools with good success, and left the hall of instruction for household duties when she was twenty. She married Stephen C. Arnold, of Providence, R. I , where her whole married life has been passed. S. C. Arnold is a thorough business man, is junior partner in the long established firm of " William W. Arnold & Son," and enjoys the confidence of all his acquaintances. He is Colonel of the Mechanic Rifles, and held the offices of Inspector of the State Prison, Director of High Street Bank, Director of the Narragansett Insurance Company, Director of the Gaspee Insurance Company, Clerk of the Sixth Ward, and is Trustee and Treasurer of several property holding societies of Odd Fellows and Masons.

Stephen C. Arnold is a descendant in the 5th generation from Stephen Chapman and Zervia Sanger, who were married in 1734. This was an unusual pair. In 1735 their first child was born, and, in 1760, the last of 21— all at single births—21 children in 25 years. Stephen Chapman died in 1770, his wife survived him 42 years, and died at the ripe age of 94, in 1812. Col. S. C. Arnold's two great grandmothers, his father's grandmother, and his mother's grandmother, were two of this family ; Hannah Chapman, who married Simeon Arnold. and Lucia Chapman, who married Reuben Blanchard, he is, therefore, justly entitled to his name, Stephen Chapman Arnold. They have four children, one dear girl, Alma Stone Arnold, is in the Spirit land, she died aged ten years, and they have three sons, the oldest, William Edmonds Arnold (462). aged 16, is in his second year of the High School, in the city of Providence.

NOTE 85.

Alma Stone (445) was born in Oxford, and learned to read almost in infancy, reading the New Testament through in course before she was five years old. Her education was received in the schools of Bridgewater, the Academy at Framingham, and the High School of her brother, at Fall River. She taught school in Sherborn, Fall River, and was, for several years, assistant in the Summer Street Grammar School, in the city of Providence. She married Thomas Metcalf, of Wrentham, Mass., a graduate of Bridgewater Normal School, and Professor of Mathematics and English literature, in the " State Normal University of Illinois," located at Bloomington, where they now reside. Prof. Metcalf was, for several years, teacher of the High, School, in West Roxbury. Mass ; from that place he removed to St. Louis, Mo. and was appointed Principal of the High School, in that city. From St. Louis, he accepted the position he now occupies, where he has been four years. They have three children living, the remains of their oldest two sleep in the Cemetery, at Forest Hill, near Boston.

NOTE 86.

Richard Butler Stone (446) was born in Oxford, Mass., but, when five years old, was removed with his parents to West Bridgewater, and subsequently, when thirteen years old, to Sherborn. In that town, and at Framingham Academy, he received a good English and mercantile education, and entered a store in Boston as salesman and accountant, where he remained two years. Becoming dissatisfied with city life he learned the trade of carpenter, and in a few years emigrated to Olean, Alleghany County, N. Y., where, after a year or more in the lumber trade, he took a yearly school, and taught with good success nearly two years. At this time his health failed, and he was obliged to seek respite from labor, mental and physical, in order to regain his health, at the " Water-Cure Establishment," in Worcester, Mass. Within

a year, his health so far recovered, that he he resumed business, in Chicago, where he has for the last ten years resided. He has, most of the time, been in the lumber trade, for which his long acquaintance with the article, his order and method in yard arrangement, and his ease, fraukness, affability and knowledge of the world, as a salesman, admirably fitted him. He married when at Olean, Miss Ellen Russell, daughter of Mr. Josiah Russell, of Oxford, a young lady of good education and cultivated mind, who was, for some time, a teacher in the High School, in her native town. They have five children, one has been called above, four are still with them.

Martha Stone (447) was born in Oxford, and early in childhood was removed to West Bridgewater, where her father was settled in the ministry. In the schools of West Bridgewater and Sherborn she received the rudiments of her education, but studied much with her brother, at " Fall River, where she was qualified as a teacher. Her first effort in teaching was in Fall River, next in Taunton, then on the island of Martha's Vineyard, where she taught a year or more, and finally, in one of the Grammar School of Roxbury she closed her labors, and bid adieu to the school-room, with all its anxieties, perplexities, and joys. She at that time married Mr. Robert C. Metcalf, a graduate of the " State Normal School," at Bridgewater, and, at the time of their marriage, also a teacher in Roxbury. Soon after, Mr. Metcalf was invited to the " Adams School," East Boston, one of the largest and most important schools in the city. To this he has been appointed Principal, and it is not too much to say that, as a methodical, energetic, active, and popular teacher, he has no superior. He is a ready speaker, interesting, humorous, and when called out, on almost any occasion, rarely fails to please. They have three children, all living.

Mary Stone (448) was born in West Bridgewater, and when seven years old removed with her parents to Sherborn. Her education was mainly obtained with her brother, in Fall River, effectively begun however, in the District school of her native town. Her first effort in teaching was in Mansfield, Mass. Subsequently she was appointed teacher in the Chapman Grammar School, East Boston, where she remained several years, and until her health failed, and she was obliged to leave teaching altogether. For six years she has been an invalid. Disappointment seemed stamped upon all her surroundings; her eyes refused her the alleviation of reading; and, thrown upon her mental cultivation and her firm faith in God, she still endured with cheerfulness, though sometimes with tearful smiles, her long years of weariness and debility. She was engaged to be married to Thomas Slade, of Fall River, Mass., a graduate of Brown University, now a lawyer, in suc-

cessful practice in Bloomington, Ill., and when she removed to the home of her parents, in St. Louis, he sought employment in the same city, and kindly, faithfully, affectionately, sought to soothe, alleviate and encourage her, during her long years of suffering and trial. But she has truly grown better, been drawn nearer to God by her privations and disappointments;—a Christian before, she is nearer God now. For more than a year she was under the skillful and judicious care of Dr. Pallen, of St. Louis; the year after, she spent the warm season in the healthy breezes of Minnesota, and the year following, from April to December, she was under the skillful care of Dr. Gleason, at that delightful summer retreat, the " Elmira Water Cure," N. Y. During the last three years, her health has gradually, but almost imperceptibly improved. Last December she was married, and her friends cherish the hope that her life may, many years, be continued. They reside in Bloomington, one of the most beautiful of the prairie towns in Illinois, the county seat of McLean County ; is the site of the " State Normal University," and several literary institutions, and located on the St. Louis and Chicago Railroad, and nearly midway between those two cities.

Note 89.

Charles Henry Stone (449), the youngest son and youngest child of Richard C. Stone (436), was born in West Bridgewater, Mass., spent the earlier part of his life in Middlesex County, and moved with his parents to Manchester, N. H., where his father was then in the ministry. When fourteen he entered the High School, in that city, and commenced the study of the classics. Here he remained a year; his father then removing to Missouri, Charles Henry went to Providence, entered the High School, and continued the course commenced at Manchester, preparatory to entering Brown University. His progress was good, and when nearly ready for admission, his father consenting, he turned his course to other pursuits. He went to Missouri, gave his attention to mercantile objects until, in 1861, the country issued her call for volunteers, to hold the State among the loyal, in opposition to a strong rebel host which was rising up on every side. He was among the first to respond, enlisted under the brave and generous Lyon, and on the 10th of May was among the boys who took the *first* rebel prisoners during the war, at Camp Jackson, in the suburbs of St. Louis. He was with Lyon in his march to Springfield, and after his death returned with the retreating army to Rolla. In the autumn of that year, his term of enlistment having expired, he was mustered out, but retained as recruiting officer and military instructor, until December. It was, during this period of service, that he was fired upon by a squad of skulking traitors, and his coat pierced, with two holes, both made by the same ball. Soon after this he received the appointment of assistant in the Post Office, at Cairo, Ill , where he remained until 1863, when he was transferred to the mail agency, on the Illinois Central Railroad, his route lying between Centralia and Chicago. While

mail agent on this route, he met with what came near a fatal accident. The cars ran off the track, detached the mail car from its couplings, turned it end for end, tumbling it down an embankment of ten feet, where it rested on its roof. The mail agent was taken out from under a stove and two tons of mail bags, with only the small bone of the leg fractured, and somewhat bruised. The mail bags saved his life, or at least, from serious injury. In 1865, he removed to Hamburg, Ill. He has a large farm, mostly located on the table lands, skirting the East bank of the Mississippi River, and 100 feet above its waters, where he is extensively engaged in stock-raising, and fruit-growing He married Miss Maggie M. Barber, of St. Louis, a lady of superior education, and fine musical culture. She has taught several terms of school, was organist in the Baptist Church, at Centralia, and has extensively given lessons in music where she has lived. They have two children.

NOTE 90.

George Stone (482) was probably born in Scituate, R. I., but spent his youth and early manhood in Foster, where his father had removed. Here he remained till about the time of his marriage with Miss Naomi Bennett, when he removed to the State of New York, in Chenango County, we believe. In his New York home he has married a second wife, by whom he has one or more children. His son, George Stone (497), is a Baptist preacher, in the State of New York.

NOTE 91.

Betsey Stone (483) married Thomas Hill, and lived in Rockland Village, Scituate, R I. Mr. Hill was a miller and farmer, and the family are respected and esteemed. Their eldest son, William Hill (501), is a preacher, in his native town. James Stone (486) married Phebe Greene, and for his second wife, Mary Whitford, both of Coventry. He lives in Scituate, near the line of Foster, and is an industrious farmer.

NOTE 92.

Asahel Stone (487) was born in Foster, and has lived in Providence County, R. I., through his life. He has been twice married: 1st., to Betsey Harrington; 2d, to Dolly Burnham, of Connecticut; he is a carpenter by trade, and is an enterprising, useful man. He resides in Clayville. R. I., and has reared an active and respectable family. Lyman B. Stone (515) married Emily Trowbridge, and resides at Spragueville. Almira G. Stone (516) married Edmund Potter, and resides near her father. Betsey M, Stone (517) married Thomas Burgess. Charles A. Stone (518) married Celinda Howard, daughter of Rev. Gardner Howard, of Foster, and lives in Clayville. The youngest son, George A. Stone (520), lives with his father.

Note 93.

Israel Stone (188) was born in Foster, and in early manhood moved to Coventry. When about thirty years of age he purchased a farm near Coventry Centre, where he has ever since lived, a hard working, industrious, economical man, always saving part of every dollar he earns. His prudence and activity, in doors and out, would, ere this time, have made him a very wealthy farmer but for the never ending " Stone law case," which has been stereotyped on the legal record of Kent County, with yearly additions and improvements for between thirty and forty years. In this law suit he was the most active, unflinching, and persevering of the parties; a lull was felt for a few years in this controversial breeze; the old lawyers, Gen. Greene, Atwell, Cozzens and Bowen, died off, glad to escape a contention which, *even they,* tried to settle by reference or adjustment, without effect; and a new batch of attorneys has been got up to attend to the interests of that unlucky farm, and a new set of jurors have been born and raised to adjudicate upon its travelled ways, and its river rights. He is still confident of having matters settled " *right,*" and looks forward to days of quietude and peace. He married Miss Eliza Burlingame, of Coventry, R. I., a woman of more than ordinary intelligence, whose active brain, and busy hands, have aided him in every department of his eventful life. We believe, although they have mainly failed; she has never counselled an abandonment of what they have considered their rights, and would now, if it were her last words, say with the lamented Lawrence* " don't give up the ship." They have, we believe, met all their law liabilities, and now own their farm, free of debt. They have had but one child, Mary Ann Waterman Stone (531), a girl of fine promise and intelligence beyond her years. She died, aged sixteen.

Note 94.

Jeremiah Stone (489) married Ellen Barber, and a few years since, moved to Minnesota. Mary Stone (490) married Aldis Borden, and reared a large family, who resides in Providence County, R. I.

Note 95.

Cyrus Stone (545) was the eldest son of Samuel Stone (328), and married in due time, as almost all his relatives have done before and since, as we can recollect, no man, among this large collection, who failed in this respect—and died a bachelor. He married Miss Eleanor Smith, whose buoyant temperament, genial disposition, and loving heart, shed a radiance over their common home, and tinged his own staid sobriety even, with relaxation and smiles. They commenced life in Johnston, a little west of the noted " great elm," and here most of their nine children were born. Disposing of their property in that place, he purchased a farm and moved to Pomfret, Conn., where he lived but a few years, when he sold out and went to Philadelphia.

16

Here he engaged in manufacturing. In this, however, he was unsuccessful, and he returned in a short time, and settled down in his native State, where he has ever since remained. His wife died a few years since, much lamented and beloved, while he, some 74 years of age, is enjoying good health, a fine representative of the ancient stock, lives with his daughter, Caroline Stone (556), now Mrs. Littlefield, in the town where he was born. His eldest son, Henry Stone (550), married Miss Elizabeth Hodson, from Maine. They reside in Providence, where he is engaged in the manufactory of jewelry. The second son, Charles Edward Stone, is a blacksmith, and lives in Olneyville. He married Miss Caroline Sweet. They have six children. William G. Stone (553) married Miss Sophia Ann Fiske, and resides in Providence, and is also a jeweller. Benjamin B. Stone (555) is superintendent of of manufactory of jewelry, in the same city, and a young man of moral worth and ability; four have died in early maturity, much beloved, and the five who still remain, by their industry, filial love, and moral worth, cheer the heart of their surviving parent as he travels the path down into the lonely valley.

NOTE 96.

George K. Stone (546) married Susan Child, and died in middle age. William Stone (548) has been, we believe, twice married, but his history is not known, nor is that of his family.

NOTE 97.

Almira Stone (549) married Daniel Greene, and died at the early age of twenty-eight, leaving five small children, the eldest nine, the youngest an infant. Seven years afterwards the father also died. The children thus left in double orphanage, were kindly cared for by their relatives, and especially by their liberal uncle, the late Dutee Greene, of Providence. They have all been rendered affluent by the disposition of his large estate, and bid fair to make a good use of the inheritance so liberally devised. The eldest daughter, Abbie Ann Greene (577), lives in Central Falls, R. I., a manufacturing village near Pawtucket.

NOTE 98.

Charles Henry Greene (578) early manifested a disposition to rove. The seas became his highway of travel for several years; visiting the East and West Indies, and the various seaports of Europe, California at length became, for several years, his home, where he married Miss Marian Buck, and in a few years visited his native State. He now resides in Providence, R. I.

NOTE 99.

Phebe Greene (579) was but five years old when her mother died, and soon went to live with her uncle, Dutee Greene, of Providence, an enter-

prising apothecary and merchant of that city. Phebe, though a double orphan, was a child peculiarly favored of fortune; in her uncle's family were no children, and she had all the educational advantages of the city, joined to the blessings of a genial, virtuous, Christian home. She married Stephen G. Henry, a worthy and enterprising man, who was for years the confidential clerk and fiscal agent of her Uncle Dutee, in managing his large estate, and enjoys the confidence and esteem of all who know him. He is now a member of the City Council, is in affluent circumstances, and renders his wealth a blessing to himself and others.

Note 100.

Andrew Jackson Greene (580) was but three years of age when deprived of a mother's care. The family were kept mainly together till the death of the father, some seven years afterwards, when Andrew went to live with a relative. Here he found a comfortable home, and at a proper age he was apprenticed to a trade. With merited success he learned the jewelry business, and, we judge by his subsequent course, that he read and believed that sensible remark of Dr. Franklin, "He that hath a trade hath an estate, but the trade must be worked at." He entered into the employment of " Sacket, Davis & Potter," in whose employ he had satisfactory success, for he has been there twelve or fourteen years. He has realized in his life, and family position, the reward of industry and prudence. He married, in about 1850, Miss Emma M. Chapman, a lady of cultivated mind and refined taste, a lady who, for several years, was Principal of one of the Intermediate schools in the city of Providence, and gives evidence that a transfer from the school-room to domestic life is by no means inconsistent with home enjoyment. Andrew J. Greene is, and has been for years, a prominent member of the Franklin Lyceum, and, by his energy and liberality, has contributed much to enlarge its library, and give it the rank which it now holds among the literary institutions of Providence. They are in affluent circumstances, and have two sons, of fine promise, whose names appear on page 30.

Note 101.

Ray Greene (581) was but an infant at the death of his mother. A few years residence at home, and he lived with a farmer, in Johnston, until he was twelve years old, or rather I should say, all the time except while making two coasting voyages; for at this early age the sea seemed to offer him many attractions. At twelve, he went a year or more to North Scituate Academy, and then commenced learning the trade of a currier, in the city of Providence. Ray, even at this age, had learned, there were some things which he liked, and some that he disliked. He disliked the currier's trade much, and his employer more, and on the whole, as he preferred pulling up whales to pulling up hides; as he preferred working oil out, to working it in, he

left the currying knife for the harpoon, and shipped for a two years whaling voyage, as an able seaman before the mast, though but fourteen years old, a big boy with the pluck of a man. This voyage completed, he had grown two years older, but with no more love for the currier's shop than when he left, and so he enlisted for three years on board the U. S. frigate Brandywine. This time he mostly passed on the Brazil station, and, at its close, with the character of an able seaman and a worthy young man, he started for California. A short stay at San Francisco, and he crossed the Pacific, doubled the Cape of Good Hope, and stood, when a little passed twenty, on the soil of his own native State. Here he spent two years or more, in which time he married Miss Sarah E. Aldrich (305)—Note 51. Since then he has been twice to South America, as mate of merchant vessels, and on one occasion, was cast away, about forty miles above Buenos Ayres, on the La Platte. For the last few years he has kept a livery stable, in the city of Providence. For other particulars, see Note 51.

NOTE 102.

Amasa Stone (547) was one of those men whom nature has endowed with peculiar powers; a mechanic possessing a genius, both imitative and inventive. There were but few difficulties that he could not overcome, and when he left his native State for Philadelphia, the mechanics and manufacturers felt that a power was withdrawn from their midst. His most useful invention, the one which has most advanced the interest of mankind, is the "Stone motion," as it was called, attached to power looms; and although it has been, we believe, succeeded by something more valuable, yet the first invention overcame the main difficulty, and enabled, as is often the case, a common mechanical mind to make the needed improvement. Having brought his invention into active use in his own land, he went to Europe and introduced it there. It attracted the attention of Baring Brothers, of London, and, by their influence and money they aided him in his object. An English mechanic, Wainwright, a man of large influence, at once saw the utility of his invention, and generously introduced him to several large manufacturers of his acquaintance. A Mr. Greer, an American gentleman of influence, also materially aided him. But English pride and prejudice is a strong barrier to American talent on English soil, and the young American inventor, while he was treated with courtesy, found it difficult to overcome the obstacles which continually rose up before him, and, after four years of effort and labor among the weavers in Europe, years in which he visited France, Scotland and Ireland, as well as England, years in which many flattering attentions were given, many beautiful presents made. among them from one of the nobility, was a pair of suspenders, with gold buckles and clasps; notwithstanding all this, he returned to his native land, his mind enlarged by travel and observation, but his pockets but little heavier than when he left. Here, too, he was destined to meet with another repulse,—he found that

some change had been introduced, and his patent infringed upon in his absence, and those very manufacturers which were growing rich through the action of his inventive mind, had united together to avoid the justice which his helps and mechanical inventions demanded. He resorted to the law for redress, and the case was finally decided against him in the Circuit Court. He retired from the law, satisfied that an army of well-discipled millionaires is a difficult host to conquer. In some few instances he reaped, from a few honest men, a small compensation for his great invention, but it was mainly lost; he afterwards invented machinery for weaving circular lamp wick, and he also invented, a kind of air-tight jars for preserving fruits. His labors and inventions always afforded him a competence but failed to give him the affluence which his genius and labors demanded. He married Miss Sarah T. Dana, the daughter of Capt. Colville Dana, who was lost at sea many years ago on his return from Europe to America. Miss Dana is a lady, virtuous and intelligent, and their home was one of love, virtue and peace. They have but one son, Walter W. Stone (547), a young man of fine promise. Amasa Stone (547) died in Philadelphia, March 26th, 1864.

Note 103.

Betsey Stone (588) married Henry King, of Cranston, in the village of Knightsville, where her husband built a large public house, and where they spent the closing portion of their lives. She died in 1858, the mother of eleven children. Her second daughter, Eliza King (599), married Sylvester C. Stone (61), she is mentioned in the biography of her husband, (Note 23.)

Note 204.

David Stone (590), eldest son of Edmunds Stone (330), married Betsey Potter, of Scituate, and soon after purchased a small farm, and built a snug house, in Foster, near the line of Scituate. Here he lived, managing his little farm, and working at his trade, a custom shoemaker, till 1827, when he sold out and moved to Sterling, Conn. In this State he lived twenty-seven years, and died as he lived, a worthy man and pious Christian, in 1854. His wife died five years before him. They had four children, noted correctly on page 85. Three are living : Jason Stone (617), who is married, is a machinist, and lives in Oneco, Conn., where his children are married and reside. Nathan Stone (618) is married, and lives in Coventry, Conn., he is an enterprising farmer, and has one daughter, who is married, and lives in the same town. Laura Stone (620), between whom and her youngest brother there is sixteen years difference, is still unmarried, she is a girl of fine abilities, of highly cultivated mind, and for several years a successful school teacher, in which employment she is now engaged.

Note 105.

Richard Stone (592) was born in Cranston, in sight of the spot where his ancestor Hugh (1) died and was buried; he lives in Washington Village, (Coventry), R. I., has been three times married, and sustains the character of a quiet, industrious man. he has had a large family, who have mostly died in early life. Edmand Stone (631), a son by his second marriage, contrary to the general character of the race, was quite a wanderer; he had been in most of the European ports, and was a marine in the British service during the Russian war. When men were wanted to sustain our own liberties, he enlisted in the land service, in the first Rhode Island Volunteers, was in the army of the Potomac, and was killed at the battle of Antietam. Amey Stone (593), see Seneca Stone (170).

Note 106.

Edmand Stone (594) married Julina Congdon, and lives in Putnam, Conn., where he owns a house and lot, and is employed as a stone mason ; he has three children, all married, and living near him ; he is an industrious and respected citizen. Robert ,Stone (596) married Sarah Taylor, and died at the early age of twenty-seven ; his remains lie on Sockonossett hill, by the side of his father and grandfather.

Note 107.

Joseph Ralph Stone (595) was born in Cranston, on Sockonossett hill, where his remains now rest by the side of his ancestors. His early opportunities for improvement were, like other farmer boys in Cranston, and he learned the trade of a blacksmith. In early life, however, he gave evidence of a clear head and a practical mind ; military affairs and political interests engrossed his attention, while a decided legal bearing, united to an easy expression, and social temperament, rendered his advice and society much sought. He was a Justice of the Peace for Providence Country, and Brigadier General of Rhode Island Militia, at the time of his decease, which occurred when he was 33 years of age. He married Miss Catharine Congdon, of Newport, a lady of intelligence and worth, by whom he had two children,—one died in infancy, the other, Christopher Congdon Stone (639), lived to the age of nineteen. He was a young man of good education and fine promise, when the consumption blasted his own and his friends' expectation, by an early death.

Note 108.

Samuel Stone (597), the youngest son of Edmand Stone (330), married Abbie Bennett, and is a farmer, residing in Scituate, near Swansicnt pond. His eldest son, Samuel (611), has been twice married.—See page 33. His second son, Albert Stone (642), enlisted in the army, and died at Portsmouth Grove. They all, as we learn, sustain a respectable position in life.

NOTE 109.

Zilpha P. Stone (356) married a man by the name of Cobb, and lived in Chenango County, N. Y. The father, and his only son, Henry C. Cobb (377), enlisted among the brave boys, and left their homes to defend their country against a rebel host. Sickness visited them both, the father died in the camp hospital, much lamented, and Henry C. died of an inflammation of the lungs, and was buried with military honors.

NOTE 110.

John Stone (4), the third son of Hugh Stone (1), was born in old Warwick, where he lived till the year 1712. He was a wheelright and chairmaker by trade, and built a house on his father's land, now called the Barlo Greene farm, near "Mark Rock." The lot of two acres was deeded by Hugh to his son John, Oct. 16th, 1706, and is described as the lot on which "John had built his house." The same year, Sept. 29th, 1706, Thomas Barnes, by will, bequeathed his son Thomas to his brother-in law, John Stone, until he was twenty years of age. Between 1812 and 1815, his first wife, —— Barnes, died, and he married Abigail Foster. The boy, Thomas Barnes, was taken from his care and placed under the guardianship of an uncle Barnes, in Warwick, where he probably remained when his uncle, John Stone, removed to "Mashantatack," where his two older brothers had already settled. John Stone (4) was an active and industrious man, possessing by gift and purchase, a large real estate, and was much respected by his acquaintances ; he was a man of genial temperament, mirthful and sportive, even to the close of life, and left a large family in good circumstances for those early times, from whom has descended a large posterity of much intelligence and moral worth. He had three sons by his first marriage, all of whom have many descendants ; and eight children by the last marriage, all settled in Rhode Island. He died about the year 1754.

NOTE 111.

John Stone (656) was born in Warwick, and removed with his father to Cranston, when seven years old ; we judge that he lived mostly from home, as his name is not mixed up with any trades, among father, brothers or uncles, as are most of the others. He was, however, a land and mill owner, and his name appears in several land conveyances up to the time of his death. He was accidentally shot while fowling in Providence river, near Pawtuxet. There were two in the boat, himself and another man ; the arrangement was that both lie flat in the boat; the partner was to fire first, and he immediately after, at the same flock of ducks ; so anxious was he to be " on time," that he raised his head just as his partner discharged his gun, and received the shot in his head. He married Hannah Olney, and left a family of nine children, two of whom have each a large offspring. Phebe

Stone (668e) married John Gorton, a descendant in the 5th generation from Samuel Gorton, the founder of the Colony of Warwick. She left no children. Olney Stone (668a) married Phebe Arnold, daughter of Simeon Arnold, of Warwick, April 25th, 1782, and went West, all knowledge of him and his descendants are lost.

NOTE 112.

Anne Stone (659) married William Colgrove, her descendants reside in Scituate. Abigail Stone (660).—Descendants, not known. Alice Stone (662) married Daniel Fisher,—descendants in Rhode Island. Benjamin Stone (663) married Mary Strait, the daughter of John Strait, of East Greenwich. He lived in Warwick, near the sheet of water now known as "Ben Stone's pond,"—they left no descendants. Lydia Stone (665) married Wilson Spencer. Prudence Stone (666) married Robert Vaughan,— no descendants known of either.

NOTE 113.

Oliver Stone (667) was born in Cranston, near Pawtuxet; he spent most of his life in Foster, he was a man of good habits, we believe, but was a farm laborer of very moderate circumstances. He married Phebe Brown, a worthy woman and a good mother. Caleb Stone (671) married Amey Thornton, and lived and died, we believe, in Cranston, near the well known " Fenner ledge." His two daughters are both dead.

NOTE 114.

Benoni Stone (673) was born in Glocester, and married Susannah McIntire, in 1798, they lived together almost fifty years, he dying at 80 and she at 66 ; they had five children, four of them married, and what is singular, there is not a grandchild in the family. Lewis Stone (684) resides at Blackstone, Mass. He was born at Limerock, and he resided at Lonsdale, Albion and Blackstone, where he owns a house, and has for some years lived ; he has met with some successes and discouragements, but still is in comfortable circumstances, a worthy man, and a good citizen. He is a dresser-tender, and has, for years, been connected with some departments of manufacturing. The brothers and sisters are living at Limerock, or at some of the manufacturing villages on the Blackstone, and are all esteemed and respectable. See page 36.

NOTE 115. •

William Stone (674) married Elizabeth Brown, and lived a portion of his life in Foster, near the Connecticut line ; William has ever maintained the character of an industrious man and worthy citizen. He has heeded the command " multiply and replenish the earth." Of eleven children, one

died aged fourteen, ten lived to mature age, most of them have families of children and grand-children, and are a worthy part of the bone and muscle of New England.

NOTE 116.

Waity Stone (695), the oldest daughter and oldest child of William Stone (671), is a woman of intelligence and virtue, and much beloved by a large circle of friends. She married Rev. Daniel Greene, a Baptist clergyman, of energy and ability. He is pastor of a church in the East part of Killingly, and West part of Foster, and his labors are attended with success.

NOTE 117.

Simon Stone (697) married Sally Smith, and resides in Southbridge, Mass. He is a farmer, as also are his sons; his son-in-law, Charles Biggs, is connected with an iron foundry; his sons-in-law, James Barlow and Otis Barlow, are wheelwrights ; another son-in-law, George L. Avery, is overseer of a weaving-shop, and all reside in Southbridge, and in that portion of Worcester County. The family of Simon Stone (697) is peculiar. We know of no family who deserves its country's gratitude like this. It is a large family, and it has largely contributed to the overthrow of treason, and the suppression of rebellion.

Charles E. Stone (712), enlisted, served a year, was wounded at Antietam, and discharged.

William J. Stone (715), served two years, and was mortally wounded at Cold Harbor. See extended notice below.

George N. Stone (714) served two years, and came home without a scratch.

Charles Biggs (706) enlisted, served two years, was sick of a chronic dysentery, and was discharged.

Henry C. Biggs (a), page 38, died of sickness in the army hospital.

James Barlow (709) enlisted for three months, and again for three years, was wounded at Antietam, in the hip, and was discharged.

Otis Barlow (711) served in the army two years, and came home safe.

George L. Avery (710) entered the army, and was shot through the foot, and discharged ; after it healed he enlisted *again*, and stayed two years.

Another son of Simon Stone enlisted, but was rejected by the surgeon.

William J. Stone (715) died at Armory Square Hospital, Washington, D. C., of a wound received at the battle of Cold Harbor. Extracts from a letter, and Obituary notice, by the regimental Chaplain, and another friend, will be read with interest.

OBITUARY.—Died, of wounds received in the shoulder, at the battle of Cold Harbor, June 24th, Corporal William J. Stone, aged 22 years. The following letter will be of interest to the many friends who mourn the loss of this brave soldier, and excellent young man :

17

WASHINGTON, D. C., June 19th, 1864.

DEAR BROTHER ABBOTT:—According to your request, I have searched for, and found, Mr. William J. Stone, Company C, 25th Mass. He is at the Armory Square Hospital, in the armory ward, 3d floor, bed 60. He is badly wounded, the ball entering at the shoulder, and passing through his back. I found him calmly trusting in Jesus He desired his wife to come to him as soon as possible. He has but little appetite; but such things as he can relish, or wants, are supplied him. May God bless this dear suffering Christian soldier and his anxious wife. Yours in much love,

O. P. PITCHER.

His wife spent the three last days of his life with him, and was consoled by the knowledge that he had all the care and attention furnished by the sanitary commission which he could have had at his home. The deceased entered the service in the autumn of 1861, as a volunteer for three years. Last January, he re-enlisted for a second three years (or during the war), and came home on a furlough of thirty days. We had a pleasant interview with him during that time, and shall long remember the grateful feelings which swelled our hearts as we gave him our hand at the parting. Our prayer to God was, that he might be returned to his many friends unscathed —their blessing and pride. But alas ! God, in his inscrutable Providence, has ordered otherwise. And *now* our prayer is. that they may have the strength to resignedly bear this sore bereavement, and be comforted with the thought that he died at the post of duty, serving his country and his God.

To Mrs. Lottie A. Stone (Roper), wife of George N. Stone (714), the writer is indebted for the statistics of this family, and the interesting facts connected therewith. —Statistics, see pages 37, 38 and 85.

NOTE 118.

William R. Stone (699) was one of the three sons of William Stone (674) who married into the Grayson family—three brothers, " Stones," married three sisters, " Graysons " He removed from Rhode Island to Thompson, Conn., where some of his family now reside, worthy, industrious, and respected. Abbie Ann Stone (700) married Silas Cole, and lives in Foster. They have but one child, a son.

NOTE 119.

James Stone (704) married Sarah Grayson, and lives in Foster, R. I. They have three sons, young men of intelligence and promise ; the eldest, Richard G. Stone (834) has an excellent education, and has been, for several years, teacher in his native town, with good success. James Stone (701) owns a valuable farm, and sustains the character of a worthy, industrious man.

Note 120.

John R. Stone (705) is the youngest son and youngest child of William Stone (674) and Elizabeth Brown, and married Susan Grayson, another of the three sisters, mentioned in Note 118. John R. has lived in Providence, where he was engaged in the wholesale meat business, and a few years since removed to his native town, Foster. There he now lives, partly engaged in farming and partly in cattle buying. He has four children, all daughters, three of whom are married, and living in the vicinity of the parental home. They are in fair circumstances; genial, and courteous, and enjoy the confidence and respect of the community in which they live.

Note 121.

George A. Stone (718) married Melissa C. Stone (930). He is in successful business as a butcher, in Spaingfield, Mass , and is an enterprising, business man. Samuel H. Stone (727) married Julia A. Stone (931), and resides Thompson, Conn., is partly engaged in farming, and partly in the manufacture of shoes; prosperity and industry are inmates of their home, and promises a hopeful future. William G. Stone (721) married Ellen M. Stone (932). They live in the north part of Thompson, near the line of Webster, Mass., and near Samuel H. (720). Here, too, is a quiet, industrious home ; the husband is a shoe manufacturer; the wife, a lover of domestic duties. Here Ellen's mother, now the widow of Pardon F. Stone (908), finds a retreat from life's dark cloud-blasts, as she is beginning to walk down into the lonely valley. There is a marked peculiarity in the three families mentioned in this Note. Three brothers, named " Stone," married three sisters, named " Stone." The husbands and wives are 4th and 5th cousins : thus—

		GENERATION.	
John Stone (4)	John Stone (4)	1	Common ancestor.
John Stone (656)	George Stone (657)	2	Brothers
Oliver Stone (667)	Ezra Stone (815)	3	1st cousins.
William Stone (674)	John Stone (821)	4	2d cousins.
William R. Stone (699)	John Stone (834)	5	3d cousins.
George A. Stone (718)	Pardon F. Stone (908)	6	4th cousins.
	Melissa C. Stone (930)	7	5th cousins.

Thus, George A. Stone (718), and Melissa C. Stone (930), are 4th and 5th cousins, the 6th generation on his side from John (4) their common ancestor, and the 7th on her's.

Note 122.

Elizabeth Randall (741), daughter of Phebe Stone (676), was born in Foster, and raised in the home of her old grandfather, Oliver Stone (667). Her mother was the youngest child of her grandfather, and consequently, in her girlhood days, he was a very aged man. Oliver Stone could remember

his father, John Stone (656), who was shot, (see Note 111), in Providence river about the year 1757, and he could also remember John Stone (4), who died about 1750. The little girl, Elizabeth, as she sat at her grandfather's feet, listened with thrilling interest to the history of those by-gone days, which had been treasured up in the tenacious memory of this aged man. Not only events, but dates and names, and family connexions, also made a part of this ancient record, and were duly transferred to the mind of the child, and there they have been securely kept with wonderful accuracy. The writer of this work has repeatedly tested her accuracy, by comparing, (unknown to her), names and dates with the written records of Warwick and Providence, and has never known her to fail in accuracy; nay more, in several important statistical and historical points she has enabled him to correct several errors which he had from others, on whose correct memory he had relied, and thus saved this work from some important mistakes. She married Ira Blackmar, and lives in Providence. She is the mother of nine children, two of whom died in childhood, seven are married, and live in Providence or its immediate vicinity, and are generally reputable and respected by those by whom they are known. The lady of whom this Biographical Note is written is entitled to the thanks of the writer, and also to the thanks of the extensive circle of relatives embraced in this work.

Note 123.

John Stone (668) was born in Cranston, and son of John Stone (656) and Hannah Olney. In his early days he was resolute, active and daring. Fishing in his boyhood around Pawtuxet falls, where his brothers, Caleb and Ezekiel, were drowned, guiding the light skiff over the waters of Narragansett Bay, gave a tone of fearlessness, in action and expression, which went with him through life. He engaged in the coasting trade, became master of a vessel, and ever after went by the appellation of "Captain John." He married Phebe Greene, of Warwick, and when a little past middle life, leaving the ocean and its dangers, his native State and its attractions, he bought a valuable farm in Killingly, Conn., and moved with his family to that town, where he spent the remainder of his days. Capt. John was a man of integrity and honor, warm and generous in the lower folds of his heart, though he retained to the last the rough, prompt tone and manner of the sea captain.

Note 224.

William Stone (755) was born in Cranston, where he resided till after his marriage with Abigail Randall, when he moved to Killingly, into the neighborhood of his father. Here he buried his wife, who died leaving him with three children, under seven years old. In 1805, he married Lydia Arnold, by whom he had five children; still residing in Killingly, where he spent the remainder of his days. For many years he kept a public house in East

Killingly, and enjoyed the confidence of a generous public. He was a prominent politician of those days,—was what was then called a Jefferson Democrat in opposition to the Federalism of the old school. He was, several times elected Sheriff of Windham County, and died Sept. 19th, 1863, at the age of 91 years. He was a worthy citizen, one of the best of fathers, and was to have been baptized the day of his death.

Stephen A. Stone (758), the youngest son of Capt. John (668) was born in Killingly, on what is generally known as the Captain Stone farm, between Killingly hill and the present town of Putnam, and spent his early days in that rural valley, bordering on the Quinebaug.. Being the youngest and petted son of old Capt. John, and born when he was 51 years of age, he received more than common school advantages, attending, from time to time, the instruction of Rev. Mr. Atkinson, Con. Clergyman of Killingly, who generally received under his instruction more or less young men, who were fitting for College, or business life. From this school he went as clerk and book-keeper for Smith Wilkinson, in the town of Pomfret. While here, he married Miss Prudence Morse, of Pomfret, Conn., who lived but two years after their marriage. During these years the father died, and the old farm came into his hands. Marrying Miss Lucia Johnston, daughter of Jotham Johnson, of Thompson, Conn., he went back upon the farm, and commenced farming. Here he remained a few years, when he sold out, and we find him at one time farming, in Thompson; at another a book-keeper, in Providence,—then an inn-keeper in Killingly, and again residing in Providence; always active, always honest, and industrious, but never quite satisfied with his present position; not a builder of air-castles, but somewhat inclined to examine and try those built by others. In 1847, his wife, Lucia, died of a consumption. She was a woman of great excellence, fervent piety, an affectionate mother, and true friend. Though quietly cheerful, she was constitutionally disposed to look at the shady side of life, and yet, its shadows were always tinted with the sunlight of a happy spirit-land. He subsequently married Miss Lydia Douglass. and died of a paralysis, Aug. 28, 1853.

NOTE 126.

Olney R. Stone (759), the oldest son of William Stone (755), removed soon after his marriage, to Marion County, Ohio, where he became wealthy, and died suddenly of the cholera, in 1850. He was living with a second wife at the time of his death, and was a worthy man, and faithful Christian. He was blind of one eye from his childhood, and is remembered with interest by those who knew him in his early days. He has left no posterity. Godfrey G. Stone (761) died of a sun-stroke, in 1825.

Note 127.

John Stone (760) married Mary Colwell, a lady of intelligence and energy, and lived in Providence, where he was engaged in the oyster business. In 1853 he was found fallen from his boat and drowned, in shallow water. He probably fell overboard in a fit. He was an active, worthy man, and much beloved and lamented ; his widow resides in Providence, most of her children are married,—some of them are in California. Sally Stone (763) is not married, and resides with her brothers, sister, and relatives, the welcomed inmate of all their homes.

William A. Stone (764) married Miss Charlotte Dutcher, and resides in Danielsonville, Conn. He is engaged in the staging business, which has been his occupation most of his life. William A. Stone is a worthy, industrious man, and much beloved by his acquaintances. Abbie E. Stone (766) is a worthy, intelligent woman, and an excellent mother. She married John W. Richards, of Ashford, Conn., who is now, and has been, engaged in staging. They have lived in Danielsonville and East Killingly, and have resided, for the last seven years, in Providence.

Note 128.

Elisha Stone (765), the youngest son of William Stone (755), received the early educational opportunities of Connecticut boys, aided by the advantages of Academies and High Schools. These opportunities he improved to good advantage, and has taught common schools and schools of higher grade, in New England, and was Principal of an Academy, in the State of Ohio. His health failing he went to Hayti, where he remained through the cool season, and, unlike many who have sought the West India isles, he returned with improved health. He married Miss Olivia P. Eastman, a lady of taste and refinement, while a resident of Lowell, Mass., and has since removed to Boston, where he now resides. He is connected in business in a music store, and has an appointment in the Custom House.

Note 129.

Phebe Ann Stone (806) was the oldest and only surviving child of Stephen A. Stone (758), by his first marriage. In disposition she was mild, genial, amiable, and yet not lacking in energy ; her home was a home of love and peace. She married Henry Dresser, who removed soon after their marriage to the West. Their home was first in Springfield, Ill., afterward they removed to Naples, on the Illinois River, where the wife died, in 1853, of an attack of the congestive chills. Her family statistics are on page 42.

Maria H. Stone (811), the youngest daughter of S. A. Stone (758), lived with her father in Thompson and Providence, up to the time of her marriage with William O. Darling, in 1847. She possessed much energy of character, and a strong love of virtue. Her husband lived but a few years after their

Pardon M. Stone

marriage, leaving Maria a widow and one child, Ida Olney Darling, born
———— ——, 1855. In 1856, she married Rev. John Howson, a clergyman
of the Methodist connexion, of much ability and good clerical standing. She
died in 1865.

NOTE 130.

Pardon Manchester Stone (807) was born on the "Captain Stone farm,"
in Killingly, Conn., and received the advantages of the Connecticut Free
Schools, only in the Winter terms, working in the cotton mills of the Quin-
nebaug Valley ever after his capacity permitted, until, when thirteen years
old, he attended one term at the Woodstock Academy. In the year 1836,
when eighteen years of age, he commenced learning the trade of a jeweller,
which he completed at the close of three years. At this time he began to
be impressed with the idea, that his ability and business talent would enable
him to manufacture, as well as make jewelry, and his subsequent career has
proved that he did not miscalculate. About a year of journeywork, and in
1842, he commenced the manufacture with a partner, under the firm of
" Stone & Weaver." This partnership was continued eighteen years, and was
a happy financial success. In 1860, it was dissolved, and another formed :
the firm of " P. M. Stone & Co.," in which he is now successfully engaged.
Few men have evinced a clearer view, a steadier aim, and a more untiring
perseverance in business pursuits, than P. M. Stone. And these qualities,
joined to an unflinching integrity, have given him the success and affluence
which he now enjoys. His prosperity has mostly been gained by the steady,
well-regulated manufacture of jewelry ; occasionally, he has dipped moder-
ately into the attractive speculations of the day ; but, saving a few thousands
realized from speculations in Providence real estate, he has lost more than
he has gained. Nor does the glitter of success bewilder, or the almighty
dollar eclipse, with him, life present or life future. He is not the man to
enquire, first and foremost, " *what will it cost?*" Not a man of one idea ! The
beauty and convenience of his spacious dwelling, situated on Broadway, that
beautifully broad and shady avenue, in the city of Providence ; his extensive
gardens and shrubbery, ornamentally and tastefully arranged in beautiful
borders, shady arbors and serpentine walks, skirted here and there with
climbing vines, and spanned by floral arches, evince the man of taste, and
speak to you of talent, generous and appreciative. Not only in his own
home, is his activity and love of the beautiful displayed, but is seen in all
public enterprizes for the improvement, convenience and advancement of
the City. In the support and advancement of religious truth he ever stands
prominent. Before he came to the city he made a profession of religion, in
the Methodist church, and, in 1850, united with, and took an active part in
carrying forward the interests, fiscal and religious, of the church of that
order, on Matthewson Street. Since that time, he has *there* paid more than
$5,000. Other objects, literary and religious, have largely received his aid. To

the Providence Conference Seminary, at East Greenwich, he has donated $1500; and Missions, foreign and domestic, have shared his attention and liberality. His activity and munificence has called out the expressed confidence of an appreciative public. The boy, who came empty handed to Providence, twenty-nine years ago, apprenticed to a jeweller, is now acting an important part in the various departments of human life. He has held the office of Treasurer of the State Temperance Society; is Treasurer and Trustee of the Providence Conference Seminary, located at East Greenwich; $140,000, much of it raised by his exertions, has passed to that institution through his hands; is Finance Committee of the Wesleyan Camp Grove, at Martha's Vineyard; is Director of the Bank of America: is Director of the Firemen's Insurance Company; is Director of the Union Horse Railroad Company; has been a member of the City Council for three years; is one of the representatives for the city of Providence in the Legislature of the State, and has been one of Governor Dyer's staff, with the rank of Colonel. P. M. Stone married, in 1847, Miss Mary F. Mason, of Fall River, daughter of Perez Mason, a lady of cultivation, refinement, and piety; one well calculated to make his beautiful home double attractive. Her health, not very firm, somewhat checks her native activity, but her aid and encouragement show her interested in every good work, and render her beloved by all who know her.

NOTE 131.

George Stone (657) was the second son of John Stone (4), and was, probably, born in old Warwick, before his father moved to Mashantatuck. He married Rest Clarke when about twenty-five years old, and commenced life for himself. It is believed that George Stone (657) lived in Scituate, as no home of his has been traced, in the neighborhood of his father, and tradition says that his son emigrated from Scituate; be that as it may, George (657) died with his son Ezra Stone (815), in the extreme north-west corner of the State of Rhode Island, "aged eighty-eight years and five months, wanting three days," as shown by the family record of Ezra, the son. The following is Ezra's record of the death of his mother: " The 19th of the 4 month 1793 mother Died, Aged 77 years "

NOTE 132.

Ezra Stone (815), the eldest son of George (Note 131), married Freelove Howland, a Quakeress of Rhode Island. There was a strong religious affinity between them, for either, he being a Quaker, was drawn by the power of sympathy to seek a Quaker wife, or, attracted by a sweet Quaker face, he was carried body and soul into the denomination; probably the latter, as this is the only pair of the name, so far as we can learn who were ever enrolled among the followers of George Fox. They were a worthy and God-fearing pair, and their descendants can look back upon these their ancestors

without a blush. He is still remembered by some of the most aged of his offspring. One, now himself advanced in life, informed the writer, that he believed his grandfather Ezra had a marked vein of silent mirth, beneath his sober exterior ; that he recollected the old man once gave him *two cents* to stand still *two minutes,*—and while he was going through the trial, by certain slight muscular movements ot the old man's face, he was sure that he enjoyed the fun more than the boy. Not many years after their marriage, he purchased a tract of wild land, about a mile square, bordering on "Alum Pond," and bounded North by Massachusetts, and West by Connecticut. To this distant country, nearly forty miles, they prepared to remove. " Distant country ! "—" forty miles!" Nay, smile not, gentle reader; miles were longer in those days than now. When the trees are to be felled, and the pathway cleared, a mile is a different affair from what it is on smooth, well-worked roads,—and a different affair still, from a mile on the railroad at almost lightning speed. Get on board the cars, if you will, settle yourself quietly down into your soft-cushioned seat; roll on and on and on, till, in less than three days, you stand on the banks of the Mississippi, and then sneer with ineffable contempt at the ignorance and narrow-mindedness of your ancestors. Forty miles ! yes, and twenty of that forty had to be cut out, that the team of Ezra Stone might go ouward, to their habitation in the wild woods of Burrillville. When they started, neighbors and relatives came to bid them farewell, and many were the invocations offered, and many the kind wishes expressed, and many the tears shed, as this family moved off to their forest home. Record of the family is ; The 29th of 6th month 1805 then Freelove the wife of Ezra Stone deceased, aged 68 years and four months. The above record was made by the husband. The record of the old man's death, was made by a hand of another faith, probably by his son, Ezra Stone (823), who was a Methodist preacher, and has not the Quaker style. The 20th of April 1816 Ezra Stone died aged eighty years and twenty days.

Note 133.

James Stone (820) lived in Gloucester, now Burrillville, and sustained the reputation of integrity, intelligence and moral virtue. He was an active officer, and for many years a Justice of the Peace. He has left no children.

John Stone (821) was a blacksmith, and lived in Thompson the greatest portion of his life. His wife, Hannah Eddy, was an excellent woman, and an affectionate mother.

Ezra Stone (823) married Lucina White, and lived near his father, in Burrillville. He was an able preacher, of the Methodist connexion. His life was an example of piety and faith, and many can trace their first religious impressions to the earnest, and persuasive eloquence of this worthy man and faithful Christian. Oziel Stone (825) married Nabbie Bowen, of Gloucester, and on the second day of February, 1859, left New England for Greenfield, New York.

18

George Stone (828) married Mollie Humes, and lived in what is now Burrillville, near " Alum Pond." His wife died in 1808, leaving him with five children. He afterwards married Polly McDonald, by whom he had five others,—(see page 49). George Stone was a man of intelligence and moral worth, a peace-maker among his neighbors, and a large portion of his days . was engaged in the transaction of town business. He was remarkably sedate, and, unlike his father, no vein of silent humour ever disturbed his quiet face. He died July 31st, 1826, aged 53 years and ten months.

NOTE 134.

Joseph Stone (831) was the oldest son of John Stone (821), and married Anne Foster, Dudley, Mass., a girl of mild temper, genial and kind, not deficient in intelligence, and said to be the most beautiful girl in Dudley. A few years subsequent to their marriage, they removed to Putnam, where he engaged as teamster, to an extensive trader, in that section of Connecticut. No railroads, no engines, in those days, rolled the heavy freight, the flour and molasses, and salt, and sugar, aye ! and rum, too, into the manufacturing villages, and the inland towns, and among the green but rocky hills of New England. Horses and oxen. and in those days mostly oxen was the power which moved the heavy luggage along our roads sixty years ago, and Joseph Stone (831) drove an ox-team, for one firm, from what is now Putnam to Providence, and back, averaging twice a week, for fourteen successive years ! and, for eleven years more, he had charge of the team, sometimes going to Boston, sametimes to other places, and occasionally stopping off a trip now and then. Thirty-one or two years he was in the employ of Smith, Wilkinson & Co., though six or seven of the last years he gave up teaming. His early opportunity for mental culture was almost entirely neglected, he had no knowledge of books and letters, and never seemed to regret or feel his want ; and yet he had an active mind, a retentive memory, and a correct judgment. In 1841, when he was about sixty years old, his daughters, Hannah (842), Polly (843), and Ann (849), all unmarried, purchased a small farm, near Daysville, Conn., and but a few miles from the cotton factories where they had long worked, for a home for their parents during the closing years of their lives Here this aged couple spent their last days, and here those three daughters weekly returned, to supply any needed want, and with filial love and affection encouraged their parents in their descent into the lonely valley. What a pity those girls did not find suitable mates ! The world needs the perpetuity of such stock ! The character of Joseph Stone was social, very sportive, with a keen perception of the ridiculous, leading him almost continually to intersperse his conversation with jokes and witticisms, and which would not always bear the test of refinement. He died when 72 years of age. His wife survived him but two years.

NOTE 135.

George Stone (844) possessed something of the sportive humor of Joseph (831), with less of that especial disposition to tease which characterized his father through his whole life. He would be called a roguish boy, but always sympathizing, generous and kind. He was, hence, a favorite among his associates, and his presence a sun-light at every excursion or social gathering. This generous, social nature almost became his ruin. Oh! how many noble, generous, kind-hearted young men, have fallen under the sad influence of the social glass, thought, in those days, indispensable, in the expressions of hospitality in every home. George felt its blighting effects before he was sixteen, and his friends trembled in view of the dark future which seemed to gather around that generous young man. On one occasion, during that early period of his life, returning home from some amusement or social gathering, he seemed in a delirium almost bordering on insanity; his sister Polly watched, as only a sister can, in anxiety and sorrow by his bed-side, through the night. In the morning, returning reason delineated on his own mind his present degradation and future ruin, and taking down the fur-cap which he wore the night previous, and addressing it as himself, he commenced a course of reproofs, instruction, condemnation, encouragement, and advice, clothed in language at once so sensible, so sympathtic, and yet so satirical, wild and sarcastic, that it called forth admiration and laughter, mingled with tears. He was evidently a young man of genius, and when nineteen, assisted by Divine aid, he turned from his former course. It was a radical change; a new world, with new objects, new duties, new enjoyments, new responsibilities, and new hopes, opened before him. He attended the district school that winter, and went the next year to Wilbraham Academy. The year following he commenced preaching in the Methodist connexion. He was a member of the New England Conference, at twenty-two, and remained so till the time of his death. He was a preacher of marked ability. The writer has often heard him spoken of by those who sat under his ministry, as an effective preacher, and one of the best of men. He died at his post in Mansfield, Mass., the first day of January, 1839. He was sick of a lung fever but a week. Late in the evening, of December 31st., he inquired what time it was, and being told it was " watch-night," he exclaimed—" glory to God, it is a good time to die ;"—he expired about fifteen minutes into the New Year. In 1829, he married Olive Cundall, a woman of strong domestic affections, virtue and piety. They had five children; the last, born two months after the decease of the father, was, in childhood, called to join him in the Spirit land; the other four are all living, and married. Joseph W. Stone (850) is a harness-maker, resides in North Woodstock, Conn., and is manager in charge, and has been for ten years, in the same shop, and for the same man of whom he learned his trade.

Note 136.

William J. Stone (*51). second son of George Stone (844), has no recollection of learning to read, or the rudiments of arithmetic. At ten he commenced work in a cotton mill, and from that time till he was nineteen, did
not average two months school advantage per year. By close attention to
business during the day, he could get released at dark in winter, and earlier
in summer. These odd hours, by dark and by light, were all saved ; saved
not for play, not for the loafer's shop, but for study and work ! For seven
or eight years, in the same village, he pursued the same course, during the
hours saved by extra industry. These he employed in cutting wood for the
family, studying mathematics, grammar, geography, philosophy and astron-
omy. In this way he studied, and from such a seminary he graduated ; graduated, as Nathaniel P. Banks recently stated in Congress that he graduated,
from a seminary, a part of which was a water-wheel and a loom. The day
he was twenty he left the cotton-mill ; sat down and renewed his studies
twenty days, and then commenced teaching a district school in the adjoining
town of Killingly. His teaching, on the whole, was a success, and the Spring
following he went to New Jersey, and taught the school at Pleasant Plains,
Morris County, one year and a half, when he returned to New England, and
studied one term at the Academy at East Greenwich, R. I., Again he set
his face for Pleasant Plains, and again he was welcomed by those among
whom, and for whose good he had labored. He remained with them, as
teacher, some two years, and then removed to Lexington, Green County,
N. Y., and engaged in the dry goods and grocery business, (no liquors).
Here he remained a year ; the business was successful, but a drawing to his
New England home, and the distant prospect of a financial crisis, induced
him to sell out and return to Killingly, which he did in the Spring of 1857.
No business immediately offering, he engaged to teach the same school in
Killingly, (compensation just doubled), which he had taught six years before. He was soon employed in Putnam, by J. W. Manning, as clerk and
book-keeper. Mr. Manning is not only a very extensive trader, but is Town
Clerk, Treasurer, and Registrar, and much of the recording of deeds, of the
reception and disbursement of town funds, and the general transaction of
the whole business passes through William J. Stone's hand ; added to this
he has been acting as Cashier of the Savings Bank, located in the same
building, for the last three years. Another labor, voluntary and without
pay, he has assumed, at the urgent request of the Volunteers and their
families, the agent to apply for, when needed, and receive the remittances
from government to the soldiers' families. In this continuous and responsible round of duties, more or less arduous, he has been engaged for nine
years, with the full confidence of his employer, and an appreciative public.
Young men, relatives more or less distant, of William J. Stone (851), read
this biographical Note. Consider his industry, and his manliness in early life.
His education was almost all gained in those sunset hours, and evenings, at home,

without a teacher,—hours which most lads throw away. Consider his energy, his generosity, his faithfulness, his punctuality, his goodness! "Go thou and do likewise." He married Miss Frances P. Sharpe, of Killingly, Conn., in 1856, a young lady of intelligence and moral worth, whose warm affection, and genial smile, lights up their home with radiant sun-wreaths, and cheers her husband along life's journey.

NOTE 137.

Ruth Stone (833) is a woman of intelligence, one who observes and profits by the affairs of life which are continually passing before her. Not born to affluence, but to the better inheritance, to earn her bread by the labor of her own hands; and, faithfully in her sphere of life has she fulfilled her duty. She married Ransom Upham, a worthy industrious man, and in the County of Windham they have reared a healthy, industrious family. Emeline Upham (867) married P. Copeland, and lives in Putnam. Angeline Upham (900) married William Arnold; she lived but a few years, and passed away to the "better land." The husband, with two children, left in widowed loneliness, married a sister of Angeline, Elmira M. Upham (901). They live in the Quinebaug valley at Fisherville, a few miles above Putnam, worthy, industrious and virtuous.

NOTE 138.

John Stone (835) married Esther Curtiss, and lived mostly in Thompson, Conn., where he reared a large family of children. Of their particular history we are not informed, except that they generally sustain the character of worthy men and women, and good citizens. Pardon F. Stone (908) died a few years since, in or near Webster, Mass., his widow and daughters live in the same neighborhood. Rebecca B. Stone (909) married Wilson Cutler, and lives in Webster, Mass., they have but two children living. Mary Stone (911) married Capt. Caleb Brown, who was, we believe, for a time in the war. Sarah E. Stone (912) married Horace Gay, who is a carpenter by trade, a worthy man, and a professing Christian. Hannah E. Stone (913) married Eddy Pray, and lives near Chestnut Hill, now called East Killingly.

NOTE 139.

Marvin Stone (904) married Zilpha Dunham, lives in Webster, and is a blacksmith by trade. Charles E. Stone (905) is a farmer, and in good circumstances, and reside, we believe, in Charlton, Mass. Of the residence of Otis E. Stone (906), we are not informed, but his son, James Stone (922), is a dresser-tender, and lives in Willimantic, Conn. This worthy young man was a Sergeant in the army during the war; he enlisted first for three years, and afterwards as a veteran. He came home unhurt, a faithful soldier and loyal citizen.

Note 240.

Hannah Stone (960) was the daughter of Ezra Stone (823), the Methodist preacher, and was born and lived with her father in Burrillville, then Gloucester, until she married, about 1820. Her husband was Richard Thayer, by whom she had four children; the youngest son, Richard (976) is blind; Nathan Stone (963) married Ada Phillips, and was drowned when crossing Alum pond on the ice, near his father's. He was a worthy man, much esteemed for his virtue and sobriety, and his untimely death cast a sadness not only over their household, but over the town in which he lived.

Note 141.

Olive Stone (964) married Amasa Esten, a respectable man and worthy citizen. His wife, Olive, died in 1830, leaving three children, and, some years afterwards he married her sister Lois Stone (966); by both marriages he has had ten children, a worthy, industrious family. William Stone (967) was a preacher in the Methodist connexion, and a man of talent and standing. Thus, Ezra (823), the father, and William (967), the son, were both preachers of the gospel in the same connexion, son and grandson to Ezra (815), the Quaker.

Note 142.

Ezra Stone (977) was the eldest son of Nathan Stone (963), who was drowned in Alum pond, and lived, we believe, with the grandfather after the death of the mother, which occurred but a few years subsequent to the decease of the father. The following account is given by the relatives and witnesses to the facts: When seventeen years of age, Ezra (977) was sick with a fever, and, rapidly sinking away, to all appearance died. The friends assembling to prepare the corpse for burial discerned a slight breathing ; some doubted, some were confident; all preparations, however, were deferred until next day. Next day came, there was no perceptible pulsation, the livid hue of death was there, the death-glare was on the eye, the limbs were relaxed, but not rigid,—still, some by close observation, could detect the same slight respiration as before, and thus matters passed on, some insisting that he was dead, while others were sure he was living. So things remained until he had lain in this trance-like state nine full days, when he aroused like one from sleep, spoke, was free from pain, and soon recovered. While he lay in that condition several tests of life were applied, such as pricking, pinching, &c., without eliciting the least sense of feeling. Soon after he aroused, he sent for his uncle William, who was a Methodist preacher, and held a long conversation, in which he stated that he had been in heaven, had met his father and mother, that they were very happy, and that heaven was a delightful place. In subsequent life we learn he was unwilling to speak of the matter. As a physical fact, it did then, and does still, awaken

inquiry and wonder; as a matter of spiritual or mental phenomena, it is still farther beyond our comprehension. That it was all *free* from pretence or collusion, no one knowing the parties can entertain the shadow of a doubt, but that it proves any point, or brushes away any cloud which hangs over the awful future, no sensible man will affirm.

> "God has locked up the mystic page,
> And curtained darkness round the stage." [See App. No. 2.]

NOTE 143.

Elisha Esten (986) stepped out into life with but little love of the spade or plow, and might, by those who regard digging, and plowing, and chopping, as the only action proper to be called work, have been considered a lazy boy. But nature formed some men for mechanics, as Arkwright, and Fulton, and Ericsson, and some for bankers and financiers, as Baring & Rothschild, and some for physicians and surgeons, as Harvey and Rush, and happy is the man who can find his *proper place* in life. Elisha Esten thought his was in the medical box, and bent all his energies, contrary to the advice of his friends, to get into that position, and he has admirably succeeded. He has received a diploma from the Medical Faculty at Philadelphia, and is now in successful practice in that city, after having been, for some time, surgeon in the army of the Potomac. He married Miss Hannah Wilson, a lady of great energy of character, of fine social powers, cultivated intelligence, and well calculated, by her love of domestic life, to make the home over which she presides attractive and lovely; and now, when Dr. Esten returns to make his yearly visit to the place of his nativity, not one of the old neighbors can recollect that Elisha ever was a lazy boy! no, he always was a fine fellow.

NOTE 144.

Amos Stone (993), the son of George (828) and Mollie Humes, was born in Burrillville, when his father owned a part of the large tract, a mile square, bought by Ezra Stone (815). He received a good education, and became a teacher. He was a man of more than ordinary capacity, and was appointed a Justice of the Peace, and possessed facility of doing almost anything which he undertook, and doing it well. His talent, however, was decidedly mechanical, and to mechanical pursuits he has devoted himself, not for want of capacity to succeed in other pursuits, but because the exercise of his remarkable skill gave him the most pleasure. He is a ready worker of iron and steel, but especially has he given his attention to gun-making. He married Miss Julia Angell; they live in Burrillville, in or near Pascoag. Chloe Stone (995) received an education superior to the girls of her age, and early gave evidence of a mind intellectually superior to the ordinary. Genial, social, and much beloved, she taught school several years, until leaving the school-room for household duties, she became the wife of Dr.

Erastus Robinson, of Northbridge, Mass., a man of extended reputation, and large medical practice. Chloe (995) is now a widow; her husband died respected and lamented, and she, esteemed and beloved by all who know her, with an unwavering trust in God, is beginning to descend the shady side of that mountain which connects with the lonely valley.

Azuba Stone (996) married Brown Angell, who lives on Alum Pond Hill, the North part of Burrillville; they are a worthy pair, and have a large family of nine children, who are all worthy, intelligent citizens.

Cynthia Stone (1001) is a lady intelligent and virtuous. Her husband, Stephen Emerson, is a manufacturer, esteemed, religious, active; with a pious faith in God, they realize, in some degree, that their union is for time and eternity.

Arnold Stone (1002), the youngest son and youngest child of George Stone (828), married Miss Philinda Aldrich, and, allured by the rich, cheap and fertile lands of Minnesota, set his face for the "Far West," where, in affluence and prosperity, the prosperity incident to new countries, (for there are always some debits as well as credits to be entered to the account), he is living and enjoying life with his numerous family.

NOTE 145.

Asahel Stone (997) was born in Burrillville, where he spent most of his early life. His genial mirthfulness, and lively appreciation of whatever is amusing, gathered around him a large circle of genial spirits, and made him many friends. Nor was he unmindful of the fact that life is a great reality, and such has been his course in training his family of eleven children, nine living, that they all honor their parentage and their country. He married Miss Sarah Battey, a worthy, lovely woman, and an excellent mother, who died in 1852. She is the mother of all his children. Since her death he married Mrs. Esther Pierce, a woman intelligent, courteous, and social. They live near Harmony Village, in Gloucester, and are now engaged in farming, successfully and prosperously. Some portions of Asahel's life has been spent in trading, in Burrillville, where, for a number of years, he was successfully engaged in merchandize. He is now on the topmost point of life's acclivity, begins to look over to the descent, where the shadows are beginning to lengthen, but the same sportive temperament, the same appreciation of wit, still marks his almost every word, and every look; he can stand still more easily than when his Quaker grandfather gave him "two cents to stand still two minutes," but we think he appreciates the joke now, when the man of sixty, better than he did then when the boy of six.

NOTE 146.

Almira Stone (1019), oldest daughter of Asahel (997), is a woman of good mind, genial and domestic in the relations of life, and a worthy mother.

She married Henry Timothy, a man of clear head, and cultivated mind. His reading has been somewhat extensive, and his memory enables him to treasure up the reasonings, the facts, and the descriptive relations of other minds with which to gather material to enrich his own. He is what is termed, in manufacturing parlance, a "boss weaver," and commands the most responsible positions in the largest mills. They live at the Arctic. Emeline Stone (1020), second daughter of Asahel (997), is a woman amiable, intelligent and virtuous, and her conversation is marked for clearness and perspicuity. The writer is indebted to her for much clear and intelligent information, of that branch of our family with which she is especially connected. She married Edmund W. Hawkins, a man of much mechanical skill and moral worth. He is a "pattern maker," a grade of mechanics demanding the highest imitative mechanical skill. They are industrious, economical, prudent, enjoying life's comforts while they have the prospect of an abundant competence when they shall step down into the vale of old age. They reside in Providence.

George Stone (1021) is an industrious mechanic, one of that class of men who are the bone and muscle of American prosperity; the men who not only *can* do the mechanical labor, but men who *do* do it; men who not only *can* put a shoulder to the wheel, but men whose *shoulder is there* every day. Such a man is George Stone (1021). He married Mary F. Mott, a woman of neatness and good taste, one whose genial smile and cordial welcome makes for her husband a happy home. They live in Providence.

Stephen Stone (1023) is a good mechanic, and an excellent man; what is said of the character of the elder brother George may, with equal propriety, be said of him. He married Miss Carrie Carpenter, a woman of social and domestic virtue, and with her husband not only looks to life's journey, but to a union continued in the spirit world. They reside in Providence, and are both members of the Baptist church, at Olneyville.

Of the five of this family, not already mentioned, found on page 50, the two girls, Fanny (1024), and Emily (1025) are both worthy members of the Methodist church; and the three boys, Clovis (1026), Albert (1028), and Charles (1029), are young men of fine promise, and bid fair to follow the good examples of their older brothers.

NOTE 147.

William Stone (658) was born in old Warwick, the year before his father moved to Mashantatack. In this neighborhood he spent most of his life, his sons and daughter reaching maturity, and settling as heads of families in the same neighborhood. It is very probable that John Stone (4) died with this son, as he, William (658), owned and lived upon the farm which Hugh Stone (1) bought of Susan Lawrence, and which, at Hugh's death, passed into the possession of John (4). On this farm William (658), lived till the year 1779,

'when he sold the farm to Dr. William Aldrich, and with his son, Jabez Stone (1050), moved to Coventry, where, seven years afterwards, he died, aged 74. His remains now rest in a wall-enclosed cemetery, in the South part of Scituate, on the farm where his son Jeremiah Stone (1051), lived and died. Capt. William Stone, as he was usually called, was a man of talent and integrity, and, in his day, was highly respected, filling many important military and civil offices. He married Miss Eleanor Westcott, who died before he removed to Coventry. The following is copied from the family record, now in the hands of a great grandchild : " Died, in Coventry, on Tuesday, February the 21st, Capt. William Stone, in the 74th year of his age, after a long and tedious illness which he underwent with great patience and fortitude of mind. A kind husband, a tender parent, and a respectable neighbor,—one whose company is much lamented by all.

NOTE 148.

William Stone (1048) married Lydia Westcott, removed from Cranston to Coventry, some time about the year 1770, and spent the rest of his life on a farm near Coventry Centre. On this farm was a corn mill, which, during his life, and years after, was the principal manufactory of corn or Indian meal, for a large circle of surrounding farmers and mechanics. The estate has recently been purchased by Pardon S. Peckham, an enterprising manufacturer, and the prospect now is, that a large manufactory will occupy nearly the site of the " Old Mill," and a village of mechanics and artisans take the place of the four or five houses, which, for the last hundred years, has overlooked that valley. William Stone (1048) was a man of correct business habits, and his education above the ordinary young men of his day. He was a Justice of the Peace before leaving the town of Cranston, and the strictly moral principle and correct judgment by which he acted, gave him influence in all the relations which he sustained. Soon after he removed to Coventry, he was elected Town Clerk, which office he held for many years ; held until his age and infirmities led him to resign, and retire from those public duties which he had so long and so satisfactorily performed He died about the year 1819. He was an active Christian, of the Baptist denomination, and among the first to establish the church in his neighborhood.

NOTE 149.

William Stone (1053) was born in Cranston, and removed to Coventry with his father, when a lad 12 or 14 years old. In this portion of Rhode Island, educational advantages then were far less than now, and his opportunities for improvement were, consequently, very limited. They were all, however, well improved, and in point of literary attainment, he entered upon life somewhat in advance of the young men of his age. He was for some months in the army of the Revolution, in battle on Rhode Island, under Sul-

livan, and finally settled in life on a farm near his father, where he lived and died. On this farm, a portion of which he purchased of his brother West-cott, was a saw-mill, which engaged him somewhat extensively in the lumber trade during the years of his middle life; but he was not the man to venture upon rash speculations, always in comfortable circumstances, never oppressed with debt; cautious, always sounding a stream before he attempted to cross it, he pursued life through, in the "even tenor of its way," and died when eighty-two, beloved and respected. He married Miss Lucy Scott, daughter of Joseph Scott, of Coventry, a worthy woman, and an affectionate mother. William Stone (1053) was, many years, President of the Town Council of Coventry, repeatedly held the office of Justice of the Peace, and several times represented the Town in the General Assembly of the State. For nearly forty of the closing years of his life he was deacon of the Baptist church, at Coventry Centre, and as there had been *three* William Stones, father, son, and grandson, for eighty-two successive years, with two short intervals, he was called, for distinction's sake, " Billy," and hence, known far and near through all that region, as " Deacon Billy."

NOTE 150.

Welcome Stone (1059) married Susan Hudson, and many years since removed with his family to Luzerne County, Pennsylvania. He was an industrious and worthy man, was mostly engaged in custom-shoe manufac-turing while in New England, but, we believe, devoted himself to agricultural pursuits in his western home. Nancy W. Stone (1065) married Charles Bailey, and resides near " Bailey Hollow" Post-Office, Pa.. They have a large family, highly esteemed, and among the most affluent and worthy of the section where they live.—Statistics, page 53. Ira B. Stone (1067) mar-ried Content Ryan, is a man of respectability, and lives in the same section of the State. Ethan A. Stone (1068), also, bears a good character, and lives in Pennsylvania.

NOTE 151.

Eliza Stone (1066) married James Williams, of Worcester County, Mass. Eliza returned from Pennsylvania in her youthful years, and lived with her grandfather, deacon Williams (1053). She is a worthy, intelligent woman, and lives in Pawtucket, R. I. Calvin Gay Williams (1069) is a machinist of high rank, has had the oversight of the extensive repair shop of the Long Island Railroad, and now occupies a similar post on one of the principal Railroads in New Jersey. Mary E. Williams (1070) married Henry L. Dean, and died within a few years, leaving one child. Lucetta Williams (1071) is a young lady of marked ability and superior attainment; she is a graduate of the Bridgewater Normal School. The husband of Eliza (1066) is an in-telligent mechanic, and by his industry and economy, united to correspond-

ing qualities in an excellent wife, has rendered life a success, and they both have the consciousness, that when they pass away, they will leave the world better for having lived in it.

NOTE 152.

Artemas Stone (1060), the second son of William (1053), has lived, during his married life, on a portion of the farm owned by his father, including the saw-mill, mentioned in (Note 149). He has been engaged mostly in farming and fruit-growing, connected, more or less, with the lumber manufacture and trade. He is a social, genial hearted worthy man, taking the world easy, and feeling far less than many around him, the ripples, and eddies, and rough currents of life, as he floats down the stream of time. He married Miss Mahala Henry, a woman of much energy of character, and highly esteemed. They have seven children, two died in childhood, five are still living. Sallie Stone (1093) married Edwin Manchester.—(See Note 156). Ruth Stone (1094) married Charles Hawkins, an active, enterprising man ; they reside in Mansfield, Conn. Few ladies fill their position in life better than the daughters of Artemas Stone (1060), as wives, as mothers, as daughters, intelligent, cultivated, refined ; while their husbands, respected for integrity and enterprise, are making life, in its pecuniary relations, a success.

NOTE 153.

Dexter G. Stone (1089) married Miss Elizabeth Lillibridge, has lived in the State of Rhode Island, most of the time a trader or an inn-keeper. He now lives in Pawtucket. His oldest son, Dexter S. Stone (1097), is a graduate in the Commercial Course of Brown University, and is a young man of much energy of character and fine promise. His youngest son, John T. Stone, is cashier, we believe, in one of the manufacturing establishments of the city, a young man of confidence and trust, and esteemed by his employers. Leonard R. Stone (1091), the third son of Artemas (1060), unlike most of the name, is a rambler. Leaving home in early life, he has been in the Florida war, and in most of the Southern and Western States. He is now, as is supposed, somewhere in the South.

NOTE 154.

Benoni Stone (1061) was born in Rhode Island, and went, previous to his marriage, to Scott County, Penn., where he married Aurilla Blanchard, and settled in life. He was marked as a young man of easy address, of strong social proclivities, and ready intelligence. He has been, we believe, mostly engaged in agricultural pursuits. He still lives in Scott County, and is respected, for intelligence and integrity. He has a large family, numbering ninety-seven. Found on pages 54, 55, 56 and 57, of this work.

Note 155.

Lucy Stone (1062) married Earl Manchester, and removed, during their early married life, to Abington, Penn. The husband was a chair manufacturer, and had machinery for wool-carding and cloth-dressing. He sustained the character of a virtuous man, and an industrious worthy citizen. He was, for many years, deacon of the Baptist church. He died in 1850 or 51. His widow is still living. Samuel G. Manchester (1185) was born in Coventry, R. I., and commenced life as a mechanic, and worked in a shovel manufactory, in the vicinity of his present home. Some twenty years since he purchased a farm, and is now successfully engaged in the cultivation of the soil. He is a man of activity and intelligence, and is respected by all who know him. He married Miss F. P. Reynolds, a woman virtuous and domestic, and their home is a home of peace and love. The writer is indebted to much of the statistical information of the " Stone family" in Scott and Luzerne Counties, Pa., to the information furnished by Mr. S. G. Manchester. Amey S. Manchester (1187) was born in Abington, Pa., and married A. A. Nichols, a respectable farmer, of her own town. Almira Manchester (1180) married Myron Dean, of West Abington, a man of active business talent and enterprize. He is successfully and extensively engaged in farming, has flour-mills, and besides, a large store of dry goods and groceries, (no liquors). Mr. Dean has many irons in the fire, but we believe none of them burn. William E. Manchester (1190), the youngest son and youngest child of Deacon Earl Manchester, was born in Abington, and there he has spent most of his life. He married Miss Mary Hazzard, and is successfully engaged in farming, highly respected and esteemed as a virtuous man, and a faithful Christian. He has recently been elected deacon, the mantle of the departed father resting down upon the son.

Note 156.

Henry W. Manchester (1186), and Edwin H. Manchester (1188), sons of Earl Manchester and Lucy Stone, both reside in Providence, R. I., and have been associated in business for twenty years or more. They are, and have been, steadily and perseveringly engaged in the daguerreotype, ambrotype, and other forms of human immortalization. Their judgment and artistic skill has given them a widely-extended reputation, and placed their photographs, especially, among the very best artists in America. Henry W. (1186) married Miss Sarah Hodges, a lady of cultivation and refinement ; they reside in Elmwood, a beautiful and healthy suburb of the city. Edwin H. (1188) for his 2d wife married Miss Sallie Stone, they reside in the city. (See Note 152.) His first wife was Miss Sarah Potter.

Note 157.

William Stone (1064), youngest son and youngest child of Dea. William (1053) and Lucy Scott, was born, and has ever lived, in Coventry. He is

the 4th William Stone, in direct descent, father and son, and, consequently, the 4th generation from Capt. William, who moved, in his old age, from Mashantatack to Coventry, and the 6th generation from Hugh (1). Like most Coventry boys of that age, he commenced with no superior educational advantages, married Candace Henry, a worthy, industrious woman, and commenced his married life on the farm where he was born and bred. Here he remained until the death of his parents, when circumstances favoring he sold out, and purchased a valuable estate in Washington Village, a few miles below the old homestead, where he now lives. The life of this worthy couple has been useful, and, on the whole, happy, and but for one sad and long-continued affliction, would have been unusually so. Lucinda Stone (1191), their oldest child, lovely, amiable, virtuous, intelligent, was attacked by a disease of the brain; every effort was made, medical skill was exhausted, but the disease settled down into a hopeless insanity, of the most interminable and most uncontrollable type. More than twenty years have passed away, years of confinement, watching and anxious care, and their dear suffering child seems no nearer relief in any form. Patiently they watch, and hopelessly they wait. May this trial, severe and protracted, be especially blessed in drawing them nearer to the Divine Hand, which governs and directs, a universe in wisdom and love.

Two sisters, Celia R. Stone (1193) and Susan R. Stone (1195) remaining at home, to care for, and watch over their afflicted sister, exhibit a love and devotion which may truly be termed heroic, while they encourage and comfort their parents, now aged and infirm. Too much respect cannot be awarded to such sisterly and filial devotion. William Stone (1064) has repeatedly received evidences of respect from his acquaintances and fellow-townsmen. Among other offices, civil and military, he has been a member of the Town Council of Coventry, and a Lieut. Colonel in the Rhode Island Militia. He is in easy circumstances.

Note 158.

Harris H. Stone (1192), son of William (1064), is a man of active brain, a quiet tongue, and a noble heart. For several years he was a successful teacher, and was then employed as agent and confidential clerk, by an extensive cotton manufacturer, in Clayville; and when, in early life, his employed died, Harris was made his executor and constituted trustee of the whole interest, and guardian to his young family. A stronger testimonial of confidence, both in the integrity and ability of any man, was never given. He marries Miss Abbie Ann Parker, daughter of Joseph Parker, of Coventry, R. I., a lady, intelligent, cultivated, very social, and every way worthy the position she occupies. They reside in Clayville, R. I. William A. Stone (1196), and brother of the above, is a young man of ability, activity and enterprise, social, genial, making many acquaintances and many friends. He has been engaged in merchandizing, and has a general tact for general trade.

He married Miss Sarah Whipple, daughter of Gov. Thomas Whipple, of Coventry, a lady, amiable, refined, and lovely; domestic in her tastes and habits, a wife, mother, friend, to be remembered and loved. She died in 1865, of a consumption, trusting in Him whose grace had moulded her life, and removed the sting of death. Amarilla A. Stone (1194) married Edwin W. Potter, and resides at the little village called Black-Rock, in Coventry; her husband is a manufacturer of machinery, and carries on an extensive business. They have two children, and a home rendered pleasant by health, intelligence, refinement, virtue and social love.

Note 159.

Westcott Stone (1054) was born in Cranston, and removed with the family when they moved to Coventry. In earlier life he gave evidence of a more restless and adventurous spirit than his brothers, his conversation and reading evinced more disposition to step out of the lineal traces of his ancestors, and when quite a young man, although having no classical education, he commenced the study of medicine, and made considerable proficiency under the instruction of Dr. S. Stearns. While he remained in Rhode Island he was an active man,—farming, practicing medicine, engaged in the lumber trade, and a deputy sheriff, all at the same time. In middle life he sold out his property to his brother William (1053) and removed to Abington, Penn. There he passed the remaining portion of his life, mostly, as we believe, engaged in agriculture, and in the practice of medicine. He married Miss Abbie Smith, of Rhode Island, by whom he had two children, whose statistical record is found on pages 58 and 59.

Note 160.

Arthur Stone (1057) was born in Coventry, R. I., and was a young man of fine mind, and, for those days, highly cultivated. His health was feeble, disease fastened upon him with unyielding grasp, but the best medical skill, and the aid of two seasons spent at Saratoga Springs, was all of no avail; he died when twenty-five years of age.

Lydia Stone (1055) married Asa Knight, who moved, in middle life, to Abington, Pa. She has left a family, esteemed and respected.—[Statistics, page 59].

Ruth Stone (1056), late in life, married Daniel Bennett, of Coventry. She has left no descendants, and died November 22d, 1852.

Note 161.

Asa Stone (1058) was the youngest son and youngest child of William Stone (1058), and was born in Coventry, where he lived until he was 86 years old. His opportunities for early education were very limited, but of them he made the most, and upon all subjects to which business called, or

duty directed, he rarely made a step in the dark; and hence, although he was never a scholar, or a close student, he never, during his long life and extensive public business, attempted that for which he had not previously prepared himself. Combined with a clear perception, and excellent judgment, he possessed great simplicity of character, which set off, as in bold relief, those characteristics for which he was eminently distinguished. To clearness of perception, promptness in execution, accuracy in thought and expression in all the business relations of life, he united, in an eminent degree, a sympathy with childhood, and a high sense of the value and worth of intelligent, inquiring, earnest, youthful life. As a business man, in the usual acceptance of that phrase, he had very little talent. His farm and his mill commanded his attention, and his large caution ever prevented his stepping out into the business current of the world; but, as an accurate, recording, financial, judicial or executive officer, he had few equals, no superior. He was Justice of the Peace, Town and Probate Clerk, and Town Treasurer, many years; and, considering the large amount of business, controversial and otherwise, which passed through his hands, he has left more friends, and fewer enemies, than any man we ever knew. Affable, courteous, frank, liberal-minded, he secured the confidence of his fellow-citizens, and when, at the close of 1865, he passed away, the voice of the community in tones of affectionate remembrance, was: "Mark the perfect man, and behold the upright for the end of that man is peace." To other attainments were added those of a mind, pious and devout. For more than fifty years he was a worthy member of the Baptist church, and was deeply interested in the benevolent object for the improvement of the race. He married Miss Phebe Greene, a woman of good mind, very domestic in her habits, an excellent wife and mother. They lived together sixty-two years. Her funeral was the sixty-second anniversary of their marriage. Asa Stone, Esq., was about five feet eleven inches in height, lean in figure, and although not round shouldered, was a little inclined to stoop, features rather thin, lines distinctly marked, eyes blue, and light brown hair. He had not the form nor features of the "Stone family;" is in countenance and form no type of the race, but strongly resembles the Westcotts from the maternal side. He died in Mansfield, Conn., and his remains rest in his old town, Coventry, on the land owned by his grandfather Westcott, and near the site of Werden's meeting-house, near Coventry Centre.

NOTE 162.

Lydia Stone (1221), oldest daughter and oldest child of Asa (1058), was born, and has lived, till within the last four years, in Coventry, R. I. She is a woman of good mind, continually improving from books and observation. Nor has she ceased at this late period of life. Almost every form of human progress and change is by her seen and examined, and if she ever fails of a correct judgment it is owing to the impression of types set in early life. Un-

like most of the world, she approves nothing, because circumstances have rolled it to the top of the wheel; it must pass the ordeal of examination, but in this she is not illiberal, and weighs most things in the scales of liberal common sense. She is decidedly a woman of superior observation, and excellent memory, though a little inclined to severe censure, where virtue, truth and justice, appear to be wanting. Joined to a well-improved mind, she has a good heart, and those who know her best most appreciate her virtues. She resides in Coventry, Conn., and has never married.

Arthur F. Stone (1222), the oldest son of Asa Stone (1058), was a young man of good character, and much executive ability. He was ripe and capable beyond his years, and gave promise of a useful future. He died when about twenty.

NOTE 163.

Lowry Stone (1224) was born and lived in Coventry, R. I., until, when fifteen or sixteen, he left for Providence, to learn the trade of a tailor. This he completed, and worked for a few years in Oxford, Mass., and Providence, R. I. The sedentary habits necessarily connected with his trade, and his naturally active inclinations induced him to abandon it altogether, and engage in farming, upon the old homestead. There he lived some twenty-five or thirty years, much of the time harrassed by legal troubles, in which, circumstances beyond his control involved him, until, in 1864, he sold out to Pardon S. Peckham, and purchased a large farm in Mansfield, Conn., where he now resides. He married Miss Mary Arnold, an excellent woman, mild, amiable, beloved by all who know her, one who fills her station in life with credit and respectability. This worthy couple have two children, of fine promise, a son and a daughter, just ripening into maturity. We shall be much disappointed if Lucetta A. Stone (1234) and Robert Earle Stone (1235) do not deserve the reputation for virtue, industry and integrity, which has been sustained in their direct line of ancestry, for 7 generations.

NOTE 164.

Asa Stone (1227) enjoyed advantages above the boys of his day, and the faithfulness and energy with which he applied himself, and the ease with which he mastered the studies in which he engaged, gave evidence to his father, that both time and money were not wasted. He attended the Academy, at Plainfield, Conn., and the High School, at Oxford, Mass., and, when quite a young man, taught schools, in East, North and West Bridgewater, for several successive years, with good success. He then engaged in merchandizing, in company with William F. Brett, in West Bridgewater, where he remained one year, when he sold out and opened an extensive trade in Phenix Village, his native town. Here he remained several years, when, again disposing of his stock, he removed to Providence. He has been, for the last fourteen years, book-keeper and confidential clerk for D. C. Jencks,

20

South Water Street, Providence, an extensive dealer in lime, cement, bricks and articles in that line. His position in that house is a sufficient testimonial of his integrity and ability. Asa Stone (1227) has been twice married,— first to Miss Diantha Eames, of North Bridgewater, a woman of good mind, genial, affectionate, domestic; second, to Miss Judith Hodges, of Foxboro', a lady of well educated mind, of much reading, and decided literary taste. He has two sons by the first marriage, Arthur F. Stone (1236), a young man of cultivated mind, and much literary ability. He has taught school two winters with good success. Edward L. Stone (1237), of less disposition to study, is a young man of intelligence, and deeply interested in farming and stock raising. They live with their Aunt Lydia (1221), in Coventry, Conn.

Note 165.

John Enos Stone (1223) married Susan Potter, and died some ten years since, in Plainfield, Conn. His family are respected and esteemed. Their statistics are found on page 59.

Mason P. Stone (1228) has been four times married. The fourth wife is unknown to the writer. The statistics of this family, so far as known, are found on pages 59 and 60. He resides in the State of Maine.

Note 166.

Jabez Stone (1050), second son of William Stone (655), usually called Captain William, was born in Mashantatack, Stoneville, and commenced life on the old farm bought of Susan Lawrence by Hugh Stone (1). This property he owned with his Father, and joined with him in the sale to Dr. William Aldrich. On this farm old John Stone (4) made chairs and machinery for making cloth, &c., woolen and linen wheels and looms; and in the same machine shop, the grandson, Jabez (1050), worked at the same business, until, in 1779, he removed to Coventry, upon a farm some two miles Southwest of Coventry Center, where he lived until the time of his death, which occurred January 7, 1820. He was a man of industry and virtue, went through life comfortably, and left a hard, rocky, sterile farm of one hundred acres to his youngest son. He was twice married: first to Miss Sarah Taylor of Cranston, and afterwards to Mrs. Waitstill Greene, widow of the la e Jedidiah Greene of Coventry; he had seven children by the first marriage and one by the last.

Joseph Stone (1242) married Mary Bowen, the daughter of Joseph Bowen, Esq., of Coventry; and, in their early married life, removed to Paris, Oneida County, New York. Here he lived many years, and reared a large family, the eldest of whom married and settled around him. (See Appendix 86.) He afterward arranged his affairs in Paris, and, with his younger sons, removed to Wetherfield, Gennessee County, where probably he died. His younger sons, Charles and Joseph, now live in Grand Rapids, Michigan,

and the family generally are respected by their fellow-citizens by whom they are known. Ambrose Stone (1244) married Miss Lizzie ——. They lived in several places in the State of New York. At the close of his life, he was an innkeeper in Burlington, Oneida County, where he died. We believe he left no children.

Daniel Stone (1246), the youngest son of Jabez Stone (1050), married Miss Polly Gorton of Warwick, and removed to Oneida County, New York, we believe, where he lived till the time of his decease. He reared a large family,—ten children,—and died when the youngest was in childhood. After his death, his widow came back to Rhode Island with several of her younger children, where they found connexions and still live. We believe the family generally are reputable and virtuous.

NOTE 167.

Sarah Stone (1245), second daughter of Jabez Stone (1050), married Matthew Manchester, and in (1806 or 8) came to reside permanently in Coventry, Rhode Island. She was a woman of unusually amiable manners, and of great beauty, which she has transmitted to her daughters. She is the mother of Deacon Earl Manchester, mentioned in (Note 115). Her husband was a man of genius and talent, somewhat inclined to castle-building, but one of those who, more busy with their brain than their hands, strike out the sparks of thought and action which warm and stir the world, more to the advantage of others than themselves. He travelled far into the then Western Territory, now the State of Ohio, when marked trees were the only road, and Indians the general inhabitants of the forests, and made investments which, we have no doubt, if wisely managed, would have rendered his children independent. He bought and put in operation a valuable water power in Coventry. He introduced the spinning of woolen yarn by machinery driven by water power; but failed to make any of his investments afford him more than a competence. He was, for several years, a Justice of the Peace; was an interesting companion, respected by his fellow townsmen, and died of an apoplectic fit, about the year 1818. Job Manchester (1264) lives in East Greenwich, Rhode Island. He has been married to Miss P. Fry, and to Mrs. —— Congdon, widow of the late Peleg Congdon of Warwick. Almira Manchester (1265) married —— Gorton, of East Greenwich, where she lived till the death of her husband. She died, in 1865, in Bristol, Rhode Island. Phebe Manchester (1266) is an estimable woman and married Thomas R. Greene, of Bristol, Rhode Island. He is a manufacturer, and is highly esteemed for his ability, integrity and consistent religious course.

NOTE 168.

Isabella Stone (1247) was a woman of warm heart, an excellent mother and kind friend. She was twice married; first, to Captain John Hammett,

of Warwick, master of a vessel in the foreign trade. He was a worthy man and died in their early married life, leaving his widow with two children. A. R. Hammett (1302) married Eunice Ledyard, lives in Coventry, and is generally respected by his fellow citizens. They have two children,—a son and a daughter,—much esteemed for their intelligence and moral worth. Clorinda Hammett (1303) married W. E. Rice, and died a few years since, beloved by all who knew her. Isabella Stone's second husband was Daniel C. Goff, a man of intelligence and virtue. He held most of the offices in the gift of the people,—town clerk, treasurer and Justice of the Peace,—and was extensively employed as a land surveyor. His mathematical knowledge was good. He had a lively appreciation of the beautiful, and his drawings and plans of real estate partake more or less of the ornate. They have six children,—all still living,—generally respected and esteemed, upon whom the mantle of the father and mother now rests.

NOTE 169.

Jabez Stone (1243) was the second son of Jabez (1050), was born in Cranston, in the same house, probably, certainly on the same farm, where Hugh Stone (1) died some forty years before. When fourteen or fifteen years old, he removed with his father to Coventry. He married Miss Free-love Manchester, a woman generally beloved; still, quiet and home-loving. Jabez (1243) was a man of a social nature, but lacked the force and energy to make life a success. They had but two children who arrived at maturity. Wanton Stone (1251) married Miss Freelove Knight and reared a large family of children, who are generally respected and esteemed. Charles D. Stone (1262), youngest son of Wanton Stone, married Almira A. Arnold, and is a man of much ability and energy. They reside in Coventry, near the Black Rock village, and are in good circumstances. Freelove M. Stone (1253) has been married, but is now a widow,—a woman beloved,—upon whom the mantle of the departed mother has gently fallen.

NOTE 170.

Jabez Stone (1268), the eldest son of Daniel Stone (1247), married Miss Zilpha Adams, a woman of virtue and intelligence, and a worthy member of the Baptist Church in Athens. She died March 28, 1864. Her husband is a man of Christian virtue and general intelligence, and, although denied, in his boyhood days, the educational light of the present time, he has, through a long life, aimed at an onward and upward course. His social nature has gathered around him many friends, and he has the satisfaction of knowing that most of his surviving children are journeying, in Faith, towards the shining shore. Jabez (1268) lives in Athens, Bradford County, Pennsylvania, a town located almost on the North line of the State, nearly South and not far distant from Elmira, New York. Himself and three of his sons are shipwrights, and the family are among those who, by active energy, are

building up the prosperity of our nation. The statistics of this family are found page 62.

Daniel J. Stone (1276), the youngest son and youngest child of Daniel (1246), was born in Oneida County, New York, and came with his mother back to the native State of his father and mother. Here he has spent most of his life, and here reared a fine, healthful and promising family. He is a man intelligent and social, lives in Warwick, about two miles from Pawtuxet, and appears to have and enjoy a genial and happy home. He married Miss Harriet E. Chase, a woman of prepossessing appearance and fine social powers, and their children are smart, full of genial, buoyant life, and promise well for the happiness of their parents and their country. Stephen Dexter Stone (1292) is married,—is a young man of uncommon energy and bids fair to make life a success.

Stephen Stone (1218) was the youngest child,—in fact, the only child,—of Jabez Stone (1050), by his second marriage with Waitstill Greene, and was born when his father was sixty-one years old. His boyhood opened much like other boys of that age in the neighborhood around him, save that an unusual indulgence marked his early life, and lent no aid to the life-trials which must more or less be met by all. He married, before he was eighteen years of age, Miss Phebe Comstock, a girl who aimed to discharge life's duties,—for she was, indeed, but a girl, and her husband but a boy,—and hence this fact,

> " The early days of wedded life
> Are oft o'ercast by childish strife,"

Was somewhat realized in the beginning of their connubial relations, and yet they were *neither* decidedly bad, but *both* decidedly human. The main difficulty was the demon of the cup was coiling, coiling its damning folds around the young man, and gradually crushing out the husband and father. Oh! how many young men of good mind, of generous hearts, in that neighborhood,—boys and young men who were schoolmates, as was Stephen, with the writer—how many have fallen into the snares of intemperance! Stephen struggled along nearly twenty years, from the time of his marriage, and died. His wife, all the way on during her married years, did not sink, but bore up like a noble woman, and it was plainly perceptible that, as the husband *sunk*, the wife *rose*. There is some granite that is full of gold. There are some minds that need hard trials to bring out their excellence. Phebe's was one ; and well did she profit by the twenty years experience, during the life of her husband. She is an energetic, strong, virtuous woman, has brought up her children to industry and virtue, and commands the respect and esteem of all who know her. Her children are all married and, we believe, are mostly doing well

158

Freelove Stone (1049) was the only daughter of Captain William Stone
.(658), was born in Cranston, and removed to Coventry, either before or
after her marriage with Ephraim Westcott, a wealthy farmer, and extensive
owner of the water privilege and several hundred acres of what is, and what
is around, Potterville, near Coventry Center. They had a family of five
children, whose statistical record is found page 63. Most of them settled in
Rhode Island. Ephraim Westcott (1315), their oldest son, settled on a part
of the old farm, married his cousin Freelove Stone (1321), and lived and
died esteemed and respected. He was much interested in the cultivation of
fruit, and reared a very fine orchard on the southern declivity of Nipmuc
Hill, much of which, though old and decaying, is still standing. Zilpha
Westcott (1330) married Nathan Bailey and moved to Abington, Pennsylvania. Her descendants are among the most wealthy and respected in that
place. Nathaniel Westcott (1335) married Miss Abigail Albro and lived
for a time on the farm where he was born. He, in boyhood, united with the
Baptist Church in his own town; and when some twenty years old, imag-
ined he received a call to the ministry, but his subsequent mental development and success gave no evidence that he understood himself or his duty;
he sold the farm and finally removed to Luzerne County, where many of
his relatives had found a home. His wife was a worthy woman and a good
mother. She died in Pennsylvania, some years since. The husband again
married, still resides there, and maintains the character of a man of integrity.

NOTE 174.

Jeremiah Stone (1051) was born in Cranston, Mashantatack, and learned
the trade of a tanner and currier, a business which he followed, more or less,
most of his life. When but sixteen years old, he married Dinah Knight,
daughter of Nehemiah Knight, Esquire, of Cranston, and some ten years
afterwards bought a tract of land in the South part of Scituate, adjoining
Coventry, and commenced life, in earnest, as a farmer, and tanner and currier. Here he passed a long life; here reared a family of seven children,
who reached maturity, who all became heads of families and reflected honor
upon their parents and their God. Of the descendants of Jeremiah Stone
(1051) and Dinah Knight, there are more than six hundred, including those
with whom they are intermarried, settled in every State in the Union, from
Massachusetts to Missouri. One is in Mexico, in the army of Louis Napoleon; and, with very few exceptions, are among the most virtuous and trust-
worthy of the nation. He was a man of ability and energy, inclined to
impatience; social, religious, economical, with little inclination to study or
read; with but few aspirations for improvement, and a great lover of home,
which was always rendered attractive by one of the best of wives. He was
much respected in the town, and was, for some years, a Justice of the Peace.

Jeremiah (1051) was a very fair sample of the "Stone" character, spiced with a little Westcott nervousness. He survived his wife some twenty years and, in his old age, married Mrs. Esther Fry, widow of the late Benjamin Fry, of Foster. He died when about eighty, and his remains rest in a wall-enclosed cemetery on the farm where he lived and died, and by the side of his father, Captain William (658).

NOTE 175.

Charles Stone (1322), the oldest son of Jeremiah (1051), was born in Cranston, and came with his father, when a boy, to Scituate. His opportunities for education, in that early day of Rhode Island History, were very limited, and, consequently, as the father saw no necessity of his son's becoming better educated than he himself was, no efforts were made to help on the boy Charles, although he was decidedly a boy of superior mind. With no early encouragement or culture, he or his father, looked forward to nothing higher or beyond the level upon which his ancestors moved. True, he would not fall back behind and below, though little expectation was entertained of his advance. He disappointed his friends. His first step was advance. His father married when sixteen; Charles waited till he was eighteen, and then married Rachel Knight, a very worthy woman, commenced life in the same occupation of his father, and on a part of the same farm. It was not in his nature, however, to rest down in the current level around him. He would rise, he would improve; not because he would ambitiously excel, but because he felt, intuitively felt, intellectually felt, that the God-given nature of man is progress, and this idea went with him through life, and more or less guided his conversation, his reflection and his reading. He was the student of human nature as developed in our fallen and redeemed race, and graduated only when he passed over to the "Shining Shore." Previous to 1795, his attention was called to the subject of religion; he experienced a work of grace and became a member of the Baptist church in the West part of Coventry, under the pastoral care of the Rev. Caleb Nichols. How long before the above time his conversion dates, or how long before, he made a public profession of Faith in Christ, the writer is not informed. But, March 20, 1795, we find a petition signed by twenty-two members, to be set off and called "The Second Separate or Independent Baptist Church of Christ, in Coventry." Among these petitioners were Jeremiah Stone (1051), Charles Stone (1322), Henry Stone (1324), Mercy Stone (1326), William Stone (1053), Dinah Stone (1327), Dinah Stone (Knight), the wife of Jeremiah (1051); Rachel Stone (Knight), the wife of Charles (1322), and Lydia Stone (Blackmar), the wife of Henry (1324). The prayer of the petitioners was granted the July following, and, on the first day of August, 1795, the petitioners assembled at what was called Werden's Meeting House, and organized the church by the choice of William Stone (1053), Clerk; Nathaniel Price, Elder, and Charles Stone (1322),

Deacon. The recognition of this church by the sister churches took place September 11, 1795. The record of which was signed and duly certified by Francis Fuller, Messenger of the church in Foster, Council Scribe. Rev. Nathaniel Price remained with them only till March, 1796, when he was, by mutual arrangement, dismissed. For more than a year, the church was without a settled pastor. Much of the time, however, they enjoyed the instruction and labors of their worthy deacon, whom they appointed on the day of their organization. On Saturday, December 23, 1797, they passed the following vote : " Chose Brother Charles Stone to be their Elder, declaring his qualifications to be satisfactory to their mind ; they also believe him to be called of God and set apart to that work."

The Ordaining Council met on the 20th day of June, 1798, and, after a very methodical examination ; First, of the church, in " their leanings of mind toward the candidate as their watchman and minister." Second, of the candidate, " his call from nature to grace," " his call to the ministerial work," " his call to the pastoral care of this church ;" the vote was unanimous in the affirmative, and the act of ordination took place on the next day, June 21st. Of this church, he was the Pastor nearly forty-six years, up to the time of his death, though he had assistance for a few years near its close. His labors were mostly at one place, in the same house, its name changing, by common consent, from " Elder Werden's Meeting House" to " Elder Stone's Meeting House," a name which it still retains, though the foundation where it once stood now only remains. Rev. Charles Stone, as a preacher, was a man of much argumentative and persuasive power, easy, fluent in expression, though his style of delivery was somewhat antiquated, and his discourses possessed more of logical deductions and reasoning, than those generally of his day. He was not an extensive reader, nor did he ever become a man of general science. His study was God and man, as revealed in the " Divine Word," and the great truths which it reveals of man's duty and destiny. He was a Calvinist, rather of the Emmons or Hopkins school, and dwelt with an extra reverence on the writings and arguments of the Apostle Paul ; but his was the Calvinism of a generous and expanded liberality, rather than the Calvinism of a diminutive, nutshell exclusion. He was a man far in advance of his age. He did not believe that the world, with its Christian Philosophy, or its statements of Christian scientific truth, or its understanding of gospel order and Christian duty, was fully understood, completely developed and stereotyped, when he was born. No ; he believed in advancement, some new development of man's capacities to be learned and brought out, some new truth to be discovered and made plain, and hence a noble charity tinged and beautified his whole mind. He did not view, with any degree of interest, the exclusive communion of the denomination to which he belonged. The following incident was related to the writer by the Rev. Charles himself. Two men called at the Church Covenant Meeting, on Saturday, introduced themselves to him as Congrega-

tionalists and Agents for the Bible Society, and he courteously invited them to stop and take part in the meetings. They did so, remained over Sunday, stopped to the Communion Service, were waited upon by the Deacons, and received the Sacrament. Some three days after, his brother called and the following dialogue ensued:

Br. Charles, did you know that those two men who communed with us last Sabbath were Congregationalists?

Elder C. Yes.

Br Well, what are you intending to do about it?

Elder C. Well, I guess not much.

This shows, better than a volume could have done, his hearty fellowship for all those who love the Lord and are engaged in his work. He was decidedly in favor of improvements,—a practical man. The denomination, in his day, generally cherished the idea that study and preparation, especially written preparation, was inconsistent with a dispensation of Gospel Truth. He early saw and threw aside this foolish idea. He himself related to the writer the following fact. "I was going to an exchange," said he, "to the 'Tin Top,' (a church near Warwick line,) when I overtook an aged man of some years' acquaintance. 'I am going,' said the man, 'to hear you preach. I don't go to hear these College chaps, with their book-learning and their *written sermons*, but I heard *you* were to preach, and I am going.' I felt happy to meet him, though I had a prepared sermon for the afternoon. I went into the pulpit, which, fortunately for my friend, was quite elevated, and preached my sermon as I had intended. As I came out of the house, he bade me good bye, saying, 'There, that is what I call preaching; but if you had had one word written, I would have left the house.' I did not think it best to spoil his enjoyment of what he called a 'good sermon,' by giving him the facts." Elder Charles was one, while he gathered up and examined life in all its relations, that *never grew old*, but cherished a lovely freshness of spirit. Children knew him only to remember and love, and his easy, familiar approach never failed to secure their confidence, and remove the distance which too often obtains between the old and the young. As a social, genial companion and friend, he had few equals, no superiors. His conversation was vivacious, always tinged with religious trust, easy, fluent, very frequently interspersed with illustration and anecdote, but never overstepping the bound of religious propriety. As he approached the close of life, his Faith brightened into a brilliancy, and he was almost permitted to look beyond the veil, and listen to the echo of angel voices from the temple-arches of the New Jerusalem; and, in cheerfulness, in bright, beaming hope, he heard the voice, "Child, your Father calls, come home."

He died, 1844. His wife, Rachel Knight, was an excellent woman, of strong, social habits; of earnest, confiding faith, a loving companion, a firm friend, and an excellent mother. She died April 8, 1842.

Note 176.

Nathan K. Stone (1338), the eldest son of Charles Stone (1322), was born in Scituate, Rhode Island. The moderate circumstances of the father opened no opportunities beyond the ordinary range of Rhode Island boys, and daily toil among the rocks and in the sterile soil of his native State, was the commencement of his youthful life. The schools of Rhode Island, in those days, were few and far between, but neither distance, nor wind, nor snow, kept him from all the schools within his reach ; and, with a strong grasp of the sciences taught in those days, the boy Nathan ripened into the man of more than ordinary scientific acquirements. He taught several schools in his own neighborhood, with good success, and entered upon manhood's life in advance of all the boys who started with him, on the same line. His aptness for and love of music made him chorister in his father's church, many years ; and the same native trait is seen developed in his family. He married Cilda Matteson, daughter of Job Matteson, Esq, of Coventry, by whom he had ten children. See pages 64 and 65. Of this large family, not one, either by misfortune or misconduct, has brought disgrace or grief to a parent's heart. In 1839, the worthy wife, the excellent mother, with whom he had lived thirty years, died, and subsesquently he married Rhoda Cooke, with whom his family had been acquainted for many years,—a lady every way worthy and well qualified to smooth the down hill of life. They are both living ; the one very infirm, the other nearly blind, though cheerful and happy, awaiting the call of the Master they have long loved and served. The ability and moral worth of Nathan K. Stone (1338) has been acknowledged by his town and State. For many years he was Justice of the Peace and several times Representative in the General Assembly of the State ; and many, in various portions of New England, cherish, with interest, their acquaintance with this worthy man.

Note 177.

Alban M. Stone (1343), the oldest son of Nathan K. Stone, evinced, even in boyhood, those traits which now render him a worthy man. In fact, the boy is the father of the man,—was in his case,—is almost always. His mind was improved, enjoying somewhat more than ordinary advantages of study ; and was refined and matured, and rendered practical by the conversation of his father, and especially of his grandfather, the Rev. Charles (1322). In his early life, he taught several schools, with good success, and when about twenty, engaged as overseer in a cotton mill a few miles from his home. Here, his faithfulness and ability displayed itself, and, for a few years, he was employed in different mills, but always with good success, and to the entire satisfaction of the owners. He has soon earned and saved some five or six hundred dollars, when he was induced, by the representations of others, and, perhaps, partially by the desire to set up for himself, to engage in trade at the Washington Village, Coventry. He was unsuccessful; and, in

a short time, he had lost every dollar he was worth. He was not discouraged. He had earned what he had lost; he knew how to earn more. More than this, his observation and experience rendered him fitted for a higher position. From an overseer he became "Super," and was, at length, engaged as Super and Agent for one of the smaller mills of the Union Manufacturing Company, a wealthy corporation in the easterly section of Connecticut. His success in that smaller mill, at Marlboro', Connecticut, sent him, in the employment of the same corporation, to one of their largest, in Manchester, Connecticut, where he ever since has been. He married Miss Mary A. Morse, of Coventry, a woman of much mental culture and business talent; social, genial and not deficient in domestic taste. They have made life, in its pecuniary relation, a success. Affluence has crowned their faithfulness, and the respect and esteem of a large circle of acquaintances show that honesty and virtue, in this world, meets its reward. They have been, for years, active members of the Baptist Church, and are living for the life present and life future. They have but two children living; James B. Stone (1354), who is married, and resides in Hartford, and is there engaged in business; and Sarah A. Stone (1356), who resides in Mansfield, Conn.

NOTE 178.

Cynthia P. Stone (1344) is now a widow, and resides with her son, John King (1366). He is a worthy son of an excellent mother. Minerva Stone (1345) married David H. Wightman. Their statistics are on page 65. D. H. Wightman is a farmer and a worthy man; Deacon of the Baptist Church, and Superintendent of the Sunday School. This whole family honor a worthy ancestry. Phebe Stone (1346) has left but one surviving child, Phebe B. Smith, a young woman of quick perception, and much reading and observation. To these, she unites strong social powers; and now, in the comfortable home of her infirm and aged grandfather, and her blind grandmother, she labors, with cheerfulness and love, to smooth their pathway adown the declivity of life. Melissa C. Stone (1349) was a woman of excellent mind, and married Stephen Whitman. She died in early life, beloved and lamented. Harriet P. Stone (1351) subsequently married the widowed husband of her sister. Their record is found on pages 65 and 66 The name of the husband is sometimes spelled Wightman, sometimes Whitman. Alice H. Stone (1350) was a lovely girl, and died Feb. 19, 1853.

NOTE 179.

Horatio A. Stone (1347) was the second son of Nathan K. Stone (1338), and was born in Scituate, Rhode Island, where he lived, working at farming and sawing lumber, until he was nineteen years old, when he entered, as clerk, into his brother's store. This clerking business was short, as one year wound up his brother's small capital, and both wisely gave up an employment, which had so far been unsuccessful. Horatio soon found employ-

ment as overseer in one of the many cotton mills of his native State. During this period of some two or three years he was interested in the operations of machinery ; it was constantly before him, until he left his position, as overseer, and entered the machine shop of Levalley, Lanphear & Co., to learn the trade of machinist. In this matter of learning the trade, he got more than he expected or bargained for. He expected to get the trade ; but, with it, he got a wife, Miss Hannah Lanphear, sister to the principal business operator of the firm for which he was working. His trade was now learned, but another opening presented itself, more remunerative and more attractive. He was offered the " Super's " place in the Crompton Mills, a large cotton establishment in Warwick, near Coventry line. He accepted, and remained in this position four and a half years, to the mutual satisfaction of both parties, when he bought an interest in the firm where he learned his trade, resigned his position as Super, and entered as an active partner in the old firm, where he now is, and has, for many years been. Miss Lanphear, his first wife, was frail, feeble, with a mind well cultivated, but too active and energetic for her physical frame. She lived but five or six years, leaving no children which survived the mother. His second marriage was with Miss Elizabeth Almy, of Portsmouth, Rhode Island, a woman of strong mind, clear business perceptions, affable, with strong social proclivities. She lived some two or three years, after this marriage, and died, leaving one daughter, Elizabeth Almy Stone. She is still living,—a young lady of active mind, of earnest, decided impressions, rather of strong individualism, but social, vivacious and ardent. She is blessed with advantages of general culture, no pains are spared in giving her a *good* education. Horatio's present wife is Miss Ann Eliza Whitman, youngest daughter of Martin Whitman, Esq., of Coventry. They have been married some fifteen or sixteen years. and have one son living, a lad of ten or twelve. Miss Whitman was a young woman of mind well improved; genial, warm-hearted, refined, and uniting, withal, good sense. She has great love for, and an excellent knowledge of, domestic life. Her home is a home of order and neatness. She has suffered much from debility,—is now much better,—and has before her the prospect of health and happiness. Horatio A. Stone (1347) is known and appreciated for his warm, honest heart. He is one of those, (there are some such,) that you can always see more by looking at his heart, than you can hear by listening to his tongue. He has held many offices, in the gift of people. He is a member of the Town Council, and has been Representative in the General Assembly of the State. From his earliest life, he has been deeply interested in musical science, and has, more or less, from his boyhood, practiced and taught vocal music. He has been chorister in every religious society with which he has been connected. He is a religious professor, and is deeply and earnestly engaged in every good work for the advancement of Christian truth, and for the elevation of sinning and suffering humanity. He is in affluent circumstances and has a pleasant residence, in the Phenix Village, Coventry, Rhode Island.

Note 180.

Jason P. Stone (1348), the youngest surviving son of Nathan K. (1338), was born at the old homestead of his grandfather, Charles (1322). It was a home of love, of virtue, of moral and religious worth, but it presents few rural or agricultural charms; the soil sterile, the fields abounding in rocks, and the pastures with huckleberry, it afforded a fine opportunity to develop the physical man, in bone and muscle ; and the mental, in unaspiring patience. It was decidedly an unfavorable locality in which to rear Yankees, and hence the three boys mentioned in Notes 177, 179 and 180, all left home for a more extended sphere of action, as they severally reached maturity. Jason P. first went as assistant in a weaving shop, where he remained nine months, and then accepted the position of " Boss Weaver," in the large establishment of Gov. Harris, where he remained five years. Next came the allurements of trade, and he opened a large store in the Phenix Village. Five years of " Profit and Loss,"—mostly loss,—and the store was abandoned, a manufactory in North Scituate rented, and he engaged in manufacturing cotton goods, with a partner. Firm : " Greene & Stone." Within the year, they were burnt out. He then removed to Providence, and, within a year, accepted the agency for the sale of Singer's Sewing Machines, where he has, for some ten years, been engaged, to the mutual satisfaction of all concerned. He is a man of Christian Faith, genial disposition, and good mind ; possessing much of the humorous and sportive nature, though not the vivacious manner of the grandfather, Charles (1322). Jason P. Stone has been twice married. His first wife was Miss Eliza Albro, of Warwick, a woman earnest, but very kind hearted, genial, social, but possessing much individualism. She made many friends, possessed a firm faith in God, and died about 1850, beloved and lamented by all who knew her. His second wife was Miss Sarah Weeks, of Warwick, Rhode Island. In her, his first children have found a loving, judicious mother, a counsellor and friend. She, is social, genial, intelligent, and very domestic. Her home is the home of intellectual, Christian love. They have six children, by both connections, and promise well for a hopeful and useful future.

Note 181.

Allerson Stone (1341), second son of Rev. Charles (1322), was born in Scituate. The boys of that day had moderate opportunities for education, in the country towns of Rhode Island; but, small as they were, he never exhibited unusual aptitude for book-knowledge. Mechanical science had more charms for him, and, when an opportunity offered, he learned the trade of a carpenter, and subsequently married Miss Sarah Burlingame, sister of Mr. George Burlingame, of whom he learned his trade. They have four children, all living. When near midlife, he purchased a farm in Coventry. On this, he and his excellent wife, are now living contented and happy, having reached the age of nearly eighty ; and, all the way, during their earthly

sojourn, his quiet temperament has moved him gently by the sharp corners, and over the rough surface of life, more easily than most men of his race.

NOTE 182.

Charles Morgan Stone (1390) was born in Coventry, and lived there during the days of his early boyhood. In this town, he had such opportunities as the country towns then afforded, and graduated from those seminaries when about sixteen. Having a decided leaning toward mercantile pursuits, he entered, as clerk, in a store in his native town. While in this store, he became acquainted with the principal operators and owners of a large manufacturing establishment in the South part of the State, and was invited to manage the sales and act as paymaster to their help. This situation was a responsible post for a young man of nineteen; but his fidelity and ability met the expectations of the company, and fortune held out before him brighter hopes than his most sanguine expectations had anticipated. But fortune has been called a " fickle jade," and so, in this instance, she proved. In less than two years, a financial crisis, which manufacturers in New England have so often met, swept away this company, and the hopes of the young man together, and left him free to tack ship and sail another course upon the voyage of life. The winter following found him teaching a school in his native town, and enjoying the high privilege, so common in those days, of " boarding round." To teach school and " board round " is an eventful period in the life of any young man. Every family in which he lives, if only for a week, is a new leaf in the book of life, for him to study,—in each he sees the working of new machinery, physical, mental and moral. In short, we can hardly conceive how a young man's education can be complete, till he has " kept school" and " boarded round !" The following year found Charles Morgan Stone clerk in the store of Pardon Holden, Esq., of Mount Vernon, a small village in the western part of Providence County. Shortly after this, he married Miss Mary E. Holden, daughter of his employer, a lady of virtue and intelligence, and continued with P. Holden, part of the time managing two stores; the one at home, the other at Foster Centre, distant some three miles. At this time, he was elected Cashier of Mount Vernon Bank, a position which he occupied eight years. As most of the bank business was done in Providence, he was appointed its agent and removed to the city. He continued this agency until the bank closed its affairs. In 1853, the Atlantic Bank was chartered, and he was appointed Cashier, which position he now occupies. He was, for three years, a member of the Common Council of Providence. He has two children, of fine promise, just entered upon the realities of life. Charles Morgan Stone (1393) is unmarried, resides at home, and is junior partner of the firm, " Waterman & Stone," engaged in the coal and wood trade. Anna M. Stone (1392) married Albert O. Baker. He is engaged in the manufacture of jewelry. Firm : " Fanning, Potter & Co."

NOTE '183.

Jason P. Stone (1342) was the youngest son of Rev. Charles Stone, and had, in boyhood, somewhat better opportunities for mental improvement than the boys of his age; and, when seventeen or eighteen, was clerk for several years in a large store in the city of Providence. His health being somewhat impaired, he left the store and taught school in the vicinity of his father's. Soon after, he married Miss Alice Hazzard, and entered into trade on Escoheag Hill, in West Greenwich. Here he lived many years, continuing in trade, to which he added Farming in his later years. He was a man highly esteemed by those with whom he was best acquainted, a man of few words, but of generous, noble spirit. He represented the town, from time to time, in the General Assembly; was actively engaged in the Sunday School, was Deacon of the church, for many years, and was a worthy, devoted Christian. He died much lamented, and his name and worth will long be cherished by all who knew him. He left no children.

Phebe Stone (1340), the only daughter of Rev. Charles Stone (1322), was a woman of open heart, and generous affections. She married Wanton Chase, of Coventry. They have left no children.

NOTE 184.

Hannah Stone (1323) married Dennis Knight and lived in Scituate, Rhode Island. They reared a family of six children, all of whom are virtuous and respectable. A son of Mary Knight and Joseph Parker is a graduate of Dartmouth College, is a man of fine talent, and taught in some literary institution in the Southern States, with good success. When the war commenced, in 1861, he enlisted, and was elected first Lieutenant. He served his country during the war, and came home unhurt. The statistics of this family are found on page 67.

NOTE 185.

Henry Stone (1324), was the second son of Jeremiah Stone (1051), was born, bred and lived, almost to the close of life, on the same farm with his father, in the South part of Scituate, Rhode Island. Here he reared a large family of thirteen children, eleven of whom married and became heads of families. He was a man of much moral worth, of a strong religious faith, and was Deacon of the church, of which his brother was Pastor, nearly forty years. In his early married life, he met with a severe accident in felling a tree. His leg was crushed dreadfully, and the surgeons met to perform the amputation. It was the decision, with one dissenting voice, to take off the leg. Dr. A. Waldo said, " No. I can cure it. It will be a homely thing, but better than a wooden leg." He finally prevailed, the leg was saved, and was, very much as he said it would be, "a homely thing, but better than a ' wooden leg.' " Deacon Henry, as he was usually called, was a man of industry and economy, and his children were brought up to practice the

same virtues. He had no taste for reading or study, was not a close thinker, and gave his children but little opportunity for education or mental development; and yet, few families have stepped forth into active life, with fewer proclivities to evil, or with a greater dislike to whatever was degrading or low. He married Lydia Blackmar, a woman of energy, virtue and great domestic taste. The family was brought up to obedience, and few families were better governed; both parents uniting the *love* of obedience with native ability to gain it. Toward the close of life, the old homestead was sold and the family moved to Providence, where Henry (1324) and his wife both died. Their remains now rest in the cemetery on the old farm.

Note 186.

George Stone (1405), oldest son of Henry (1324), lived in Scituate, in his earlier married life, but subsequently worked, as boss farmer, for William Almy and the Slaters, until he bought a farm in Coventry, on the Southern declivity of Nipmuc Hill, where he passed the last thirty years of his life. George Stone (1405) was twice married; first, to Miss Mary Carpenter; and second, to Mrs. Mahala Mason. They were both excellent women and faithful Christians. Toward the close of life, he was converted to God, made a profession of religion, and died in 1865. He was a man of industry and integrity, kind and obliging; a man of much dry humour, and strongly given to satire. He had many friends, and died beloved and lamented. Julia Stone (1418) married Charles Burlingame. They live in the State of New York, and are in affluent circumstances. Waldo Stone (1419) died when about thirty-five years old, in the Island of Cuba. Sallie Stone (1320) married Eric Walker, a man of moral worth, and " boss farmer" for the Slaters, in Webster, Mass. Emily Stone (1421) married Joel Vaughan. She was an amiable, lovely girl, a devoted Christian, too good for earth. God called her home. Statistics of this family, on page 68.

Note 187.

Waldo Stone (1406) received his name out of respect to Dr. Albigence Waldo, surgeon and physician, who saved his father's leg, in opposition to the advice of all the rest. See Note 185. This boy, born before the recovery of the father, was named Waldo. He was an industrious and economical man; by trade, a shoemaker, and devoted himself entirely to custom work. He bought a farm in Coventry, which he improved, in connection with his trade. There he married and raised four children, who all possessed those principles, in an eminent degree, which elevate and advance. The oldest three died before either was twenty, the youngest, just past seventeen. Not far from the death of the last, the father and mother also passed away. One daughter only,—and she but fifteen years old,—survived, of the whole family. They passed to the Spirit land highly respected, deeply lamented. The mother was Betsy Johnson, daughter of Deacon Benedict Johnson.

Note 188.

Alzada Stone (1431) married, very soon after the death of her family, with Henry B. Arnold, a worthy man, but somewhat aerial and visionary. After experimenting in various matters here, with little success, he went to California, where he remained several years. At the close of this period, he returned, his health much impaired, but without much pecuniary advantage, though he had invested somewhat extensivly in "claims," by which he yet hoped to realize a fortune. Six months stay in New England, and his health was but little improved. Again, he left tor the gold regions, but he died on the way, at San Diego, before he reached the end of the voyage, and was buried in that far off land, upon the shores of the broad Pacific. He was a man generous, manly, honest and virtuous, with an imagination vivid and glowing, but lacked judgment to discern between the practicable and impracticable ; and, with too much self-reliance, to seek and follow advice. Alzada was left a widow, and without much pecuniary aid to meet the struggles of life. She had, however, what was better,—good health, good sense, good economy, good cultivation, good boys, and a firm faith in God. She had two boys, about twelve and fourteen years old. No one ever failed when possessed of so many good things. Her life has been a *labor*, but a *success*. She has reared her sons in industry and virtue, and such has been their course thus far through life, that they have never done, so far as we know or have heard, an act which would bring the blush of shame upon a mother's cheek.

Orren Stone Arnold (1432), oldest son of Alzada Stone (1431), has lived with his mother, in Coventry, at the Washington Village and at Potterville, where, for the most of the time, he was engaged in making machinery ; and, for the last eight or ten years of his life, he has given his attention entirely to the manufacture of spools and bobbins. In this, he has met with decided success. He now owns one-half of a manufactory of machinery, of this description, in Williamsville, Connecticut, employing from twenty to twenty-five hands, with a valuable and profitable corn mill connected, where he, with his partner, is in successful operation. This water power and manufactory he owns free of debt, and he is now arranging matters to build a splendid house. More than this, when his country needed soldiers to strike down the red right hand of treason, Orren enlisted for one year, a private, in army rank of our brave boys, and nobly, faithfully served his time in the Potomac Valley. The year that he was in the army, the mother passed, in visiting the family of the writer, in the Valley of the Mississippi, when they again resumed their home in New England. Added to this, he has assisted his brother in gaining a classical education, and in his preparatory course. There has been, from the time these boys were put to labor in a cotton mill, up to the present time, an exercise of good sense, and practical industry ; working out and harmoniously mingling their studies and labors together.

Denham Arnold (1433), the younger brother of this family, was, in early

22

life, much disposed to study, and yet, never to the neglect of the labor in which he engaged. He has nobly seconded his mother and brother all the way up, and, even after it was decided that he should pursue a literary course and enter College, his intervals of time have been by no means wasted. He graduated, at Brown University, a scholar of high rank, taught one year in the " English and Classical School," at Foxboro', Massachusetts, then under the care of James L. Stone, A. M., and then accepted the appointment of Tutor in " Washington University," at St. Louis, Missouri, where he has now entered upon his third year. Statistics of this family on page 68.

<h2 style="text-align:center">NOTE 189.</h2>

Knight Stone (1407) married Miss Zilpha Matteson, daughter of Job Matteson, Esq., of Coventry, remained some ten years in Rhode Island, and moved to Abington, Luzerne County, Pennsylvania, where he engaged in farming. He settled on a somewhat unproductive farm, for that region, where he lived till the close of his life, which happened when about sixty, being thrown from a carriage and so injured that he died in a few days. He was an active, laboring man, and both he and his wife much respected. Orrilla Stone (1436) married John Bailey, of Abington, Pennsylvania. They are worthy, industrious and intelligent, and have a fine family. Statistics, page 69.

Knight Stone (1437) married Miss Fidelia P. Clarke. He resides on the farm owned by his father, is a man of intelligence and high moral worth, and has a large and much esteemed family. Statistics, page 69. Knight Stone (1407) died July, 1855. Statistics, pages 69 and 70.

<h2 style="text-align:center">NOTE 190.</h2>

Ellen Stone (1409) married Owen Arnold and lived in Coventry and Providence. She died of a cancer, in 1851, and has left no children. Cyrene Stone (1410) married Joseph Burlingame, and lived in Rhode Island. Both are dead. Alfreda Burlingame (1477) is a milliner, and lives in Providence.

Nelson Burlingame (1479) is an industrious, worthy young man, has been engaged in trade, in Pawtucket, and is clerk in a store in that town. He married Mary Sherman, a very worthy woman, who died, 1865. Cynthia G. Burlingame (1481) married E. O. Potter, a mechanic of much inventive genius and skill. They are highly esteemed, and live in Pawtucket. Albert O. Burlingame is a sailor ; was on the Amphitrite, of the British Navy, during the Russian war, and was honorably discharged. He enlisted in the War of the Rebellion, in 1861, and has not yet returned. Alma Stone (1411). See Note 80. Roby Stone (1413) married Joseph Briggs, an industrious mechanic. They live in Providence.

Melina Stone (1414) has been twice married ; first, to Charles J. Westcott,

by whom they had four children. Their record is on page 72. Melina's oldest daughter, C. A. Westcott (1511), married Allen T. Chilson, an enterprising merchant and an excellent man. They are in good circumstances, and have retired from business on account of ill health. They are highly esteemed, and members of Congregational Church, High Street. Mary H. Westcott (1513), the second daughter, married Simeon Round, who died a few months after their marriage. She is now the wife of G. E. Lyman, a merchant of Providence, a man of intelligence, virtue and Christian worth. Melina's second husband was Jonathan West, who died in Iowa more than ten years since. By this marriage, she has two sons, aged sixteen and eighteen, of good character and fine promise. Much credit is due to this worthy woman, in view of the manner, industrious, moral and elevated, in which she has reared her family. Poverty has sometimes looked in at the door, always been within hailing distence ; and yet, her children, neatly and tastefully dressed, have always walked to church and Sunday School, side by side, with the best and most respectable. Rachel K. Stone (1415) was a worthy woman, married William Andrews and lived in Providence. She subsequently married George Brownell, lived in Barrington and Smithfield, where she died. She left one child by the first marriage. Statistics on page 71.

NOTE 191.

Henry B. Stone (1416), fourth son of Henry Stone (1324), was born in Scituate, Rhode Island, in which State he spent the earlier years of his married life. He subsequently went to Philadelphia, and, for years, was Conductor on the horse cars, and died in 1864. The corporation and their employees unitedly attended his funeral.

Charles G. Stone (1417), the youngest son and youngest child of Deacon Henry Stone, was born in Scituate, but removed, in his early married life, to Providence, where he has spent most of his life. He married Miss Sophia P. Sprague, a worthy woman and good mother. They now live in Barrington, Rhode Island, and the family are reputable and respected. Their oldest daughter, Susan M. Stone (1501) married Eugene D. Burt, a young man of good business talent and education. He is Clerk, Paymaster and one of the Proprietors, of the Builders' Iron Foundry, in Providence, and his position in life promises well for the future. Martha S. Stone (1504) married Charles Tillinghast, who is in business in the city. The two younger sons are at home with the parents.

NOTE 192.

Abigail Stone (1325), third daughter of Jeremiah Stone (1051), married John Whipple, of Scituate, where she spent her whole married life, and there reared a family of seven children. She was warm hearted and genial, and died, in middle age, much beloved. Her family maintained a high

standing, for intelligence and moral worth. Richard Howard, the husband of her oldest daughter, Polly Whipple (1526), has been State Senator; and Rev. Gardner Howard is the husband of Selinda Whipple.(1529). The family, in its several branches, reside in Scituate and Foster, Rhode Island.

Mercy Stone (1326) married George Knight, of Scituate, and there lived and reared a family of three sons and three daughters. They are all reputable and in comfortable circumstances. Daniel Knight is a Baptist preacher, and lives in Exeter, Rhode Island ; and none of the family, we believe, have left the State.

Dinah Stone (1327), the youngest daughter of Jeremiah Stone, married Silas Weaver, and divided her married life between the States of New York and Rhode Island. This family are active, energetic, and somewhat marked for versatile talent. Owen Weaver (1538) lived in Providence, an industrious, worthy man. James P. (1539) lives in New London, Conn.

Charles Stone Weaver (1540) became a professing Christian, in early life, and soon devoted himself to the work of the ministry. His early opportunities for acquiring an education were somewhat limited, but close application and an enquiring mind have supplied the deficiency, and his earnestness and faithful devotion to duty number him among the most useful and efficient in his denomination. He is a Baptist by inheritance. Very few of the six hundred descendants of Jeremiah Stone ever thought of any other mode of Baptism but immersion, and very few families can number as many devout God-fearing, God-loving, people, in proportion to the whole number, as this. Charles S. Weaver (1540) married Miss Dianna Northup, a woman genial and very domestic. They have a large family of children, as we learn, intelligent, active and of fine promise. His labors in the ministry were, for many years, in Voluntown, Connecticut. He is now settled at Noank, in the same State.

Sallie C. Weaver (1541) married Joseph L. Bennett. They reside in Hartford, Connecticut. The husband is Superintendent, the wife, Matron, of the " Hartford Home " for destitute boys. Sallie C. (1541) is a woman of fine social powers, genial and intelligent. The husband is Deacon of the Baptist Church ; social, brilliant, of ready conversational powers ; a man much esteemed wherever he has lived. Nehemiah K. Weaver (1542) lives in North Swanzey,—is Deacon of the Baptist Church, in that place. Celia Weaver (1543) married Thomas D. Bentley. He is a manufacturer, and resides in New Hartford, Connecticut. Alston Weaver (1544) resided in the same place, and was killed in the cloth room of the manufactory, in September, 1865. Silas G. Weaver (1545) is a Druggist, and lives in Dundaff, Pennsylvania. Sterry A. Weaver (1546) was a Physician in Providence, Rhode Island, and died, of a consumption, 1857. Harriet R. Weaver (1546a) married Enoch Cox, is a tinplate worker, and lives in Sturbridge, Massachusetts. The wife died in 1848. The children of Dinah Stone (1327) were all professors of religion.

NOTE 193.

James Stone (1052) was the youngest son of William Stone (658), and was born in Mashantatack, Cranston, where he married Rebecca Sheldon, and soon after removed to Coventry, in the neighborhood of his three older brothers, who had settled in that then comparatively new country. He was an industrious, virtuous man of moderate abilities, and moderate expectations. His farm was poor, light, easy land. It supported him and his, in moderate competence; but, with his large family, they eat as fast as it grew, and the prospect was small for cutting up this farm of 150 acres into nine parts. " So," Robert said, " one-ninth, sixteen acres ! No, that will never do !" And he set his face for the West,—for Pensylvania. And John said no ! and Samuel said no !—all, but James (1553) and two young sisters, said no ! Away, six of the children of James Stone (1052), went, and founded a new colony, the town of Abington, Luzerne County, Pennsylvania. The worthy descendants of a worthy man. They carried with them the stern principles of virtue, in which they had been bred, and the colony grew and flourished like the Israelites in Canaan, and eleven pages of this work now number but a part of those who have grown up from this Rhode Island Puritanic Stock. Some twenty years from the emigration of his first son, Asenath Stone (1555), a lovely girl of fifteen, died. Soon after this, the father sold out, and, with James (1553), his youngest son, and Rebecca (1554), his youngest daughter, removed to the same place to which his children had emigrated, years before. Here he spent the closing years of his life, and died respected, in good old age.

NOTE 194.

Robert Stone (1547) removed from Coventry, Rhode Island. to Abington, Pensylvania, in his early married life. He found a heavy timbered forest, and, in the expressive language of the West, " pitched in." He learned a tailor's trade, in New England, but facts subsequently proved that he could " cut trees " as well as " cut coats." Four of these industrious young men, Robert, John, Lemuel and Samuel, (page 74) went, by marked trees, into the Pennsylvania woods, when, lo ! it blossomed like the rose ! Thirty years afterward, Robert (1547) has a finely cultivated farm, large orchard, and a well finished house, on one of the finest elevations in the Susquehannah Valley ; and, with pride and thankfulness, sees some hundred or more relatives, not squatters in the woods, but farmers, with large, cultivated, well fenced farms, that have all grown up under his own eye. He was, for years, a tax collector, and always carried his shears with him,—killing " two birds with one Stone,"—collecting taxes and cutting coats and pants. In stature, Robert Stone (1547) was below the middle size, active, quick ; a man of great energy and order. Everything was in its place. In disposition, he was ardent, but genial, pleasant and sportive even, and his society was always sought with interest. He married Sybil Dean, a woman physically

the reverse of her husband. It is said, husbands and wives admire in their partners, traits of character opposite to their own. Perhaps this applies to physical form ; it may be so, in this case. They certainly lived very happily. He, dwelling with satisfaction, on the noble, fat, fair and well proportioned form of his wife,—weighing nearly two hundred pounds;—and she, with equal satisfaction, on the lively, dapper, nervously active form of her husband. In one thing they were alike. They both smiled all over their faces, and you felt, in their presence, the glow of a warm, sunny heart as well as a smiling face.

NOTE 195.

James Stone (1557) was the oldest son of Robert Stone (1547), and married Sarah Stone. (See Note on last page.) He was an active and energetic man, and raised an intelligent family. Statistics, page 74.

From Almond Stone (1566), (he spells his name Almon,) the writer has received the following letter: "There is no family, in this section of the country, as numerous as the " Stone Family," that presents so little diversity of character. From the old Patriarch, James Stone, whose sons were among the first that settled in Abington, down to the latest generation, we find them an industrious, pious and devoted class ; but little inclined to travel, or seek a fortune in any new enterprise, or untried business. They are mostly farmers, owning the land they till, and living within their means ; possessing enough of this world's goods to render them independent and happy. They possess rather an even temperament and are very conscientious. At the Communion of the First Baptist Church, in Abington, the " Stones " far exceed any other family. Fathers, sons and grandsons holding sweet communing with their Maker. The families are rare that can boast of such purity of morals, and freedom from all the leading vices." Of Almon, another correspondent thus speaks: " I would mention Almon Stone, a worthy, enterprising, pious young man, and first-class scientific farmer."

Foster Stone (1565) is in business in a wholesale store, in the city of New York.

Columbus Stone (1564) studied law, and died when twenty years of age.

NOTE 196.

"John Stone (1548), with his wife, Rhoda Barney, and one child, came from Rhode Island to Pennsylvania about the year 1803. The country, then so little cleared, they were obliged to leave their wagon ten miles from their destination, and proceed on horseback, by marked trees, to their home in the forest.

They commenced life poor; but, by steady perseverance and industry, succeeded in clearing and bringing into a high state of cultivation, a large farm, and raised a large family of children, who, without a single exception, occupied respectable positions in life. He was a man of little education, of

mild and social disposition, thoughtful and sedate, yielding; strictly honest, believing others equally so, until he found, sometimes to his cost, the reverse. Rhoda, his wife, had much energy and decision of character, with a disposition hasty and impetuous, and a strong tenacity of opinion, but with a kind heart and genial, sportive manner, that made her many friends. Both were professors of religion, members of the Baptist Church, and enjoyed the reputation of highly respectable Christian people, with the confidence of their acquaintance. He died in 1841." ·

Note 197.

Rhoda Stone (1578) married H. W. Nicholson, who, in the language of another, "was a lawyer of eminence, a man of influence and wealth, a member of the Presbyterian Church." Since his death, Rhoda (1578) has married Rev. L. Jones, a preacher in the Methodist Connexion. Another extract says, "The 'Stone Family' were among the first settlers of this part of the country ; consequently, had not the facilities for acquiring an education which the present generation enjoy. Most of the name and connexion are Baptists ; some are Methodists, some are Presbyterians; some occupy positions of influence, a majority are above mediocrity."

Note 198.

John Stone (1577), the youngest son of John (1548), was born in Abington, then comparatively a new country. Like all newly settled communities, little interest was felt in schools, mainly because clearing and fencing were absolutely more needed than Geography, Grammar and Mercantile Science. Schools were thought of *then*, teachers were engaged, and most of the children learned to "read, write and cypher ;" but that was considered all to which an Abington boy had any right to aspire. John was sent to school, in the winter season, when he could be spared, but, liking his sports better than his books, made but little proficiency in learning. He was not lazy, he was quick, active, but disliking work or study ; not a thinker, but an observer and early showed a partiality for trading in stock, horses and cattle, with unusual success for one of his years. His father had been induced to enter into trade, relying entirely on the ability and honesty of his partner for success. The result was a failure, and there seemed no alternative but the sale of the home farm, to meet the liabilities. John (1577), hitherto rather a thoughtless boy, now working and now trading, more for gratification, than for the thought of an earnest life, was aroused. His brothers were on farms given by the father, for themselves, and he saw at once a crisis was before him. Something must be done, or the whole family, his aged father, his sisters and himself, would all be "flat." It aroused him. It was just the thing needed. How often our greatest misfortunes are our greatest blessings. The failure of the father *made* the son ! But for this

crisis, he might have dreamed on, in sluggish competence, through life; but it aroused the decision and energy inherited from his mother, and he went to work with a will. In a comparatively short time, the debts were all paid and the " home " saved. These few years of real life developed his capacity for trading, though he would have rejoiced if he could have improved some of those months of study, in his early life, which he mainly threw away. In 1840, he first engaged in mercantile business, and, in 1841, the year his father died, bought the homestead. He had, however, but little taste for farming, and soon resumed his store trade, which he successfully pursued almost twenty years. In the year 1861, his health, became impaired, which he has not fully regained, and he sold out his business and retired from active life.

John Stone (1577) is a man still in middle life ; genial, mild, temperate in all things, cool, persevering and in affluent circumstances. In 1841, he married Miss Esther L. Sisson, daughter of Rodman Sisson, granddaughter of George Sisson, formerly of Exeter, Rhode Island, a woman of superior mind, cultivated, refined, more by native intuition, the influence of society, and the reflections of a vigorous intellect, than by early educational culture. Her letters bear the impress of scholarship, as well as earnest thought and clear analysis, and the writer is happy to bear testimony to valuable aid, which she has rendered to her family, in this work. They have no children, but have brought up three ; two orphan children of a brother and sister, Almira L. Stone (1715) and Benjamin M. Greene (1724); the third, an orphan daughter of a deceased friend. John Stone (1577) has received repeated testimonials of respect from the people of his county. He has, many years, been Postmaster, and, in 1860, was Representative in the State Legislature. He still lives in his native village, has never travelled extensively, is strongly attached to home and the interests of his native place. Himself and wife are both members of the Baptist Church, and interested in the various benevolent objects of the day.

Note 199.

Riley Stone (1572), oldest son of John (1548), lives in Abington, a worthy, industrious man. His family are mostly dead. Barney Stone (1704) died in Syracuse, New York, in 1860, and left three little girls. Esther E. Stone (1705), and her husband, died, 1853. Mary Ann Stone (1706) died in 1861. Mortimer Stone (1707), when last heard from, was Drum Major in the army, in Kentucky. Jeremiah Stone (1574) is a farmer, and much respected. He has been twice married ; first, to Louisa Greene ; second, to Laura Rice. George Perry, husband of Emily A. Stone (1716), and George Stone Nicholson (1729), and Thomas Kennedy, husband of Hortense B. Greene (1726), all enlisted, in September, 1862, in Company B, Regiment 143, Pennsylvania Volunteers. Nicholson was wounded, in the Battle of Gettysburg, and was discharged. Perry was Sergeant, was in

fifteen battles, served till the close of war, and was honorably discharged. Kennedy was sick a year, in the hospital, and served till the Rebellion was crushed.

Benjamin M. Greene (1724), mentioned in Note 198, served three years, in the Commissary Department. Andrew J. Smith, husband of Josephine A. Greene (1725), served three years, in Company H, Pennsylvania Cavalry, as Second Lieutenant.

NOTE 200.

Mary Stone (1549), the oldest daughter of James Stone (1052), married Stephen Parker, and moved, when they had but two children, to the forests of Pennsylvania. The husband was just fitted for the place, and the place for him. Were there trees to fell? he could do it. Land to clear? he could do it. Wheat to raise? he could do it. Log house to build? he could do it. He was equal to any emergency in a new country; never discouraged, never tired. But, with all his human steam power and iron will, he wore out and finally died. Stephen Parker and wife were a hard-working, worthy couple, amassed a handsome estate; were induced to enter coal and other speculations, lost it all and died poor! Too bad!!! They reared a family of industrious and virtuous sons and daughters, who are beloved and respected. Charles Parker (1583) is a Baptist preacher.

NOTE 201.

Lemuel Stone (1550), son of James Stone (1052), removed to Pennsylvania, in early married life, and, for that age of America, and the means given, has made life, in its various relations, a happy success. He reared a large family of worthy, intelligent children; eight or nine lived to marry. He was a carpenter and farmer, and became affluent; for the country, wealthy. He was the first Justice of the Peace appointed upon the incorporation of the town of Abington, and transacted a large amount of business through life. He was the first Sabbath School Superintendent in the town of Abington. He was the first man who did his haying and harvesting, without whiskey, in the town of Abington. In fact, he led off, in Abington, in every good word and work. He married Anna Colvin, of Coventry, Rhode Island, in 1803, who was the mother of all his children. She was a good wife and excellent woman. Lemuel Stone (1550) was a man of even temper, a firm friend, of excellent judgment, conscientious and just. His farm, his shop,—everything around,—showed a large development of order. Himself and wife were both, many years, exemplary Christians, and members of the Baptist Church.

NOTE 202.

Philip Stone (1590), oldest son of Lemuel (1550), married Sarah Northup. They had two children; both are dead. Their oldest, Emanuel

23

(1598) married and left two children. Statistics, page 76. Meriam Stone (1591) was a woman of lively temperament, genial, social. She married Reuben Sherman. Statistics, page 74. Pardon Stone (1592) lived in Abington ; his son, George L. Stone (1606), served three years in the Cavalry, and was honorably discharged. Edwin Stone (1593) lived in Abington, and is a worthy, industrious man. His son, Thomas W. Stone (1628), enlisted in Company 11, Pennsylvania Volunteers ; was in the Battle of Mechanicsville, and again, at Gaines' Hill, where he was wounded, June 27th, 1862.

Hannah Stone (1194), third daughter of Lemuel (1550), is a woman of superior mind and attainments, for her opportunities. Her husband, Leonard Batchelder, is a native of Massachusetts, and graduate, we believe, of one of the Eastern Colleges ; a man of marked versatile ability, and a highly esteemed citizen. They reside on a part of the homestead of Lemuel (1550), and in the house built by the father. Statistics, on page 77. Anson J. Stone (1596) married Rachel Stevens. Statistics, page 77. Louisa L. Stone (1597) married Joseph Chase. She was a worthy woman, and died, much lamented, but a few years after their marriage, leaving one child.

Note 203.

Lora W. Stone (1395) was the son of Lemuel (1550), and has, in all the relations of life, sustained the character of a worthy citizen and reliable man. Not subject to impulsive emotion, and yet possessing energy and perseverance, he has made himself acquainted with the principles of Agricultural Science. These principles, with a wise, judicious application, he reduces to practice, and his farm bears testimony to his success His abilities and worth are appreciated. He has been elected Captain of Pennsylvania Militia, and has held almost all the offices in the gift of the town where he lives, and of the church to which he belongs. He has been severely tried, in his domestic relations ; has followed to the grave two excellent wives, and four children. He is now living with his third wife, and has but two surviving children. S'atistics, page 77,

Note 204.

Samuel Stone (1551), son of James (1052), left Coventry, Rhode Island, in the early years of his life, and, with his brothers, went to Abington, Pennsylvania. He there married twice ; first to Susannah Hall ; and second, to Prudence Colvin. By these two connexions, he had twelve children ; ten of whom reached maturity and married.' In him, is seen a very full development of the race ; especially in that unaspiring quietude, which, unwilling to descend, never envies those who climb. Men who, whenever the door bell rings, are always found at home. Samuel (1551) and his posterity are included under the general description given in several letters from Abing-

ton, of this character. "Among all the 'Stone' families, there is not, and has not been, a drunkard,—not a criminal." It speaks well for the race, and better for the pioneers; for Old James (1052), and his five sons and three daughters, who have almost peopled that part of Luzerne County, with probably not less than six hundred descendants. Heavenly life, in children, is no accident, but the fruits of earnest, noble efforts of parents, blest by the Divine Mind. Among the sons of Samuel (1551), is found Hugh Stone (1641). He is the sixth generation from Hugh Stone (1), and the only descendant who bears his name. Mary Elizabeth Stone (1642b) married Amos B. Gorman, a grandson of Dr. Lyman Beecher, of Litchfield, Connecticut. He died, 1858. Sally Ann Stone (1638) married T. R. Purdy, and lives in Fond du Lac, Wisconsin.

Celinda Stone (1552) married Samson Wright, and removed to Abington, in their early married life. He was a blacksmith, but somewhat failed of success. He died about 1825, leaving a widow, six children, and a farm covered all over with debts. This position called the widow into life. Like a mariner on the ocean, she took an observation, " tacked ship," and steered for the haven of Success. She reached it in safety. The farm was paid for, the children well brought up ; every one lived, every one married respectably. We hope their names are recorded in heaven. Rebecca Stone (1554) removed, with her father, to Pennsylvania, where she married Samuel Clarke. Of her children, the writer has not learned.

NOTE 205.

James Stone (1553), the youngest son of James (1052), was born in Coventry, and lived with his father, on the "old homestead," until they sold and removed to Abington, in the neighborhood of his brothers. He was not a man of strong mind, but combined almost all the moral qualities, which go to make up the good man and Christian citizen. He was twice married ; first, to Miss Polona Greene, of Coventry, Rhode Island, a worthy, energetic woman, by whom he had six children ; second, to Miss Catherine Ackley, by whom he had seven. Ten of these children lived to maturity and married ; two died in early manhood ; the youngest daughter is, we believe, unmarried. They are all active and industrious. Nancy (1652) was rather a sober child, has ripened into a fine woman and excellent mother. She married John Miller, a man of industry and prudence, who "gathers up all the fragments that nothing is lost." Lemuel Stone (1650) has been twice married ; first, to Miss Eliza West, who died June 25th, 1855 ; and second, to Miss Susan C. Gaylord. Two of their children are married, and the whole family reside in Clinton Township, Wayne County, Pennsylvania. Five are members of the Baptist, and two of the Methodist, Churches.

Emory E. Stone (1654) is an unusually active and enterprising man. He is largely engaged in tanning and currying, the trade of Jonathan, and William, and Jeremiah and James, we believe,—four generations back. Busi-

ness, in that line, has somewhat changed, however; changed from the time
when Old Jonathan, son of John (4), took the green hides of his neighbors,
in old Mashantatack, and dressed them at the halves! Emory's is not such
an establishment. The old adage is true of the Stones; "Times have
changed and they have changed with them." He was formerly in Wayne
County; but, about two years since, purchased in Abington, where he is now
doing a very extensive business. Nor is the race, so far, as he is concerned,
about to die out. He maried an estimable woman, Miss Catharine S. Hudson. They already have five sons and four daughters; the oldest eighteen,
the youngest one year; all living and healthy. The statistics of the families
mentioned in Note 205 are on pages 78, 79, 80, 83 and 84.

NOTE 206.

Jonathan Stone (661) was the oldest son of John Stone (4), by the second
marriage with Abigail Foster, and lived a portion, perhaps his whole life, in
Mashantatack. The well called "Jonty's well," is only a short distance
Southwest of the Old Meeting House Lot. "Jonty's house," which stood
near the well, is taken down, and the field called "Jonty's Orchard" is
known now by that designation, though the apple trees disappeared before
the remembrance of the present generation. Various deeds, some of gift
and some of consideration, passed from John (4) to Jonathan, his son. He
was a tanner and currier, and his tanyard was on the opposite side of the road
from his house and well. Of his children, we learn but little, with certainty.
The strong probability is that John Stone (1684) and Abigail Stone (1685)
were the children of Jonathan Stone. The reasons are: Benjamin Stone
(663) had no children. Joseph Stone (664) had but one child, a daughter.
The families of the elder brothers, John (656), George (657) and William
(658) are all traced, with their several branches. Nor could John (1684)
and Abigail (1685) have sprung from Hugh. No male descendant can be
traced at all, farther than Thomas (9) and Oliver (10). Nor can they be
traced to Peter (3), as not a John is found from 1704 to 1772, in this branch.
Sixty-eight years, and no name of John, and not one Abigail in the Peter
(3) branch at all. Besides, we have the descendants of Peter (3), in all
their various branches. But those names, John and Abigail, would be likely
to be found, if they were the-children of Jonathan, as his father was John
and his mother, Abigail. Again: Jonathan's wife was Hannah Westcott,—
not Elizabeth Westcott, as in the Statistics,—and John (1684) named
his second daughter, Hannah. See page 80. Moreover, a granddaughter of John (1684) informed the writer she was sure she had
heard her mother say that *her* grandfather was named Jonathan John
(1684) moved from Cranston to Coventry about the time of his marriage,
in 1766, and died when twenty-five years old, leaving three children. He
was buried on the farm which he owned, and whereon he lived. His widow.

Phebe (Daily) Stone, married William King, and lived, for more than forty years, on the same farm. The statistics on page 80.

NOTE 207.

Joseph Stone (664) was the youngest son of John Stone (4), and was born, and lived, and died, and was buried, on the farm which his father bought of John King, in Mashantatack, in 1712. He was married to Anna Kent, a few years before the death of his father, and moved her home ; the father then living at the "Lawrence Farm," where Hugh Stone (1) passed the closing years of his life. In 1779, the farm on which is the " Old Stone Burying Ground," passed into the hands,—was bought by Dr. Aldrich. After this, Joseph (664), and probably those of his brothers and sisters still living near, commenced a new cemetery, on his own land, Northwest of the house, where he and his immediate relations, and those of his son-in-law, the Salisburys and Martins, were buried. The Peter Branch still continuing to use the " Old Stone Burying Ground." The commencement of one cemetery, about 1724 ; the other, 1790. Joseph Stone (664) was a man much respected for virtue and piety ; was Deacon, for many years, of the Baptist Church, worshipping in the " Old Meeting House," located but a few rods west of his dwelling, and was known, in and out of Cucumber Town, as " Deacon Joe." He died aged nearly eighty.

Abigail Stone (1689) was only child of Deacon Joe, and was somewhat lame through life. She married Nathan Salisbury, by whom she had ten children, born between the years 1771 and 1796. Statistics, page 80.

NOTE 208.

Rebecca Stone (36a), mentioned in Note 15, was daughter of Peter Stone (18), and married David Patt, of Scituate. They reared a large family. Statistics, page 84. Anthony B. Patt (1784) was a worthy man, industrious and honest. He married an excellent woman, Miss Cynthia Carpenter, who died during the first year of their marriage, much beloved and lamented.

William N. Patt (1786), youngest son of Rebecca (36a), is married to Britannia Baxter, a very worthy lady. He is a preacher in the Free Baptist Connexion; by trade, a Builder and Architect, and a man of high moral and religious standing. He has been Pastor of churches in Scituate and Cranston ; was one of the Founders of the Smithville Seminary ; the first Signer of the Temperance Pledge, in the town of Scituate ; was Delegate to the First Anti-Slavery Convention in Rhode Island, and aided in forming the first State Society. He now resides in Providence.

ERRATA.

Page 15— 296. Lyman Aldrich.

" 35— 656. Hannah Olney.

" 35— 661. Hannah Westcott.

" 48— 986. Elisha Cornell Esten.

" 68—1405. M. Carpenter.

" 72—1511. Allen T. Chilson.

" 81—1574. Louisa Greene.

Note 99. Stephen P. Henry, not Stephen G. Henry.

" 166. Ichabod Bowen, not Joseph Bowen.

DATES CORRECTED.

Page 6.—107. 1821, not 1814.

" 6. Balance of Paris Parker's family not known.

" 23.—438. 1810.

" 23.—439. 1812.

" 23.—440. 1815.

" 35. Hugh (2) 1669.

" 35. Abigail, 1667.

INDEX.

185

Esther, 918	Freelove, 822	Henry, 45
Emma Jane, 925	Freelove, 969	Henry A. 58
Ellen M. 952 121	Freelove, 1049	Horace, 63
Ezra, 970	Fanny, 1024 146	Harriet N. 82
Ezra, 977 142	Frederick, 1037	Helen, 101
Emeline, 1020 146	Frederick L. 1135	Hannah A. 115
Emily A. 1025 146	Frederick W. 1199	Harriet, 125
Ellen F. 1044	Frank, 1200	Henry, 138
Emeline A. p. 51	Freelove M. 1253 169	Henry, 150
Eliza, 1066 151	Flora, 1298	Henry J. M. 165
Ethan A. 1068 150	Freelove, 1321	Henrietta, 225
Eliza C. 1088	Frederick W. 1378	Horace Whipple, 289
Esther A. 1140	Frederick C. 1386	Hiram, 383
Emogene, 1149	Fernando C. 1462	Henry W. 428
Emery A. 1158	Frank F. 1507	Harrie Winthrop, 460
Emery D. 1159	Foster, 1565 195	Henry, 550 95
Emery C. V. 1177	Frank L. 1570	Harriet B. 636
Earl, 1206	Fannie M. 1624	Henry J. 688
Eva L. 1211	Frank Hudson, 1670	Henry, 707
Ella E. 1212	Florence, 1719	Henry C. 722
Earl M. 1226	Florilla E. 1776	Harriet E. 728
Ellen M. 1232	Fannie, 1801	Harriet Angeline, 782
Edward L. 1237 164	G.	Henry Arnold, 794
Eleanor, 1241	George, 6	Hannah, 812 134
Edwin K. 1255	George Albert, 85	Hamilton B. 869
Elizabeth W. 1259	George H. 120	Hannah E. 913 138
Emeline, 1283	George, 143	Hannah, 960 140
Edwin, 1301	George W. 163 33	Hiram, 968
Elias S. 1312	Gilbert W. 174 39	Harley, 979
Edgar A. 1376	George, 206	Henry, 990
Elizabeth A. 1377 179	George B. 443 83	Hallina, 1051
Eliza Jane, 1380	George Lewis, 455	Hiram L. 1116
Emily A. 1383	George, 482 90	Henry C. 1129
Ellen, 1409	George, 497 90	Helen G. 1134
Emily, 1421 186	George, 508	Harris H. 1192
Esther Read, 1430	George, 520	Henry Harris, 1202 92
Edwin D. 1502	George, 533	Hannah M. 1258
Emily, 1447	George K. 546 96	Harriet H. 1250
Ezra, 1560	George, 573	Henry C. 1261
Edwin, 1593	George, 657 131	Harrie, 1300
Emanuel, 1598 202	George N. 701	Hannah, 1323 184
Edwin N. 1632	George N. 714 117	Henry, 1324 185
Eddie E. 1619	George A. 718 121	Horatio A. 1317 179
Emery E. 1654 205	George Orlando, 726	Harriet P. 1351 178
Eleazer, 1660	George W. 744	Henry H. 1379
Eva Augusta, 1673	Godfrey G. 761 126	Herbert P. 1384
Esther E. 1705 199	George, 819	Henry B. 1416 191
Emily A. 1716 199	George, 828 133	Henry B. 1506
Ellen, 1769	George, 844 135	Hannibal, 1563
Elbert B. 1771	Georgianna F. 851	Harriet, 1589 a
Edward Eddy, 619	George M. 856	Hannah, 1594 202
Eliza, 1806	George, 862	Hattie, 1620
Elmer Franklin, 400	George, 1021 146	Henry L. 1631
F.	George, 1087	Harrison, 1640
Freelove, 30	George W. 1145	Hugh, 1611 204
Freelove, 53	George Alban, 1353	Henry S. 1677
Fanny E. 201	George Alban, 1358	Hattie Foster, 1678
Frank Pierce, 219	George, 1405 186	Hannah, 1688 206
Frank M. 229	George L. 1606 202	Hannah, 1753
Fannie H. 288	George A. 1626	Horace N. 1760
Frederick II 364	Gilbert, 1642	Henry, p. 88
Frank Charlton, 457	George W. 1773 83	I.
Frank Burrill, 473	H.	Isaac, 76 30
Frank Pierce, · 536	Hugh, 1 1	Ida, 90
Frank G. 562	Hugh, 2 2	Isabel, 126
Frederick A. 735	Hugh, 8 8	Israel, 488 93
Francis, 777	Hopkins, 34 17	Inez Alma, 470

24

Index (reading in column order):

Name	No.
Ida J.	601
Isaac,	516
Irving,	916
Ira B.	1067
Ira B.	1086
Isabella A.	1132
Isham G.	1213
Isabella,	1247
Isadore,	1720
Isaac,	1313
Ida A.	1617

J.

Name	No.
John,	4
John,	16
John,	31
Josiah,	49
John II.	50 b
John,	59
Joseph,	62
Julana J.	87
Jesse,	88
James R.	103
John,	144
Joseph,	146
John,	177
Jeremiah,	183
Jerome,	192
Josephine,	199
Joseph,	215
John W.	259
James,	327
Jared,	357
Julia A.	365
James L.	441
John R.	484
James,	486
Jeremiah,	488
Joshua,	496
Jonathan,	498
James,	511
James,	535
John II.	554
John Emery,	565
Joseph R.	595
Jason,	617
James,	626
John,	656
Joseph,	661
Jonathan,	661
John,	668
Joseph Nelson,	687
James,	704
John R.	795
Jacob,	714 a
Julia A.	725
James Allen,	736
John,	700
Julia Frances,	779
John Abbott,	783
James Edwin,	812
John,	817
Jane,	818
James,	820
John,	821
Joseph,	831
John,	834
James,	837

Ref	Name	No.
	Joseph W.	850
	James,	922
	John,	923
150	Julia Ann,	931
	James,	959
	Jane M.	1045
	John G.	1017
167	Jabez,	1050
	Jeremiah,	1051
	James,	1052
	John T.	1099
	Julia S.	1120
110	James,	1143
8	Josephine,	1148
13	John M.	1169
	Jacob W.	1176
	Julia E.	1181
	John M.	1183
	John Enos,	1223
	Joseph,	1242
	Jabez,	1243
	Jabez T.	1252
	Jabez,	1268
	James W.	1272
	James A.	1286
	Julia A.	1315
41	Jeremiah,	1328
	Jason P.	1342
	Jason P.	1348
	James B.	1352
61	James Burrill,	1344
	Jason P.	1382
	Julia,	1418
81	Job M.	1435
	Jane,	1493
91	John,	1548
	James,	1553
94	James,	1557
	Jeremiah,	1574
	John,	1577
	John L.	1618
	Joseph C.	1612 d
	John,	1681
107	Joseph,	1749
104	John C.	1764
	James A.	1762
111	Julia Kezia,	1770
207	Jasper N.	1774
206	John,	
123		

K.

Ref	Name	No.
	Kate Olivia,	797
11	Knight,	1329
120	Knight,	1407
	Knight,	1437

L.

Ref	Name	No.
	Lydia,	33
127	Laura,	50
	Louisa,	72
	Lyman,	78
	Louisa,	83
	Lucy,	123
	Lucy Jane,	127
133	Lucy Ann,	129
133	Lorenzo,	188
134	Lucy Frances,	205
138	Laura M.	208
	Leander,	213

Ref	Name	No.	No. 2
135	Lawton Belmont,	220 u	
139	Lucy C.	239	47
	Lydia Ann,	310	
121	Lucy B.	315	
	Lydia,	343	69
	Lucinda,	351	
	Lydia A.	355	
166	Lucy,	380	
174	Lyman B.	398	
193	Lillian Lincoln,	479	
153	Louisa,	513	
	Lyman B.	515	92
	Lucy M.	530	
	Laura,	620	104
	Lydia,	630	
	Lonisa,	635	
	Lydia,	665	112
	Lydia,	667	
165	Lewis,	681	114
166	Lydia H.	686	
169	Lizzie,	690	
	Lottie M.	692	
170	Lucy,	706	117
	Laura E.	737	
	Louisa A.	739	
	Lydia A.	742	
	Lucy Ann,	917	
183	Lucy,	962	
180	Lois,	966	141
	Lizzie H.	1038	
177	Louis N.	p. 51	
	Lydia,	1055	160
186	Lucy.	1062	155
	Laura,	1082	
	Leonard R.	1091	153
196	Lucy A. M.	1118	
205	Laura M.	1142	
195	Lucy A.	1155	
199	Lucy,	1167	
198	Lyman H.	1180	
	Lucinda,	1191	157
	Lydia,	1221	162
206	Lowry,	1224	163
	Lovicie,	1225	
	Lucetta A.	1234	163
	Lorenzo D.	1254	
	Lucinda,	1281	
	Lillian Adams,	1302	
86	Lovice D.	1389	
	Lydia,	1434	
	Lydia F.	1505	
	Lemuel,	1550	201
	Lora,	1561	
18	Lora W.	1595	203
189	Lovisa L.	1597	202
	Lydia A	1610	
	Lavina T.	1642 a	
26	Lemuel,	1650	205
32	Lydia,	1754	
	Lotta,	1761	
	Lester S.	1778	

M.

Ref	Name	No.	No. 2
	Mary,	22	
44	Mahetabel,	28	
	Mary,	36	15
	Maria,	73	27
	Mary,	113	20

Name	No.
Melissa A. F.	160
Mary A.	117
Maria,	139
Mercy M.	166
Mary Ann,	172
Mary,	191
Maria,	212
Mary,	214
Mary H.	244
Mary E.	253
Mary E.	312
Martha B.	316
Mary,	329
Mercy,	338
Mercy G.	352
Maria,	378
Minnie M.	387
Mercy,	433
Martha,	435
Martha,	417
Mary,	418
Mabel,	456
Mary,	461
Mary,	490
Mary,	514
Mary Frances,	522
Mary Ann W.	531
Mary,	590
Maria,	647
Maria,	685
Mary,	696
Mary,	710
Maria,	762
Maria Louisa,	781
Maria,	793 a
Maria H.	811
Mary,	826
Martha,	827
Mary,	836
Mary C.	852
Mary J.	859
Martha A.	860
Marvin,	904
Maria M.	910
Mary,	911
Malissa C.	930
Marcus F.	952
Mercy,	1004
Mariella,	1022
Maria,	1027
Marcus M.	1013
Mahala,	1096
Mary E.	1100
Mary A.	1141
Mary E.	1184
Mason P.	1228
Maria,	1257
Mary,	1271
Massina,	1299
Mercy,	1326
Minerva,	1345
Melissa C.	1349
Mary Melissa,	1360
Minerva,	1387
Melina,	1414
Melissa,	1446
Mary E.	1458

Pref	Name	No.
33	Mary,	1493
	Martha S.	1594
	Mary,	1549
	Meriam,	1591
34	Mary L.	1630
	Mary,	1637
	Mary Elizabeth,	1612 b
	Merit,	1649
	Milo,	1659
	Melissa,	1661
	Margaret Gertrude,	1671
	Mary Inez,	1672
58	Milton Willis,	1680
61	Myron H.	1681
	Mary Ann,	1706
	Mortimer,	1707
	Melbourne,	1717
	Malviner,	1750
76	Melissa R.	1708
87	Mary Melissa,	1772
88	Martin M.	1780
	Mary Wilbour,	1867
	Maria,	1808
94	Martha,	p. 86

N.

Pref	Name	No.
	Nancy,	52
	Nehemiah,	70
	Nellie,	98
	Nathan T.	118
	Nathaniel,	325
	Nathaniel,	340
117	Nancy,	461
	Nathan,	618
	Noadiah,	808
	Nathan,	963
129	Nancy,	1003
	Nancy W.	1065
	Nancy,	1085
	Norman E.	1130
	Norman C.	1182
	Nelson P.	1296
	Nehemiah,	1337
137	Nathan K.	1338
	Noel.	1460
	Nicholas,	1464
121	Nancy,	1652

O.

Pref	Name	No.
	Oliver,	10
	Otis,	184
	Otis,	217
	Orin,	261
	Orville E.	564
	Olissa,	632
	Oliver,	667
	Olney,	668 a
	Oliver,	683
	Olney R.	759
	Oziel,	825
	Otis E.	900
192	Otis P.	914
178	Olive,	964
178	Oscar F.	1110
	Orren,	1428
	Orilla,	1436
190	Oscar Hudson,	1676
	Oliver,	1686
	Orson,	1751

P.

Pref	Name	No.	No.
191	Peter,	3	3
200	Peter.	12	6
202	Peter,	18	9
	Prissilah,	15	7
	Patience,	20	
204	Patience,	13	
	Phebe,	21	
	Peter,	25	10
	Peter,	42	
	Peter,	45 a	
	Polly,	45 b	
	Patience,	46 d	
	Phila,	46 c	
	Peter,	48	
	Philip,	74	29
	Phebe Lavina,	121	
	Phebe,	176	38
	Phebe,	257	49
	Polly,	415	70
	Peleg A.	353	
	Phebe,	512	
	Prudence,	666	112
	Phebe,	668 c	111
	Polly,	672	
19	Phebe,	670	
25	Phebe,	678	
	Phebe,	757	
	Pardon M.	807	130
59	Phebe Ann,	806	129
66	Polly,	843	134
	Pardon F.	908	138
104	Phebe,	1000	
	Phebe E.	1010	
140	Pamelia B.	1110	
	Pamelia S.	1146	
150	Phebe,	1229	
	P. J.	1281	
	Phebe,	1340	
	Phebe,	1346	178
	Philip,	1590	202
	Pardon,	1592	202
	Polona G.	1759	

R.

Pref	Name	No.	No.
	Rebecca,	36 a	15
205	Raymond,	178	39
	Richmond J.	196	39
	Roby,	260	
41	Rilla,	284	
	Rebecca,	299	
	Rufus,	326	60
	Roxana,	381	74
	Randall H.	419	71
113	Richard	434	60
111	Richard C.	436	80
	Richard B.	446	86
126	Richard,	592	105
133	Robert,	596	106
139	Ritner W.	638	
	Robert Taylor,	640	
141	Rhoda,	668 b	
	Russell,	669	
	Robert,	676	
180	Rhoda,	698	
	Richmond,	703	
	Rhoda M.	711	117
	Richard G.	734	119

	Rest,	816			Sarah E.	912		138	Walter,	221
	Ruth,	833	137		Sarah,	919			Whipple,	263
	Rebecca B.	900	138		Susan,	921			Whipple,	282
	Roxanna,	965			Samuel,	961			Whipple,	283
	Ruth,	1056	160		Susan,	1005			Warren,	274
	Ruth,	1094	152		Stephen,	1023		146	William A.	298	17
	Rasselas,	1112			Sally,	1063			William H.	311
	Robert Earl,	1235	163		Susan A.	1080			William G.	338a
	Rachel K.	1391			Sheldon,	1090			William G.	342
	Rachel K.	1415	190		Susan R.	1095			William N.	358
	Rebecca Adams,	1359			Sallie,	1093			William G.	399
	Roby,	1413	190		Sidney T.	1109			Walter,	424
	Robert,	1517	191		Solon S.	1115			Winslow Cecil,	452
	Rebecca,	1554	201		Susan C.	1139			Warren,	453
	Robert M.	1569			Sarah E.	1141			Waldo Hodges,	454
	Riley,	1572			Susan R.	1195		157	William Loring,	471
	Rachel,	1572a			Susan A.	1231			William,	485
	Rebecca,	1573			Sarah,	1245		167	William,	518	96
	Rhoda,	1578	197		Stephen,	1248		172	William G.	553	95
	Rachel,	1579			Sarah,	1267			Walter A.	559
	Robert,	1639			Sphina,	1280			William Eugene,	570
	Robert,	1651			Sarah J.	1285			Walter W.	575	102
	Rensalaer,	1748			Stephen Dexter,	1292		171	William,	576
	Richard.	1813			Solomon,	1295			William,	628
	S.				Sarah V.	1311			William,	645
	Sarah,	13	7		Sarah Adams,	1356		177	William,	658	147
19	Samuel,	17	57		Sallie,	1421		186	Waity,	670
	Sophia,	43			Susan M. *1501*	~~1101~~		191	William,	674	115
	Sylvester,	44			Samuel,	1551		202	Waity,	695	116
	Sarah,	55			Sabra,	1575			William R.	699	118
	Sylvester C.	61	23		Sarah,	1608			William J.	715	117
	Susan P.	81			Silas L.	1609			William,	755	121
	Stephen,	114	20		Sterling B.	1623			William A.	764	127
	Sophronia,	115			S Lovisa,	1629			William,	780
	Sylvester C.	122	21		Sally Ann,	1638		204	William,	829
	Sylvester,	147			Samuel R.	1642c			William J.	851	136
	Susan,	153			Samuel,	1657			William,	956
	Sarah,	296	50		Sarah Elizabeth,	1810			William,	967	141
	Seneca,	170	14		Sarah D.	1765			William,	1048	148
	Sally Ann,	171			Stephen J.	1779			William,	1053	149
	Susan M.	226			**T.**				Westcott,	1051	150
	Seneca,	224			Thomas,	9	2		Welcome,	1059	150
	Samuel,	328	62		Thomas H. B.	162	33		William,	1064	167
	Samuel,	339	65		Thomas C.	179			Welcome,	1111
	Sally,	341	67		Thomas L.	197	39		William,	1117
	Samuel E.	354			Temperance,	258	49		Windfield S.	1147
	Samuel E.	369			Tyler Putnam,	809			William C.	1157
	Sidney S.	385			Thankful A.	1275			William H.	1179
	Sophia,	421			Thomas W.	1628	202		William A.	1186	158
	S. Hollis,	442	82		Theodore E.	1605			Walter Delmont,	1201
	Sarah,	444	81		**U.**				Westcott,	1209
	Sarah,	509			Urana,	719			Winfield C.	1210
	Sarah A. F.	519			**V.**				Wanton,	1251	169
	Sarah,	529			Violetta,	318			Waldo,	1406	187
	Sarah,	589			Vidella Jane,	730			Waldo,	1419	186
	Samuel,	597	108		Victor B.	1166			William,	1559
	Sarah,	627			Virginia,	198			Watson, D.	1607
	Samuel,	641	108		**W.**				William H	1655
	Simon,	697	117		Whipple,	32	161		Washburne,	1752
	Sarah,	709	117		Welcome,	35			Waldo,	1763
	Susan,	716			William,	46			William E.	1800
	Samuel A.	717			William,	51	18		William Edward,	1802
	Samuel H.	720	121		Waterman,	56	20		**Z.**	
	Sally,	756			William,	77	31		Zebulon,	499
	Stephen A.	758	125		William,	145			Zilpha,	668c
	Sally,	763	127		William Joy,	171	36		Zilpha P.	356	109
	Stephen M.	806a			William Henry,	194	41			
	Sarah J.	861			William,	216				

INDEX TO NAMES OF THOSE WHO MARRIED PERSONS NAMED STONE.

Whipple, John		64	Walker, Eric	68	West, Eliza	78
Wightman, David H.		64	Whitman, Albert	69	White, Elinda	79
Whitman, Ann Eliza		65	Whitaker, I. H.	70	Wight, William H.	78
Weeks, Sarah,		65	Williams, Olney	73	Westcott, Arnon	82
Whitman, Stephen		65	Weaver, Susan	74	Warren, Emeline	82
Waterman, Amy		67	Wright, Samson	74	Y.	
Westcott, C. G.		68	Wright, Frances	74	Young, Daniel	16
West, Jonathan		68	Wight, Lyman	78	Young, Rhoda	48

INDEX TO THOSE WHOSE MOTHERS WERE NAMED STONE.

Avery,	85	*51 Earl,	30	Northup,	81, 85
Anthony,	20	*52 Eston,	*48 *143	Pitts,	5, 58 ‡67
Aldrich,	*15	*53 Fenner,	*12 *46	Phillips,	5, ‡20, *18 *61
Angell,	50	*51 Fairfield,	49	Parker,	6, ‡75 ‡184
Arnold,	†24 ‡68	†84 Franklin,	56 ‡198	Pratt,	11, *4 *17
Andrews,	71	‡188 Fiske,	8 ‡199	Po ter,	14, 17, 27, 80
Brown,	8, 18, 40, 41,	Grant,	13	*97 Pray,	47
	44, 46, 71, 15	Greene,	12, 16, *30,	*98 Putney,	85
Bates,	12		‡81	*99 Purdy,	82
Burlingame,	9, 68	Gay,	47 *100	Patt,	8, *81 *208
	*70, 71 *100	Goff,	63 *101	Richards,	41
Burt,	72	Gorham,	83	Randall,	*22 *122
Briggs,	15, 71	Harris,	*12 *34	Richardson,	85
Bowen,	*21	*70 Hopkins,	13, 21	Sisson,	16
Barlow,	85	Hammond,	*16 *56	Sweet,	22
Bennett,	84	Hinkley,	19 ‡77	Sherman,	33, 76, 81
Baker,	31, 67	Hawkins,	‡23, 51, 54 ‡77	Sears,	84
Burgess,	27	Henry,	30 ‡79	Smith,	*66 *178
Borden,	28	Hawthorne,	82	Salisbury,	80
Bailey,	53, 69	Hill,	25, *26, 30 *91	Taylor,	14, 55, 57
Biggs,	*38 *117	Harrigan,	34	Thayer,	*48 *140
Blackmar,	39	Hubbard,	46, 58	Thompson,	82
Batchelder,	77	Hammett,	‡63 ‡167	Timothy,	50
Baldwin,	62	King,	*31, 65 *103	Tillinghast,	86, 72
Budlong,	62	Knight,	59, ‡67, 73 ‡184	Upham,	*44, 45 *137
Cranston,	7	Leach,	31, 32	Wightman,	65
Cheney.	9	Lawton,	33	Wheaton,	41
Cole,	*13, 18, 82 *38	Lane,	56	Williams,	9, *52 *151
Cobb,	*19, 56 *109	Ledward,	59	Weaver,	†73, †74 †192
Cutler,	46	Little,	62	Winsor,	54
Clarke,	51	Metcalf,	24, 25	Whipple,	*73 *192
Colvin,	69	Matteson,	32	White,	60 ‡190
Carr,	70	M'Clarrin,	7	Westcott,	2, 63, ‡72,
Carter,	71	Mann,	47		*64 *173
Chilson,	7	Manchester,	*61, 54, *107	Wight,	83
Crocker,	78		‡57 ‡155	Waterman,	4
Cheeseboro',	8	Martin,	72 ‡156	Young,	16
Dresser,	42	Miller,	79		
Disbrow,	65	Nicholson,	*81 *199		

EXPLANATION OF THE ABOVE INDEX.

The left column and the figures before it denote the page; the right column, the number of the note.

The figures without reference have no notes.

A reference, as *, † or ‡, show the page and note or notes which correspond.

Aldrich, 15*, has four notes, 51*, 52*, 53*, 54*.

Arnold, 24†, has one note, 84†; also, page 68‡. has one note, 188‡.

Greene, 30*, has five notes, 97*, 98*, 99*, 100*, 101*; also, page 81‡, has two notes, 198‡ 199‡.

Manchester, 61*, has one note, 108*; also, page 57‡, has two notes, 155‡, 156‡.

Births

Phillips was born January 20th 1755 —

Scott " " September 10th 1753

Phillips " " November 16— 1780

Phillips " " March 5d 1782

Phillips " " August 19 1783

Phillips " " February 18th 1786

Phillips " " March 20th 1788

Phillips " " April 16th 1790

Phillips August 26th 1795

Deaths

Died October 17th 1828 Aged 79 years

" February 19th 1828 " 74 "

Died November 28th 1858 Aged 78 years

" February 2d 1846 " 64 "

" January 1st 1841 " 57 "

" December 29th 1841 " 54 "

" April 11th 1814 " 24. "

" September 5th 1852 " 62 "

February 24 1873 " 78 - 5m - 29ds

il Dec. 11" 1 11 . . 46 1 11

om. 30 1875 " 26 4 " 10

May 18th 1865 " 70 " 10 "

7th 1856 " 76 " 5 days

Dec. 5 1861. " 70 " 10 13

March 27 1882   78 - 8 13 ds

July 11 1885   77 - 10 19 ds

Apr 24 1889   77   2 ds

Nov 11 1 75 "

an 21st 1897 " 55" 10" 11

Oct 4th 1883 " 66   14

APPENDIX No. 2.

1815. Almon A. Stone, the grandson of Edmands Stone, (330) was born 1811, and married Mary Ann Lake, who died in 1850. For the most of his life Almon (1815) has resided in Cranston, and is a " Stone Mason," both by trade and name. He has the general characteristics of the " Family," but, at one time in his earlier days, he was seized with a desire to behold more of the world than was daily shown up in the panc. ma of Rhode Island and Narragansett Bay. He entered as seaman on a whaling vessel bound for the Pacific. Here, in this voyage of discovery, like *one* much older than hims lf, he got more than he bargained for. His case vas not exactly paralle! to the old messenger of Ninevah; *he* went ' ito the whale's belly. Almon only went into the whale's mouth ; *he* was three days in his new habitation. Almon only *half an hour*, as it seemed to him,—probably ten seconds. The time he was there, however, be it longer or shorter, gave Almon the assurance that *three days* would have been in uncomfortably long visit. The facts were :—there were two whales in sight, half a mile apart, which seemed to be feeding or playing ; i. e., they :ould go down, and come up, and spout near the place where they went dov n. Two boats were manned and sent to attack them. The boat in which A on was not, was soon stove by the whale, and was in a sinking conditic .. Almon's boat, seeing the disaster, rowed up near to the disabled bo: and fastened to the whale by a harpoon and line. The wh le went down t suddenl came up with his mouth wide open, the under jaw on one ide, the junk, or upper jaw, on the other, reaching just above their heads on both sides of the middle of the boat. All jumped ; all but Almon went over. He, being amidships, i. e., the centre of the bo it, and the centre lso of the whale's mouth, was caught by the boat on one side, and by th onster's tooth on the o. . He felt the grip on his thigh as his body hu g over the gunwale, and in his meditations remembered " home" with thrilling inte st arewell," he said, " to Cucumber Town," or, he would h e said s said anything, but at that time he was more disposed to action th -making. From some cause, at that moment, the whale eased up o get a better hold, when Alm n slipped out his leg and tumble n a. The whale in a moment more closed his jaws, cutting the boat in tw parts, almost as square as if cut with a saw. Other boats took them up ; l, towards night, they secured the whale. Almon (1815) has enjoyed confidence and respect

of the community in which he has lived. He was appointed Adjutant of the 14th R. I. Militia, and subsequently was elected Colonel of the same regiment, which he commanded with respect and honor. He has had four children, Emily S. Stone, born 1836 : died aged 18 years.

John A. Stone, born 1838 ; has lived in Cranston, and was for a time engaged in the milk business, but without marked success ; since, he has removed to the city, where he now lives, and is employed in the ice business, a sober, temperate, worthy man, respected and esteemed by his acquaintances. He married Mercy A. T. Arnold. They have two children, Lillian J. Stone, born 1860, and Henry B. Stone, born 1861 ; the last died aged four years.

Josephine Stone, born 1841—married William E. Vallette, a machinist ; they have one child, Ellery Vallette, born 1865. Freelove T. Stone, born 1843, youngest child of Almon (1815), is unmarried.

ADDENDA TO NOTE 22.

Henry Stone (138) early manifested a disposition to rove ; made one whaling and several trading voyages, and subsequently went West, with a view to Lake Navigation. His sobriety and good judgment found him friends, and he was made master of a trading vessel, sailing on Lake Erie from Cleveland. But his course was short ; he died aged 34, beloved and lamented. He married Miss Eliza Canvin, by whom he had two children, Frank Augustus Stone and Mary Eliza Stone, who still live in Cleveland, Ohio.

Maria Stone married David Patt, an enterprising and respected mechanic, a painter and glazier. They reside in Providence, and have had two children, the eldest, Emma, born 1851, was called to the Spirit-home, aged two years ; Frank Herbert (142) is with them.

Amos Stone (140), at the commencement of the war of the Rebellion, enlisted in the Naval service, and was on the flag ship Minnesota, when the rebel iron-clad, the Merrimac, produced that frightful commotion in Norfolk harbor. He saw the Congress sunk and the Cumberland disabled, while our whole fleet trembled, and our whole country groaned. He, among others, waited in dread suspense and fearful anxiety as our *untried deliverer*, Erricsson's Monitor, like some huge sea-monster, rolled slowly up to the side of the exulting Merrimac, at one shot gave her a death wound, and in fifteen minutes delivered the harbor, our navy and our country, from the jaws of impending ruin. At the close of the war Amos was honorably discharged, and now resides in his native State, an active, industrious young man.

ADDENDA TO NOTE 58.

Betsey Stone (331), the wife of Thomas Hill, and youngest child of Samuel (19), died at an early age, leaving Jonathan Hill (537) a child but one

year old. Immediately on the death of the mother he was taken to his grandfather's, at Sokonossett Hill, where he was cared for by a grandmother, intelligent, kind, firm, until he was ten. Under her instruction he studied, learning easily to read, and was never at school till he returned to Foster, to live with his father. His father was a wagon-builder, and took Jonathan into the shop at ten, giving him the ordinary school advantages of Foster boys, and in the intervals, which were long between terms, he labored in the shop with a strength and capacity far above his years. At sixteen he was master of the trade, and as capable of labor, and as ripe of judgment, as young men of twenty. He married early in 1817, and reared a family of eleven children. In the easterly part of Foster, near Clayville, he purchased a farm of 115 acres, which he carried on with unusual success, and excellent judgment, ever blending the practical and theoretical in reclaiming and improving and fertilizing his farm. Almost the only agricultural mistake which he ever made in life was, in the selection of his farm; his perseverance, judgment and industry, expended on soil instead of rocks, would have placed his name among the most successful agriculturists of America. He was a man of few words, though genial and social to friends, while he was apparently cautious in the company of strangers. He was not averse to discussion, he assisted in Lyceums and debating clubs with great interest, and his decisions not hastily reached, were usually the result of thought and investigation ; but, however reached, they were fixtures in his mind, afterwards he was very unyielding.

He was a man of much reading on the common affairs of practical life, a Democrat in politics, though loyal to his country. His moral and political worth was acknowledged by his town and State; he was, many times, a member of the Town Council, for years a Justice of the Peace, was three years a State Senator, and three years represented the town in the General Assembly of the State. Although he was much engaged in farming, yet he carried on his trade to the close of life, which took place in 1865, by the inoculation of poudrette which he was using as a fertilizer upon his farm. His wife, Mary Phillips, the daughter of Capt. Abraham Phillips, of the Revolutionary army, still survives him, living on the farm where they have spent most of their married life, surrounded by her children and her children's children.

Elizabeth S. Hill, born 1817, is well educated, was a teacher several years, and married Hiram Wells, a man very social and quite intelligent. He is a farmer, but little disposed to agricultural improvements, and with no great love of order. They have two daughters married, and the family is much esteemed.

Susan A. Hill, born 1818, died 1836.

Sarah A. Hill, born 1820, lives at the old homestead.

Hannah M. Hill, born 1821, married W. B. Mathewson, and died in the faith of the gospel, in 1855, much lamented.

Mary E. Hill, born 1825, married Sheldon P. Lyon, a farmer, in the southwest part of Foster. She is a woman, virtuous, intelligent, cheerful.

Abbie Maria Hill, born 1826, died aged 23 years.

Lucinda P. Hill, born 1828, married G. B. Lawton, a man of worth, devoted to a sea life, sailed as mate from Providence, and died in San Juan, Central America. Lucinda subsequently married S. R. Briggs, a jeweller, and a worthy citizen. They live in Coventry, R. I.

Thomas W. Hill, born 1820, is somewhat like his father in disposition, though more demonstrative, and possessing much less of the "*family*" love of home. The father, true to the instincts of the "race," sought his happiness in home duties. Thomas, though a good boy, and following a father's advice, yet, when of age, he thought Rhode Island a *very* good State to emigrate from, and so he went away, spending two years in California, seven years in Minnesota, and two years in Colorado.

Almira P. Hill, born 1832, resides, we believe, at home with the mother.

James A. Hill, born 1833, a carpenter by trade, has had advantages somewhat superior to boys of his age. In addition to the Foster schools he attended the Academy at East Greenwich, where, to the common English branches, he added Surveying, and the higher Mathematical studies. He married Welthan Randall, a lady genial, social and refined, and his home in Clayville, Scituate, where he has lived for the last eight years, is a home of peace and plenty.

Clerinda E. Hill, born 1837, the youngest daughter of Jonathan (587,) married James M. Wright ; industrious and respected they live at the homestead with the mother, and they, with the family generally, combine a large share of intelligence, cultivation and esteem.

ADDENDA TO NOTE 58.

Mary Stone (329) married William Hill, and died early, leaving two children. Alice, (585) who married Josiah Bennett, and died about 1840. She left three children.

Waity, the eldest, is a worthy woman, and married Caleb Weaver. They have somewhat departed from the staid, unroving disposition which characterizes the race, seeking their fortunes in various localities of the west and east. They have now returned to their native State.

Abbie, the second daughter, is an excellent woman, industrious, genial, amiable, and has " done what she could" to make her home a home of refinement and virtue. She married Samuel Stone. (597)

William H. Bennett, the youngest son and child of Alice, has removed to Iowa.

Mary Hill (586) was early left an orphan, and when but a few days old was taken to the family of John Hill, a near relative, where she was carefully cared for, nursed, and kindly reared, till nearly three years old. Dur-

ing these years, the father having a second wife, the two children Alice and Mary were taken home, where Mary remained until she was married to Jarvis Eddy, when about twenty-two. She was an excellent woman, of much energy of character, and in appearance bearing a strong resemblance to the maternal side. The writer recollects her as one of his earliest and most loved play-mates, and the impress of her features, demeanor, and lively, joy-abounding spirit, has stamped itself upon his memory more vividly than scenes of greater importance and more recent date. She died in 1826, leaving a husband and a little boy of 8 to mourn her loss.

John H. Eddy, born 1818, though deprived of a mother's care, was blessed with a good father, who did all which a good christian parent believed was necessary for the best interests of his son. Fifty years ago the views of education in Rhode Island were far less just than at the present day. Then, among the farming yeomanry, no one looked higher than for a good *farmer* in his own family. Perchance, there might be a Justice of the Peace, now and then a School-master; most of these, however, were imported from Connecticut. With such views among the common people fifty years ago, the boys of Rhode Island started off upon the line of life. Such were about the views of Jarvis Eddy, relative to John H., and he gave him all the advantages which the common schools afforded, both summer and winter. This was better than was received by common boys. John H. Eddy improved all the advantages afforded him, and when but ten and twelve years old, of his own will, for months in succession studying his lessons in the winter season by the morning lamp, he learned grammar, and geography, and arithmetic, (for he cannot remember when he could not read,) and at sixteen years of age commenced teaching a small school in his own neighborhood. Not all the time before this had he been in school. He had been clerk in stores at Ponagansett and Richmond villages for some time previous to teaching. At twenty he passed several terms at Smithfield Seminary, where he mastered several treatises on Algebra, Geometry, and the higher English studies. He then taught one continuous year at Rockland, and commenced trading at Mt. Vernon, in the south part of Foster. While there he married Mercy P., daughter of Pardon Holden, Esq., a lady of moral and intellectual worth, and removed to Providence, where he has resided the last twenty years. The first years of his city life were passed clerking for the Providence & Worcester R. R., when he commenced the wholesale Wooden Ware trade, which, successful, and constantly increasing, is now an extensive business. One incident in his early life should not be omitted. While clerking at Ponagansett, two winters, he taught a school of operatives, from 8½ to 10 in the evening ; and, every morning during the same winters, he was up by five, studying by candle-light. Such perseverance has made life a success. He has been Colonel of the 7th Regiment of R. I. Militia, and member of a convention which finally resulted in the Constitution of the State, and an extension of the elective franchise. He has through life been

an uncompromising defender of total abstinence from intoxicating liquors, signing the pledge when he was but sixteen years of age; and through the late severe national struggle, his voice and action has proclaimed loyalty and liberty in every circle in which he has moved. In fact, no man more than John H. Eddy can claim the motto on the " Stone Coat of Arms," "*Humani nihil alienum*,"—Nothing of Humanity is foreign to me. As a merchant, he is respected for his probity; and in the Westminster Con. Unitarian Church, of which he and his lady are members, they are highly esteemed. They have two children, John H. Eddy, Jr., recently married, and Mary E. Eddy, who are both well educated, virtuous and respected.

ADDENDA TO NOTE 70.

Earl D. Barden and family were among those who felt severely the effects of the Rebellion. He had removed from Camden, Mo., where he had been in the lumber trade, to Bridgeport, Alabama, on the Tennessee river. After the fall of Fort Sumter, the Rebel winds blew an uncomfortable gale, even in Alabama. The family hastily packed three trunks, and started for the North, leaving their house, furniture, saw-mills, and a million of sawed lumber. After the battle of Chickamauga he went back, but of the whole he left, nothing was to be seen. *One cannon ball* lay where his house stood to tell the tale of war, and bear testimony to the consequences of the Rebellion.

Earl D. and Lucinda Barden (409) have one child, Dora Barden, born 1849.

Horace Bowen (418) enlisted in the 3d R. I. Reg Heavy Artillery, 10th Army Corps, in 1862, and was, though but sixteen years of age, soon promoted to be gunner, from his wonderful ability as a marksman His Captain sometimes entertained visitors by an exhibition of his skill. He rarely ever failed in the second shot of striking a window, from Fort Greggs where they were stationed, on Sullivan's Island. He was at the taking of Fort Pulaski, and in many severe engagements, but came home healthy, and without a scratch. On one occasion, Case, a mess-companion, while standing at his side, was cut down by a Sharp-shooter. On another the Rebs fired a volley of artillery as the boys off duty were at play. "*Cover !* " shouted several at once. Horace looked up, saw many shells coming. It was too late to run, he fell flat on the ground. One shell came ricocheting onward, (rick-o-shaing) and, striking four feet before him, hopped four feet over and behind him, and lay still. Fortunately the fuse was out, or Horace's bed on the sand might have been less safe. He was honorably discharged in 1865.

ADDENDA TO NOTE 52.

Amy S. Aldrich (301) daughter of Sarah Stone (296) and Lyman Aldrich, was an excellent wife and mother. She passed to the " Shining Shore" in her early married life, lamented and beloved by all who knew her.

The husband, John D. Cranston, an enterprising merchant, and his son, John Henry Cranston, now a young man of twenty, reside in Providence. Thankful W. Aldrich (302) married Thomas William Hill, (495) and removed to Iowa, where the husband, a worthy man and pious christian, soon after died. There she still remains, sustained amid her trials by a circle of worthy, intelligent, and loving children.

"STONE FAMILY GATHERING."

The appointed meeting of this numerous family came off at the "Old Farm," in Stoneville, Mashantatack or Cucumber Town, 3½ miles from Elmwood, on the Pontiac road, Tuesday, the 4th inst. The morning was enveloped in a heavy fog, so that by half past eight it was difficult to decide whether it was stormy or not. A vote was taken by those collected in the city, in which the ladies largely participated, and the decision *was unanimous that it did not storm.* A large company arrived at the "Old Farm," but at 10 a. m. the decision was reversed—it rained in torrents. During the intervals between the showers four of the largest furniture wagons, holding thirty each, were arranged before the old mansion, which is remarkably large. The south-side windows were removed, many private carriages were brought near, and the "Family" was called to order by the chairman, Rev. Richard C. Stone, of Missouri. The exercises were commenced by reading from an Old Bible, owned by the heirs of Asa Stone, and brought from England by Stukely Westcott, the companion of Roger Williams in his exile journey from Massachusetts to Rhode Island. With the descendants of S. W. the family of Hugh Stone has been largely connected. An original ode written for the occasion by Alma Stone Metcalf, wife of Prof. Thomas Metcalf, of the State Normal University of Illinois, was sung by the "Harmoneons," under the direction of Captain William Stone, of Providence. Introductory remarks were made by the chair, in which he alluded to the interest of the occasion. The spot where they stood was the farm of their common ancestor; in view were the farms of his three sons, one of which had been owned in the family *one hundred and fifty-six years.* There they lived, and toiled, and prayed, and slept at last in that lowly spot which we this day consecrate to their memory. Here we, their descendants, some of the ninth generation, (he raised in his arms two boys, George Martin Stone, of Woodstock, and Charles Isaac Stone, of Putnam, Connecticut,) have come to look upon their graves, to cherish their memories, and to imitate their virtues. The ode "A Hundred Years Ago" was then sung, prayer was offered by Rev. John Howson of Chatham, Mass., and the Chair introduced Mr. Denham Arnold the orator of the day a graduate of Brown University, now tutor in Washington University, St. Louis, Mo. He spoke about forty minutes, in which he briefly alluded to the occasion of meeting, "to bring together the scattered branches of the Family Tree, to honor the resting place of our ancestors, and learn some lessons of truth and duty." He contrasted the moral and political school in which our ancestors were trained with the advanced position of the present age, and in view of this inquired, what regiment of American freemen from such a stock would be conquered fighting under the shadow of Bunker Hill? He alluded in a masterly manner to the value of family ties, to the pernicious custom of shirking household duties amid the demoralization of fashionable hotels. He portrayed the strong love of freedom as a family type, and of their practical evidence of that love in the numbers who have responded to the call of our country. We cannot do justice to the clearness, strength and beauty of this address—every sentence disclosed the well read and accomplished scholar, while the lively touches of humor, the great practical truths, and the impressive appeals in behalf of duty and heaven, chained the attention of all who heard it. Another Ode, "A Hundred Years to Come," was sung, and (the rain having ceased) the family adjourned to the "Old Orchard," where they discussed, with lively interest, the good and substantial things of life, generously provided and cordially received, amid introductions, greetings and congratulations of old friends, newly discovered cousins and far off relatives. A few rods from the Old Orchard, and they stood in the "Old Stone Burial Ground," where the first marked date is *one hundred and fifty-five years ago.* An unostentatious granite monument was here ready for erection. The Harmoneons sung an original Ode of three stanzas, each commencing with "Here rest the dead!" On the conclusion of the Ode, a solemn and impressive prayer of consecration was offered by Rev. Charles Stone Weaver, of Groton, Conn. A copper box, containing the organization of the family in this matter, names of the trustees of the burial lot, the printed programme of the occasion, the circular addressed to the "Family by the committee, the names of all the contributors to the monument and enclosure, and the book of genealogy and biography, published by Rev. Richard C. Stone, was placed in a cavity in the base, and the shaft was settled to its place. The whole was an occasion of great interest. The company was large—between four and five hundred—but would have been more than doubled had the day been fair. Two pieces were omitted in the singing : an original hymn by Rev. N. K. Bennett, of Hudson City, N. Y., and an original ode by the chairman. Letters were received to be read from Richard B. Stone, of Chicago, Ill.; Rev N. K. Bennett, of Hudson, N. Y.; from Mr. Robert C. Metcalf, Principal of the Adams School, Boston, and from Prof. George B. Stone, of Washington University, St. Louis, Mo.; but all were omitted on account of the rain. It was truly a family gathering. Lemuel Stone, Esq., a patriarch of the family, aged 85 years, came from Luzerne county, Pa., four hundred miles. Hugh Stone, the *only* descendant who bears the ancestral name, and twelve others, came from the same section. Many from the states of Massachusetts and Connecticut were present to exchange congratulations with their relatives here, to learn the history and emulate the worth of the departed, and encourage the virtues of the living — *Providence Journal.*

STONE BURIAL GROUND.—The Trustees or the old Stone Burial Ground, on the Pontiac road, a few miles southwest of Elmwood, have recently removed the remains of three of their ancestors to that place: John Stone, (4) his first wife, Hannah Barnes, and his second wife Abigail Foster. The bones were in an entire state of preservation. The man had been buried 107 years; the first wife 151 years; the second wife 106 years. Hannah Barnes, buried in 1712, was a little girl at the decease of Roger Williams, and died when between thirty and forty years of age, and yet the skeleton was as sound and perfect as if cleansed and kept in a case. The hair, also, braided, wound up in a coil, was as sound and perfect as on the day on which she was laid down to sleep, although one hundred and fifty-four years of summer and winter have passed away, varied by Indian warfare, French conquest, Colonial struggle Revolution, Independence, growth from less than two to thirty millions, a rebellion crushed, and the Goddess of Liberty enthroned throughout the land, since that hair was braided and coiled in sorrowing kindness on the head where most of it still rests. Her descendants are and have been more than two thousand; more than half that number are now living. These bodies were buried from five and a half to six feet deep, on a small ridge of land near a branch of the Pochasset river, the bottom of the grave some seven or eight feet above the level of the branch, in a bluish, sandy clay.

ODES AND HYMN SUNG AT THE "STONE FAMILY GATHERING."

ORIGINAL ODE—BY ALMA STONE METCALF, OF ILLINOIS.

Kindred met! With our memorial
Mark we now this sacred soil,
Where are gathered home the fathers
Long since rested from their toil.

Mosses gather on the tombstone,
Crumbling o'er each silent grave;
Grass and weed and lonely floweret
O'er the ancient sleepers wave.

Back! turn back, O Time, thy pinions,
Scenes of youth and home restore;
Picture fathers, mothers, children,
Loving, loved, in days of yore.

Overwhelmed by tide of ages
Earthly hope and power, and fame,
In Eternity's wide ocean
Buried lie—without a name.

Father, stay us in our weakness;
Fill us with a Christian love;
May our life-work be an emblem
Of our work in Heaven above.

Thus may we, in faith and gladness,
To our Father's presence come,
Bearing with us sheaves of glory,
Which shalt crown our "Harvest home."

ORIGINAL ODE—BY REV. R. C. STONE.

Here rest the dead! In thought appears
The shadows dim of by-gone years:
The past—weird, strange—a phantom stands,
Dark, distant, primal, awful, grand.
The Past, ah yes! in thought appears,
Draped in the garb of former years,
When erst upon old Warwick's shore,
Our sires were found in days of yore.

Here rest the dead! No storied urn
Marks the lone spot; no pages burn
To light their shrine; but, quiet rest,
The plain, the true, the just the blest;

The men, the wives, who set with care
The plantlet Freedom green and fair.—
That tree which now with mighty sheen
O'erspreads the land with radiant green.

Here rest the dead! but every vein
Which throbs to-day gives life again
To those who sleep beneath this sod,
Although their spirits rest with God.
Aye, life with all its spirit-thrills,
As when they rambled o'er these hills;
With all its thrills of Hope and Love,
Pointing us up to Heaven above.

ORIGINAL ODE—BY REV. R. C. STONE.

Oh hark! Oh hark! the voices sounding,
'Mid vales where zephyrs gently sighing
Are rolling, rolling, deep'ning, rounding,
As o'er the dead—the moments flying,
Brothers sisters gather round--
Generations silent stand
In the graveyard where are found
Relics of th' ancestral bard.
Voices true! voices grand! voices from the
    silent band.
We will heed thee voices from the silent band.

Although no radiant towns are rising,
No gilded banners proudly waving,
The wild-flower, blooming, lights the fading
Grass which grows, the dew-drop laving.
Over forms beneath this sod!
Still their voices echo here—
"Children! live for truth and God "
Yes, we listen, and revere.
Voices true! voices grand! voices from the
    silent band.
We will heed thee voices from the silent band.

ADDENDA TO INTRODUCTION.

The records of the early settlers of New England give the names of William Stone, who appears among the Freemen of Guilford, Conn., in 1669. He had three chil., William, Hannah, and Benajah, all born before 1650; also, of Hugh Stone, who settled in Andover, Mass. He was married about 1696 or 7, as was Hugh Stone, of Warwick. He left several children, among whom was a John; their posterity, if any, is not known. Hugh, of Andover, became insane, and murdered his wife in 1689. No blame is attached by historians.

9

ERRATA No. 2.

CORRECTED MARRIAGES.

4. Hannah Barnes.
9 Patience Webb.
33 a. William Patt, a Sea Captain.
585. Josiah Bennett.
586. Jarvis Eddy.
587. Mary Phillips.
532. His 2d and 3d wives' names should have been in Roman, not Italic.
503. Joseph Nutting.
694 W. Thomas
15 3. Clara Parker.
1533. Lizzie Tinkham.
1785. His 1st wife, Alzada Steer, was the mother of his nine chil.—four not in Statistics died in infancy. Alzada was a good wife and mother, lived the life of the righteous, and died aged 58.

CORRECTED FACTS.

43 left children.
631 was married. No. chil.
634. Anna Kent. (Wid. Waterman.)
13. S S. Died 1728? "Old Burial Ground."
195. Raymond F., 9th Gen., son of G. W. S. (195.)
311 is still living.
1572 died 1848—1574 died 1853.
1511 died in childhood.
1513 is living. This family write the name Batchelor.
Note 197. L. Jones is a physician.

CHIL. OF MARY STONE (490) & ALDIS BORDEN

Henry C. Borden. 1835.
James A. Borden. 1838.
George R. Borden. 1840.
Anne Maria Borden. 1842.
Aldis Borden. 1845.
Mary Emily Borden. 1846.
Aldis Borden. 1849.
Luther C. Borden. 1851.
Nancy Maritta Borden. 1854. page 28.
483. Order of Chil.—1st. William. 2d, Jonathan. 3d, Laurania. 4th, Thomas. 5th, Roby. 6th, James. 7th, Priscilla. 8th, George. 9th, John. p 26.

AGES CORRECTED.

139—1831.
397—1849.
447—1832.
490—1810.
1708-1831.

NAMES CORRECTED.

113. Mary Ann Stone.
235. Almoran Harris.
413. Sarah J. Randall.
477. Gertrude Stone Metcalf.
142. Frank Herbert Patt.
495. Thomas William Hill.
1183. Henry N. Manchester.
1532. Althenna Stone.
1568. Dewilton Stone.
1622. Almira Stone.

INTRODUCTION, 1ST PAGE OF.

Line 17 read thirty, not forty.   Line 20 read Grandson, not son.

THE STONE "COAT OF ARMS."

The author has recently had access to the English Encyclopedia of Heraldry, with a large collection of works and drawings on Chivalric Emb'ems Escutcheons and Devices pertaining to the marks of honor and badges of the English Nobility and Gentry, as the classes are and have been distinguished, and finds that the Name has had thirty patents of Coats of Arms, or Armorial Devices granted, some to the name, some to particular individuals and branches.

HYMN

RESPECTFULLY DEDICATED TO THE "STONE FAMILY" BY REV. N. K. BENNETT, HUDSON.

Begotten of the self-same race—
A family of men in God;
Here on this dear, ancestral soil,
We greet each other face to face.

From near and far our ways have led—
With children's children we appear,
To mingle words of sober cheer
In honor of our sacred dead.

Through a long line of sturdy sires
Have we descended to this day;
We come our filial debt to pay,
To freshly stir Love's altar-fires.

The welcome Record of our past
Inspires our hearts with thankful song;
Without a stain of shame or wrong,
Tis sealed with—"Faithful to the Last."

The joyful Present fitly proves
How royal they who walked in truth;
It nerves their age—it crowns their youth—
And thrills with life the soul it moves.

To God, who is the dwelling-place
Of generations called from dust—
To Him our praise—in Him our trust—
For He has stayed us by His grace.

And while a lettered column stands
To witness for our earthly part,
Let Jesus reign within each heart.
Each name be written on His hands.

Then, Christians of the self-same race—
A family of Saints in God,
We soon shall burst this wasting clod,
And dwell forever face to face.

PROVIDENCE, SEPT. 10th, 1866.

REV. R. C. STONE:

Sir:—

At a meeting of the members of the " Stone Family," held Sept. 4th, in Cranston, R. I., on the " Old Farm," on which is located the " Old Stone Burial Ground," it was unanimously voted :

That the thanks of this meeting be tendered the Rev. R. C. Stone for his untiring efforts in compiling a Genealogy of the Stone Family, and that we fully appreciate the arduous labor in which he has been engaged for many years, in perfecting a work which is of the greatest interest to every member.

Further, That the thanks of this meeting be tendered him for the energy and active part he has taken in proposing and carrying into effect measures for protecting said Burial Ground, and memorializing, by the erection of a monument, the spot where rests the dust of our common ancestors.

Further, that he be tendered the thanks of this meeting for the able, dignified, and courteous manner, in which he presided over and conducted the exercises at the " Stone Family Gathering."

With great esteem,

Yours, &c.,

WILLIAM STONE, Sec.

FROM WILLIAM STONE (658) TO ROGER BURLINGAME.

CRANSTON, FEBRUARY, 1761.

Most honored Sir: I Send you this Paper, Charged With my Sincerest thanks for the Faviour I have Received At your hand, Acknowledging it to be very ingageing; for The angels in heaven doth Rejoice at the Return of a Sinner, and the greatest Ofender is accepted At Repentence. But yet I Cannot Set my hopes So far beyond the Limmets of Probility as to think that it Ever will Be With the youth that has exerted Every art to ovethrow me, as it was With Prodigel Son ; however I Return my ardent Thanks to you for Wishing So much Happiness to Both, as there Would Be in such a great alterration, and so Conclude With the most Ardent wishes for your health and happines. your most obliged Servent.

Being Resined unto fate,
the thoughts of Love can't burn;
for dust we art, and unto dust
We must agian return.

if we enjoy the greatest bless
on Earth that we do crave,

We Soon must Leve them all behind,
and hasten to the grave.

tho' here we Live oprest with cares,
our jurny it is short.
We soon must Leve both frind and foes,
and to the dust depart. finis.

for I am know poet.

WILLIAM STONE.

11

Addenda to Note 142.—Before writing this note the Author earnestly sought to make the personal acquaintance of its subject, but failed to succeed, as most of his immediate relatives had moved off, or died. All believed him living, but no one knew where.

In April, 1867, he unexpectedly found Ezra (977) married, and living in a quiet, happy retirement in the town of Cranston, R. I. The following statements substantially, the Author received from his own lips relative to his sickness, apparent death and early history.

His father and mother both dying when he was a child, though clearly within his remembrance, he lived with his grandfather, Ezra Stone (823) till the time of the old man's death, when he was about 24 years old. After this he left the neighborhood of Alum Pond for the central and more southern portions of the State.˙ He pronounced the statements in Note 142, relative to his sickness and apparent death, correct. He was in this trance-like state nearly ten days. For some of the time he knew what those around him were saying and doing. He was conscious of the life-tests of pricking and pinching, though they produced no pain. His mind seemed to wander anywhere and everywhere independent of his will, or to use his own language, " like a humming bird from flower to flower." The ten days mental action would, if all were written, " make quite a book," but now lies in his mind a confused mass indistinct and undefinable; still there are points clearly remembered and well defined. Among others, the fact that his mind much of the time was away, not with the body ; often in the vicinity knowing what the neighbors were saying or doing, which to their astonishment he related on his recovery. On one occasion when he had been in the trance four days, Dr. Albee and wife came to the house late in the evening, through the rain and mud; his mind or spirit was with them, saw their difficulties, heard their conversation and related it on his recovery. On another occasion, Dr. A. asked the grandfather to go to the barn for some private conversation ; when alone the Doctor asked the grandfather to consent to a post mortem examination, was very urgent in his request, said Ezra (977) was as dead as he ever would be, and earnestly pressed the subject of his burial. The grandfather said, " No! not while that place on his breast is warm." When he became conscious, he, to their astonishment, informed them of all the particulars of their private interview. At times, his mind or spirit seemed to be among those who had passed from this world away. He distinctly recollects seeing a great multitude of persons in a delightful place, and in this multitude were his father and mother ! These are among the most vivid remembrances of that wonderful period, " whether in the body or out of the body, he cannot tell."

His physical health recovered slowly, but his mind was clear soon after he

aroused from the trance-like state, and he has never been subject to absence of mind or any species of mind-wandering before or since.

The circumstances of his apparent death and restoration to life awakened much interest at the time, and hundreds visited the retiracy of Alum Pond to gratify their curiosity, insomuch that the retiring nature of Ezra (977) became annoyed, and he avoided then, and does even now, any conversation upon the subject; and, such indeed has been his silence, that scarcely one of the neighbors where he has lived has ever heard it mentioned.

The subject of this Note is about 48 years old, of ordinary mental capacity, not a business man, of unassuming manners, of few words, modest, retiring, a lover of home, and almost unknown in his own neighborhood, excepting in the little circle to which his daily labors call him, and not *half* of them know his first name. He has worked four years for his present employer, engaged as a teamster, and bears an unexceptionable moral character.

Twelve years since he married Miss Harriet F. Lovell, a lady of natural refinement, genial and social—one who renders their home truly attractive by the neatness, smiles and quiet virtue ever found within their dwelling.

Ezra (977) is a believer in the Christian doctrines, untinctured by enthusiasm or fanaticism, but is, we believe, not connected with any church, nor does he say of his trance-like state that he looked into the Spirit-world; he states the facts as they appeared to him, leaving each one to draw his own conclusions,—a man less opinionated, less imaginative, or less enthusiastic, the Author has rarely met. We leave the facts of this singular case with our readers; that they are the results of imagination, is beyond the scope of common sense; that there is deception or collusion, no one knowing all the parties, can for a moment assume; indeed, we believe that every one who carefully analyzes the facts, must admit, that it prompts the inquiry: Is there not a state, a condition of soul and body, which, while it beholds the movements of time, listens to voices, and sends its vision-scope to that "innumerable company which no man can number?" Is there not sometimes a condition of life, before the soul passes away, in which it catches glimmerings of truth on both sides of the "veil?"

ERRATA No. 3.

Introduction page VI. Rev. A. L. Stone traces his pedigree to Connecticut.

Introduction page VII. Stone Coat of Arms corrected by Encyclopedia of Heraldry—Crest, Eagle Rousant—Escutcheon per Quartre—Dexter Chief—Lone Star in Argent rising in Azure, below; three cinque foils in sable standing in Argent—Sinister Chief—Fleur de lis in Or Standing in Argent—Dexter Base plain Argent—Sinister Base, Lion rampant, in sable standing in Argent. Motto—"Humani Nihil Alienum."

www.ingramcontent.com/pod-product-compliance
Lightning Source LLC
Chambersburg PA
CBHW030111030726
47498CB00007B/2340